DEVIL OF A CRIME

A BLAKE MEYER THRILLER

BOOK 6 OF 6

C. KEVIN THOMPSON

ALSO BY C. KEVIN THOMPSON

For All Those Who Serve Our Country

*May you find true peace
in the midst of any war you face.*

"Thou hast made us for thyself, O Lord, and our heart is restless until it finds its rest in thee."
   - Augustine of Hippo, *Confessions*

As he sat, looking at The White House in Washington, D.C.: *"People think it matters who occupies that house. It doesn't. Multinational corporations and criminals run the world."*
   - Raymond "Red" Reddington

"If God were your Father, you would love Me, for I came forth from God, not for Myself or of Myself, but God sent Me. Why is my language not understandable to you? It is because you are unable to truly hear My word. You belong to your father, the devil, and you want to carry out the desires of your father. He was a murderer from the beginning, and does not stand in the truth, because there is no truth in him. Whenever he speaks, it is a lie, because lying is his native language. It is his nature, for he is a liar and the father of lies."
   - Jesus of Nazareth, John 8:42-44

C. S. LEWIS QUOTE

"How did the Dark Power go wrong? Here, no doubt, we ask a question to which human beings cannot give an answer with any certainty. A reasonable (and traditional) guess, based on our own experiences of going wrong, can, however, be offered. The moment you have a self at all, there is a possibility of putting yourself first—wanting to be the centre—wanting to be God, in fact. That was the sin of Satan: and that was the sin he taught the human race. Some people think the fall of man had something to do with sex, but that is a mistake. (The story in the Book of Genesis rather suggests that some corruption in our sexual nature followed the fall and was its result, not its cause.) What Satan put into the heads of our remote ancestors was the idea that they could 'be like gods'—could set up on their own as if they had created themselves—be their own masters—invent some sort of happiness for themselves outside God, apart from God. And out of that hopeless attempt has come nearly all that we call human history—money, poverty, ambition, war, prostitution, classes, empires, slavery—the long terrible story of man trying to find something other than God which will make him happy._

"The reason why it can never succeed is this. God made us: invented us as a man invents an engine. A car is made to run on gasoline, and it would not run properly on anything else. Now, God designed the human machine to run on Himself. He Himself is the fuel our spirits were designed to burn, or the food our spirits were designed to feed on. There is no other. That is why it is just no good asking God to make us happy in our own way without bothering about religion. God cannot give us a happiness and peace apart from Himself, because it is not there. There is no such thing.

"That is the key to history. Terrific energy is expended—civilizations are built up—excellent institutions devised; but each time something goes wrong. Some fatal flaw always brings the selfish and cruel people to the top and it all slides back into misery and ruin. In fact, the machine conks. It seems to start up all right and runs a few yards, and then it breaks down. They are trying to run it on the wrong juice. That is what Satan has done to us humans."

-- C. S. Lewis, *Mere Christianity,* Collier Books, MacMillan Publishing Company, 1943, pp. 53-54.

EZEKIEL 7:26-27

"Disaster upon disaster will come upon you.
Rumor upon rumor.
They will seek a vision from a prophet,
But the priestly teachings of the law will perish.
The counsel from the elders will cease.
The king will lament,
The prince will be clothed in hopelessness,
And the hands of the people will quake.
I will deal with them according to their conduct.
By their own principles I will judge them.
Then, they will know that I am the LORD."

DEVIL OF A CRIME

A BLAKE MEYER THRILLER
BOOK 6 OF 6

Fern Circle Books, LLC

"Where Imagination Meets Eternity"

JULY 13, 2014

CHAPTER 1

GENFORMA LABORATORIES
Outskirts of Novosibirsk, Russian Federation

Lazar Nicolescu leaned back in his chair, which sat in front of the desk in the main part of the lab. He scribbled some notes down on his clipboard, attempting to appear busy, wondering what was taking Vladimir Klebnikov so long to get there. Karina Kuznetsova had alerted him via email that Klebnikov had arrived just as they were leaving. He expected Vladimir to burst in with all the pomp and circumstance of a mob boss and muscle his way around until he had everything desired. Instead, however, it had been well over an hour, and he was running out of things to do.

He finally set the clipboard down and decided to prepare the healthy black rat in the specimen room for transport. Vladimir had stated over the phone how Lazar's "old friend," who had been with him from the beginning of the testing, would be used to help produce the vaccine alongside "the human subject."

Lazar took a deep breath and stood just as the outer doors of the decontamination unit leading out into the rest of the facility opened. He turned to see three men, all equipped with biosuits, step inside and begin the cleansing process.

Lazar took another deep breath and crossed his arms. He loathed the idea of his fellow Biopreparat scientist getting his worthless hands on all of the research Lazar had amassed just so he could save his own backside while the world burned. The more Lazar stood there and watched the three men complete the cycle, the angrier he became.

Acting the part will take very little imagination.

The inner doors opened, and Klebnikov led the other two men inside.

"Lazar, Lazar, Lazar, how are you?" Klebnikov said, reaching out his hand.

Lazar kept his arms crossed. "Sure took you a long time to get in here after your arrival."

Klebnikov lowered his hand to his side. "Keeping tabs on me, are we?"

"Word travels fast around here. Almost as fast as the diseases we house."

Klebnikov's lips twitched into a quick smile. "If you must know, we have been preparing a lab for the next phase. For some time now. We had a truck arrive and bring extra equipment. Took a little time to get it set up and operational, but it is done. We are ready for you and your work."

"What you are doing is wrong, Vladimir. Therefore, I cannot act like everything is wonderful. Nor can I assist you any longer."

"I do not believe you have a great many choices."

"I beg you. Do not continue with this madness. If your people have already released this contagion, then using this information to create a vaccine for yourselves alone will be the most devilish thing in all of human history. And mark my words, Vladimir, this contagion will find you. It will hunt down your loved ones. It will kill indiscriminately. And if my gut is right—and you know it usually is, then even your vaccine will eventually be ineffective as this contagion mutates. However, by then, it will have affected so many people, the infection rate will have accelerated to a point where even the great Vladimir Klebnikov would not be able to produce a cure in time."

"You underestimate me, my old friend, like you have always done."

"And you underestimate this contagion. You have not been working with it. I have. You have seen my notes. It will spread and kill until there is nothing left but the proverbial cockroach. Even marmots are not immune."

Klebnikov lifted his hand and raised his index finger. "Ah, but your black rat is. And in one historically ironic twist, a black rat will be the very entity that saves the human race from the greatest Black Plague to ever strike mankind."

Lazar snorted in derision. "You put too much faith in a specimen which has not been tested fully. Yes, it has been exposed to this strain of bubonic plague. However, that was early in the transmission cycle. You have no idea how the specimen will fare after the contagion has jumped from host to host for five to six cycles. It may mutate enough and transform its killing power. Even your prized rodent may not survive the aftermath."

"Lazar, you are placing too much doubt on conjecture. Just like you have always done, I might add."

"Better to be careful than to be careless."

Klebnikov allowed a wry smile to surface. "We have come for all of your notes, the black rat, and the human subject."

"The black rat is in the specimen room," Lazar said, pointing, but making it clear by his tone he was not willing to lift a finger to help. "As for 'the human subject,' whose name is Peter, by the way...Peter Zakayev...a boy really, compared to old goats like you and me. He was an innocent bystander. In the wrong place at the wrong time. Caught up in someone else's political power struggle, apparently. Simply on a trip to Moscow to meet girls, and instead, he gets labeled a dissident because of who his friend's parents were. It had nothing to do with him.

"Now, he is your legacy, Vladimir. An innocent boy being used as cannon fodder for greedy old men and women. So, they can what? Rule the world? A totally decimated and utterly chaotic world, once the final bodies fall?"

Klebnikov took a couple of steps toward Lazar. "Where is the human subject?"

"He is resting."

"Where?" Klebnikov looked around the lab. "He has been in here since the beginning. Where is he now?"

"He is in the lab in the far back of the facility. I thought it best he be placed in a clean lab while he recuperated. To simulate a true quarantine protocol."

Klebnikov motioned to the assistant on his left. "Get the rat from the specimen room."

"Yes, sir."

He then motioned to the assistant on his right. "Go get a guard and retrieve the human subject."

"Yes, sir."

"And take them both to Yuri's lab."

Both men nodded and proceeded to their tasks.

"And as for you," Klebnikov said to Lazar, "I need your notes and research."

Lazar stared at his colleague for several awkward moments until he finally waved him on. "They are in my office."

Klebnikov motioned for Lazar to lead the way.

After enduring the decontamination process in silence, without so much as idle chatter, Lazar walked into the cramped little office and unzipped his biosuit. He pulled his arms and head free and grabbed a large three-ring binder off his desk and held it out. "Everything is in here."

Klebnikov followed Lazar's lead and unzipped his biosuit as well. Pulling his head and hands free, he took the binder from Lazar and rummaged through it.

Lazar stepped aside and offered Klebnikov his desk chair. "Might be easier if you sit."

"Just point me to the pages containing the tests conducted on the human subject," Klebnikov said as he sat down in the chair.

"Look at the tabs. They are labeled."

"Ah," Klebnikov said, setting the binder down on the desk and thumbing through the multi-colored tabs.

Lazar eased back a couple of steps and opened his mini-fridge. "Would you like a bottled water? String cheese?"

"No."

"Suit yourself." Lazar grabbed a bottled water and then snatched a single syringe, which had been placed inside the refrigerator. He held the syringe against the bottled water to conceal it as best he could. He closed the door and peeked over his shoulder.

Klebnikov had just found the tab he was looking for and pulled the pages apart, opening the binder wide.

Lazar popped the cap off the syringe, turned it in his hand, and held it like a knife. With his other hand, he set the bottled water down on the desk to Klebnikov's left. The distraction caused Vladimir to turn his head in that direction, allowing Lazar to plunge the needle into the right side of his neck.

Before Klebnikov could react, Lazar had forced the plunger down.

Vladimir reached up with his left hand and grabbed Lazar's hand, but Lazar yanked it free and punched his victim in the side of the head with his clenched fist wrapped around the empty syringe.

Immediately, the injected sedative caused Klebnikov to stagger as he tried to stand and defend himself.

Lazar stepped back and watched as Klebnikov spun around, lost his balance, and collapsed to the floor, striking his head on the side of Lazar's cot.

He hit the floor with a thud and at once seemed lifeless.

Lazar stood in a fighter's stance, his hands held up, like he was ready for round fifteen. But his opponent was down for the count.

With a relieved huff, Lazar tossed the syringe to the floor and snatched a pair of scissors from the lap drawer of his desk. He walked around and grabbed his desk from the side and slid it out away from the wall. He unplugged the phone jack and snipped the end off and allowed the severed wire to dangle in place. He slid the desk back to its original position and held up the now separated jack. "Sorry, my old friend, but in case they turn the phones back on, I need you to not have the capability to make contact with the outside world."

Lazar then searched his new enemy and found his smartphone tucked away in his front right pants pocket. He yanked it out, set it and the phone jack on the desk, and put his biosuit back on.

Giving one last tug on the zipper before covering the zipper with the Velcro flap, he knelt down and unzipped Klebnikov's helmet from his biosuit. He turned it upside down, tucked it under his arm, and tossed the smartphone and phone jack into it before reentering the decontamination unit.

You are almost done. Play the part. Look convincing. We don't know who is watching...

And with a little luck, Klebnikov will not be able to proceed any further.

Lazar stepped out of the decontamination unit and pulled Klebnikov's smartphone and the severed phone jack out of the helmet. He set the helmet down on Peter's metal table and placed the phone jack next to it so Klebnikov could see it, if he were to look out the window of the cramped office where his friend had been sentenced to live for months.

Lazar faced his office. *But I am keeping your phone, Vladimir. The information on this may prove valuable.*

He turned and walked directly toward the other decontamination unit. The one leading outside his lab. The one he had never been allowed to enter for months.

Until now.

Nervous and sweating, he endured the unit's process, hoping no guards were outside the lab.

This might be a short trip.

The doors opened, and Lazar walked out like he had done it a thousand times. He took a turn to his right, toward Yuri's lab, and marched down the hallway until he reached the control room.

With a key provided to him by Karina, he gently inserted it into the lock and opened the door. As he and Karina had hoped, the control room was empty.

It seems Joseph found a way to leave...

Good for him.

Lazar closed the door and locked it. Then, almost in a dash, he crossed the room. He used the other key on the ring and opened a clear plastic box hanging on the wall. He lifted the lid of the box on its hinge and pulled the lever inside.

Instantly, red lights flashed, and an alarm, sounding like nothing Lazar had ever heard before, blared inside the control room. Lazar allowed the plastic box to fall back into place. He walked over to the bank of monitors and watched as flashes of light filled every monitor. Joseph had told Karina that when the lever was pulled, what was happening in the control room would occur in every other room in the facility, including the custodial closets and maintenance rooms. Even the guard shack outside.

"When someone pulls the lever," Joseph told Karina, "everything stops. Nobody goes anywhere. Nobody gets out of the room they are in at that time. Nobody moves until government personnel from the Vector Institute come in and clear each and every room. It has never happened since I have been here," Joseph continued, "but I am told it could take days before we are given the all clear. That is why there are cases of bottled water and packages of army rations in each and every room. Each room is stocked with a fifteen-day supply."

Lazar monitored the screens as the people in each room became more and more frantic. They pulled on doors. They pressed the buttons for the decontamination units to open. They pressed call buttons, and those alerts—one at first, then two, then four, then more than Lazar could count, came into the control room. The lab technicians, military guards, the cooks, and everyone else wanted answers. They looked up at the security cameras with raised hands. Lazar couldn't read lips, but he really didn't need to. He knew what they were saying, but he didn't respond. Instead, he flipped the switch marked "Silence Alarms" and continued to watch.

What is done is done, Vladimir.

I have been exposed now...in more ways than one.

But nobody else in this facility has to die today. They will live once the quarantine is lifted.

The good news is, my old friend, you cannot hurt others ever again.

CHAPTER 2

Supervisory Special Agent-in-Charge, Julee Scarfano led her fellow Supervisory Special Agent-in-Charge, Sheridan Fox out of Kurt Bowker's interrogation room and down a long corridor toward Fox's office. She hadn't been doing this job for very long—just a few hours, really—but yet it felt like she'd been the AIC for months. Even years. Those feelings were not based on experience. They were based on the constant, high-pressure situations she had faced, crammed into a small window of time. Coupled with the lack of sleep, she suddenly felt overwhelmed and exhausted more than ever before.

She stopped and turned to face Agent Fox. "Sheridan, how do you do it?"

"Do what?"

"Sit in your chair. Day in. Day out. You've been doing this job for what now? Ten years?"

"Thirteen."

"Okay. Thirteen. And you seem so calm. So composed. Like dealing with Kurt Bowker is nothing different than a cop dealing with a twelve-year-old shoplifter at a local convenience store."

"Hey, don't let my stunningly good looks and ageless complexion fool you. I'm just as nervous as you. You saw the internal memo go out about Las Vegas, same as me. I've got a sister who lives in Reno. People trek back and forth between Reno and Vegas every day. She'll be right in the line of fire, if this contagion gets outside the quarantine zone."

"Sheridan, I am so sorry."

"And you know as well as I do, I can't even call her and give her a heads up. I just have to trust the people handling that crisis will make the correct decisions and keep her, along with everyone else, safe. So, in the meantime, we do this part of the job and nail these people to the wall. Put an end to this madness, once and for all."

Julee nodded, as if being convinced to act by some motivational speaker. "I need to call the president."

"Yes. You do."

"Okay, but stay here. Two heads are better, right?"

"Depends on the heads, but in this case, yes."

Julee smiled and opened her smartphone. Selecting the correct number, she dialed and turned up the volume so Agent Fox could hear without putting it on speakerphone.

"Agent Scarfano," President Gilmore said. "Please tell me you have some good news."

"I do, Mr. President. We have caught a major player in this coordinated attack and have him in custody."

"Yes, Kurt Bowker, if I'm not mistaken. Director Jameson told me all about him. So, is he going to be able to help us?"

"I think so, sir. He claims he knows where the contagion is being housed."

"Really? Well, if he's correct, then that is huge indeed.

However, I'm guessing he wants something in return for that information."

"He does. He wants an immunity agreement and freedom from prosecution."

President Gilmore chuckled into the receiver, but it sounded tired. "He's got a lot of nerve."

"That he does, Mr. President. And my take on him is he's not going to give up the information until he has the immunity paperwork in his hands."

There was a long pause. Julee looked at Agent Fox and shrugged. "Sir, did you get that last bit of—"

"He's not getting anything, Agent Scarfano. Do I make myself clear? We do not negotiate with terrorists. I've already been down that road. I was willing to meet their demands of releasing the six hundred families. I was not going to alert any government employees about an impending attack. And I was going to lift the ban on air fresheners. And look where it got me? They released the contagion in Las Vegas anyway. And they claim they have the ability to replicate the feat all over the country. So, forgive me if I seem a little terse and uncooperative. I've bent over backwards to meet these terrorists' demands...against my better judgement, I might add. And all they did was double cross me."

"Sir, I don't think Kurt Bowker knows about or had anything to do with what's happening in Vegas."

"That's not what Director Jameson told me."

"Sir?"

"Jameson said this Bowker character has been working with all sorts of unsavory sorts, including Arina Filipov. Jameson also said he was responsible for hacking into our systems and mirroring your computer. Was he, Agent Scarfano?"

"Yes, sir, but—"

"I don't want to hear any excuses, Agent. I've made up my mind. You can tell Mr. Bowker he has been betrayed by his compadres. Therefore, his only play in this game of chess is to give up the information on the location of the contagion. And only if his information leads us to the complete seizure of said contagion, will I entertain the possibility of commuting his certain sentence of the death penalty to life without parole at Gitmo. Otherwise, he can burn in hell."

Julee looked at Agent Fox with pleading eyes.

Agent Fox shrugged, as if the president's answer was to be expected, not to mention final.

"Are you still there, Agent Scarfano?"

"Yes, sir. I was just trying to think of any other way. Kurt Bowker is prepared to die. He's on a bit of a mission of his own, seemingly. So, without an agreement of immunity, I don't expect him to give us much of anything."

President Gilmore sighed heavily into the phone. "Then, let me make myself as clear as I can, Agent Scarfano. Either you extract that information from Mr. Bowker, or I will send my people there to do it. And if I do, they will not only get the information from Bowker, but they will take him to ground zero, strap him to a row of slot machines in the middle of the Bahama Bay Casino, and let him breathe in death first hand.

"Then, my people will also relieve you of your duties as Supervisory Special Agent-in-Charge and the point person on this operation."

"Does this directive mean I have presidential permission to use any and all means necessary to extract said information from the enemy combatant?"

"Desperate times call for desperate measures, Agent Scarfano. So let me ask you this: If you were in Las Vegas right now, what would *you* want you to do?"

Julee peered at Agent Fox. "Understood, sir."

"Good. I'll leave you to it, then. You have one hour, Agent. We need that information."

The line went dead.

Scarfano pocketed her phone. "You heard the man."

"I did, and I can't believe my ears, frankly."

"What do you mean?"

"That any president would give an FBI agent *carte blanche* when it comes to interrogation tactics."

"You heard him. Desperate times, right?"

"These are desperate times, for sure. But, to violate your oath as an FBI agent puts you—puts us—on some shaky ground. If things go wonky, we'll be the ones at Gitmo. You know that, right?"

"Okay, so, what do you suggest?"

Agent Fox slipped his hands into his pockets. "We give the man what he wants."

"What? You mean give Bowker an immunity agreement? How? The president just said it's off the table."

"We can still give Bowker what he asked for. An immunity agreement. A fake one, but one nevertheless."

Julee pointed at Agent Fox and grinned. "You see? Experience. That's what you bring to the table, Agent Fox. And we just might be able to win this little battle without having to fire a shot."

"Like my daddy always said, 'Big brains always beat big fists.'"

CHAPTER 3

OVER Europe
   En Route to the United States

Supervisory Special Agent Blake Meyer, facing the front of the Gulfstream, sat on the opposite side of the plane from his fellow soldiers. The five men had risked their lives to get him to this point of being able to hold his children again, and he would be forever thankful.

Jacob sat on his left. Little Sara on his right. She had fallen asleep and was still snuggled up close to her father. A little bleary-eyed, Jacob peered out the window, looking down as best he could at the western European landscape.

Blake placed his arm around his son, causing Jacob to face him and smile. "Hey, you want to call your mom? Let her know you're okay and on your way home?"

"Can I?"

"I wouldn't have offered it if you couldn't." Blake snatched the satellite phone off the small table in front of him and disconnected the power cord. He punched in the phone number by heart and put the device up to his ear until he heard it ring before handing it to Jacob. He glanced at his watch. "I'm not sure who is going to answer. It's around lunchtime in Vermont."

Jacob grabbed the big phone with both hands and held it up to his ear.

* * *

"Yeah-lo?"

"Grandpa? Is that you?"

There was a short silence on the other end. "Jacob?"

"It's me, Grandpa. Is my mom there?"

"Uh, yeah. Yeah. Let me get her." Jacob could hear his grandfather groan, like he was getting up out of his recliner. And the noise sounded muffled. "Sara? Sara!"

Jacob heard more muffled sounds, like something was rubbing up against the phone. Then he heard other voices.

"Jacob? Jacob, sweetheart? Is it you?" Sara Meyer said.

"Mommy! It's me. It's Jacob." He looked up at his dad and smiled. "Daddy saved us. We're okay. He came with some other men and rescued me and Little Sara."

"He did?" Jacob could hear her crying. "That is so wonderful, baby. Are you okay? Did they hurt you?"

"No. We're okay."

"Is your sister there?"

"Yeah, but she's asleep. She's sitting next to Daddy."

"Oh, then let her sleep. She must be exhausted."

"Yeah. I am too."

"I'll bet you are."

Jacob could hear his mother cry even more, but it was mixed with happiness.

"I have missed you so much, little man. I can't begin to tell you how worried I've been. I'm so glad you're safe now."

"I've missed you too. And Sara missed you. She would cry and scream and tell the bad guys to let us go so we could go home."

There was another pause on the other end of the call, but Jacob could tell it wasn't disconnected. He could hear his mother crying and sniffling. She even sounded like she was having trouble breathing. He could hear Grandpa's voice in the background, asking a question, but his mother said she was fine.

"It's okay, Mommy. You don't have to cry anymore. We're safe now."

"I know. And I'm happy for both of you. I'm just sad Mommy was not there to protect you and keep all of this from happening to you and your sister."

"It's not your fault, Mommy. It's the bad guys' fault."

"Why don't you hand the phone over to your daddy and get some sleep, sweetheart. I'd love for you to be wide awake when you get back so I can kiss you all over your face."

Jacob smiled and looked at Blake again. "You know I'm getting too old for that, Mommy. We've already talked about this."

"I know, I know. But under the circumstances, I thought you would allow me to kiss you just this once."

"I guess," Jacob said with a sigh.

"Good! Because I was going to do it anyway. I'm your mother, and I'll kiss you all over your face whenever I feel like it. Especially today."

Jacob peered at Blake and rolled his eyes.

"She's gonna kiss you to death when we get back, isn't she?" Blake said.

Jacob nodded with a mortified grin.

"Be glad you have a mother who can kiss you, son. You almost lost her forever, you know."

Jacob thinned his smile and nodded his understanding.

"Is that your dad's voice I hear in the background?" Sara said.

"Yeah. Here's Dad."

"I love you, Jacob."

"Love you too." Jacob pulled the phone away from his ear and held it up. "She wants to talk to you."

* * *

Blake took the phone from his son and inhaled deeply. He winked at Jacob and allowed the breath to expel before pressing it to his ear. "Hey, Babe. How are you doing?"

"I'm doing a lot better now. I can't believe you found them so quickly."

"There's a bunch of people in our corner," Blake said, looking at his fellow soldiers. "Lots of helping hands, you know?"

"Please tell them 'Thank you' for me?"

"I will."

"How are Jacob and Sara? I can't imagine what they've been through."

"To be honest, better than I expected. I think it's because they were in the hands of an Albanian government official during the last leg of their journey. As it turns out, he intercepted them in the Cape Verde Islands and was with them every step of the way from there. He was working undercover to catch the people who had abducted them. He was not going to allow anything bad to happen to them. Trust me. He had me and my men arrested and was ready to ship us to an Albanian prison before I could convince him I was Jacob and Little Sara's father."

"It all sounds so messed up..."

"It is. I'll fill you in on all the details later. The important thing now is you are safe, and so are the kids, and we're heading home. We plan to land at the Northeast Kingdom International Airport in approximately four hours. I'll call you when we are about an hour away. Can you meet us there? Everyone will need a ride back to your parents' place."

"Of course. Is there anybody else with you besides the kids?"

"I have five men with me. They'll be staying with you all until this whole ordeal is over."

"So, you're gonna leave us again?"

"I have to, Sara. I have to put an end to this. But mark my words, it won't take long. A lot has happened since I left the Navy ship."

"Who are these men with you? Can they be trusted?"

"I trust them with my life. You'll be in excellent hands until I return."

Blake could hear Sara sigh, and it reminded him of how tenuous their relationship was right now. "Look, Sara, I want you to know that no matter how this turns out, I love you with everything in me. I'm sorry my past has caused all this, but I promise, once this is over, I'm done being Blake Meyer, SSA. I'll do whatever it takes to keep us together as a family. I'll flip burgers or walk people's dogs, if I have to."

Sara chuckled in a nervous way. "If only I could believe you."

"You can. You will. You'll see...soon enough."

"It's not that I don't believe *you*. You've never done anything to cause me to doubt you. It's the people you work for who worry me. And it's the people, like Colin Murphy and Pavel Morozov, who worry me even more."

Blake understood. His past would never be fully eradicated, regardless of how far away he ran from the FBI and the military. Even if they went into witness protection or something like it, if people wanted to find him, it was only a matter of time.

"However, Blake," Sara continued, "what really has my stomach twisted up in knots is I feel like I don't know the man I married anymore. I know the part I've seen with my own two eyes. I know how we met. I know how we have become a family. And

I've seen you love me and the kids the entire time, providing for us, protecting us..." Her voice trailed off for a moment.

Blake almost said something, but his words seemed so empty, so meaningless.

I wasn't able to protect them...

"But now," Sara said with a flutter in her voice, "things have changed." Blake could hear her squelch the rising emotion in her voice. "Yesterday, Mom and Dad got a call from the Duval County Medical Examiner's office. They claimed they had my sister's body in the morgue along with all the other guests at Little Sara's party." Blake covered his eyes with his free hand as Sara whimpered, trying to keep her composure. "They needed Mom and Dad to fly down and identify the body."

Blake wiped his eyes, as they, too, gave way to sadness. "Tell them I'll do it. I have to go back to the Jacksonville field office. I'll go by the ME's office. It'll be the first thing I do when I get to Jacksonville."

"I'll tell them you offered. They were talking about getting online and purchasing plane tickets. They may wish to do it themselves."

"Of course. Just let them know I am willing."

"I will."

"Sara, I am so, so sorry."

"Now," Sara said, as if Blake's last few words didn't register, "we have to make plans for how to handle my sister's funeral. I suppose they'll have the body flown up here. Dad called Longmont's Funeral Home out of Burlington. They're supposed to call back and set a meeting to make all the arrangements."

Blake didn't know what to say.

"And they have to go to my sister's house and see if she had a will, look into her bank accounts, bills, everything. It's going to take weeks to sort it all out.

Blake had no words. All he could muster was a shaky "I'm so

sorry." His erratic breathing, a loud sniff, and a wipe of the eyes caused Jacob to look up at his dad.

"Daddy, are you okay?"

Blake shook his head. "No, son, I'm not. Daddy's heart hurts right now."

Jacob frowned and placed his hand on his daddy's chest, softly patting it. He then leaned over and rested his head on Blake's side.

Blake closed his eyes and pinched them together as the father inside had collapsed to the floor and was sobbing.

"Will you be done with whatever you have to do in time for the funeral?" Sara said.

"Just call me at this number," Blake said, giving Sara the satellite number, "and let me know when the funeral is going to be held, and I'll be there."

"You promise?"

"I promise. Even if I have to hand this investigation off to someone else for a couple of days."

"Okay, well, we'll see you in a few hours at the airport?"

"Yes."

"We'll be there, waiting."

"I know the kids are looking forward to it. And so am I, Sara. I love you."

"I love you too."

"See you at the airport."

And with her last words, Blake heard a click, ending the call in silence.

He set the phone down on the little table and covered his face with his left hand, fighting back the tears.

"Daddy, is Mommy mad at you?" Jacob said.

Without removing his hand, he shook his head. "No, buddy. She's just sad because of everything that's happened."

Blake felt a small hand slide down his right forearm and eventually clasp his hand. He sniffed and wiped his cheeks.

Little Sara, whose eyes appeared puffy and sleepy, smiled up at him.

He patted her arm and smiled back, sniffing again.

"Are you okay, Daddy?"

"Daddy is dealing with some stuff, sweetheart. He hopes everything will be okay."

Little Sara wriggled around in her chair and sat up straighter before resting her head against Blake. "Once we see Mommy, evewyfing will be okay."

Blake closed his eyes and wrapped his arms around the children, pulling them close.

From your lips to God's ears, baby girl...

From your lips...

CHAPTER 4

MARFA REGIONAL MEDICAL Center
  Marfa, TX

Detective John Forde of the Wichita County Sheriff's Office sat in a chair, attempting to write his witness statement the way he was ordered. Captain Theodore "Harley" Harlan, Forde's supervisor, had given permission to start his narrative with the meeting in Shafter, Texas, between the dirty INS agents, an FBI's Ten Most Wanted List member, his little SUR-13 lap dog, the exchange of people for cash, the explosion, and Willis's injury, followed by the attempted murder of his partner in the hospital. There was no need for Forde to include the auto accident involving the van carrying the Jimenez family, driven by two terrorists, on their way to Orlando, Florida, several days ago. Everyone knew about it now. However, the story of Hector Jimenez and his brutal murder? Forde was instructed to omit it for now. "Because we don't know who knows what exactly," Captain Harlan said over the phone, "nor who is compromised, we need to keep the details of this investigation as close to the vest as possible. Put in too much information, and our enemies will tie everything together. You can always go back and amend your statement later. Got it, detective?"

"Don't have to tell me twice," Forde said.

Forde was also not allowed to mention Guillermo Castaneda by name. He could mention Pedro Arroyo for obvious reasons. He was in police custody. Chained to a gurney, according to the officer taking Forde's statement, in surgery, having his abdomen repaired from the gun shot Forde inflicted. Ballistics would match the bullet found in Arroyo's gut to Forde's gun. They would match the two bullets lodged in the wall and television of Detective Willis's hospital room to the gun Forde wrestled from Arroyo's grasp. And Arroyo's "lunchbox," which had been found just ten minutes earlier, would contain a tablet inside, Forde told the detectives who had arrived on scene. Also, Forde believed Arroyo had floor plans of the hospital, not to mention information on exactly which room contained his partner. All this evidence meant Arroyo was not only connected, he was toast.

However, Guillermo Castaneda was off limits to the statement being written because he was in the wind, and nobody wanted him more than Captain Harlan.

"You don't try to murder one of my detectives and get away with it," Harlan said to Forde over the phone. "He's all mine."

"I want him just as much as you do, Cap," Forde said. "He tried to kill me too."

"Point taken."

"When are you getting here?" Forde said.

"We turned the chopper around just as soon as you called for backup. Should be there well before you finish writing your statement for the locals."

And he was correct. The Captain walked into the hospital as Forde started the third page.

* * *

After Forde completed his seven-page statement and handed it to the Marfa Police officer, he walked down to the main lobby where he and his boss agreed to reconvene their meeting from earlier.

Captain Harlan was sitting in a comfortable-looking lounge chair in the far corner. No doubt so he could see everything going on, everybody who walked into the area.

Forde zigged and zagged his way around rows of stiff-backed chairs and tables filled with old magazines and plopped down into the nearby love seat.

"Just got back from checking on Arroyo a few minutes ago," Captain Harlan said, taking his eyes off his smartphone. "You did a number on him, detective. Nurse told me he's gonna be a while. Gut's all tore up. Surgeons are having trouble finding a bleeder. Got some cuts to stitch up on his head too."

"He's lucky I didn't empty my clip when I had the chance."

Harlan stood. "Coffee? I know I could use some."

Forde nodded and yawned. "With a shot of espresso, if they have it."

"This ain't one of those froufrou coffee houses. It's a hospital cafeteria. You're lucky if it's dark enough to be considered coffee and not mistaken for tea."

Forde stood with a groan. "The stuff we had in the other waiting room wasn't too bad."

"True. Where is that waiting room?"

"Follow me," Forde said. "I know the way."

Harlan nodded and walked with Forde toward the sign pointing down a hallway, telling patrons the emergency room was straight ahead.

"So," Forde said, "did you get ahold of that Dennis guy from Homeland?"

"I have not been able to raise him yet. Just tried callin' again right before you arrived."

"How well do you know him?"

"Forde, I am a lot of things, but a bad judge of character is not one of them. Dennis Morrison is a straight shooter. He's just as much baseball, apple pie, and Fourth of July as I am. He'd never switch to the dark side. I'd bet my bottom dollar on it. He's probably knee deep in some meeting with a bunch of big shots at Homeland."

"Then, Captain, we have a bigger issue. Somebody in Homeland Security has a Sinaloa Cartel member on his or her payroll, or he or she is on Sinaloa's books. That's the only explanation for how Arroyo was able to even know about Willis, let alone know where to find him."

"I'm hoping Dennis can shed some light on the subject for us."

"And if he's dirty?"

"Then, I'll arrest him myself. But before you act as the judge, jury, and executioner, give Dennis a chance to exonerate himself. If he can't, and he gives us the runaround, acting all guilty and everything, then I'll bring him in for questioning. Just that alone should get him talking. Because if I did bring him in, Sinaloa would know about it. All I'd have to do is tell Dennis he's free to go. He'd be dead within forty-eight hours."

Forde pointed at the sign, indicating they needed to turn left at the hallway intersection. "You'd set up an old friend for his certain death, Cap?"

"I'd do that to my own grandmother, if I proved she was helping an organization like the Sinaloa Cartel. I have very little patience for people who help organizations destroy people's lives with drugs and human trafficking, for money, no less."

Forde led the captain into the little room with the individual coffee maker. He motioned to his boss. "After you."

"No, you first. I insist. I wasn't the one shot at this morning."

Forde shrugged, but he wasn't going to argue.

* * *

Captain Harlan's phone rang to the sound of a motorcycle engine being revved by the driver. Harlan plucked the phone from its holder and checked the screen. He held it up for Forde to see and then slid the green phone icon sideways. "Dennis?"

"Harley, man, I am so sorry. My phone says I have eight missed calls from you. What's going on?"

Harlan watched Forde finish making his coffee. "You tell me, Dennis. I think we have a major issue to address."

"What kind of issue?"

"Well, it's like this. We sent you all those photos of Mr. Castaneda and his little SUR-13 lap dog, Arroyo, right?"

"Right."

"What did you do with those pictures after we hung up?"

"I...uh, I'm...not following, Harley."

Harlan pointed at the coffee maker and then himself, asking Forde to make his coffee for him. "We sent you those pictures, and over the phone, you said you identified the four men in those pictures. Remember? Two of the men, you said, worked for a group." Forde picked up two of the options, one a breakfast blend and the other a dark roast, and held them up. Harlan pointed at the dark roast. "The Hands of...something. Aladdin? Alabaster? Alabama?—"

"Allah. The Hands of Allah. Yeah, I remember."

"Right. Allah, Arab group. And the other two men identified were Guillermo Castaneda and Pedro Arroyo. You told us Castaneda had been a ghost, and you didn't have any good photos of the man, et cetera, et cetera. The other guy, Arroyo, was a member of *Surenos*-13 and Castaneda's right-hand man."

"Yes, yes. I remember. So, what about it?"

"So, I'm asking you. What did you do after we sent you all those pictures?"

"Uh,...I ran all those photos through facial recognition software. Just to make sure they were the same people in each one. I also wanted to positively identify the two dirty INS agents, which I did, by the way."

"What did you do after that?"

"Harlan, why are you asking me all these questions?"

"Just play along, Dennis," Harlan said, taking his coffee from Forde. "I have my reasons. I'll fill you in when I think I have the answer to our issue."

Harlan could hear Dennis sigh. "I notified my superior. The man who runs the Dallas area office."

"What's his name?" Harlan said, setting his coffee down on the counter and pulling out a little notepad and pen.

"Larry Montrose."

"Spell the last name for me?"

"M-O-N-T-R-O-S-E."

"And how long has he been in that position?"

"Ever since this office opened, which was shortly after DHS was created. He's the only one left of the original DHS Special Agents-in-Charge. We can trust him, if that's what you're wondering."

"Who else did you send the pictures to, Dennis?"

"Once Larry looked them over, he instructed me to send them to the director."

"Patricia Williamson?"

"Uh, yeah, she's the director, last time I checked."

Harlan didn't appreciate the sarcasm in his friend's voice.

"Harley, what's this all about?"

"Dennis, we can't talk about this anymore. Not on the phone. Can you meet me?"

"I'm an analyst, Harley, not a field agent."

"I need to talk to you in person, but it can't be at your office. And I would just a soon keep it out of mine for now." Harlan took a sip of his black coffee just as a voice came over the intercom of the hospital, asking for Doctor Twelve to report to the emergency room.

"Are you still at the hospital?" Dennis said.

"We are."

"I thought you were heading back to Wichita Falls?"

"I was, but something came up. I had to turn the chopper back around. Hence, my need to talk to you in person."

Dennis Morrison was silent on the other end for several seconds.

"I wouldn't ask, Dennis, if it wasn't important."

"And we can't discuss it over the phone? Or teleconference over a computer?"

"We don't have any way to make sure those connections are secure."

"This is a big deal, isn't it?"

"It is."

"You aren't the kind of person inclined to make these kinds of requests for run-of-the-mill information."

"See? You know me too well. And trust me, my friend, what I need to discuss may just be a major case endangering our national security."

"Okay, I'll see what I can do."

"Bring your laptop, all those pictures we sent you, and the most secure method of accessing information you can muster."

"Anything else?"

"How long will it take you to get here?"

"If I can get a chopper, about three hours. If I have to drive, eight or nine."

"I strongly suggest getting the bird, Dennis. If your supervisor needs to talk to me, then have him call me."

"Will do."

Harlan hung up and looked at Forde. "Where's the creamer? This coffee needs some help."

"Too strong?"

"No such thing. I'm a percolator-on-the-stove kind of guy."

CHAPTER 5

Blake Meyer told Jacob and Little Sara he needed to use the restroom on the plane. He stood and allowed them to sit comfortably in their seats as he made his way to the back of the plane.

Closing the door and moving the latch from "vacant" to "occupied," he flopped down on the toilet seat. He rested his elbows on his knees and covered his face with his hands. The wrestling match inside between the soldier, the FBI agent, the husband, and the father had taken its toll. His conversation with Sara went about the way he expected. He knew she'd be ecstatic to hear her children's voices and know they were safe now, but she'd be defensive when she spoke with him. He knew she'd be disapproving of him showing up and leaving again. He knew she'd be hesitant, even perturbed, about having five strange men in her parents' house.

However, it was Sara's words, about her sister, and the funeral, which proved to be the proverbial straw. He pictured Little Sara's party on that fateful Friday evening...just two days ago...even though it seemed like two years...all the people who had arrived...jubilant, smiling faces...presents in hand...joyous discussions wafting out onto the deck as he flipped hamburgers and hot dogs on the grill...silly laughter as Little Sara's friend's father told knock-knock jokes to the kids...his own trip to the shed to get his little girl's present...hours spent making it incognito...then, the shot in the neck...awakening to the dizziness...trying to stand...the explosion...

He imagined the party guests sitting in the house, scared to death, no doubt, as armed gunmen stormed inside and took his wife and children.

Although he wasn't awake at the time, he'd read the reports Harrison had sent him from the Jacksonville Sheriff's Office. And he'd already watched the footage from the commandeered satellite spying on his home.

The reports pieced together a gruesome scene of a firing squad-like killing of the guests as they sat huddled together, protecting the children as best they could. According to the reports, this took place simultaneously as the satellite footage caught the other gunmen carrying his children and his wife out of the house.

Then, they were placed in inflatable rafts. The gunmen pushed the boats into the surf, and angled toward the north, just as the house erupted into a fireball...

The soldier inside tried to brace the dam. The FBI agent inside, who had tossed his credentials aside several hours ago, lent his aid as well, but to no avail. The flood waters were too strong.

The husband and the father inside fell against the wall of Blake's heart. Stone-still, all they could do was replay Sara's words until the wall of tears burst forth.

All Blake could do now was weep.

* * *

Fifteen minutes later, a knock came at the door to the bathroom.

"Captain Meyer, everything okay in there?" It was Captain Davis.

Blake wiped his eyes and examined his face in the mirror. "Not really, but I'll be okay."

"Just checkin'. Your kids were getting a little concerned out here."

"Tell them I'll be right out."

"Good, 'cause I think your daughter needs to use it next."

Blake smiled and opened the door.

Captain Davis examined Blake as he stepped through the small doorway. "Captain, don't take this personally, but you look like—"

"Hey, Sara," Blake said, eyeing his fellow soldier as he did. "You need to use the bathroom?"

"Yep," she said, whisking past him and closing the door without another word.

Captain Davis covered his mouth and winced.

"Don't forget to wash your hands," Blake said. He then pointed at Davis. "And don't forget to wash your mouth out with soap."

"I didn't say anything bad."

"Thanks to me."

"But you do, Cap. You look horrible."

Blake patted Davis on the shoulder. "That's because I feel horrible, captain. Physically. Emotionally. Psychologically. I'll be the first to admit I'm a mess."

"Understandable."

"But I need to get a grip. This thing isn't over yet."

"What's our next step?"

"Let me make a phone call, then we can talk about where we go from here."

"Ten-Four."

Blake walked back to his seat and picked up the satellite phone. He looked at Jacob and smiled. "I have to call someone. You doin' okay?"

"Sure. I'm a little thirsty, though."

"There's some stuff in the little fridge over there. Go check it out."

Jacob hopped from his seat with a bounce in his step.

"Hey, Captain, can you help him with that while I make this call?"

Davis nodded. "Sure."

"And when Sara gets out, see if she wants anything."

"You got it."

Blake dialed the number by heart.

"Blakey, me boy, am I glad to hear from you. How are you doing? Did you find Jacob and Sara?"

"Yes. They're with me. We're on our way back to the States now."

"Praise God! Thank you, Father. This is such wonderful news."

"You're tellin' me."

"Answer to prayer, my friend. The enemy means to do harm and destroy. But God loves and creates."

"Thank you for praying."

"Well, Blakey, I'm not gonna stop just yet. A lot has happened since we last talked."

"That's why I called. We need to get up to speed so we know what to do next."

"Are you sitting down?"

"That bad, huh?"

"Let's just say you might want to have something to jot all this down."

"Oh, okay, then." Blake opened a drawer and searched for a pad of paper.

"Whatcha lookin' for, Daddy?" Jacob said.

"Something to write on, sport," Blake said, pulling a pen from the small pocket in his shirt.

"Over here, Cap," Alwin Nefarje said. He held out a small pad.

"Thanks. Okay, Harrison, go ahead," he said as he sat down across from Jacob.

"Remember when you gave me access codes to Sorensen's computer?"

"I do."

"Sorensen's information has proven to be very helpful. I have identified the person responsible for accessing Julee Scarfano's laptop. Turns out, he's been responsible for a bunch of stuff, including helping Arina Filipov."

"We knew she had help. There was no way she could access the places she'd infiltrated without someone on the outside running interference."

"Well, it gets better. Her guy running interference is none other than Kurt Bowker."

Blake watched as Little Sara exited the bathroom and slowly walked toward him. He was staring at her, but his mind was trying to process what Harrison had just said.

"Sara, are you thirsty?" Jacob said.

"Yes."

He held up a bottled water. "You can get one from the fridge over there. That's about all that is in there. Except some beer."

Little Sara wrinkled her nose and sat down in her chair. "I don't want any water right now."

"Blake, you still there?" Harrison said.

"Yeah, uh...Are you sure, Harrison?"

"Julee has already traveled up to Atlanta and met with the devil. They have him in custody. He's all but admitted to everything. Helping Filipov. Helping Markus Sorensen and his group called The Consortium. Commandeering the satellite which was positioned over your house. He's turned into a computer geek for hire, it appears."

Blake remembered being introduced to Kurt once when he was about ten years old. Conrad had just taken the job with MI6, and Kurt had come along for the ride to London. Yet, now that Blake thought about it, Conrad never talked about his family much, unless they were in the news and being—in Conrad's estimation—brainwashed by Russian operatives. Then, Conrad told the world about it. In his blog.

"I also have voice recordings from Sorensen's computer, Blakey. I believe they are the people who make up this Consortium."

"Have you identified them yet?"

"I asked Julee to give me access to their voiceprint database, but she was in the middle of an operation at the InterHealth Medical Center at the time and couldn't help me."

"And you spoke to her how long ago?"

"I don't know. Four, maybe five hours."

"We need those people identified, Harrison."

"Uh, yeah. But all I can do is ask. I even threatened her by saying I would tell you and have you order her."

Blake smirked. "What did she say?"

"In so many words? Uh,...she was in charge now, and even the mighty Blake Meyer could not persuade her to do anything she didn't deem necessary or feel capable of doing."

"Eh, she's just overwhelmed. I can't imagine how she feels right now. Being thrown into this mess as a new AIC? Never having done the job before? Better her than me."

"You're being way more forgiving than I thought you'd be."

"She's good people, Harrison. I'm sure she's making the best decisions she can under the circumstances."

"Oh, I didn't say she was doing a bad job. I just think she's allowing the tail to wag the dog. I mean, I'm right there with you. Identify these voices, and we'll be able to bring this entire network down to its knees." Blake heard Harrison shuffle some papers. "Hey, that reminds me...," Harrison continued, groaning like he was reaching for something. "Speaking of bringing networks to their knees—and even Julee doesn't know this yet, but I just uncovered two big pieces of information from Sorensen's computer in the last hour. This should help you guys immensely.

"The first thing involves a phone number we uncovered way back toward the beginning of this investigation. It's a Russian phone number. 011-7-93832-555-7891. Remember that one? We pulled it off of Sergei Botinkin's smart phone?"

"I do. There was a text message back and forth between Sergei and the person the number belonged to. They had Sergei all set up to leave the country, sail to the West Indies, and wait for what I assumed was a Soviet sub scheduled to take him to Venezuela."

"Good memory. Well, are you ready to learn who the user was of said phone number, Blakey?"

"Using it how?"

"Using it, as in...it's his phone, and he has been calling some very shady characters with it."

"Of course."

"You sure? It's gonna blow your doors off and grind your gears, all at the same time. Might even make you say some things your kids should probably not hear Daddy say."

"I don't have any doors left, Harrison. And my gears are about as ground up as they can be, so just tell me. I'm tired. I'm frustrated. I'm—"

"Okay, I get it."

"Then, spit it out."

"You still sitting down?"

"Harrison!"

"Okay, okay. The owner of the Russian phone number is none other than Benjamin Franklin Jenkins, President Gilmore's Chief of Staff."

Blake's head almost exploded. It quickly started replaying conversations he'd had with Jenkins, both one-on-one and in the presence of the president. Suddenly, like a hologram, with a gentle turn of the image, another one came into focus. Each one more sinister, more devilish than the last.

"I can tell by the silence. You did have some doors to blow off after all," Harrison said.

"How certain of this are you, Harrison?"

"Ninety-nine-point-nine percent."

"How can you be so sure?"

Harrison sighed heavily into the receiver.

"I'm sorry, buddy. I'm doubting your skills again, aren't I?" Blake said.

"Some things never change."

"I'm just asking, Harrison, because if I waltz into the White House with a crew of secret service agents and arrest the president's chief of staff, and we are somehow wrong about it, then it gets ugly for us in the snap of your fingers. Besides, we don't have the entire list of who he's working with. We could arrest him and inadvertently hand him off to an accomplice, for all we know."

"And that's why I need those voice recordings identified. The person who owns this number contacted Sorensen multiple times. In all of those recordings, he used this number. All of them were the same voice. And I am convinced it is Ben Jenkins's voice. Sorensen even calls him by his first name in five of those recordings."

"But Jenkins could easily say it's another 'Ben' being referenced, not him."

"My point exactly. Hence, the need for the voice match. Match *his* voice, and it would, at least, give you and your contacts within the alphabet agencies the right to dig into his life unobstructed."

"Okay, so let me contact Julee and see what I can do."

"Good on ya, cobber. Now, the second thing I found out is even bigger, if you can believe it. I have the location of the contagion. The bad one. The real one. The one in the air fresheners. The one they made their initial threats with. I know where they are storing it until the ban is lifted."

"The president hasn't lifted the ban yet, has he?"

"No. I don't think so."

"Send me the address, but send it to our D-mail, not over our phones or through text messaging. I'll alert local authorities at the proper time to lock the area down and wait for my arrival."

"You got it."

"And what's the news on Las Vegas?"

"You heard about Vegas, did ya?"

"Yeah. Is it bad?"

"It is. All flights to Vegas are being rerouted, and nobody on the ground is being allowed to enter or leave the city. President just ordered the National Guard to go in and help keep the peace."

"Not good."

"Apparently, whatever happened in Vegas, the government wants to keep it in Vegas."

"Oh, you're a comedian now?"

"Gotta lighten the mood, Blakey. It's getting pretty grim around here."

"Understood. Keep me posted. We're taking Jacob and Little Sara to Vermont to meet up with Sara at her parents' house. I'm going to leave these men with her and the kids, just as a precaution. Until everything is over.

"In the meantime, before we land, I'll contact Scarfano and get you access to that database. We will need those voices identified. And of course, if you pull any additional information off of any of those files, let me know. I'm not going dark anymore, so reaching me shouldn't be a problem."

"You got it."

"And I've got one thing I need you to do for me."

"Which is?"

"The transponder signal from Morozov's yacht...I need you to give it to Arina Filipov."

"Have you gone troppo?"

"I'm not sure exactly what that means, but she's the only one who can track these people down and make them pay."

"Whatever happened to arresting them and bringing them to justice?"

"To be honest, Harrison, even after what I've been through in the last seventy-two hours, I was on the fence with this. But your information about Ben Jenkins just pushed me over to Filipov's side in cases like Morozov. It appears we have some quote-unquote good guys who are in bed with Morozov, no pun intended, as well as others like him. How can we expect them to bring people like Morozov to justice when it means incriminating themselves? Yet, they cannot be allowed to continue. There are too many innocent lives at stake, and many of our government leaders are apparently just as guilty. So, when the enemy perverts justice, the Arina Filipovs of the world become necessary."

"I'll see what I can do."

"I'll put her number in the D-mail. All you have to do is call her and let her know you are fulfilling a request for me. She'll let you know where to send all the information."

"But then I'll be seen as working in a lurk with an international terrorist. Her name is all over the chatter, Blakey. Our government has every agency on the planet looking for her."

"Then, I suggest you use those mad skills you're always throwing back in my face and do it discreetly."

Harrison huffed. "Okay. But this is the first thing you've ever asked me to do which didn't make sense, you know."

"Harrison, it's because she's the only one who can take down these human trafficking rings. We have government and world agencies spending hours and days at conferences—*on human traf-*

ficking...it is their sole reason for meeting—and all they can do is argue about the definition of 'human trafficking.' How can you get bogged down in the definition of human trafficking? Defining it should be one of the easiest things to do because, allegedly, all of these countries are against it. However, truth be known, they aren't against it. They profit from it. Oh, they hold their conferences, and they pass their laws and statutes, and they hand out awards to leaders who pass such things. But so many of them are on the take. There's too much money involved.

"And for many government leaders and corporations, they even use the services provided by traffickers. The sex industry. The farming industry. Supplying maids and butlers. Millions of slaves exist right under our noses, and generally speaking, we happily ignore it all.

"The world is broken, Harrison. The system of society and government is broken. And it doesn't matter if it's dominated by capitalism, communism, a monarchy, a tribe of elders, or a dictatorial regime. Slavery has been prevalent throughout history, and it's very much alive and well today. Maybe more so now than ever.

"So, when you're dealing with a broken system, which employs people who work extremely hard at keeping it broken, all you are left with is to send in someone who will simply burn the building to the ground. No more system, no more damaged goods in the form of innocent, broken people.

"And if there is one thing I've learned about Arina Filipov, she has a singular focus. She was going to kill me, because she was led to believe I was part of the system she seeks to destroy. When she learned the system was going to kill us both—because she was viewed as a loose cannon and I was viewed as a threat to their way of living—she killed the killers and set us both free."

"But if Kurt Bowker can no longer help her, then she's much more vulnerable than before, right?"

"That's her business. Just don't let her recruit you when you call. She's very impressed with your skills, Harrison, and she will probably make you an offer that will make you choke on your vegemite."

"Wonderful."

"Just tell her you're not interested."

"I'd rather not have to talk to her at all."

"She's not as bad as everyone has made her out to be. I mean, she's done some despicable things, don't get me wrong. But she saved my life. She's simply one very angry Russian assassin who wants to put human traffickers out of business and save the women and children being held by those people."

"Well, since you put it like that..."

"So, you'll call her then?"

Harrison huffed again. "Enough with the earbashin'. Yes, I'll phone her."

"Good on ya, cobber. I said that correctly, right?"

"Yes, but it sounded funny coming from a yank."

"One step at a time. At least you didn't refer to me as a 'seppo.'"

"Ah, no. Doesn't apply to you, my friend."

"That's good to know. I'll call again to get an update after I leave Vermont, but if something pressing comes up between now and then, call this number."

"Aye."

"In the meantime, make sure you contact Filipov."

Harrison sighed. "*Da Svidaniya.*"

CHAPTER 6

Blake Meyer hung up and peered at his children. Both of them looked at him and smiled.

"Who was dat, Daddy?" Little Sara said.

"An old friend, sweetheart."

"Is his name Harwison?"

"Yes. Why do you ask?"

"Mommy was tawking about him at my birfday party. The day the bad men came to our house."

Blake tried to smile at her comment, but he found it difficult to do so when he really wanted to cry. "What was Mommy saying about Harrison?"

"Mommy told Aunt Salwy she thought Harwison would be a good boyfwiend for her."

Blake looked away for a quick second. "She did, did she?"

"Aunt Salwy told Mommy her old boyfwiend was a putz," Little Sara said with a shrug. "Whateffer that means."

"Ah, well, I know about her old boyfriend. He's not a very good person. So, if he breaks up with Aunt Sally—" Blake suddenly realized what he was about to say. He closed his eyes and beat back the emotions raging inside. "It would be a good thing for her."

Little Sara nodded in her five-year-old way. "I hope Aunt Salwy finds a boyfwiend just like you, Daddy."

Blake stared at his daughter as tears formed. Her words were sweet. She meant them for good, but they made him feel ill.

She doesn't know...

She and Jacob must have been taken from the house before the guests were...

"Are you okay, Daddy?" Little Sara said.

"I am now, pumpkin. You and your brother are here with me."

Little Sara jumped from her seat and ran to her father, plowing into his chest.

Blake wrapped his arms around her and almost hugged the life out of her. He then tickled her.

She squealed with excitement.

Jacob inched up onto the edge of his chair and chuckled as he watched them play.

Blake noticed and reached out his arm. With a wave of his hand, Jacob lunged toward his father, and it quickly became a game of Daddy playing his infamous role as the Tickle Monster.

* * *

A couple of minutes passed before Blake leaned back in his chair, breathing more heavily than he should. He winced at the discomfort in his abdomen and the stinging sensation in his chest area, but he tried not to let his children know he was in pain.

The five soldiers watched and laughed as their fellow brother-in-arms enjoyed his life as a Dad, even if it was for a brief time.

Eventually, the commotion subsided, and Little Sara ended up on Blake's lap. Jacob had sat back down in his chair and grabbed his bottled water.

"Are we going home now?" Little Sara said.

Her words, simple and innocent, shattered Blake's glee.

"Uh, sweetheart, we're actually heading to Grandma and Grandpa J's house. Mommy is there waiting on us."

"But why can't we go home?"

"Did something happen to our home, Daddy?" Jacob said. "I overheard some people on the boat say something about our house. I couldn't hear everything, but one of them said they heard it got blown up."

Little Sara, listening to her brother, jerked her head around. Her sudden, scared expression bored holes into Blake. Her voice went up an octave, and a quiver rattled the words. "Daddy...is dat twue?"

Blake pulled his daughter close. A tear streamed down his face, and a knot in his throat kept any words from escaping. All he could do was nod.

Little Sara buried her head into his chest and burst into tears of her own.

Jacob's disbelieving look scrunched his brow together, and his features, soft when he asked his question, turned hard. Bothered. Angry.

Jacob slammed his fist down on the armrest of his chair and jumped out of his seat.

"Jacob. Wait." Blake said.

Jacob stormed toward the back of the plane without a word and entered the bathroom. The door slammed shut.

Blake allowed his head to flop back against the seat. Tears

flowed for his children. The only home they'd ever known was gone.

Blake wasn't sure they'd ever be able to live there again. Even if they rebuilt everything...put everything back exactly the way it was, the memories would still remain. Each room would haunt them. Little Sara's birthday would be psychologically catastrophic. It would be remembered as the event which started it all.

Besides, he knew Sara would never approve.

For those very reasons.

It was now the place where her sister was murdered.

It was the place where Blake's past ruined their lives, never to be the same again.

It was a place they'd never be able to revisit.

Little Sara whimpered in Blake's arms, as he replayed those images in his head over and over. He knew she was wondering if Mr. Panda, her stuffed bear who wore a tuxedo, was okay, or did he get killed too.

Blake wiped his face and his nose with his hand and clenched his teeth. A seething rage was building, and he needed to squelch it before his children saw a side of him they may never forget.

He motioned at Sergeant Spanarkle to come over and sit down beside him.

"Hey, sweetheart, I promise you, we'll find Mr. Panda."

"You promise?"

"I promise. When Daddy is done with his job, he will personally go find Mr. Panda."

She mustered a slight smile but said nothing.

"Listen, I need to go check on your brother. I've asked my friend to sit here next to you, in case you need anything. Okay?"

She nodded but appeared hesitant.

"His name is Sergeant Spanarkle. That's a funny name, isn't it? But you can call him Nark."

She nodded again.

"I'll be right back." Blake got up and went to the back of the plane.

He leaned against the wall and rapped lightly on the bathroom door. "Hey, buddy, you okay in there?"

"I'm fine," Jacob said.

"You don't sound fine."

"Okay, so I'm not fine."

"Can you open the door?"

"Why?"

"So we can talk."

Blake heard what sounded like water running. Then, some banging. Then the latch flipped from "occupied" to "vacant" before the door opened.

"It's okay, Daddy. I was just mad. I hate those men who did this to us."

Blake knelt down and placed his hands on Jacob's shoulders. Gently, he used his thumbs to wipe his son's cheeks. "Jacob, I get it, but nobody is angrier than me. Those bad guys attacked me and my family. And you don't pick a fight with Blake Meyer and expect to win. I will get every last person responsible for what they did to us. I promise you."

Jacob pressed his lips together. A slight nod made the tuft of hair on his head bounce.

"But just remember, all the stuff we had...the house...our beds...your toys...the food in the fridge...everything...everything can be replaced. But I can't replace you. Or your sister. Or your mom. You guys are all I need. You're all I care about. We could live in a tent in the middle of nowhere, and I would be okay with it, so long as we have each other."

Jacob's face changed from calm to perplexed. "But we're not really gonna live in a tent, right?"

Blake chuckled and allowed his hands to slide down to Jacob's arms. "No, son. I was just trying to make a point so you understood how much I love you guys."

"Good, because my friend, Josh, went on a camping trip with his mom and dad and his two sisters last summer. He said they got all bit up by mosquitos, and a bear crashed their tent and ate all of their food while they were canoeing on the river. They had to leave early, because they didn't have anything to eat. And they were afraid the bear would come back."

Blake snickered as Jacob told his tale. He loved hearing his son forget about their troubles for a few minutes. "Well, if we go camping, as a family, we'll get a hotel room. Sound like a plan?"

"Will it have a swimming pool?"

"If you want one, sure."

Jacob threw his arms around Blake's neck. "Thank you, Daddy."

"I love you, sport."

"I love you too."

"Let's go back and sit with your sister."

"Okay," Jacob said, relinquishing his dad's neck.

Blake led Jacob back out into the common area.

"So, when are we going to go camping in the hotel room, Daddy?"

"Once I catch all the bad guys, buddy. After that, we can make it one of the first things we do. Deal?" Blake held up his hand.

Jacob reared his hand back and slapped Blake's with considerable force. "Deal!"

CHAPTER 7

OVER THE ATLANTIC

En Route to the United States

Blake Meyer asked Jacob and Little Sara to sit next to each other and try to get some rest, for once they got to Grandma and Grandpa J's house, sleep would be hard to come by because of all the hugs and kisses they would get from Mommy and Grandma and Grandpa J.

The two little tikes agreed and curled up in their chairs with blankets around them.

Blake then went to the back of the plane and sat down. He unplugged his satellite phone from the charger and called Julee Scarfano.

"Blake? Is it you?"

"Yes. Despite any rumors, I'm still alive."

"It is so good to hear your voice. Were you able to find your children?"

"I was. They're with me now. We're on our way back to the States. Should be in Vermont soon."

"That's where your wife's parents live, correct?"

"It is." Blake rubbed his face as fatigue slowly gripped him. "Where are you?"

"In Atlanta."

"Right. I've already talked to Harrison. He filled me in on a bunch of things, one of which being why you had to travel up there."

Blake could hear Julee give somebody a muffled directive. "Listen, if this is a bad time, I can make this short, but I do have some important things I need to cover with you."

"No, no, we're just getting some things lined up here before I head back to Jacksonville."

"What kind of things?"

"Frankly, Blake, I don't know where to begin. So much has happened since we talked last."

"Does it have to do with Kurt Bowker?"

"Harrison told you about Bowker?"

"He did."

"Then you probably know Bowker was the hacker who was watching my computer station."

"Yes. He also told me Kurt is the one who set up the satellite feed for the people who watched my family get abducted...and they watched my house blow up." Blake grunted. "And he mentioned how he's been helping Arina Filipov for years too."

"Okay, good. You're up to speed on the Bowker situation for the most part."

Blake could hear more voices in the background.

"Did Harrison discuss Sorensen's computer at all," Julee continued, "and how he's pulling data from it?"

"Yes. And that's why I called."

"Did he also inform you of our joint decision to allow you to break the news to Conrad Bowker about his son?"

Blake allowed a tired chuckle to escape. "No. He failed to mention it."

"We figured it would be best received coming from you, since you know him personally and all."

"That conversation will have to wait. We've got a bunch to get done before then."

"You're telling me."

Blake inhaled deeply and allowed it to escape in a measured breath. "Harrison thinks he located the contagion. The one they've been threatening to release the entire time."

"Are you serious?"

"Yes. I need you to choose two of your—"

"Hey, Agent Fox," Julee said, interrupting Blake. "Stop the presses on the immunity agreement."

"What immunity agreement?" Blake said.

"Kurt Bowker said he would tell us where the contagion was, if we gave him an agreement."

Captain Davis strolled up to Blake with a bottled water in his hand.

Blake reached out his hand. "Did the president approve it?" Blake mouthed the words "thank you" as Davis gave him the bottle and a thumbs-up.

"No. But we were going to draw up a fake one, have him give us the location, check it out to verify, and then explain to Bowker how he'd been duped."

Blake unscrewed the cap and took a swig of water. "Risky. His lawyers would probably have all the information gathered thrown out of his court case."

"Maybe, but at least we'd secure the contagion and save lives. And besides, with the Who's Who List of criminals he's been working for, all we have to do is get the word out he helped us in so many ways. He'd be dead inside of a week. But, if Harrison is correct, then there's no need for this charade to continue."

Blake took another swig and screwed the cap back on the bottle. "Harrison's information is solid. It's straight from Sorensen's own files. Therefore, we need to handle this next phase carefully. We don't know who we can trust, Julee. And once we let the cat out of the bag on the contagion's location, if whoever we work with isn't trustworthy, then the contagion could disappear. If that happens—"

"Then we probably won't get another chance to seize it before it gets released," Julee said with a sigh of frustration. "I know."

"Look, Julee, we're gonna get these guys. We're close. Real close."

"Are you aware there has already been an attack? They've already released some of the contagion."

"Ambassador Lew told me. Director Jameson confirmed, at the time, it was only one location, and they only had one confirmed case of illness. An elderly woman, I think? She was there with her husband, if memory serves."

"Correct. Bahama Bay Hotel and Casino. She was the first case. However, there have been seventy-two more since then."

"Seventy-two..." Blake blew out a big breath. "How many people are in the resort?"

"Well over a thousand. CDC representatives just arrived on scene. Local medical authorities are turning it over as we speak. Reports are saying the contagion has been weaponized. It incubates in a matter of a few hours and shows symptoms immediately. And Blake, medical authorities on site have confirmed. It's bubonic plague."

"But we have antibiotics for the plague. It can be cured, if caught in time. Are they giving the victims the antibiotics?"

"Yes, but I've been told it's too early to tell if they will have any effect."

"Julee, if those drugs don't work, then we will know they used the contagion they've threatened to use all along. The one with no known cure."

"We are well aware, Blake. That's why they have the hotel and practically the entire city quarantined. They said it's a waiting game now."

Blake turned his water bottle sideways and then held it upright again, watching the liquid change shape. His mind, however, was somewhere else. "Did they figure out how this Hands of Allah group got the contagion into the facility?"

"Not yet. The people who have contracted it so far were booked on different floors, and as far as anyone can tell, they didn't have any contact with one another."

Blake set the bottle down. "We've got to stay focused." He rubbed his forehead, trying to keep his blood pressure from bursting one of the vessels. "Okay. First things first. There's not much else we can do for the situation in Las Vegas at this time. However, we can prevent a massive attack on the country. Are Ryker and Sandburg still in Jacksonville?"

"Yeah, but they're out on assignment. They're following up on an important lead."

"What about Agent Williams?"

"He's with me. Why are you asking about them?"

"I need agents I can trust to meet me in Chicago."

"I'm sure there are some in Chicago you can trust."

"You do remember that's where Connell worked years ago, right?"

Julee sighed. "Yes, but I also recall he made enemies there too. Listen, let me make some calls. I know of some female agents who hated Connell. They felt about him the same way I did. I think they would be solid choices for you on this operation. I should be able to get at least one of them to volunteer."

"So, why can't Williams meet me there?"

"Frankly, I need him here. With me. I need people I can trust, too, you know?"

"Fair enough." Blake nodded, as if Julee could see him. "What about Agent Charles or Agent Stevens?"

"You haven't heard about them, have you?"

"No. What happened?"

"The sting we ran at the InterHealth Medical Center? Kurt Bowker knew about it. He was working with someone and allowed their personnel to enter the building, access the floor, and plant bombs in the room next to where we had Agent Getty set up to play the role of an injured Colin Murphy who survived the bridge attack. We had another room here at the FO set up as the 'undisclosed location' of one Blake Meyer, who would conduct the interrogation of Murphy, because Murphy had stated he would only talk to you. We thought we would take advantage of those wishes.

"Agent Charles was also in the room with Getty when the bomb went off. They both had to have surgery. They are in stable condition, last report I received, which was about an hour ago. Agent Stevens had his eardrum blown out and has been sent home to heal. Only Agent Chavez survived the blast and didn't get injured."

"Then, send Chavez."

"I can't, Blake. I'm down three agents. I need all hands on deck right now."

Blake huffed into the receiver. He was too tired to mask his frustration, but he fully understood her stance. He would have done the same thing, if the tables were turned.

"Okay. Make your calls. When I'm ready, I need those agents from Chicago to meet me at the airport when I arrive."

"To do what exactly?"

"To form a team and secure the warehouse said to contain the contagion. We will need to secure the building and perimeter without those guarding it noticing our presence and alerting their superiors. Besides preventing the contagion from being trucked out of there before we arrive, we also have to avoid a gun battle. We can't afford having the contagion's packaging compromised."

"Understood."

"Once we have everything secure, then we will be able to let CDC officials go in and test it to make sure it's the real deal. And because Sorensen's files stated the amount of contagion was considerable, we have to assume the warehouse is being guarded by some of Sorensen's men. So we will need to monitor all communications to and from the personnel working the perimeter."

"Okay. You'll have to give me some time to track down those agents."

"Julee, it's imperative that these agents are straight as arrows. If just one of those agents is in on this, she could give the bad guys a play-by-play of our plans and help them at least escape, in the best-case scenario. Worst-case scenario? We start a gun battle in the heart of the Windy City. These people are running scared now. They are off script. Therefore, their plans are being developed on the fly, and safety continues to deteriorate in these types of situations with each passing moment."

"Understood. And once you confirm we have the contagion in hand, then I can officially tell Kurt Bowker there will be no deal."

"Oh, I'd love to be there to see the look on his face."

"I'll have Mitchell video record it."

Blake smiled. It was good to smile. "Julee, there is one more thing I need you to do immediately as well."

"Just one more?"

"For now. Give Harrison access to the FBI's voiceprint database. He can possibly identify everyone who was working with Sorensen. And my gut is telling me the list of names is going to be a star-studded list of politicians, businessmen, and dignitaries that will shake up the world. However, we can't do anything legally until we can get matches on those voices. Once we do, then we can request a bunch of warrants."

"I'm on it. I told Harrison I'd give him access after the sting at the medical center was done. Then, the bomb went off, and the Kurt Bowker information came to light, and I've been driving here and flying there, interviewing survivors and storming condos ever since."

"Just have Agent Mitchell contact Harrison. Between the two of them, they should get those voices identified in no time."

"I will."

"And when they've identified all the voices they can, they need to notify you and me at the same time. However, under no circumstances are they to give this information to anyone else but us. Not yet anyway. So, no reports are to be written. No other phone calls made. No sidebar conversations around the water cooler. Just a call to you and me only."

"Can I ask why?"

"Because after talking to Harrison earlier today, our pool of eligible, trustworthy personnel shrank considerably, but I don't want to discuss it over the phone. I'll have to tell you in person."

"Can't wait."

"And can you keep me posted on the Las Vegas situation?"

"I thought you said there was just one more thing for me to do for you. That's two."

"You want to sit in that AIC chair? Get used to it."

"But I thought I would be the one giving the orders around here?"

Blake laughed. "I know you, Julee. I'm sure you've already given your fair share."

"I do my best."

"But remember, you may be running point as the AIC of the Jacksonville field office, but I've been tasked, by the president himself, to run point on this entire contagion operation. I have three people to answer to: The president, his chief of staff, and Director Jameson."

"Aye, aye, captain."

"And Julee, *be careful*. Just because we have to answer to certain people doesn't mean we can trust them."

"Are you trying to tell me something without saying it?"

"I can't talk about this over the phone. Just watch your back, and only give out information to people you know you can trust. That's the best we can do right now."

"Got it."

CHAPTER 8

HK JET LTD.
Hong Kong Business Aviation Center

Arina Filipov never expected her personal mission—some would call it a vendetta—to go as fast as it did. She expected to have a lengthy conversation with Miss Kim. She had planned to have Tam give her access to the company's computer system and find out just how far reaching Miss Kim's tentacles spread. She knew a woman like Miss Kim had suppliers. Someone was capturing girls like Chan Ming and bringing them to Hong Kong, and in her experience, those people always supplied to more than one organization. They sometimes even sold to the highest bidder. Held auctions, if you will, parading the girls in front of the organizations' liaisons to the sound of the auctioneer's mounting dollar amount.

However, Filipov never got that far in her little talk with Miss Kim. She wasn't going to be able to follow the "organizational chart," like she did with Boris Baranovskaya's organization, systematically taking out every person who didn't heed her warning. Filipov went back to the office area and tried to hack into Miss Kim's computer system once she left Tam and Miss Kim sitting opposite each other. However, with her computer geek not answering his phone, she knew it would take hours she did not have to figure out a workaround, so she unscrewed the back panel of the computer she deemed as Tam's and removed the hard drive and stuffed it into her bag.

Heading back downstairs, using the same stairwell she used going up, Filipov pulled the fire alarm closest to the back door of the Kowloon City Hotel and waited for the guard outside the door to step inside and check out the commotion. When he did, she shot him in the chest, dropped the silenced pistol inside her duffel bag, and exited through the back door.

Walking briskly across the outdoor sitting area, she hopped the waist-high railing and angled across the back corner of the hotel property until a line of bushes shielded her from direct eyesight of anyone working for Miss Kim. She continued walking away from the hotel, when she noticed a garbage can to her right, fifty meters away.

She stopped, knelt down, and fished the shirt stained with Miss Kim's blood from her bag. She zipped up her bag, stood, and walked in a straight line, tossing the garment in the can as she strolled by, attempting to appear as nonchalant as possible.

When she reached the corner of the block. With a quick turn to the left, she jogged down the sidewalk and around the next corner until she spotted a taxi idly motoring around, looking for its next fare.

She flagged the driver, and the cabbie pulled up along the curb. Opening the back door, she didn't even allow time for the driver to ask about her destination. "Hong Kong Business Aviation Center," she said in fluent Cantonese. "And hurry. I have a plane to catch."

The driver shifted the car into gear.

"Get me there in under an hour, and I will double your fare," she said.

The cabbie eyed her, using the rearview mirror. He gave her a slight nod, and Arina felt the car jerk forward.

* * *

Forty minutes later, the cab driver whipped into the parking lot of the Hong Kong Business Aviation Center and pulled up to the front doors of the terminal.

Filipov was on her smartphone, checking some information she had received from Kurt Bowker earlier in the day, giving her the receipt and itinerary of the company jet she was to use to get out of town.

She pulled a wadded up sum of cash from her bag and asked the driver for the cost of the fare.

When he told her the amount, she thumbed through the bills, making sure she doubled it. She handed the wad of cash to him and thanked him as she climbed out of the back seat.

"Thank you," he said, grinning and exposing his imperfect set of teeth.

Filipov rushed inside the terminal and handed the woman at the counter her smartphone, displaying the boarding pass QR code.

"What is your destination, please?" the woman said.

"Beijing. I have business there tomorrow."

The woman nodded and picked up the scanner, resting in its little holder. She aimed it at the screen, and within a second, the beep was heard. The woman returned the scanner to its perch. "Only one passenger?" the woman said. She looked around, acting like she had missed someone.

"Yes. My fiancé has been delayed," Filipov said with a pout. "He told me to go on ahead, and he would catch up."

The woman offered a sorrowful frown. "May I see your passport?"

Filipov handed her the one matching the scanned registration.

The woman peered at the document and looked up at Filipov. "Very good," she said, handing it back. She typed some things on the keyboard and tapped the monitor with her index finger several times until Filipov heard a paper ticket printing and then watched it slowly emerge from a slot in the machine to her left.

The woman waited until the printer stopped before ripping the paper loose. She held out the thick, card-stock like ticket, and Filipov took it. "Here you are, Miss Melius. Your plane is located in hangar number three. It is in the far back corner. Go through those doors to your right, and when you get to the hangar, they will instruct you further."

"Thank you."

Filipov exited the terminal and walked briskly toward far corner of the airport.

The doors to hangar number three slid open as she approached, and inside sat what appeared to her as a brand new Gulfstream. The cabin door was open, and the steps leading up to the plane were draped with a red carpet, which spilled out onto the hangar floor and extended from the aircraft for another twenty-odd feet. On either side of the carpet were a row of stanchions, ornately decorated in a gold-plating and hooked together with a golden rope.

Filipov entered the hangar and scouted the area. She expected to see terminal personnel, bag scanners, and the rest of the usual things found at airports. She was ready to offer whoever a large amount of Hong Kong dollars to allow her to carry on her bag with no questions asked. Instead, she didn't see anyone. Not even one attendant standing at the bottom of the stairs, holding a tray of crystal flutes filled with champagne.

Suddenly, an Asian woman appeared in the doorway to the Gulfstream. "Miss Melius?"

"Yes."

"Welcome to HK Jet Limited. Please, come aboard. We have everything ready, just as you requested."

Just as I requested, huh? "I believe my fiancé requested this," Filipov said as she cleared the stanchion on the far end and walked up to the stairs. "But I do not think I will mind."

"We believe you will appreciate our attention to detail. It is what sets us apart from other airlines."

Filipov reached the top step, and the Asian woman led her into the heart of the cabin. She took a few steps and then spun around like a girl modeling for a fashion show. "How did we do, Miss Melius?"

Arina quickly scanned the cabin and noticed how brilliantly new everything seemed to be. "Is this a new aircraft?"

"Almost. Her maiden voyage took place two days ago. You will be her second flight." The Asian woman motioned toward Filipov's bag. "May I?"

"Uh, no. I am fine carrying it myself."

"As you wish. Please, sit. Make yourself comfortable. My name is Huáng, and I will be serving you today."

Arina picked the chair giving her the best view of the front and back of the plane.

"Would you like something to drink? Wine? Tea? Coffee?"

"How about some water?"

"We only serve the finest water from the Fiji Islands. I will get you some."

Arina nodded and watched Huáng disappear into the back part of the plane.

Less than a minute later, Huáng entered the cabin with a bottle of water and a glass filled with ice cubes. She set the items on the small table in front of Filipov. "Our flight will take approximately two hours and thirty minutes."

Filipov glanced at her smartphone.

That puts me into Beijing before midnight. Perfect.

"You are free to get some rest, if you like," the flight attendant continued. "There is also a television behind the wooden panel. The control next to you reveals and turns on the television all at the same time. The channel guide is also there next to you. If you prefer, there are headphones under your seat in the pouch, sanitized and prepared for your pleasure. And if you wish to have something to eat, we have a small menu available as well. If you need me, just push the red button on the wall behind you. Is there anything else you need from me before we taxi to the runway?"

"There is one thing. My fiancé said he had purchased an item? And that it would be here, waiting for me?"

"Oh, yes, of course. I am glad you said something. It is not every day we have such requests." The flight attendant walked over to a cabinet, opened the small door, and pulled out a rectangular-shaped box, gift-wrapped in a bright blue paper. She walked across the cabin and handed it to Arina.

Filipov shook her head in an animated fashion and laughed. "He does spoil me. And he never ceases to surprise me."

"Will there be anything else?"

"No."

"Very well. We will be exiting the hangar and taxiing to the runway shortly."

* * *

Three hours later, midnight, local time, Filipov sat in the Shìjiè Coffee House, sipping a strong cup of Shangrila Farms coffee, one block away from the Tonghui River and the business offices of the

Emperor Pharmaceuticals Corporation. Her hair color had changed slightly from the fake, jet black wig to a dyed, natural brown color, compliments of the wrapped present in blue paper her "fiancé" had provided on the plane. Her clothes had changed, too, from a Japanese model to a European business woman in slacks and a blouse. Her duffel bag, secured in a locker at the Beijing airport, was replaced by a briefcase big enough to hold all the essentials.

On her tablet, according to the information the computer geek sent to her a day ago, the president of the Emperor Pharmaceuticals Corporation was nowhere to be found on the web, although a website existed for the company.

However, the computer geek was able to obtain some legal documents, and on those, the president was listed as Ju-Long Zou. Also, he was listed as a member of The Consortium, Sorensen's clandestine group of movers and shakers.

Oh, Mr. Zou...I wish I had not seen this...

You should choose your friends and business associates more carefully.

In her reading of the dossier on the plane, she learned everything she could about Mr. Zou.

Former military general-turned-businessman. Compliments of the Chinese government.

His company, although owned and operated by Zou, was diversified to some degree. One of his business operations was Chōngtiān Airlines. With at least two flights each day between Beijing, Shanghai, and Los Angeles, California. Many flights between China and Europe. Some back and forth to the Middle East, Africa, and Russia. However, it appeared he allowed a business partner to see to the day-to-day operations while he simply monitored the overall company.

Zou also owned a shipping company called the Consolidated Shipping Corporation.

Zou's companies paid their fair share of taxes to the government, all part of the pay-to-play arrangement to which most companies had to agree, if they wanted to profit from the growing Chinese economy.

Communism and capitalism in perfect harmony.

CSC was responsible for shipping goods to America and elsewhere.

At least one ship, containing over twenty-one thousand shipping containers, left port each day, and at least one returned each day.

CSC seemed to get a great many directives from the government as well. Some of which involved being told what to ship, how many, and where those goods needed to go.

Other directives were more secretive with few details to help determine the nature of business. Filipov surmised at least one cargo ship a week took care of the pharmaceutical side of the business, and there was no telling what was in those shipping containers.

But she had her suspicions, like heroin, opium, and fentanyl, stashed inside shrink-wrapped crates containing blood pressure medication, diabetes syringes, and bottles and bottles of off-brand acetaminophen and ibuprofen, just to name a few.

She also scrolled through a series of photos taken by American, Russian, and European operatives of Mr. Zou. In about half the pictures, she noticed Zou was with another man who was always smartly dressed, often wore sunglasses, and was often on his smartphone. According to the information, he was believed to be Zou's bodyguard and went by the name of Mr. Li, but no one knew for sure what his role entailed. There was no first name ever mentioned, and there was scant information about him, because he seemed to know when people were following him. That's when he ditched them and disappeared.

A man I could admire...

Filipov read a little further before minimizing the page of the dossier and tapping on another page containing nothing but a phone number. She opened her smartphone and entered the phone number into an app the computer geek had created. It was much like a phone finder app for any of the major cellular service providers or smartphone manufacturers. You typed the number in and hit the "Find" button. If the phone was on, the computer geek's app would pinpoint it within a one-hundred-foot radius.

She took another sip of her coffee, waiting while the series of circles in the middle of the screen turned, each circle turning in the opposite direction of the circle around it.

Several minutes passed until the screen blinked and displayed a satellite image map of the Beijing Central Business District. A red dot formed in the middle of a building along the Tonghui River, and coordinates, latitude and longitude, appeared at the bottom of the screen.

Filipov studied the app for a moment and went back to the dossier. She swiped at the screen until she found it.

Emperor Pharmaceuticals Corporation. Rents the twenty-sixth, twenty-seventh, and twenty-eighth floors of the Wěidà de Guówáng Office Building.

The red dot is in that building...

On the twenty-eighth floor...

Zou must be in his office.

Filipov then swiped the screen of her tablet until the floor plan for the first floor of the Wěidà de Guówáng Office Building appeared.

CHAPTER 9

President Gilmore sat at his desk in the Oval Office, reading report after report on the ongoing and growing dilemma at the Bahama Bay Hotel and Casino in Las Vegas. All of them were sketchy. Most of them were incomplete, warning the reader to be careful not to make any concrete decisions until more reliable information was available. The CDC had arrived, according to his press secretary, Jonas McCormick, so maybe, he thought, they would start getting some solid answers soon.

He flipped the folder shut and grabbed another just as a knock came at the door.

It opened, and FBI Director Sam Jameson walked in, followed by Jonas McCormick. "Mr. President, we have a situation," Jameson said.

"That has to be the most overused statement I've heard in the last few days, Sam."

"Well, sir, I would have to disagree this time. You know how we have been looking for a mole? Someone working on the inside, in a position of authority, possibly inside the government, and possibly the mastermind behind this entire contagion affair?"

"Please tell me you caught them."

"I'm not sure if this person is the mole, but she is definitely a very high-profile person of interest."

"She?"

"It's Merina Parker, sir."

"What?" The president fell back into his chair. His arms flopped over the armrests and hung down beside the chair. "I can't believe...Merina Parker? She's many things, but she's not a terrorist, or a traitor."

"Sir, I would've agreed an hour ago, but now, I'm not so sure. Local law enforcement in Las Vegas just found the device used to spread the contagion at the Bahama Bay Hotel and Casino. It was inside one of the air handlers. CDC has it now and is testing it as we speak."

"The reports I was reading said they thought it might be bubonic plague."

"It's been confirmed, sir. It is bubonic plague. What they are testing for now is *what kind* of bubonic plague we're dealing with. Is it the run-of-the-mill plague from centuries past, or are we dealing with some modern, weaponized version of it? Whichever it is, we are up to 134 confirmed cases now. Some of the earlier victims are already starting to show signs of the plague. The buboes under the arms, in the groin, other such signs."

"Are the antibiotics making any headway?"

"'Too early to tell,' was the answer I got about ten minutes ago. They have started giving everyone in the hotel antibiotics, even if they are not showing symptoms, just as a precaution and an effort to help prevent the spread. Those who are in advanced stages are being given the antibiotics intravenously. However, they feel everyone will need to have the medication administered that way, which makes the logistics of doing so an issue."

President Gilmore stood and rounded his desk. "So, how does this connect to Congresswoman Parker?"

"The device they found was detonated remotely. They used a cell phone connected to a power cell. The power cell can last up to twenty days, so now we know the device had to have been installed within the last three weeks.

"Also, the call history of the phone lists one number. However, there were two calls made to the device from the listed number. The first call was made over two weeks ago. The second call came through early this morning, Las Vegas time. Both calls, sir, came from the phone number assigned to Parker's *personal* cell phone."

"You've confirmed this, I assume?"

"Yes, sir. We've even checked her phone records with her service provider. They show the two calls being made at the same times showing up on the device's call history."

"Why so long between calls?"

"We believe the first call was to test the system, to make sure it was working properly. The call this morning was to activate it and release the contagion."

The president leaned against the front of his desk, hands in his pockets. "So, what do we think her role in all this is?"

"We're not sure yet."

"However, Mr. President," Press Secretary McCormick said, "I just got word from one of my contacts about fifteen minutes ago that Congresswoman Parker has already been arrested, as has her aide, Samantha Springer."

President Gilmore lifted his eyebrows. "That was quick, wouldn't you say? Maybe a little too quick? Especially considering the FBI just found out the number tied to the device was hers."

"That was the other reason I came immediately, Mr. President," Jameson said. "She was arrested by *FBI agents*. I was totally unaware of any of this until just minutes before we came in here. So, I have to ask, Mr. President. Were they following orders from this office, like James Connell was?"

"No. This is the first I've heard Congresswoman Parker's name associated with anything besides blocking the release of those six hundred families." The president crossed his arms. "Speaking of which, have you heard from Agent Connell? He went dark shortly after he got to Paris. Haven't heard from him since."

"No, sir. I have agents flying to Paris as we speak to inquire as to his whereabouts. The authorities in Paris have pledged full cooperation."

"Good, because I would like to know what he discovered."

"Likewise."

"So, gentlemen, our mole appears to have jumped the gun. He —or she—made a mistake. Tipped their hand. How can you arrest a sitting congresswoman with information that has not been made known to anybody yet?"

Director Jameson nodded. "Precisely."

Gilmore looked at both men. "Our adversary is getting desperate. You start making mistakes when you have to go off script. Therefore, let's throw another *sabo* into the machinery, shall we?"

"What do you have in mind?" McCormick said.

"Jonas, I need you to draft a press release. I'm going to issue an executive order within the hour. All cities with populations of one million residents or more are to have all government buildings, all hotels, all casinos, all airports, and all tourist destinations searched, specifically the HVAC units in all buildings. Photos of the device found in Las Vegas are to be circulated to these city, county, and state municipalities so they know what they are looking for. They are to use extreme caution, as we do not know what is in these devices or if they can be detonated in some other way."

"Sir," McCormick said, "there is a growing press presence in Las Vegas. When this executive order gets issued and we only send out a mere press release, fear will undoubtedly spread, along with press speculation. Those two things together without facts will be catastrophic."

"So, what you're saying is I need to get out ahead of it? Hold a press conference?"

"Yes, sir. Speculation in Las Vegas has already grown exponentially. All the talking hairdos are wondering why you have not already addressed the nation."

"I haven't said anything, because we didn't have anything to tell them. Except that we believed we were under attack, but we didn't know by what kind of contagion, where it would surface, who was truly responsible, nothing. Only now, in Las Vegas, have some of those questions been answered. That's why I haven't held a presser yet."

"I fully understand, sir. But again, those outside the inner circle are left to wonder."

The president massaged his forehead. "Maybe you're right. Maybe now's the time. Get the press release ready and make sure it says something about an upcoming news conference. I'll have Mr. Jenkins work on the executive order. We'll reconvene in an hour and determine how best to set up the conference. Agreed?"

Both men nodded.

"And Director Jameson, I need you to find out why and how Ms. Parker was arrested so soon after the release of the contagion by your department."

"Already on it, sir."

"Good. Now, have either of you seen Mr. Jenkins? He's been gone for a while now."

"He was in the kitchen earlier, sir. Said he hadn't eaten anything all day."

"That makes two of us. I'll call down and see if he's still there."

"Very good, sir," McCormick said.

And both men walked out.

CHAPTER 10

OFFICES OF EMPEROR *Pharmaceuticals*
   Beijing Central Business District
   Beijing, China

Ju-Long Zou knew something was going on. They rarely met face-to-face. Most of their transactions occurred over the phone. A few took place over a secure, video chat-like app on his smartphone. The two men could count on one hand the number of times they had met in person over the last eleven years of Mr. Li's employ with Zou and the Emperor Pharmaceuticals Corporation. An arrangement designed for a specific purpose.

Anonymity.

This "organizational plan" had worked to perfection over the years, allowing Mr. Li to drift in and out of company business when needed, able to apply pressure, gather information, or act as a certain, needed person, like a business associate, for example, making decisions for the company in Mr. Zou's absence. It added a layer of protection for Zou, proving to be fruitful on numerous occasions.

However, on this day, Mr. Li needed to see his employer in person. The business was in jeopardy, unlike anything they had ever faced, and with it being his sole purpose to protect their interests from all threats, both domestic and foreign, doing so over the phone or in a video chat would not suffice.

Zou watched his computer screen as one of the security monitors showed Mr. Li step into the elevator with his phone pressed against his ear.

Zou tapped a key on his keyboard, and the picture shifted from the lobby to the inside of the elevator when his smartphone rang.

Mr. Li pushed the button for the twenty-eighth floor. "I am here. Getting on the elevator now."

"Very well," Ju-Long Zou said and hung up.

A minute later, Mr. Li knocked on the door and heard a voice telling him to come inside. He opened the door, peered inside, and saw Mr. Zou sitting at his desk. He entered and closed the door, locking the deadbolt as he did.

"Are you not being a little paranoid, my friend?" Zou said in Mandarin.

Li walked up to his employer and bowed slightly with a nod before sitting down in front of Zou's desk. "I wish I could say so."

"Is it the Russian woman?"

"Yes. One of my contacts informed me she was spotted at the Hong Kong Business Aviation Center."

Zou bit the inside of his cheek and pondered Li's statement. "She could be flying anywhere."

"Yet, here I sit."

"You know for sure she is coming here?"

"No. My contact saw her board a plane, but he was not able to find out its destination. It would appear HK Jet Limited is a private airline that prides itself in keeping its passenger manifests and destinations private and unattainable from a person outside the air traffic controllers."

"You have no one on the inside who can find out where she is going?"

"I used to, but he was found out and is now imprisoned at Qincheng."

"I see." Zou frowned with a slight shake of his head. "What makes you think she is coming here?"

"She has breached Sorensen's computer. He is a careful businessman, so this act of espionage was no small feat. He had redundant systems, layered one on top of the other. He also was a bit paranoid when it came to technology. I hear he liked to take copious notes, transcribe conversations, that sort of thing. I understand he had one secretary who printed all of these things and filed them in a clandestine location as part of Sorensen's insurance policy against traitors.

"And I do not need to tell you Sorensen had access to the same server we do. When I witnessed Filipov's actions toward Mr. Sorensen, I contacted Mr. Ping, our man at the telecommunications company. He confirmed for me that the data stored in Sorensen's file on the server has been accessed. Someone is going through all of it as we speak. It will take days, but eventually, they will have seen it all."

Zou's eyes widened. "If Sorensen's data has been compromised, then can we assume the data on the server in America has as well?"

Li gave Zou a sharp nod. "It is only a matter of time before they find out everything about The Consortium. As I said, Sorensen was a careful businessman. Maybe too careful."

"You believe, then, he kept information stored which can incriminate us?"

"I know he did. Ping would check into it for me from time to time. Not everything was there, but enough. I could only assume Sorensen kept the rest of the information on the server in Utah. Being the person he was, I believe he split the information so it would be hard for outside parties like Filipov to use it against any of us, unless someone was able to breach both servers and piece the information together."

Zou pushed his chair away from the desk and stood with an air of frustration. He walked over to the window and looked down at the highway and river below. Several disparaging moments passed before he spoke. "If what you are telling me is true, then we are operating on borrowed time. Call Klebnikov and get a status report on his progress."

"I tried calling him on my trip from the airport to here. He did not answer."

Zou looked over his shoulder at Mr. Li. He then spun around and pulled his smartphone from his pocket and dialed.

"The subscriber you are calling is unavailable at this time," the automated voice in Chinese said, "Please leave a message at the tone."

Zou waited for the beep. "Vladimir, call me back as soon as you get this. We have a situation."

He hung up and stared at Mr. Li. "Vladimir was traveling to Genforma to retrieve the components necessary for creating the antidote and subsequent vaccine."

"Maybe his reception inside the lab is not good."

Zou turned back to the window. "Perhaps."

"Sir, because we are not certain of Agent Filipov's where-abouts, and because of the breach of Sorensen's computer, I suggest you vacate the building."

"And where am I supposed to go?"

"I would suggest one of your many vacation properties."

"And if I refuse?"

"Then, it would be imperative for you to barricade yourself inside this office."

Zou continued to gaze out at the river and highway below. "Mr. Li, I am not going anywhere. I will not run from this woman. If I do, I will only have to continue to run while she chases me incessantly."

"Can I make a suggestion?"

"By all means."

"Release the contagion and notify the Americans you have done so. When you do, they will have no other recourse than to forget about catching you, or Sorensen, or anyone else who was involved."

Zou let out a little smirk. "I already have, Mr. Li."

"You released the contagion they shipped from the Jìnzhǎn Corporation?"

"No. Once that contagion left China, Sorensen did not allow any member of The Consortium to know its whereabouts. He did this so no one could take it and use it for his or her own purposes." Zou gave a slight shrug. "I released one of our Plan B devices instead."

"When?"

"A few hours ago."

Mr. Li pinched his eyebrows together and appeared to be trying to wrap his brain around the information he had just received. "You realize Filipov may know the location of the original contagion now, including the Plan B devices."

"I have already considered it. But do not despair just yet, Mr. Li. I have always had a back-up plan. We still have some time. The release of one device may be containable by the Americans and their health organizations, but it will become much more difficult when I release multiple devices across their fruited plains."

"Where did you set off the first one?"

"In Las Vegas, Nevada."

"So," Mr. Li said with a shrug, "the contagion has been released after all."

"Yes, but in a much smaller quantity than what our original plan was supposed to accomplish."

Mr. Li stood. "What are your orders now?"

Zou turned to face his loyal employee. "It would seem we need to neutralize Agent Filipov before she causes any further harm to our cause. She has inflicted enough damage already, would you not agree?"

Mr. Li nodded as he thought how exhilarating it would be to finally meet her, face-to-face. "Wholeheartedly."

"Therefore, since I believe she is on her way to us, I will barricade myself here. You, on the other hand, do what you do best. I will trust whatever plans you devise."

Mr. Li bowed and nodded. "Give me an hour," he said before exiting the office.

CHAPTER 11

U.S. Congresswoman Merina Parker sat across the interrogation table from her lawyer, Templeton Drake. For years, he had served the congresswoman and her constituency with honor and expediency as the founding member of his own forty-year-old law firm. With just him and one secretary-slash-legal assistant in the beginning, the firm had now expanded to twenty-seven lawyers in his D.C. office alone. Fourteen other offices dotted the east coast from New York to Miami with almost four hundred lawyers and over a thousand full-time and part-time employees all calling Drake, Mumford, Hill and Associates their home away from home.

In his early sixties, Mr. Drake had already pulled the trigger on early retirement. He was known for only taking on one, maybe two, very high-profile cases a year, especially when it involved established clients who had helped him build his business.

Known to Merina and his other clients as Clyde, which was his middle name, taken from his maternal grandfather, they were the only ones allowed to call him by that name besides his wife. To everyone else, it was Mr. Drake.

"Clyde," Merina Parker said with a twinge of anger in her voice, "this whole thing wreaks of Walter Gilmore. I have been a thorn in his side for years now, and this latest episode involving the six hundred families and the injunction has obviously forced his hand. If he can end my career, once and for all, then there will be few people who will stand up to him."

"You know I'm on your side, Merina, and I agree. I know the president. I know you two are not destined to be drinking buddies anytime soon. However, looking over this warrant, we've got some serious things to get ironed out first, before we can accuse anyone of anything."

With handcuffs around her wrists, attached to the large ring welded to the table, Merina fidgeted with her fingers and wondered if this was how true criminals felt. "I know. Those FBI agents grilled me pretty good before I asked to make contact with you. They seem convinced I made some phone call, activating the device at the hotel in Las Vegas. In our cabinet meeting, President Gilmore stated the device supposedly released a contagion inside the hotel. Although they couldn't confirm it, they led me to believe it's the contagion we have been looking for."

Drake adjusted his glasses and scanned his notes. "You're probably not aware yet because you've been locked up in here, but I caught a few minutes of some news coverage before I left the house. Apparently, the hotel in Vegas is completely locked down. Nobody is allowed to leave or enter a ten-block radius right now." Clyde turned his chair slightly so he could cross his left leg over his right. "Now, I have to admit, I'm a little behind on the uptake concerning this whole ordeal. Not being in the proper circles, I was unaware our country was being threatened by anybody."

Merina proceeded to give him an up-to-the-minute briefing on everything she thought she'd be allowed to tell him so he could represent her properly. "Of course, Clyde, you cannot divulge a word of this to anyone, or it will be one more thing they'll accuse me of. Not to mention, it will paint a target on your back as well."

"I will definitely step carefully. Always do." He smiled, trying to allay her fears a little. "There is one thing, though, not adding up for me."

"Just one?"

"Well, there may be more, but for now, yes. It's the timeline. You were in the emergency cabinet meeting when?"

"I was there at five o'clock sharp. The meeting started a couple of minutes past five."

"Okay, so in the timeline of events, your meeting was at 5:00 a.m., give or take a couple of minutes. And how long did it last?"

"Approximately twenty minutes. I remember looking at my phone as I walked out to my car. It said 5:24 a.m."

"Okay, good." Clyde jotted some notes down. "Then, you did what?"

"I called Samantha and asked her to meet me at my house. Then I got in my limo and went home."

"And you got home when?"

"Around six? The trip took thirty minutes, give or take."

"All right. So let's say six o'clock," Clyde said, scrawling down more notes. "And how long did it take Samantha to get there?"

"She told me it would take more than thirty minutes when I called her, so around ten after six? Maybe six-fifteen? It wasn't long after I got home."

"So, let's say ten after six. And how long, after Samantha arrived, did it take the FBI to show up."

"Like five minutes. No more than ten."

"The FBI showed up at approximately twenty minutes after six?"

"Yes."

Clyde scribbled more notes and then twirled the pen between his fingers. He flipped back some pages of his notepad, scouring previously taken information. "You told me a few minutes ago about how an FBI agent by the name of Agent Arleth read to you from the warrant he had, and I quote, 'Approximately thirty minutes ago, your cell phone number was confirmed to be the number used to detonate the device which allegedly released some sort of contagion in Las Vegas, specifically at the Bahama Bay Hotel and Resort.' Is this correct?"

"Yes. I distinctly recall his words."

"This means around the time the cabinet meeting ended, your phone was allegedly *confirmed to be the number used in the attack in Las Vegas.* If this is so, then you would have had to make the call earlier, well before the cabinet meeting, correct?"

"I guess so."

"And were you alone for any length of time during the hours leading up to the cabinet meeting?"

"Of course I was. Samantha was in and out of my office. So was I, for that matter, but...yeah. I was alone at times."

"Long enough to make such a call? Around the time they are alleging?"

"I'm not believing this, Clyde. You sound like the lawyer for the prosecution."

"Well, that's what he or she is going to say, Merina. That's probably what the FBI is thinking. So, it is extremely important we get all the facts straight and spread out before us."

Merina let out a defeated sigh. "It's not looking good, is it?"

"We're just gathering details and evidence right now. We've got a long way to go before I'll even think about answering that question."

"But they told me they are charging me with—"

"Merina," Clyde said, holding up a copy of the charges. "I have the list right here. Although they are serious charges, you are still like every other person in this country. Innocent until proven guilty."

"When can I get out of here then?"

Clyde twisted up his expression into one Merina didn't like. "Now, that's a different question to answer. You know I will file for an immediate hearing for later today. But, looking at these charges...and if our country truly has been attempting to stave off a terrorist attack behind the scenes so that the general public doesn't panic—as they allege, and as the news reports seem to indicate, then getting you out on bail may not be possible. They will see you as a flight risk."

"A flight risk? You know I'd never go anywhere with all this happening. I want to catch these terrorists just as much as anyone else."

"You know that. I know that. But they won't look at it the same way, Merina. They'll paint you as a terrorist sympathizer."

"That's insane."

"You are the person who got the injunction from Judge Carlton, correct?"

"I got it to save the lives of those six hundred families."

"But that's not how the prosecution will paint the picture. They will say you were attempting to aid and abet this...," Clyde flipped the page and looked at his notes, "Hands of Allah group. In addition, they'll ask you point blank if you ordered your aide, Samantha Springer, to spy on the president. Or, at least, ask questions, such as, what does the president know concerning the contagion? What has the president learned about the organization known as The Hands of Allah? Who has been calling the president? Who has the president been calling? And they will also inquire about Samantha asking for visitors' logs for the White House..." Clyde lifted his left eyebrow as he peered at his client.

Merina dropped her chin to her chest and muttered an expletive. "We're in trouble."

"You know I will do everything I can. If there isn't anything else you can tell me at this time, I need to go and file for that hearing. In the meantime, I'll be investigating to try and find any holes in their theory of you being an aid to these terrorists. I mean, spoofing phone numbers is easy enough these days, but I need proof."

"Right." Merina's sullen temperament caused her to fall back into her seat, only to have her arms stretched to their limit by the handcuffs. She blurted out another expletive and leaned forward again.

"If you think of anything else, let me know."

"Sure."

Clyde reached over and cupped Merina's hands. "Merina, I've known you a long time. And although we may not always agree politically, I know you're not a terrorist, nor would you help terrorists. Therefore, I am heading into this investigation under the assumption you are being framed.

"In all my years of doing this job, I have only had one case which would rank up there with this one. I wondered if the man was guilty, but I really believed he was being framed by a person who was a master at it, because for the longest time, I could not prove he had been framed. All the evidence pointed at my client, and it was pretty much ironclad.

"I finally concluded my client may have been indeed guilty after all. I lost the case, and he went to prison for murder.

"Then, about eight years later, some DNA evidence came to light, proving he was innocent after all. He would have received twenty-five years to life had he confessed when the first trial took place. Instead, he got life without parole, because he kept pleading his innocence. The judge wanted the death penalty, but thank goodness, the jury couldn't come to a unanimous decision."

"Is this story supposed to make me feel better?" Merina said.

Drake chortled. "Said all that to say this: In order to frame someone, you have to account for every contingency. And in my dealings over the years, I have reached the conclusion that framing someone in an ironclad manner is impossible, simply because one cannot account for every contingency. Even the best laid plans cannot account for sudden, unexpected changes in a person's routine. It cannot calculate with utmost precision the actions of multiple persons, if the effort to frame a person must involve many individuals. And of course, no one has the prover-bial crystal ball they can look into and predict changes which take place years later. The kind no one could ever foresee. No framer in the history of framers is that good." Clyde pulled his hands away and slid his notepad inside of his briefcase.

"How did you prove the man was innocent then?"

Clyde stopped momentarily and looked up at Merina. "It was a tennis ball which caused investigators to find the DNA I spoke of earlier. The ball had been thrown across a lawn of a newly built home in an area no one ever thought would be developed because of a nearby flood zone. The ball bounced and rolled until it went down a small hill and lodged itself in a patch of weeds. The dog chasing the ball suddenly started barking incessantly when she reached the edge of the property. As it turned out, the body of the missing man—the quintessential smoking gun, as it were—had been uncovered by years of weather, erosion, and foraging animals, but was shielded from view by trees, tall grass, and weeds. It was a wonder construction crews who developed and built the properties never saw the body. But eight years later, a dog chasing a tennis ball did. The DNA proved to be from one of the real murderer's victims...the same victim my client was accused of killing. He'd been framed with her blood, but the body was never found. The body miraculously still had the real murderer's DNA preserved from when he assaulted her, subsequently setting my client free."

"And that's supposed to be applicable to me how?"

"Merina, it's simply a story to explain how the truth will come out eventually. Time is on the side of truth. So, if you're guilty, better to come clean now. If you're being framed, someone somewhere at some time will make a mistake, and that mistake will be their undoing. And as it has been said, 'The truth shall set you free.'"

"I *am* being framed, Clyde." Merina laughed in a nervous manner and looked up at him. "So, tell the judge that later today, will ya? I have to get out of here. I'm no good behind bars."

"Again, I'll be shocked if they grant you bail, unless I find something extremely convincing between now and then, which doesn't leave me much time. If I don't get this filed soon, it may be tomorrow morning before we can see a judge."

"Go then. Do whatever you have to do to get me out of here."

"You're not hearing me, Merina." Clyde locked the clasps on his briefcase and stood. "The judge will be told you are a flight risk. The prosecuting attorneys will look into all the overseas trips you've made over the last ten years. They'll question who you were in contact with during those trips. And unfortunately, a couple of those trips have been to countries who do not like to extradite people, especially to America."

"How do you know where I've been?"

"I'm good at what I do. Besides, why do you think it took me so long to get here?"

Merina shook her head and sniffed before wiping her nose with her hand. "Then I'm stuck in here."

"Until they move you."

"Move me? Where?"

"Depends. Could be a federal detention facility. Could be the Arlington County Jail. Could be anything in between. We just don't know yet how they're going to read these charges. Everything is conjecture at this point, and if you know me at all, you know I don't operate in a courtroom on conjecture."

Merina shook her head and waved him on. "Well, you know where to find me."

"We'll be in touch."

CHAPTER 12

RIVERVIEW DRIVE
Van Buren, Maine

Harrison Kelly patiently waited for Supervisory Special Agent-in-Charge Julee Scarfano to call him. He needed access to the voice-print database. He could possibly name everyone who participated in Sorensen's Consortium so Blake could fly around the country and round them up. Cut the head of the snake completely off.

If he could identify who they were...

He contemplated hacking in and gaining access to the database himself, but he didn't want to jeopardize the subsequent arrests by giving the lawyers for those Consortium scuzzballs a ticket to the golden parachute of freedom by having all his hard work thrown out of court on one glaring technicality—that all the evidence he had tirelessly amassed was illegally obtained and thus inadmissible in court.

However, there was one other important note to consider...

He didn't want to be the one going to prison.

His days of laying it all on the line for Uncle Sam were over. Or for any other country, for that matter. Including his home down under.

The only "land" he was willing to die for these days was the kingdom of heaven. He admitted this to anyone who would listen, because it was true. His new leader, the carpenter from Nazareth, who claimed to be the Messiah, had asked him and all His other followers to die to self. Be willing to die for the sake of the call. For the gospel. The Good News, as it is called. However, he also acknowledged how the Messiah was the only leader he ever served who was willing to die for him, too, and actually did so.

And He did His dying first. While Harrison and every other person on the planet was His enemy. "Sinners," He called them.

Sure, the generals who ordered Harrison into harm's way during his service to the military all had to be willing to die, at some point in their careers, as they moved up the ranks. But they did so for Uncle Sam and the ideals we call "freedom" and "liberty." Or maybe for their careers. Or possibly both. But not solely for Harrison. Definitely not before he enlisted. And absolutely not for others considered enemies on the battlefield.

Also, once they reached a certain status, like general, for example, and especially if they were part of a major board or committee, like the president's cabinet, then ordering troops into harm's way while watching it all unfold on a monitor was as close to the action as they got. Unlike their counterparts of old, they no longer rode into battle on their trusty steed, leading the charge.

Yet, the Messiah did. He was already a king, and He rode into battle for His enemies, years before any of them became His disciples.

And He rode all the way to Golgotha.

And He will ride again one day soon.

In Harrison's eyes, it was the mark of a true leader. Be willing to do whatever you ask others to do. Unlike the politicians and military leaders of today, who order people around, telling the masses to give up things like their SUVs while they themselves fly around in private jets.

"They all do it," he told a friend a couple of months ago. "It doesn't matter who they are affiliated with, who they represent, who they are in charge of 'protecting.' Doesn't even really matter which country it is. Ultimately, those in power have one goal: to protect their own interests, as they use their 'subjects'—that's us—to help themselves. And that's why I don't serve Uncle Sam anymore. Even though America is a great country compared to most, and the freedom to move around as you wish is the envy of many around the world, it's still filled with corruption."

Harrison thought about this little theological lesson as he rummaged through the files from Markus Sorensen's computer, the contrast between Jesus of Nazareth and the generals of today was never louder, never brighter. *One "general" was actually a king,* he wrote in his little digital diary, of sorts, earlier that morning:

And He gave it all up to become a slave (Philippians 2:5-11), so others could become part of His kingdom. Equal shareholders even. He blazed a trail which reveals how one gains entrance. All while spilling His own blood to accomplish it. In contrast, earthly generals engage in conquests and win battles with other people's blood while reaping the benefits. And in our day and age, they do this from thousands of miles away, in the comfort of an office, a war room, or a bunker.

What a contrast of leadership styles.

That's why it amazes me how brave men and women can line up, sign on the dotted line, and be willing to spend their most valuable currency—their lives—for people like earthly generals. To accomplish what? Gain a freedom that really isn't free? Gain a freedom that is freer than most freedoms in other countries, but is dwindling by the day and is always under attack from government types who desire to strip us of the very freedoms we watch our brothers and sisters die for?

Yet, if you talk to them about a different kind of general, specifically Jesus of Nazareth, they want to blow your head off and view you as the enemy of all enemies.

It doesn't make sense. Especially when earthly generals are willing to allow terrorists to wipe out millions of people around the world without regret as they try to position themselves at the top of the food chain in a new world order.

God was right. He told Samuel, in First Samuel 8, to tell the Israelites that if they wanted an earthly king, they had better be ready for tyranny. He told them how the king would take their sons and make them serve in the military, either by fighting on the front lines or making the weapons of war. Those not assigned to the military would be forced to farm for the king and his forces. The king would also take their daughters and force them to serve him in various ways.

The king would take their land and money and give it to those who support him, and when the people grew weary of it and cried out, God would not answer...

Yeah, I'll pass. Give me Jesus. You can have your generals. Your politicians. Your earthly kings.

Good luck with this kingdom of men.

Come, Lord Jesus. I'm ready.

Harrison held his fresh cup of coffee and opened a new folder from Sorensen's computer. This one was labeled "Other Resources." When he clicked on it, another file appeared titled "Plan B."

"So, Markus," Harrison said out loud, "been working on a contingency plan, have we?"

He clicked on the file, and immediately, a list of file names cascaded down his screen.

Each file started with "Z-Detonator."

That's not ominous at all...

However, after the initial designation, each file was different. Each one had a name of a city attached to it. All in alphabetical order.

Z-Detonator: Albuquerque

Z-Detonator: Atlanta

Z-Detonator: Austin

Z-Detonator: Baltimore

Z-Detonator: Boston

Z-Detonator: Charlotte

Z-Detonator: Chicago

Z-Detonator: Colorado Springs

Z-Detonator: Columbus

Z-Detonator: Dallas...

Harrison paused his inspection of the files and leaned back in his chair, taking a sip of coffee.

What's so special about these places?

He continued to scroll down the list...

It seems like a hodge-podge of—

He stopped when he saw one specific file and almost spit his coffee onto the monitor.

Z-Detonator: Las Vegas.

He set his cup down and did a quick online search of the most populated areas in the United States.

Oh, man...I hate it when I'm right.

The list of the most populated cities matched the list of files exactly. All the way down from Albuquerque to Las Vegas.

Harrison opened the Las Vegas file, wanting to know more about the attack already launched against the hotel there. Several documents appeared in files of their own. Some were PDFs, with instructions on how to build and detonate that specific device. Others were scanned invoices for parts, scanned payment agreements between parties. Still others were copies of bank transactions. From what he could decipher, it seemed there were two payments made over the course of about a month to two men. One appeared to be an upfront payment of fifty-thousand dollars. The second payment was for the same amount a month later.

Two-hundred grand total.

The initial up-front money...and payment upon completion.

The other documents consisted of a complete set of floor plans for the Bahama Bay Hotel and Casino. Another contained the schematics for the HVAC system in the hotel itself.

Harrison opened the next file down: Z-Detonator: Los Angeles. In it, the kind of documents found were almost identical. There were only two differences he could see. The recipients of the payments were different. Either it was two different guys, or the same guys went by aliases for some reason. The second difference was the location of the device. In this file, the 777 Center in Los Angeles appeared to be the target.

He opened the next file on the list, and a similar pattern emerged.

Z-Detonator: Louisville.

Two different recipients. Two payments of fifty-thousand dollars each. Per person.

Target: Muhammed Ali International Airport.

I have to give Sorensen credit. He was one for consistency.

He scrolled down and found files for Washington, DC: Capitol Hill, The "T" Building, and Union Market. He opened the files, and within the information, he found the target of the first one to be exactly what it said. The heart of the United States government itself. The second file gave up the meaning of the "T": the *Treasury* Building.

The heart of the government's finances.

The third file struck at the heart of the people, Harrison thought. *Want to strike fear in Americans? Attack the places where they buy their goods, their food, and their entertainment.*

Want to start a mass panic and exodus from the capital of a country? Tell everyone they can't go to work, can't get home, can't get to school, or can't go anywhere without becoming a victim...without helping it spread...without being part of the problem...while watching loved ones become infected...

With a slight shiver racing down his spine, Harrison continued down the list opening each file, looking for locations, until he reached one not on the list of most populated cities.

Z-Detonator: Wichita, Kansas.

Target: Epic Center.

He researched the location.

Business building...Tallest one in Kansas...houses some banks, lawyer firms...

He clicked on another web page and froze...*and it houses the Secret Service and a field office for the FBI...*

And it is in the heartland...

He leaned back in his seat, peered at the black screen of his smartphone, and then glanced at the time in the lower, right-hand corner of his monitor.

"I can't wait any longer for Julee to call me."

He reached for his phone when it rang. He pulled his hand back and felt needle pricks stab his neck and race down his back and into his arms. He sighed heavily as he realized what just happened.

You're losin' it, mate. Paranoid schizo, you are.

He grabbed the phone with a little more fervor, wondering who had frightened him so.

Agent Scarfano.

Harrison took a deep breath and blew it out in a slow, measured manner.

Good timing.

CHAPTER 13

Supervisory Special Agent-in-Charge Julee Scarfano hung up from talking to Blake Meyer.

"Why do you look like you just got word your granny is dying?" Sheridan Fox, Supervisory Special Agent-in-Charge of the Atlanta field office, said.

"Sheridan, of all the people you have here at this field office, and of all the people you know within the Bureau, and of all the other people within the government itself, how many of those people do you trust? I mean, really, really trust?"

Agent Fox lifted one eyebrow. "Is this some kind of test?"

"Not at all. I'm legitimately asking you a question."

He uncrossed his legs and turned his chair so he could lean forward, elbows on the desk. "I guess it depends on what level of trust we're talking about here."

"Meaning?"

"I trust everyone here at this office to do their job. That's why we hired them. And I trust they are doing it until it is proven otherwise. I mean, when it gets right down to it, I trusted the other drivers in their cars this morning when I came in to work. I trusted them to stay in their lanes or on their side of the road and obey the traffic laws."

"Okay, let me rephrase the question. I'm not looking for a philosophical debate here. What I want to know is, when your life is on the line, or at least your job, who do you unequivocally trust?"

Agent Fox leaned back in his chair again. "Now that's a tough question to answer. Again, I trust the men and women in this office to have my back, and each other's backs when they find themselves in harm's way."

"But what if one of them is a spy? One of them is working for the enemy? Then, how would you answer my question?"

"Are you saying you have that problem in Jacksonville, SAC Scarfano?"

"I believe we did when Agent Connell was running things. Now that he is missing, I trust the others, but I have to admit... what I trust them with varies, based on how well I know them personally."

Fox nodded as if he understood. "So, you're asking me the same question?"

"Pretty much."

"Like you, it's based on how well I know a person. Trust is earned, and the higher the security level, the thinner the herd gets."

"And what if a rogue agent or person working for the enemy is even higher up the food chain than you? Then, how do you handle things?"

"What are you saying, Julee?"

"This stays in this office, Sheridan."

"Understood."

"We have a mole. I mean, the U.S. government does. He or she has been working with the terrorists over the last several days."

"And how do you know this?"

"Agent Meyer. We've uncovered scads of evidence. Now with the apprehension of Bowker, we have uncovered a ton more. However, this mole has been able to successfully hang in the shadows the entire time. As person after person gets caught, the mole's hiding place gets harder to locate."

"Until now."

Julee peered at her colleague. "I don't have any names, and I'm still not sure who it is, but apparently Blake does. And if I heard him correctly, he has it narrowed down to three people."

"Three big fish, I presume?"

"These fish are whoppers."

Fox sat up straight in his chair. "All the more reason to get crackin' on this then. If there's one thing I despise, it's crooked government officials. Makes all of us look bad."

"You and me both."

Agent Fox nodded and pointed at the fake immunity agreement. "So, we sit on this for now? I'd sure love to walk into that interrogation room and rip it up in front of his face, after he read it, of course."

"Oh, so would I. Most definitely, and we may still get the chance to do so. But, I would wait on it. If the contagion Blake is investigating turns out to be gone or was some kind of wild goose chase, then we may still need Bowker's help."

Sheridan pursed his lips and nodded. "Then, I'm gonna get a cup of coffee. Want some?"

"Yes, please."

He walked out of the office and allowed the door to close behind him.

Julee found Harrison's phone number and dialed.

"Oy, I was just about to call you. My hand was literally reaching for the phone when it rang. Scared the daylights out of me. I've still got goosebumps."

"Sorry."

"My total lack of sleep, coupled with the deep dives into computer files of Kurt Bowker and Markus Sorensen, has me wondering where I can purchase an uninhabited island, build a big fence around it, preferably with a moat filled with gators and crocs, and hunker down until it's time for me to go home."

"That bad, huh?"

"You don't know the half of it. But I am assuming you are calling to help me blow the lid off this Consortium group?"

"I am, at Blake's urgent request."

Harrison harrumphed. "I apologize if it looks like I tried to do an end run, Agent Scarfano. Not my intention at all. I relayed information I found in Sorensen's files to Blake, and he asked me what I needed to continue, so I told him."

"It's okay, Harrison. It's been a little crazy around here. But as an AIC, you always have multiple plates spinning on those thin poles, right? You have to keep them all spinning. Can't let one crash to the ground. So, to keep your plate spinning, I am going to call Agent Mitchell as soon as I hang up. He will be instructed to call you and help you gain access to the voiceprint database. Blake wants the two of you working on it together to speed up the results. And then, once you two determine the names of the people in those recordings, you are to only notify me and Blake. He doesn't want any reports. Don't take any notes that can be read by anyone. Keep it as clandestine as you can possibly keep it."

"You got it."

"Okay, good. I have to go and call Agent Mitchell—"

"Julee," Harrison said with a bit of volume, "don't hang up. I need to tell you something."

"If it's an apology for—"

"No, it's about the contagion in Las Vegas."

"What about it?"

"I think I found a list that contains all the locations of all the devices like the one used in Vegas."

"Does Blake know?"

"No. I just found the list. It's an alphabetical list targeting the forty most-populated cities in the U.S., and one very strange addition: Wichita, Kansas.

"Each and every file lists the city, the target, and documents showing monetary transactions to the goons who installed the devices, payment for parts, floor plans for each and every target, and schematics for the HVAC systems of each floor plan. Julee, there are a bunch of those devices out there. Las Vegas was just one of them."

"I need you to send me those files, Harrison."

"Will do."

"Does it say anything in those files about the contagion being used?"

"No, unfortunately."

"Of course not."

"Oh, and one more thing. There's one listed for Atlanta and one listed for Jacksonville."

"Wonderful." Julee inhaled and blew out the breath with some anger behind it. "And I assume Chicago is on the list too?"

"Oh, yeah..." Harrison's voice trailed off for a moment. "Blake must have told you about the location of the original contagion."

"He did. Do you happen to know where the device is located in Chicago? And tell me where they are in Atlanta and Jacksonville, too, while you're at it."

She could hear Harrison tapping furiously on his keyboard. "Atlanta's is Atlanta International Airport."

"Hartsfield-Jackson?"

"That's the one."

"Great."

"Chicago's is located in the Franklin Center."

"One of the largest buildings in the city."

"And it houses some big-named corporations."

"And where's Jacksonville's located?"

Julee could hear him tapping more keys. "The international airport there as well."

"So, they used airports, which would be the best way to spread a disease like this, but not in every city, just to keep everyone guessing."

"And they would have, if I hadn't been given this information."

"All right then. It appears I have some additional phone calls to make now."

"Sorry."

"Oh, no, this is good news, Harrison. If they can lockdown these devices and deactivate them before the bad guys get a chance to set them off, then think of the millions of people we will have saved."

"Right-o. I'll let you go. Make the call to Agent Mitchell quickly so you can notify whoever you need to about these device locations. And once Agent Mitchell and I identify the voices in these recordings, we'll let you know."

"Until then."

"It shouldn't be too long."

CHAPTER 14

OFFICES OF EMPEROR Pharmaceuticals
Beijing Central Business District
Beijing, China

Ju-Long Zou, sipping on another glass of soju, stood in the middle of his spacious office, watching one of the major American news agencies on the fifty-five-inch flat screen television mounted to the wall. It was mid-morning in Las Vegas, and the reporter prattled on about what she had witnessed since she arrived the night before. She described how she was now inside the quarantine zone of "an apparent outbreak. It has forced local law enforcement, with the help of the National Guard, to lockdown the city and prevent anyone from entering or leaving the ten-block radius around ground zero. The epicenter was confirmed just moments ago to be the Bahama Bay Hotel and Casino."

The reporter said she had obtained information, confirming over a thousand people were inside the resort when an unknown substance was allegedly released inside the hotel. She and other reporters were awaiting news from the governor of Nevada or the president of the United States to get an update. The good news, however, was there had yet to be any reported deaths as a result of the outbreak. In addition, CDC officials were arriving and beginning the process of administering antibiotics to all the patrons and workers inside, but the reporter noted she had yet to learn which antibiotics were being administered or for what exactly.

Zou flipped to a different channel, and another reporter from a different news agency, standing in a different area, said almost the same thing.

He changed channels and located three other news agencies, one of which was from England, all spouting similar statistics and information.

It can't spread if they keep all these people locked up. He lowered the volume and tossed the remote onto his desk.

Downing the last couple of ounces of his drink, he walked over to the built-in bar and poured another.

Glancing up at the clock, he did a mental calculation of the time zones.

A little after nine o'clock in the morning in Las Vegas. That would make it a little after noon on America's east coast.

I thought releasing it while people slept would be the best time...and releasing it near the west coast...in a place people would soon leave to travel to other locations around the city and country...I would have thought it to be the best means of spreading the contagion...

It simply proves you cannot trust other humans, can you? They always disappoint. Especially when it comes to dying when you want them to...

He took another gulp of his drink.

I need to release another one—

Suddenly, like a man who just remembered he had a very important appointment with a doctor and was already ten minutes late, Zou set his drink down on the mini-bar counter and opened the lap drawer of his desk, retrieving the burner phone he had used earlier. Scrolling through his list of contacts, he found the one labeled "Z-Detonator: Washington, DC – Union Market."

He remembered his suggestion to The Consortium, but he thought about changing the location. He almost moved up a couple and opened the one titled "Capitol Hill," but after glancing at his watch again, he knew very few, if any, of the members of congress would be in their offices on a Sunday around noon.

But Union Market? Noon on a Sunday? Plenty of people will be there, and by the time they realize what happened, they won't be able to lock it down like Las Vegas.

Zou tapped on his first choice, and the green phone icon appeared.

Let them play detective and figure out where everybody got sick, Zou remembered saying to The Consortium.

They'll say to themselves, "Did someone bring it to Union Market? Or did they get it from there?"

And by the time the contagion manifests itself, people will have come and gone from there a hundred times over.

Zou grinned. *You won't be able to quarantine this one, Mr. President.*

Zou picked up his glass and took a long swig. He glanced at his watch again.

It's lunchtime in Washington.

The perfect time.

To keep the Americans busy.

Zou pressed the green phone icon, and an immediate dial tone gave way to a series of rings. He entered the same passcode he'd used for the Las Vegas incident and tapped the speakerphone option, allowing the next set of mechanized sounds to override the mumbling of the reporters on the TV screen.

On the sixth ring, a click emanated from the phone, faint but distinct. It was followed by a high-pitched whine, as if someone started a small, mechanized series of gears.

The whine blared from the speakerphone, and Zou, remembering the last time, lowered the volume on his phone so it didn't pierce his eardrums like it did before.

Seconds later, the sound of a light bulb breaking gave way to the slow, methodical winding down of the machinery until it could be heard no more.

Then, a busy signal alerted Zou the deed had been done.

Washington, D.C. will never be the same again. He downed his drink like a shot of liquor.

"And if they press me, grandfather, I will activate the remaining devices one right after the other until none are left to choose."

CHAPTER 15

OVAL OFFICE
Washington, D.C.

President Gilmore stood, looking out the window of the Oval Office. He and Ben Jenkins, his Chief of Staff, were ironing out the last minute details on the executive order to have all major cities and tourist destinations search every HVAC system in an effort to find all the devices like the one found in Las Vegas. Pictures of the device, dimensions, everything needed would be given to aid the search.

They were just about to wrap things up when Jonas McCormick knocked on the door and opened it. "Mr. President, there's something you need to see."

Gilmore waved him inside. "I hope it's good news for a change."

McCormick entered with his laptop in his hand. "I'm not sure there is a good news or bad news here. But it could become one or the other."

The president rolled his eyes at Ben Jenkins. "I hate it when people say things so cryptically."

"Sorry," McCormick said, setting his computer down and manipulating the mouse pad. "I'm just saying I'm not sure where you're gonna want to go with this after you see it."

"See what?"

McCormick turned his laptop around so the president and Ben Jenkins could see and clicked on the Play icon. A news report from one of the major news outlets came to life, and a well-known reporter by the name of Morgan Mayhew stood in the middle of an intersection with a street sign notating her location as Las Vegas.

"Just moments ago in Washington, D.C., well-known D.C. attorney Templeton Drake issued a statement in response to a breaking story we first reported to you just an hour ago, concerning Congresswoman Merina Parker, of the U.S. House of Representatives, and her arrest on charges of conspiracy to commit acts of terror. He would not elaborate further into those charges, but did make a statement before the press."

The picture switched from Morgan Mayhew to Templeton Drake, who was standing outside, on some courthouse steps in Washington. "As many of you have already heard, my client, Congresswoman Merina Parker, has been arrested. She is being charged with multiple counts of conspiracy, but we believe this act to be a conspiracy in and of itself against my client, and we are going to fight these outlandish charges."

"What leads you to this conclusion?" asked one reporter off camera.

"Simply put, she was arrested at a time and with a warrant which could not have possibly been legitimate. The information contained in that warrant, which led to her subsequent arrest, wasn't even known nor confirmed by law enforcement until hours later. Therefore, I have filed a motion to have the charges thrown out of court. I am also urging the judiciary committees of both bodies of the legislative branch of our government to launch complete but separate investigations into this matter."

"Are you saying Congresswoman Parker is being framed?" asked another reporter.

"We have nothing further to say at this time. Thank you." Templeton Drake walked away from the barrage of reporters, surrounded by staff members and personal security guards of his own.

The video stopped, and McCormick closed his laptop.

President Gilmore glanced back and forth at both men. "Gentlemen, I do not have to tell you how incriminatory this is on my administration, not to mention the FBI."

"And the judge who issued the warrant," Ben Jenkins said.

"The judge would just say he or she was given bogus information," Gilmore said.

"I've reached out to Drake's office as well as Parker's," McCormick said. "No response yet. However, according to the warrant, they arrested her long-time aide, Samantha Springer, because she had been doing some investigating of her own, at the request of Parker."

"What was she looking into?" Jenkins said.

"She had requested visitor's logs for the White House. She was also asking about who you, Mr. President, had been calling, and who had been calling you as well."

Gilmore grunted. "Trying to see if I had anything to hide or any ties to these terrorists, no doubt. Sounds very Parker-esque."

"And sir, when Drake's office gets organized, they will paint a picture of retaliation by this office against Parker. They will say she was investigating you, and apparently, they were getting too close to the truth."

"Oh, Mr. McCormick, I know too well what Merina Parker is capable of. You don't have to spell it out like the idea is new. She also will probably have them mention how I got upset when she handed me the injunction to prevent us from deporting those families, in an attempt to honor the demands of the terrorists." Gilmore snorted and shook his head. "Optics." The president pulled his chair out and sat down. "But don't despair. It's just Washington politics at its finest. Or maybe at its worst."

"Well, Mr. President, as you can imagine, my office has been flooded with calls. My phone has blown up with over nine hundred text messages in the last hour. We need to get out in front of this sooner than we were planning."

"Agreed," Gilmore said. He motioned back and forth at himself and Ben Jenkins. "We were just wrapping up the language on the executive order we discussed earlier."

"Yeah, and I'm still a little leery about how invasive this order is going to be. And now with this Merina Parker business coming to light, an order like this just might blow up in our faces."

"The problem is, Ben," President Gilmore said, "we just don't know how many of these things are out there. Or where they are. Las Vegas could be the only one. And there could be a hundred. We can't just wait to see if they threaten us again."

"He's right," McCormick said. "If it gets out that we knew, even generally speaking, where these devices might be hidden and what they look like, and we sat on that information, this presidency would be—"

The president's phone rang. He held up his finger and waited before pressing the button. "Yes."

"Sir, you have a call waiting. It's Agent Scarfano."

Gilmore lifted his brow. "Send it through."

"Yes, sir."

"Maybe she's got some good news for us." Gilmore waited for the phone to ring and picked it up instead of using the speakerphone. "Please tell me this is something good."

"Very good, sir," Julee said.

A surprised look spread across Gilmore's face. "Really?" He looked up at the other two men.

"Sir, we have uncovered information from Markus Sorensen's computer files indicating the location of all the devices, like the one used in Las Vegas at the Bahama Bay Hotel and Casino. These devices were labeled as 'Plan B,' which we have reason to believe was a back-up plan to the release of the air fresheners. This list contains over forty device locations."

Gilmore pulled the receiver away from his mouth. "Scarfano says she thinks they know where the other devices, like the one in Las Vegas, are located." He raised the receiver to his mouth. "This is excellent news, SAC Scarfano. I will need you to send me the list of locations. We were just about to send out an executive order, asking all major cities and tourist destinations to search their grounds for a device. I am assuming this list will help us narrow the search considerably?"

"Yes, sir. And three of those locations are in D.C."

President Gilmore tapped the speakerphone button so the other two men could hear. "Where?"

"Based on the names of the files we uncovered, the three locations in Washington are Capitol Hill, the Treasury Building, and Union Market."

"My God," McCormick said. "They would devastate this entire city and paralyze the government at the same time."

"Sir?" Julee said.

"Uh, I've got you on speakerphone, Agent Scarfano. My press secretary, Jonas McCormick, and Ben Jenkins are here with me at the moment."

"I see. Well, I was going to add that each of these files contains a named target, floor plans of the target, schematics of the HVAC system associated with said target, and some other documents, showing payment to the people responsible for installing these devices as well as cost for parts."

"They were thorough," Gilmore said, peering at his chief of staff.

"Yes, sir."

"Good work, Scarfano. Send the list to Ben Jenkins and Jonas McCormick. They will need the location information for what I am about to ask them to do next. In the meantime, please notify Director Jameson and inform him."

"He was my next phone call."

"Very good. Keep me posted."

"Will do, Mr. President."

The line went dead, and the speakerphone light went out.

"Gentlemen," Gilmore said. "I don't think we need an executive order any longer. Ben, contact Homeland and direct them to set up a coordinated, synchronized assault on these locations with any and every governmental organization they deem necessary. I want each team, in each of these forty-odd remaining locations, to have the information contained in the pertinent file, so they can locate each device as quickly as possible. I expect all devices to be found and neutralized within the next," he glanced at his watch, 'five hours. I want to be able to announce to the world by the evening news cycle of our success. And Ben, remind them, they are probably just like the one in Vegas, so they are to take extreme precautions."

Ben Jenkins stood with a bit of a smile. "Yes, sir."

"Oh, and Ben, I want those responsible for physically planting those devices in those locations arrested and charged with everything we can throw at them. She said their names were listed in other documents. I suspect there will be money trails to track as well. Tell your FBI contacts in each location I want those people found."

"You got it."

"And Jonas," Gilmore said, "let's set up our press conference for two o'clock. We can use the remaining time to prepare, as I am sure Merina Parker will be an additional topic they all will wish to discuss."

"Will you want to let the press know about these newly found files?" McCormick said.

"No. I don't want anyone outside of this government to know we found those files or have any knowledge of the device locations. If our enemies find out we know, they will undoubtedly release the remaining devices in a frantic attempt at causing chaos."

McCormick stood and picked up his laptop. "Very good, sir."

CHAPTER 16

NATIONAL POLICE - CENTRAL *Police Station of the 8th District*
  Paris, France

Conrad Bowker sat on a small bench on the far side of a holding cell in a prison jumpsuit. His clothes, bloodied and torn from the accident, were what he wore on the trip from the hospital to the police station. All of his belongings—his mobile phone, his wallet, and the other items he had in his rucksack in the van—were gone. He'd had them at the hospital, but they were confiscated and bagged as evidence on the way.

When he first arrived, he scanned his holding cell and surmised it had probably been built in the eighteenth century, but definitely no later than the mid-nineteenth. He noticed signs of remodeling, several times over actually, and was now tiled from floor to ceiling, including newer, more modern material on the floor itself. The ceiling was still a slick, painted plaster with small cracks angling across two opposite corners, forming a jagged triangle in each. Despite the shiny ceramic squares on the walls and the modern flooring, the room still had a dirty, Napoleonic prison feel to it.

Conrad wondered how many incarcerated souls had died inside these walls over the decades.

Some at the hands of the guards.

Some due to excruciatingly prolonged stays, overcoming their heart's desire to remain on this planet.

Some because of disease and malnutrition.

These places weren't always Geneva Convention-compliant...

With one window above his head, at least twelve feet high and too small for any normal-sized human to utilize for escape, the dimming light streaming across the room informed him the time of day was nearing sunset. Or at least the sun had settled behind the building across the street casting its shadow upon his situation.

He had demanded he be allowed to make a phone call when he was still at the hospital. The demand resonated off the walls and down the hallway as he was led away from his room in handcuffs. Shoved into a sedan, similar to the one camped outside the safe house, he was transported from the hospital to the police station, the demand was made every thirty seconds or so. Then, when he was escorted to the holding cell, the demand continued roughly every two minutes. He yelled it as loud as he could.

"I need to make a phone call!"

* * *

Several hours had passed, and he was beginning to wonder why he was left alone for so long. In his lengthy career experience, investigators—whether it be local police detectives or the federal types, couldn't wait to interrogate their prisoner. In so many cases, they rushed the process, causing themselves extra work and unnecessary headaches. However, in this case, the pendulum had swung almost completely in the opposite direction. It had been several hours, and not so much as an offer of a cup of water had been made. The federal officers never said another word after they slapped the handcuffs on him, except for suggestions to watch his head when they forced him into the car or to disrobe and put on the jumpsuit after they arrived at the jail. It was one of the strangest episodes Conrad had ever witnessed.

Another fifteen minutes passed before a different officer opened the iron-barred door and stepped inside. His broad shoulders brushing against the jambs on both sides. Two additional officers stood out in the hallway. One held the door.

"Agent Bowker, my name is Officer Fabron. You have requested to make a phone call, yes?" the officer said with a heavily-accented French tone.

"Only ten thousand times."

"The director has granted your request. However, please note, we must identify the person to whom you wish to speak. Therefore, you will give us the number, we will call it, and if it checks out, then you will be allowed on the line. Do you understand?"

"Why all the hullabaloo, if I may ask?"

"You are being classified as an international terrorist. Because of this, the rules change for you as a prisoner."

"An international terrorist? Are you insane?"

"Agent Bowker, we are just following orders. I am sure you will have your day in court."

Bowker cursed. "And where shall this day in court be held? Here? In Paris?"

"I do not know. I do know we have been given orders to extradite you to England after the French government has decided what they wish to do with you. You committed a capital crime on French soil. Such actions are not taken lightly."

"What you're telling me then, is I won't live long enough to see my homeland as a free man."

"Those concerns are for later. Right now, we must give you your phone call."

"Good." Bowker huffed in a frustrated, yet relieved manner.

The officer motioned for Bowker to step toward him and hold his hands out, wrists together.

"I will admit, I cannot remember the phone number off the top of my head," Bowker said as he allowed Officer Fabron to secure the cuffs. "I had it in my mobile phone, but they confiscated it from me. It was dead anyway, so..."

"I am sure we can assist you. Now, follow these officers. They will lead you to the room."

Bowker eyed Officer Fabron as he locked the handcuffs. "You have more pressing matters?"

"Oh, no. I will be following you."

Bowker grunted. "Lead the way then."

The two officers outside led the little parade down a corridor and around a corner before coming to a large, solid metal door. One of the officers pressed a button, and the door's latch clicked, releasing its grip. The first officer, his hand already on the handle, yanked the door open wide and waved for Bowker to enter the small vestibule which had another, metal-barred door on the other side.

Once all four men were inside, another motorized click sounded, and the first officer pushed the metal-barred door open so the others could follow him down another corridor and around another corner. The hallway ended at another solid metal door.

Next to the door was a large, shatterproof-glass window which gave those standing outside full view of the room. Inside the room was a lone table and two chairs. On the table was a phone, a landline with a cord draped off the other side of the table and connected to a phone jack.

Bowker was taken inside and allowed to sit in the chair on the opposite side of the table.

"So, how do you expect me to call a number I cannot remember?" he said.

Officer Fabron sat down across from Bowker and pulled a small notebook from his pocket and a pen. "Who were you wishing to call?"

"The United States FBI field office in Jacksonville, Florida. I need to speak with the Agent-in-Charge there."

"What is the individual's name?"

"Her full title is Supervisory Special Agent-in-Charge Julee Scarfano." Bowker spelled it out for him.

Officer Fabron jotted down the information and picked up the phone. He punched one number and waited. "Did you get all that?"

Bowker pinched his brow together and looked for a microphone but didn't see one.

"Okay...understood," Officer Fabron said. "I will wait."

Bowker looked up and spotted the small LED camera in the corner of the room, near the ceiling. He frowned. *They're going to record everything said.*

"Just send it through when you have verified the call." Officer Fabron hung up.

"You know I am entitled to privacy when it comes to my phone call."

"But this person is not a lawyer, is she?"

"No, but she might as well be."

"Once your call comes through, I will exit the room."

"And what about your *compagnons* watching me through the eye in the sky?" Bowker nodded in the direction of the camera.

Officer Fabron twisted his frame and glanced up until he saw what Bowker was referencing, then he faced him again. "See the red light?"

Conrad nodded.

"When it goes off, so does the microphone. Our two countries may not have the best of histories, Agent Bowker, but we can still act civilized, yes?"

"It's a start."

Officer Fabron nodded and exhaled, like he didn't have anything else to say and was now dreading the long silence until the phone rang.

Bowker allowed a slight smile to appear. "Waiting is the hardest part, eh?"

Fabron nodded again just as the landline rang. He answered. "Yes...Very good. Put the connection through."

Bowker watched as he listened for Julee's voice.

"Agent Scarfano, my name is Officer Jean Fabron. I work for the *Gendarmerie Nationale* in Paris, France. We have a person in custody by the name of Conrad Bowker. He claims he knows you? Is this true?" Fabron nodded as Julee confirmed it. "Very good. I will then hand the phone to Agent Bowker. You are free to talk as long as is needed. However, Agent Scarfano, once your call concludes, you will no longer be allowed to contact Agent Bowker without going through his legal counsel. Do you understand?" Fabron looked up at Bowker with a confirming smile. "Very good. Please hold for Agent Bowker." He held the phone out, and Conrad took it.

Officer Fabron stood. "We will be outside."

Bowker covered the mouthpiece and nodded, waiting for him to exit.

He glanced up at the camera and eventually saw the red light disappear. With a deep breath, he put the phone to his ear. "Julee?"

"Agent Bowker? What is all this about?"

"Let's just say my days are numbered, and I have some things to get off my chest before I get railroaded into a deep hole in the heart of France."

CHAPTER 17

RIVERVIEW DRIVE
  Van Buren, Maine

In the kitchen, Harrison Kelly snatched a bottled water out of the refrigerator and lamented it being the last one. Having never been given the time to leave the house and go shopping since his arrival, and having to leave his home in Maryland in a bit of a rush, the only food and water he had was what he brought with him. A stop at a local convenience store along the interstate on his way from North Kensington secured a fountain soda and two bags of potato chips. The soda was a distant memory. The bags of chips were more recent casualties. Another stop at the big supermarket in Houlton, Maine, gave him the twelve-pack of waters, the three bags of ground coffee, the frozen pizzas, the pound of deli meat, the package of provolone cheese, the loaf of bread, the necessary condiments, the half-dozen apples, the gallon of milk, the paper plates, plastic ware, napkins, and the five boxes of cereal. The drive-thru at the Tim Horton's gave him the needed caffeine to complete the remaining ninety-minute journey.

He sat down at the kitchen table and checked the time on his smartphone. The trip from Maryland seemed like days ago. So much had happened since he arrived in Maine. But in actuality, it had not even been twenty-four hours yet.

Harrison had been in front of the computer the entire time, and his eyes were now conking out. They burned and were having trouble focusing. It felt good to close them.

He stood and moseyed over to the couch. He set the bottled water and his phone down on the coffee table and sat down. Grabbing the lap pillow from one end, he laid down and jammed it together with the lap pillow on the other end of the couch and fluffed them until they felt just right under his head.

Repositioning his neck, it took only mere seconds before exhaustion overwhelmed his desire to remain conscious.

* * *

Harrison awoke to the theme from his favorite movie, growing louder each time it repeated. He wasn't sure how many times it had played. He wasn't even sure where he was, or why his phone was ringing and vibrating at the same time.

Slowly, feeling like a bludgeoned boxer who'd been out for the count in the middle of the canvas, he slapped the coffee table several times until his left hand found his phone. He picked it up and had difficulty focusing on the screen.

I don't recognize the number, but the area code...it's Jacksonville...

He pressed the green icon and cleared his throat. "Hello?" he said, with the words coming out like gravel.

"This is Agent Mitchell from the Jacksonville FBI field office in Jacksonville, Florida. I was asked by Supervisory Special Agent-in-Charge Julee Scarfano to call. Is this Harrison Kelly?"

Harrison rolled over on his back and wished the wave of nausea away. "Yes, yes. It is."

"It sounds like I woke you up."

"You did, but no worries. I've been asleep for…" Harrison pulled the phone away from his ear, "all of forty-five minutes. That would explain why I feel a bit bodgy right now."

"Does that mean 'tired'"?

"What? Bodgy? No, it means, uh…you blokes here in the States would say you 'don't feel very well,' and as a result, you're not going to be of much help."

"So, 'bodgy' means 'worthless'"?

"Sort of. Not quite so harsh, but close. Anyway, that's exactly how I feel right now."

"Would you rather I call back later?"

"No, no. I just need to get up off the couch." Harrison rolled onto his side and pushed himself up until he was sitting up.

"Well, if it's any consolation, I know how you feel. I slept Thursday night for about four hours. Got another six hours Friday night, only because I went to bed early. And since then, two one-hour cat naps. And a ton of caffeine."

"Oh, well, it seems we're in the same boat, mate. I go through a half-pot of coffee about every four hours. If I make it any stronger, it'll pour like molasses."

"Agent Scarfano said you needed help matching some voices to names?"

"Yeah, yeah," Harrison said, groaning like an old man as he stood. "If we can identify these people, then we will have figured out who is behind this entire affair."

"You think it's going to be that easy?"

Harrison snagged his water bottle and staggered over to his computer. "Yes, if you have these blokes' and sheilas' voices already in your database."

"That's not what I meant. How did you acquire these voice-prints? And are they reliable?"

"Oh," Harrison said, plopping down in his comfy office chair. "You're afraid I obtained these illegally?"

"No."

"So what? Off the back of a milk carton then?"

"Uh, sort of."

"Trust me, Agent Mitchell. These are as authentic as they come. So much so, Markus Sorensen was willing to store the incriminating evidence on his own personal computer and back it up to two different servers. One in Bluffdale, Utah, and one in China." Harrison set his phone down, placed it on speakerphone and unscrewed the cap on his water bottle. "If you ask me, he wanted to make sure he had this information for any contingency." He took a long swig.

"That does make me feel better."

"And because Mr. Sorensen felt so adamantly about keeping meticulous records, I believe the people represented in these voiceprints have a great deal to lose."

"Honor among thieves?"

Harrison slipped on his headset and positioned the micro-phone in front of his mouth. "Trust is such a fragile thing in the field of espionage." He synced his phone with his headset and entered his password into the computer before opening the neces-sary files. "Hence, the reason I believe these audio files will blow the lid off this case."

"How do you want to do this, exactly?"

"It's your database. Your call."

"I have been authorized to give you access, if I deem it neces-sary. And since time is crucial, I think doing so would be the fastest way."

"All right then. Send me whatever you think best. There are a bunch of files. He recorded every conversation pertaining to the eventual release of the contagion. Therefore, he literally has hundreds of calls stored. Now, the good news is he also catalogued them all under some weird names." Harrison opened one of the files. "For example, this one is named 'Porthos.'"

"Oh, a Three Musketeers buff, is he?"

"Well, not exactly. Some of the files have more generic names, like 'The Monk,' and 'The Elf," and 'Sir Knight.' Others are even more inconspicuous, like 'Driver One,' 'Driver Two,' and so forth. He has a bunch of those. Goes up all the way to 'Driver Forty-six.'"

"Are they code names?"

"Could be or simply a way of knowing who it is without having their names blatantly listed for us."

"How many files are there total?"

"Including everything? Almost a thousand, but not all of them are audio files."

"Seriously?"

"Already counted them earlier, waiting for your call."

"Then, we'll need to split these up."

"Agreed, but only after we are done listening to the audio files of The Consortium members. This has to be our first and only job until we can identify all the players. Blake and Julee need this information yesterday. Once we have completed that task, then I can send you everything else. But, Agent Mitchell, it needs to be saved in a place *only* you and Agent Scarfano have access. I can't stress how important this step is."

"Because we don't know who we can trust, right?"

"Yeah. Wish I had a dollar for every time I've heard such a phrase this week."

"Ditto."

"Okay, first thing first. Just in case our efforts get separated somehow and we have to divide and conquer, go ahead and send me the link to the place you wish me to upload these files, and I'll send you the audio files we need to identify. Then, I'll send everything else to the same location after we complete our task. And by the way, you're gonna need about a one hundred petabytes of storage space for all of these files."

"And where am I supposed to put that much data where nobody else can access?"

Harrison winced. "How many flash drives do you have?"

"Very funny."

"I'm sure you'll figure it out. That's why they pay you the big bucks, right?"

"The bucks they pay me don't cover all the stress of the last week."

"And send me access to the voiceprint database as well. Again, if we get separated, we can split the remaining files up and handle them ourselves."

"Shouldn't we go ahead and do that anyway? Cover more ground."

"True, but Blake wanted our two sets of ears on it. You may hear something I don't or know something I don't, and vice-versa. He was adamant about how we had to get these names correct. He didn't want to have warrants issued for the wrong people or anyone who may be innocent."

"Makes sense."

Seconds later, Harrison received two notifications of two separate links. He clicked on the first one, and it gave him an official FBI screen.

"You should have received a link to our database and a link to the database. If you'll—"

"Already there. Gonna open the database first. Just need the username and password."

"I'm going to have you log in as me. Once we're done, then I'll change my password."

"Ah, Agent Mitchell, you don't trust me?"

"Agent Scarfano does. Agent Meyer does, so that's good enough for me...for now."

Harrison laughed. "Don't feel bad. I'd do the same thing." He poised his fingers over the keyboard. "Okay. Shoot."

Mitchell relayed the information. "You in?"

Harrison clicked the login button, and the page flashed and loaded a screen with one field and one place to upload a file in the top half. In the bottom half was a configuration similar to a fancy radio off to one side. The rest of the screen contained a box with fine lines running vertical. "Yep. Now, let me minimize this for a second." Harrison clicked away and tapped on the keyboard when necessary. "All right. I have these files being put in a zip file. I'm clicking on the second link as we speak."

"It will open a password box. Use the same password I just gave you."

Harrison tapped and clicked away. "Okay, the file is sitting in your folder. Might take a few minutes to get through all the virus protections and then unzip. So, while we wait, I'm going to upload the first file and listen to it. Want to eavesdrop?"

"Sure."

"This file is called 'Di Tura.'" Harrison spelled it for Agent Mitchell. "This particular recording was dated June 12, 2010." Harrison turned up the volume and pressed the Play button once it appeared.

"Hello?"

"Good evening. You're late with your update."

"Depends on your perspective, Markus."

"No, it depends on how much money we are spending, Mr. Murphy. And what time zone we are referring to, which in this case, is the Eastern Time Zone. My time zone"

"Well, forgive me. I'm a little isolated right now. They're just a touch behind on the technology in this part of the world. I had to wait until I could get a signal. Even the satellite phones have a hard time out here."

"So, before you lose your precious signal, tell me what's going on."

"It's been two days since we released it. We used ten households in the middle of the city, spread out over a ten-block radius. We also used people from varying backgrounds."

"For what purpose exactly?"

"We are trying to simulate how the final event will occur, so we studied the city. Learned who lived where. What job they had. How many people worked at the hospital. What kind of medical system they had in place. Number of ambulances, et cetera, and so forth."

"Very good. I am assuming then the demographics chosen were done to maximize efficacy?"

"As much as we could. One of the families has a father who is a worker in the nearby hospital. Another family has a mother who is a teacher in the largest school. Another has a mother who owns her own little produce market in the square. Varying backgrounds. Varying jobs. Some are rich by Bunia standards. Others enjoy a moderate wealth. And some are poor. We hit every demographic we could with only ten available devices."

"And the incubation period is how many days?"

"Anywhere from two to six days. However, I am told two days would be unlikely in this first test run. The shorter incubation periods would become more of the norm once the contagion jumped from its third or fourth host to the next victim. It is designed to speed up the incubation period as it jumps from host to host and mutates."

"So, nobody has shown signs yet?"

"None have gone to the hospital yet. My colleague is monitoring those sites. Now, we could have some in the bush who have fallen ill. They could simply not be sick enough yet to warrant a trip into the city. However, I am assured that once they do manifest full-blown symptoms, they will know they are sick."

"*Very well. Please allow me to remind you, Mr. Murphy, this plan of yours was designed to be completed by July 4th, 2012. I know that date is over two years away, however, I am assured by some of the best immunologists in the world two years in the world of immunology is like a week to us. In other words, they will need sufficient time to develop a vaccine of this magnitude. In order to do so, they first must know what kind of bug they are dealing with.*"

"*Mr. Sorensen, do I need to remind you? I'm the one who came up with this plan. Therefore, you can rest assured I am going to carry it through to the end, with or without your money. So, you would be wise not to cut me out of the picture. I have protocols in place. Therefore, if you or one of your hedge fund buddies gets too greedy and decides to exclude me in any way, the contagion will be released in whatever present form it finds itself. And if you do not have your precious little vaccine made by then, good luck. You're gonna need it.*"

Sorensen blurted an expletive. "*I do not take too kindly to threats, Colin.*"

"*That wasn't a threat, Markus. It was a promise. We have locations all over the world, strategic locations, mind you, already targeted and ready to go at a moment's notice. My colleague has several superbugs from which to choose. Everything from glanders to anthrax to smallpox to the Marburg virus... Oy! What a winner, that one is. By day fifteen, it literally melts away your insides, Markus. Prevents your blood from being able to coagulate. Not a pretty sight.*"

Sorenson groaned. "*Okay, Murphy, you've made your point.*"

"*Have I?*"

"*Yes.*"

"*Good. Because those bugs are our protection until this one is perfected. Once it is, then this one will take their place.*"

"*All I ask is that you keep me updated.*"

"*Have I ever let you down yet?*"

"*Oh, and Murphy?*"

"*Yes?*"

"Never threaten me again."

"Or what, Dad? Are you going to ground me? Permanently? The six-feet under variety? Am I supposed to be scared of a tough-talking pharmaceutical CEO?" Murphy laughed. "I've dealt with lunatics with machine guns and British commanders with armies at their disposal—"

"All I'm saying is, just watch your step, and do your job."

"Yeah, sure. Don't want to step on your polished wingtips now, would we? Goodbye, Sorensen."

The line went dead.

Harrison watched the audio file end and go back to the beginning. "So, just as I thought, the man who initiated the call was Sorensen."

"Right," Mitchell said. "And the other guy is Colin Murphy. We not only had them both call each other by name, we got a voice match on both as well."

"And they are referencing an incident which took place in the Democratic Republic of the Congo. Bunia, to be exact. That region of Africa had over fifty percent of all bubonic plague cases worldwide from 2004 to 2012."

"What a great place to hide biological testing."

"Just what Blakey...I mean, Agent Meyer thought."

"But this call was four years ago. And they're still working on the vaccine?"

"Agent Meyer thinks they were delayed by those creating the vaccine. And because of the delay, he surmised the deadliness of the contagion must have been ramped up higher than what is considered normal. Otherwise, they would have already released it by now."

Mitchell groaned and sounded as if he was reaching for something. "Well, Murphy pretty much confirmed it for us, stating the incubation period gets shorter each time it moves from one person to another."

"Scary stuff."

"What better way to make a contagion increase its mortality rate than by increasing the rate of infection."

"True. And from what I know about these things, you increase the fatality rate amongst the first responders too. And when first responders are infected, it speeds up even quicker because there are less people to care for the sick once they succumb to it."

"Thus making a vaccine so crucial. Antidote's take time to work."

"If you get them to the patient in time."

"But if you had a vaccine and were already immune..."

"Exactly." Harrison blew out a breath and grabbed his water bottle.

"Okay, so, 'Di Tura' is Colin Murphy. And we know the other guy was Sorensen. Open up another file. We've got to identify these people before they release this thing again."

Harrison manipulated the mouse and clicked on the next file with another weird title. "This one should be interesting. It's labeled 'Polecat.'"

"Polecat?"

"You can't make this stuff up."

"Okay then."

Harrison chuckled and cleared his throat. "Polecat! Come to the stage! You're the next contestant on the Price is High."

CHAPTER 18

NATIONAL POLICE - CENTRAL Police Station of the 8th District
Paris, France

Conrad Bowker spoke normally, almost softly, not wanting his words to be heard and understood by the goons standing outside the window. They were talking, often peeking inside to check on their suspect, but he wasn't sure how soundproof the room was.

"Listen, Agent Scarfano, I need to talk to Blake. He's the only one who can help me at this point."

"He's not with me. I'm actually in Atlanta right now. We had a lead in the case, and it led me here. I'll be heading back to Jacksonville soon, but I'm not sure when I'll see Blake again."

"Have you heard from him?"

"Yes. He's on his way back to the States as we speak."

Bowker bobbed his head up and down. "That means he's found his wife and kids. Brilliant."

"How would you know?"

"I know Blake Meyer. He'd never leave wherever he was until

he found them...unless they were brought back to the States, and he's in pursuit."

"You're correct. He did find them." Julee huffed. "Agent Bowker, is there anything I can help you with until Blake's available to talk? I'm a little busy here at the moment."

Bowker shifted the phone to his left ear and turned slightly, away from his guards. "I told you before I didn't want to share any of this information over the phone, and I'd only share it with Blake. However, it would appear my ability to share it face-to-face with anyone is in peril. Therefore, I am left with no choice but to tell you what I know now."

"Which is?"

Bowker hesitated. "As you have probably figured out, I've been arrested by the *Gendarmerie Nationale*."

"I figured. The call from an Officer Fabron kind of gave it away. Why have they arrested you?"

"Major General Botinkin is dead."

A silence crept into the room.

"Did you kill the man, Agent Bowker?"

"No." Bowker swore under his breath. "Even *you* think I may be guilty. So, how am I supposed to convince *them*?"

"You know I have to ask, Conrad. So, what happened?"

Conrad explained how he had kept the major general in a safe house and monitored things from afar so as not to have anyone follow him and eventually get to the elder Botinkin. A *pro bono* service for Agent Meyer. He then explained the day's events and how he was now being accused of poisoning the men in the van, including the major general.

"And how would these authorities know to stake out your safe house? How would they even know where it was?"

"I don't know. But somebody tipped them off."

"And why follow you? Only to commit this act and frame *you*, of all people? Why not just kill you too? Seems like giving you all the same water would have made things easier for them."

"I've been wondering the same thing. It would appear somebody wants me alive for some reason."

"So, what are you thinking then? Surely you have some theories."

Bowker glanced over his shoulder. The three officers were still standing outside the window. All three were watching him. He lowered his voice. "It may have something to do with Agent Connell."

"Agent Connell? You told me he was dead. You just never told me what happened."

Bowker allowed a morbid chuckle to escape. "I'm sure he's right where I left him, unless these goons found him too."

"So, you *did* kill Agent Connell."

"It was either him or me, love. He said he was looking for me because he thought I was with Major General Botinkin."

"Well, for your information, I do know he was sent by our president to find the major general. I can confirm that much."

"Oh, I bet you can. Blake warned me some rats might show up, and Agent Connell was at the top of the list. He told me, under no circumstances, was I to allow the major general to leave Paris with any of them."

"How did Blake know Connell would go to Paris? Even the director of the FBI was caught off guard by Connell's sudden disappearance."

"You and I both know Blake has eyes and ears all over." Bowker chuckled a little harder. "He's probably listening to our conversation right now."

Julee allowed a nervous laugh to escape. "Why did Connell want the major general? What did he tell you?"

"He claimed he was sent to bring Botinkin back to the U.S., so the president could give him immunity in exchange for information. The major general knew what kind of contagion was most likely to be used by these terrorists you people are battling."

"But you didn't believe Connell?"

"Not after he explained to me how his children were being used against him. According to Connell, he was sent to save the major general. I believe he was sent to kill him. Silence him. Whoever sent Connell did not want the major general to talk. Otherwise, why threaten Agent Connell's children?"

"Yeah, that doesn't make sense to threaten them, if he was simply to bring Botinkin in," Julee said. "Where is he now?"

"In an apartment in Paris."

"I need the location and apartment number."

"Only if you can help me get out of here."

"This isn't a hostage negotiation, Conrad."

Bowker smirked. "I beg to differ, Agent Scarfano. In this case, however, I'm the hostage. I'm being set up to take the fall." He swore. "The two men the *gendarmes* are claiming I poisoned, the driver and passenger in the van...I had never met them before. I had only hired them the day before they showed up. They were recommended to me by the men who watched the safe house for me. There is no way the driver or his mate could have...could have known...they were..." Bowker shouted another expletive.

"Conrad? Are you okay?"

Bowker's mind, addled as it was, cleared some memories out of the way. It was as if a fog was being lifted, ever so slowly, and things he had forgotten—because they seemed so insignificant— were becoming clear...

He switched the phone to his other ear and leaned forward. Resting his elbow on the table, he lowered his head into his hand. "The water bottles."

"What? What water bottles?"

"The ones the driver of the minivan and the passenger had."

"I'm not following."

"Once we left the safe house, the driver and the passenger... they had water bottles."

"So? They had water bottles. And?"

"You don't understand. The *gendarmes* claimed the tea I had made Botinkin earlier, before we left the safe house, was tainted with poison. They were doing labs on all three men. How much do you wish to wager, Agent Scarfano, that all three men died from the same poison? And somehow, the same poison was administered to their water bottles. That's the only way all three men could have been killed with the same poison under the circumstances."

"But how could someone poison those two men and Botinkin without you knowing?"

Bowker tried to listen to Agent Scarfano, but his mind needed more silence. Visions of past conversations jockeyed for position.

"Conrad? You still on the line?"

He gripped his forehead with his other hand and squeezed it, as if the pressure would somehow cause the fuzzy pictures in is head to magically focus and organize themselves.

"Agent Bowker?"

...the two men...in the safe house...I heard them talking about Warin and Nikolas the other day...

"Conrad? If you're still on the line, say something."

They must have known each other...

So, could this be some kind of revenge?

"Okay, Agent Bowker, I appear to have lost you. Call me back when—"

"No, wait!"

"Bowker, what's going on?"

"I think I just connected the dots, as you Americans fancy saying."

"How so?"

Bowker ran his hand over the top of his head and pulled down on his neck, trying to relieve the building pressure. "Blake had warned me about Agent Connell. Said he might show up and try to kill me to get to Botinkin. And as is often the case, Blake was correct. Connell showed up...at the hotel I was personally using as a home base. He followed me across town. I wasn't sure who to trust. Wasn't sure who worked for whom. Therefore, I made a split-second decision and eliminated the two men who had been monitoring the major general from the apartment I mentioned earlier.

"The two men, Augustus Warin and Nikolas Berriger, never saw it coming. I slipped poison into their coffees—"

"Poison, eh?"

"Ah, love, don't you go there too."

"You have to admit, Conrad, it looks suspicious. Very suspicious."

"That's why I keep telling everyone I'm being framed."

Julee sighed into the phone. "So, what happened to Connell? Poison him too?"

"Oh, you are a right corker today." Bowker paused and drew in a deep breath. "Connell came barreling into the apartment, gun drawn, but I was three steps ahead. I captured him...and I questioned him."

"You mean you tortured him?"

"It didn't start out that way, but when he started spewing misinformation about my family, I lost it."

"What misinformation?"

"He claimed my nephew was lured by the Russians to give up intelligence in exchange for an arranged marriage with a Russian woman."

"I see." Julee paused again. "So, let's get back to how Agent Connell connects to your arrest."

"I'm not sure he does. I mean, I killed Warin and Berriger, because I thought they may be working with Connell and whoever sent him. Then, I went to the safe house and sent away the two men who had been watching Botinkin since the beginning."

"Why didn't you kill them too?"

"You mean, how did I know they weren't in on it?"

"Exactly."

"I've known those two blokes for over twenty years. Used them multiple times. They're not the brightest mercenaries, but they are the most trustworthy of the bunch."

"Are you sure?"

"In this business, Agent Scarfano, who can trust anyone fully? But yes, as far as mercenaries go, they were the best of the best."

"We both trust Blake. And I trust him fully."

"Blake Meyer is the exception, not the rule...and he's no mercenary either. And by the time all this madness ends, he may be the *only* exception. Period."

"Where did those two men from the safe house go after they left you?"

"I don't know. They said something about hitting the town and tying one on. If you knew them, you'd know it all sounded legitimate. Make a ton of money and then drink it away in the presence of lonely women has been their *modus operandi* for years."

"And who says chivalry is dead?"

Conrad chuckled. "But they would never cross me, because they know what would happen, if I ever caught up to them."

"And that's just it, Conrad. You can't catch up to them, if you're in custody."

Bowker knew she was right. *And they would have been able to get into the safe house after we left...they knew where we kept the key...*

But that means they would have had to set up the two men they recommended, the driver and the passenger...

And if they did plan all of this, who are they working for?

And why would they want revenge for killing Warin and Nikolas, yet, freely kill two other recommended mercenaries?

None of this makes any sen—

"Conrad, I'll see what I can do. From what you're telling me, the evidence seems circumstantial, but it also seems overwhelming. And if they find the location of that apartment and the three dead bodies inside, and if they can prove you killed them—and I'm assuming your fingerprints are all over the apartment?—then you being framed for the death of Major General Botinkin and the other two men will not be your only worries."

"If those two blokes in the safe house pulled all this off, then they're much more intelligent than I ever gave them credit. But I still have a hard time believing it was them."

"I'm gonna need their names."

Bowker tried to recollect all the times he'd used the two men, but it was literally more than his muddled memory could recall...

If I give her their names, they'll be arrested.

But if they did frame me, then who can I trust anymore? And why help them?

And in my state of health, what does it matter if I give up names?

If they come after me? If the Russians do? The Americans? The British? The French?

Seems I've made some powerful enemies over the years...

And I'm never leaving prison. Even if I make it to trial, my days are numbered...

So, why not come clean?...

"Conrad. I need their names."

He rattled them off. "And now that I have sold my fellow mercenaries out, I might as well tell you the rest of the story. At least, the parts you'll want to hear. Then, maybe, much of what's happened over the last few days will make more sense. It has to do with the contagion used in the original incident in 1999...Operation Abydos."

"Okay. I'm listening."

CHAPTER 19

NATIONAL POLICE - CENTRAL Police Station
  8th District
  Paris, France

"I am assuming Blake has explained Operation Abydos to you?" Conrad Bowker said.

"He did." Julee yawned. "Way back at the beginning of this ordeal. He held a meeting with the president and a bunch of department heads. All of our agents here is Jacksonville were present as well. The operation sounded like a mess to me."

"You don't know the half of it." Bowker turned and noticed one of the officers standing outside the room was gone.

I wonder where he went...

Bowker faced away again and leaned his right shoulder into the chair back. He held the phone to his right ear with both hands and lowered his voice. "I was approached by my supervisor in 1999, who has since passed away, so don't bother trying to track him down. He asked me to be a part of a mission, so clandestine at the time, even leaders of the countries involved supposedly had no idea it was happening."

"When you say 'leaders,' you're talking about the presidents and prime ministers?"

"As well as directors, ministers of defense, the people who ran the organizations we were a part of, so for me, it was MI6. It was on a need-to-know basis. Plausible deniability was important, I was told." Bowker chuckled. "I almost backed out, but when I had heard one agent already did and was immediately reassigned as a field agent in Morocco, I decided being able to live in London, rather than just being able to say I was from there, was more important."

"Go on."

"I admit...I found it hard to believe our prime minister and members of our parliament who serve on the foreign affairs committees, and even the head of MI6, didn't have a clue. However, we were taught to be good little Brits and not ask too many questions. So, I played my part.

"My role in the mission was to pretend to be a black market arms dealer and travel to Russia to meet up with an old, supposedly retired KGB agent named Ivan Chernov. He was to secure a new and improved, 1999 version of the biological agent *Yersinia pseudotuberculosis* combined with myelin toxin, which he did." Bowker cleared his throat. "I met with Chernov, secured the contagion, and brought it to England. There, I was to hand it off to the contact for the group of IRA radicals who were eventually to be eliminated with the help of Colin Murphy and Liam Clarke.

"What I didn't know until much later—nor did the Americans, for that matter—was Ivan Chernov had assigned Arina Filipov to act as a Russian asset and infiltrate the IRA radicals. It was a Russian intelligence mission running concurrently with the one I was on."

"Could someone have tipped off Chernov, giving him information about your plan? Sending in Filipov could have been his way of gaining an advantage."

"I wondered the same thing, Agent Scarfano. But no. I've checked on multiple fronts. The Russians, too, wanted to destabilize the region, which has always been a main staple of the Russians' covert diet. However, the Russians were looking to affect all of Europe, not simply the British Isles. So, when they found out about our plan to use the biological weapon, they were all too happy to oblige."

"You think their willingness to help would have raised some red flags."

"Ah, love, freelance biothreats were just getting started in those days. It was becoming the method of choice because governments had been through so much over the decades since World War I. So many wars with conventional weapons, boots on the ground, and dead bodies to go around.

"Even though many countries have biological weapons programs, it's hard for them to utilize those resources without someone pointing fingers. So, they outsource it. Get the freelancers to do their dirty work for them while keeping their hands clean. Someone else fires the gun, so to speak, and the gunshot residue is on their hands, not yours.

"For example, the Rajneeshees in Oregon using *Salmonella typhimurium* is one such group. The Red Army in France attempting to use *botulinum* is another. And Aum Shinrikyo and the attack on the Tokyo subway using sarin gas...these groups are just the tip of the iceberg. The Shinrikyo cult actually had their own bioweapons facility, and had acquired anthrax, botulinum toxin, and Ebola virus. They even had three unsuccessful biological attempts prior to the subway incident. Point is, Agent Scarfano, this stuff doesn't cause anyone to have palpitations anymore, unless these bugs are used against your own."

Julee sniffed. "Because it could kill the people politicians and government officials are supposed to serve. It could kill even them, for that matter, and it also threatens them in an election cycle."

Bowker grunted an "uh-huh" each time Julee made another statement. "So, you do understand how it works."

"Some things never change."

"Regardless of the latitude or longitude too. Now, back to my story. Chernov sent Arina Filipov to Ireland to play the part of a disgruntled, female British soldier who became disenfranchised with the government's ways and who believed the IRA was right about everything they believed. Her vocal detestations caused her alleged subsequent, dishonorable discharge from the British Navy. She even had the forged, dishonorable discharge papers to prove it. Therefore, her role in all this became very simple: to exact some retribution against the British government by helping the IRA radicals release a contagion which would undoubtedly spread across the British Isles and eventually to the European continent, causing serious fallout amongst the members of the Good Friday Accords and cause a major rift amongst European allies.

"Filipov, using another name, became my contact for the IRA radicals, because she convinced their leader she could deliver something more potent than they even believed possible. I heard they were skeptical at first about everything she proposed and challenged her at one point by forcing her to kill one of their own who had been caught stealing from the group. It was a bit of a steep punishment for stealing a couple of thousand pounds worth of semi-automatic rifles, but it was just as much a test for Filipov as anything else. Without hesitation, she did it. With precision, I was told. So much so, it impressed the leaders of the group, and they tasked her with the job of training them in firearm training." Bowker sighed. "At this time, I had heard of Filipov, but I had never had any previous dealings with her. And can I say she sounded convincingly British over the phone?"

"The Black Mist moniker hadn't been invented yet?"

"Oh, it was starting to surface, but she was a master of disguise and could speak multiple languages fluently, so she could blend in like a chameleon."

"Conrad, how did Chernov know to send in Filipov? Originally, he was to supply the contagion to you, get paid, and then leave, right? The only way he would suddenly take such a vested interest in what was happening would be if he found out something he didn't know before. Something to give him a distinct advantage. Otherwise, why risk it?"

"I wondered the same thing and investigated it. As it turned out—and we learned this much later—someone in the U.S. government tipped off Chernov about the upcoming plan, so like a good KGB agent, he took advantage of the situation. However, we also learned much later about Filipov. Although she was being used by the Russians and Chernov, she had started to do some freelancing herself. There was speculation she was there just as much for her own purposes as Chernov's or the Russian government's, but we were never able to totally confirm it nor learn what those purposes were."

"There isn't much honor among thieves, is there?"

"Not much at all, love." Bowker chuckled. "Once I had secured the contagion from Chernov, I was told I would be contacted by one of the IRA radicals to make arrangements for the drop. Guess who that person was?"

"The man Filipov killed?"

"You're good, love. I was told the man had become very ill and was being replaced with another individual. Filipov, acting under her British alias, contacted me and set up a drop point for the contagion, but we never met face-to-face. It was handled over the phone. I made the drop. She picked it up and notified me of being in possession, as per our agreement. The money was deposited into my account. We followed the money, but it came from a shell corporation that was shut down two hours after the payment was verified."

"Conrad, you realize you just confessed to participating in terrorist activity?"

"It was a plan to destabilize the region. The Good Friday Accords were working slowly at bringing parties together. It was a real *Kum-ba-yah* moment. However, it was negatively affecting the price of oil, among other things, all of which were important to the power merchants on both sides of the ledger. Thus, destabilizing the region would bring the prices back up and set everything 'right' again. It was all about money and power. Nothing more. Nothing less."

Bowker could hear Scarfano shush someone in the background.

"What was your backup plan," Scarfano said, "if the IRA radicals actually succeeded in releasing the contagion?"

"We had no intentions of allowing that to happen. There were several safety protocols in place, both from the American side and from the British side. Those who planned the operation simply wanted the news cycles to report about how some IRA radicals, who planned to release said contagion, were killed in order to bring about fear. This news would affect the stock market, which ultimately would affect the price of oil." Bowker sniffed. "You would be surprised how many 'incidents' simply occur around the world...done for this one, singular reason. All one has to do is watch the stock market after an incident. It tells you exactly what the power brokers are up to. Find out who is selling out before the incident happens, and you now know who is involved." Bowker laughed. "But, I digress.

"To help prevent the radicals from actually using the contagion, the Americans' role was to send an elite black ops team into Ireland to take out the radicals. They would kill the radicals, secure the contagion, and then burn it with jet fuel for the purpose of creating a conflagration hot enough to kill it completely. The burning houses would become part of the news cycle. Remnants of the contagion would be 'found' in the subsequent investigation of the houses. The IRA radicals would be identified. The pieces of information would be conveniently woven together, and the fear factor would escalate exponentially, accomplishing the overall purpose of the mission without any catastrophic fallout from the contagion itself. And the Good Friday Accords would be severely scared, never to negatively affect the price of oil again.

"Also, I found out from Blake much later," Bowker said with a cough, "about how the Americans had learned about Arina Filipov infiltrating the radicals' group. So, they wanted to kill all the radicals, but they wanted to capture her."

"But she escaped before they arrived," Scarfano said. "Blake told me about it. She switched her clothes with some ditzy redhead who was there, because she was in love with the leader of the group, right?"

"Correct."

"So," Julee said with a question in her tone, "how did Filipov get tipped off about Blake and his team coming for her? And why would she leave all the radicals to die?"

Bowker snorted a laugh. "You want my theory?"

"Of course."

"Filipov was tipped off by Chernov, who was tipped off by probably the same person who gave him the information about the plan in the beginning."

"The American? The one in the U.S. government?"

"Yes. And as for why Filipov allowed those radicals to be killed, I believe she was saving her own backside while allowing 'The Plan' to move forward as the Americans and Brits envisioned it. If Blake and his team had not shown up, I do believe she would have assisted them in carrying out the Russians' plan instead, which would have been much more devastating. But either way, the region would've been destabilized. Blockades would've been reinforced. Bad blood between England and Ireland would've wiped out any good will the accords provided up to that moment, and all of Europe would have been on their guard, because the Russians would have been linked to the affair, although they would have denied it vehemently while the price of oil went up. And those in the know would have made millions on the backs of the little guys."

"Incredible."

"Now, what I have just told you, Agent Scarfano, is information some people know. Some people know other parts of it. However, very few know all of it. I know for a fact Blake was unaware his country was responsible for working with my government for the purpose of securing the contagion. He was led to believe Filipov and her people were responsible."

"That's why he was so adamant about catching her."

"That's one of the reasons. But it *is* the reason why he's tracked her all these years and followed her career with interest. If he ever finds out I was the one who actually supplied the contagion to Filipov for the IRA group, I'm not sure how he will react."

"He's probably going to find out eventually."

"If he does, I'd like to be the one who tells him."

"Well, I'm sure that can be arranged once all this is over. From what I hear, he has some information to share with you as well."

CHAPTER 20

"Vladimir? Are you there?" A silence followed. "Vladimir? Say something!" Another pause. "Mr. Klebnikov? Can you hear me?"

The words, faint and muffled, registered in Vladimir Klebnikov's mind, but it was like a dream. He didn't know where they were coming from, how he was hearing them.

"Vladimir! Where are you?"

Visions of being on a beach...on his back in the sand...with his arms and legs extended...making sand angels...

"Vladimir?"

His father calling out from the balcony of their vacation home...

He smiled and opened his eyes, expecting to see the sky above him...clouds, puffy and white, flowing overhead...making shapes only his imagination could define.

But instead, he was looking at something gray and dim.

He squinted and blinked, repeating the process multiple times, expecting his eyes to refocus on a blue sky and unencumbered clouds. However, the more he did so, the more the gray and dim object came into focus.

"Vladimir! We're trying to get to you!"

It looks like a floor...concrete...

Klebnikov turned his head to the right and saw a door...and a chair...and a small table. He looked the other way and was immediately confronted with metal...a metal frame of some sort, just fifteen or twenty centimeters away from his face.

The closeness of the frame startled him, and he pushed with his left foot and arm, attempting to roll over onto his back. The effort to do so shocked him, taking every ounce of energy and extreme concentration to get the message from his brain to his limbs.

He finally flipped over and realized where he was.

Lazar's office...what am I doing in—

He didn't need to ask...

It all came back to him.

The trip inside.

Looking at Lazar's notes.

The pain in his neck.

The scuffle—

Klebnikov heard something. It sounded like someone was breathing. Not in a normal, regular, regimented way. It sounded raspy. Erratic. It was mixed with the sound of a small motor of some sort.

He pushed himself up just enough to look on top of the bed, but nobody was there. He dropped back to the floor with a thud.

There's the breathing sound again...

It sounds...

Wet.

Like lungs filling up with fluid...

And the motor...a fan perhaps?

Klebnikov rolled over again and forced himself to his hands and knees. He scanned the room. He was correct. A small oscillating fan, sitting on top of a small dingy refrigerator, held its position fast, aimed toward Lazar's desk.

The breathing sound still registered loud and clear.

And it seemed to be coming from the same corner of the room where the fan and refrigerator were located.

He used the small table to help himself to his feet and staggered over to the breathing sound. A cardboard box sat on the floor, in front of the fridge. He peered into the open box and saw a glass cage with an animal in it.

And the cage's top had been removed.

A wave of nausea sloshed against the inside of his head. Trying not to vomit, he grabbed the cardboard box and pulled it toward him. He wanted to slide it all the way over to the chair so he could sit down, before he puked and passed out. However, the side of the box gave way, revealing the cage. And actually, it wasn't a box at all. It was just a partition to conceal the cage.

Vladimir's mind flooded with questions as to why Lazar would do such a thing.

Inside the cage, a marmot in its final stages of necrosis, lay on its side, foaming at the mouth and wheezing horribly. Blood oozed from its nose and mouth, and its body twitched every few seconds.

Klebnikov spun around and almost fell sideways into Lazar's cot. He held out his hands, like a man doing a balancing act on a wire, and kept himself from falling to the ground.

Once the room stopped spinning, he slipped his arms into the sleeves of his biosuit and pressed the button on the wall, so the doors to the decontamination unit would open. He reached back to grab his helmet and suddenly realized it wasn't there. Pulling frantically on the fabric, he craned his neck...

It is not there...

He noticed the doors to the contamination unit hadn't opened yet either. He pushed the button again several times, but nothing happened.

Then, it struck him.

Quarantine protocols must be in place. The doors would be forced to close and lock automatically.

He pulled on the override lever to his left, but it didn't budge.

With an increasingly ill feeling washing over him, he stepped over to Lazar's desk and looked out the window into the lab.

There, on the very table Peter Zakayev rested upon as a test subject earlier in the week, sat his helmet.

Lazar must have unzipped it from my suit when I was unconscious.

He snatched the phone from Lazar's desk and picked up the receiver. The line was dead. He punched the button, trying to get a dial tone, but instead, silence remained.

The protocols should not affect the landlines...

He held the phone up and examined it. *Why is it not working?*

Putting the receiver back in place, he used his hand to pull on the wire protruding from the back of the phone and disappearing over the side of Lazar's desk.

The wire wasn't connected to the jack in the wall.

It had been severed.

He slammed his fist down on the desk and yanked the desk out from the wall in anger. He got down on his knees to look for the missing piece.

Where is it?

He stood and peered out the window again, and there, next to the helmet, sat the detached phone jack, preventing him from rewiring it back together.

He unzipped his biosuit and reached inside his pants pocket for his smartphone, but it was gone too. Klebnikov let out a yell and cursed his friend. The phone was not on the table next to his helmet either.

Maybe it is inside the helmet...

Or Lazar took it with him...

And if so, we are in trouble...

He would have all my contacts' information...

In a bewildered state, he flopped down into Lazar's desk chair and looked up at the clock on the wall. He did a mental calculation.

It has been over two hours since Lazar sedated me...Almost three.

Lazar said the incubation period sped up when the contagion jumped from host to host...

He watched the marmot's stomach rise and fall with each, infected breath.

But which host is he? The beginning of the experiment? The middle? The end?

It was in this moment when Vladimir remembered Lazar Nicolescu's warnings about the inadequate ventilation system in the lab. *"If this contagion gets out,"* Lazar said, *"you will have started a pandemic in the heart of your own Motherland."*

Lazar's words sent a shockwave through his torso, and he immediately felt feverish. Panic gripped him, and a burning sensation flooded his extremities.

Vladimir rose from his chair, hesitant at first, and walked into the small bathroom off the back wall of the office. He stepped inside and looked in the mirrored door of the medicine cabinet.

"Oh, no," he said, as a thin red line trickled down from his nose and over his top lip.

He grabbed a nearby towel and wiped his face clean, but seconds later, a fresh, thin red line appeared.

Realizing what was happening but not wanting to believe it, he pulled his arms free from his biosuit. He reached under his left arm with his right hand, examined the area, and immediately closed his eyes. His breathing escalated as the emotions swirling inside forced their way to the top.

"This can't be happening."

He unbuttoned his shirt and slipped his left arm free. Lifting it high into the air above his head, he saw it in the mirror, and his hand fell immediately to the top of his head as he closed his eyes with a hopeless realization.

Tears trickled down his cheeks as he evaluated his underarm with his fingers. A small lump, like a squishy marble, was forming there, indicating how the end was near. And with no vaccine or antidote, Klebnikov thought, he now would get to experience what he and his associates were going to inflict on the world.

CHAPTER 21

RIVERVIEW DRIVE
Van Buren, Maine

With Agent John Mitchell on the other end of the line, Harrison Kelly pressed the Play button to reveal the person behind the name, "Polecat."

"Hello?" a man's voice said.
"I hope your day is going better than mine, Vladimir."

Harrison jotted down the name onto his notepad with a question mark next to the words, "last name."

"Did your precious stock prices fall?"
Sorensen sighed. "I wish it were something so mundane. But it's Colin Murphy."
"What did he do now?"
"Nothing really. I just don't like the man. He's not trustworthy."

Vladimir growled an exasperated sigh. "When you contacted me and asked if I would speak to him, you knew this plan was his, remember? He had already been working on it for some time, making alliances with groups that hate Americans, like The Hands of Allah, the cartels out of Columbia and Mexico, and other assorted, underground slime. You know the IRA is included in his list, yes?"

"Yes, I know."

"Then, you should not be so shocked when he talks down to you. Ultimately, he is using you just as much as he is using those other groups and we are using him. If he had his way, everyone in America would die, including you, Markus. He is not one to play favorites, and you represent the worst of the worst in his eyes. However, you are a necessary evil he must tolerate until the end."

"Hence, the reason why I don't trust him."

"And 'hence the reason' The Consortium decided to terminate him once he delivered on his promises of getting all the target families in place, getting the contagion made and into my hands, and getting it delivered to the designated target locations."

"But did you know he has an alternate plan in place?"

"What alternate plan?"

"He claims he has different contagions distributed in the areas of each Consortium member. Things like anthrax, small pox, and Marburg virus. He claims if anything happens to him, he has protocols in place to release those contagions in an effort to harm us."

"Look, Markus, Murphy is a mercenary. He was betrayed by your government and has no known relatives left alive as a result, except for an estranged sister living somewhere in Canada, I think. Therefore, he is, by definition, a 'madman.' He has nothing to lose by releasing any contagion. Therefore, we have to be strategic when it comes to handling him. And the time will come when The Consortium can. But in the meantime, ignore his little rants and allow him to deliver on his promises. There is nobody in our group who wants this contagion to be released in America more than Colin Murphy. So, we use this fact to our advantage for as long as necessary."

"Of course. You're right. I just need to consider the source." Markus sighed into the phone again.

"Do you wish to hear the update I have for you? It might cheer you up."

"Yes. Proceed."

"I am in the process of locating some colleagues I worked with years ago. They were some of the best in the world. They will be tasked with creating the antidote and vaccine to whatever Murphy's team is cooking up in their lab. Once I find them, I will offer them a deal they cannot refuse."

"Are you sure you wish to use friends, Vladimir? Would you rather use qualified people you don't know?"

Vladimir laughed. "Why would I wish to use people I do not know?"

"Because whoever works on this project in your labs will know everything there is to know about the contagion. More importantly, how to beat it. Therefore, we who are members of The Consortium have already determined how those people cannot be allowed to live once we have confirmation the antidote and vaccine work. They will know too much."

Vladimir groaned, as if a sudden thought came to mind. "But what if they wish to be on our side? What if they vow to help us in the aftermath? They would be valuable assets in a new world order, yes?"

"I'm sorry, my friend, but if they were not cleared at the beginning, it is doubtful they will be added to the approved survivor list now. Too much is at stake. The Consortium is keeping the inner circle small for a reason."

Vladimir sighed. "I understand."

"None of these people you are considering have inquired about becoming part of the survivor group, have they?"

"No. I was simply proposing a hypothetical. And to be honest, I was so happy to know good men in the field, qualified men, knowledgeable men, who would make the job so much easier to accomplish, it never occurred to me they could inquire about such things. But you are correct. They would know too much. Therefore, as it is, I am hiring these individuals for their last job."

"Yes. And because of the nature of their work, isolation in a quarantined lab would be essential to completing the plan without incident. This is bound to raise questions. Therefore, communication with the outside world would need to be heavily monitored. This isolation from friends and family will most definitely cause you issues, so you must be prepared with a believable response to every inquiry. People they know will want to know what their loved ones are doing inside your labs, why they can't get ahold of them twenty-four-seven—"

"And we cannot give these men and women I enlist the opportunity to divulge such information. I understand."

"Exactly."

Vladimir blurted out some expletives in Russian. "This will, unfortunately, narrow the pool of candidates considerably."

"I thought it might."

"Well then, I have one candidate who may be the perfect choice. He has cancer, so he has only a few years left. He is not married. No children. No family left, either, I do believe."

"He's not the only candidate, I hope. This job is too big for one person, right?"

"It could be done. It would take a little longer. But in this line of work. There is a great deal of waiting involved, so the down time would give him plenty of time to do other tasks."

"Give me your best guess, then. How long would it take one man to create the needed antidote and vaccine?"

"Markus, there are too many variables involved to make such a prediction. We do not even have the contagion perfected yet. How long will it take Murphy to get it to us?"

"They are testing it as we speak. They released it and are waiting for the first victims to arrive at the hospital."

"So, it could be another six months, perhaps a year, before my people get their hands on it, yes?"

"Possibly. That is probably a realistic timeline, unless this test going on in Africa turns out some great results."

Harrison heard what sounded like ice cubes clanking against the inside of a glass, but he couldn't tell who was either getting himself a drink or drinking one.

"Markus, keep me informed on Murphy's work, and I will contact my friend. I know him. If I throw a truck full of rubles at him, he will do anything I ask. I would just need to know when to ask him to report to my lab in Novosibirsk."

"Put a hold on that for now. Let's see how this test in Africa works first. The results will tell us if we can proceed—and thus have you contact your friend, or if we should wait until the contagion is perfected."

"Agreed. I do not want to contact him too early. He may say something and jeopardize our plans."

"Indeed. I will update you within the next few days."

"Very good."

The men said their goodbyes and then the line made a clicking sound. The audio file ended and flipped back to the beginning.

"Tell me you got something, Agent Mitchell," Harrison said.

"Got a 98.9% match to a Russian bioweapons expert named Vladimir Klebnikov."

"What do we know about him?"

Harrison heard a keyboard being manipulated.

"Worked within the Biopreparat program for over twenty years and was instrumental in helping the Iraqi military stockpile hundreds of thousands of gallons of liquid anthrax at a germ warfare facility in Al Hakum. That stockpile was destroyed by allied forces in 1996.

"Klebnikov is also responsible for supplying terrorist groups with information and knowledge. He directed several terrorist leaders, like Aum Shinrikyo and Larry Harris, for example, to an American website called the American Type Culture Collection. On this website, all sorts of germs are available for sale. Some Iraqi scientists, at Klebnikov's direction, purchased strains of tularemia and Venezuelan equine encephalitis for the low-low price of thirty-five dollars each."

"You're joking," Harrison said.

"Wish I was. Says here the tularemia and Venezuelan equine encephalitis were once targeted for weaponization at Fort Detrick back in the day, but the program got scrapped when President Nixon passed a resolution, promising the United States would no longer produce biological weapons. Instead, they would focus on—"

"Finding treatments for the bioweapons that could be used against us."

There was a pause.

"Uh, yeah, that's right. How did you know?" Agent Mitchell said.

"It was that very program which forced me to rethink my military status. I eventually requested a discharge."

"Really? Are they still working on—"

"Yep," Harrison said, remembering the woman in the bar...the afternoon which changed his mind about serving Uncle Sam. "And the participants are sometimes less than willing."

"Isn't that against the law?"

"Not when they are the ones writing the laws. Look, Agent Mitchell, if there's one thing I've learned over the years, and especially during this crisis, it's how this country may be a great place to live with all of its freedoms, but there are some scary, troubling, even downright heinous things going on behind the scenes. 'Stranger than fiction' kind of stuff, you know what I'm saying?"

"Yes, I understand completely. I've seen some pretty alarming and horrible stuff doing this job. Especially over the last few days."

"I bet you have." Harrison harrumphed. "Therefore, we need to move on to the next file called Vector. These three names keep coming up in much of the investigating I've done since Blake called me the very first time. And now we know two of the three people involved in this whole affair from what seems to be the beginning, besides Sorensen."

"I'm ready when you are," Mitchell said.

"This next file is the very first one in the folder, yet, it's dated two years later than the earliest ones, so I'm not sure why it is out of order. It's dated July 18, 2012." Harrison opened the file and readied his cursor over the Play button. "Oh, Vector...come out, come out, whoever you are..."

CHAPTER 22

OFFICES OF EMPEROR Pharmaceuticals
Beijing Central Business District
Beijing, China

Still dressed as a European businesswoman, carrying a black leather Underwood briefcase with a biometric locking mechanism, Arina Filipov finished off her coffee and exited the little all-night café. From studying the floor plans of the office building where the Emperor Pharmaceuticals Corporation was located, she noticed the lobby was in the front, and according to the information supplied by the computer geek, it was manned by a desk clerk at all times. The lobby was also under surveillance, and she believed, although she didn't have any proof, this Mr. Li—or somebody who reported to him—probably monitored those cameras religiously.

With some cosmetic appliances applied to her face, Filipov had made her nose seem bigger than it actually was and the bones above her eyes a little more pronounced. Coupled with her strong

German accent, her recently dyed brown hair, and the up-to-date German ladies' watch strapped around her left wrist, she felt the disguise would at least get her to the eighteenth floor, where a German stockbroker by the name of Hans Kilner housed his Asian bureau.

She strolled into the lobby and walked directly to the main desk, exuding the vibe she had been there before on multiple occasions.

The desk clerk, reading a magazine, looked up and watched Filipov walk across the lobby. He waited until she stopped at the counter before addressing her. "How may I help you?" he said in Mandarin.

Filipov handed him her passport. "Please excuse my language," she said in broken Mandarin, trying to make it sound like a German woman having trouble with the dialect. "I no speak Mandarin good ever."

The clerk examined her passport and then compared it to her face. "What language do you speak?"

"Germanic."

The desk clerk winced with a smile. "I do not speak German."

"No worry. I from Munich. I here to visit Hans Kilner. We have...uh, relationships?...in business to discuss."

The clerk chuckled slightly and handed Filipov her passport and checked his registry. "Hans Kilner, of the KSG Financial Group? Is that the correct business?"

"Yes."

The desk clerk tapped some keys on the computer keyboard and clicked the mouse a couple of times.

A machine next to the computer whirred to life, and a white pass with dark black script, written mostly in Chinese, printed.

When it was done, the clerk ripped it free and handed it to Filipov. "Please display this on your person at all times while in the building," he said, tapping his chest on the left side.

"Everyone who sees you will know you have been authorized by me."

Filipov peeled off the sticker and slapped in on her chest. She wadded up the paper backing and held it out. The clerk took it and threw it away.

"Thank you," she said.

"KSG Financial Group is located on the eighteenth floor. Office 18-04. When you get off the elevator, there will be a sign pointing the way. The elevators are over there." The clerk pointed to back of the lobby. "The two on the left go to the eighteenth floor."

Filipov laughed. "Do not two on right go up as well?"

"Not to the eighteenth floor. Those are private elevators. They require a key."

Arina faked a surprised look and nodded as she walked over to the elevators on the left. She pressed the button labeled "up" and glanced back in his direction, but the clerk had already picked up his magazine and was reading it again.

The elevator announced its arrival, and the door opened.

Filipov stepped inside and saw the surveillance camera in the back corner in her peripheral vision. She pressed the number eighteen, waited for the doors to close and the car to ascend. She kept her back to the camera and remembered where the cameras were located in the hallways of each floor, according to the information provided by the computer geek.

I wonder what happened to him? It is not like him to avoid my phone calls...

The elevator reached the eighteenth floor, and the doors opened. She stepped out and examined the listing of offices on the far wall, acting like she'd never been there before.

Noting KSG Financial Group's offices were located down the hallway, around the corner to the left, and past the first doorway leading to the stairwell, she turned and pulled out her smartphone, keeping her head down while she walked, thumbing the screen, giving her a reason to keep her face concealed without it appearing too obvious.

As she approached the stairwell, she pocketed the phone. Then, with one quick jolt, she pushed the crash bar and slipped inside before allowing the door to close behind her.

She knew the cameras would be positioned at each landing. One facing the stairs going down, the other looking up toward the next floor. With her head down, she reached inside her pocket and yanked out a scarf as she set her briefcase down. She opened up the scarf and stretched it until it was completely unfolded. With a flick of her wrists, she flipped the scarf up and over her head, wrapping it over the top and then around her face like a hijab.

Once she felt the garment was secure, she picked up her briefcase and ascended the stairs.

* * *

When she reached the landing of the twenty-sixth floor, she paused and eased back against the wall, out of the immediate view of the cameras. The stairwell ended there, though she knew the building had two additional floors.

Zou must have his own private stairwell…just like his own private elevator…

Apparently, I will have to do this the old-fashioned way.

Setting the briefcase down, she opened it and pulled out her nine-millimeter pistol, screwed in the silencer, and jammed it in her waistband, allowing her blouse to conceal it. She then retrieved two holsters from the case. One held a small, twenty-two caliber pistol. The other held six perfectly balanced throwing knives. She strapped the one holding the knives to her right calf, and the gun holster to her left. One last reach into the briefcase produced a retractable garrote, which she placed in her front, right pocket.

She closed the briefcase, stood, and peered out the embedded window in the door with the number twenty-six on it, written in Chinese.

She opened the door slowly and peeked out into the hallway. Both ways appeared clear as she stepped out of the stairwell. Holding the door and easing it closed so as not to draw attention in the dead quiet, she snuck her way down the corridor to her left until she reached the corner. Checking the hallway behind her to make sure she was alone, she peeked around the corner and saw one man, wearing a business suit, standing at the far end of the hallway. He was positioned in the corner so he could see anyone coming from two different directions. One of them being hers.

Filipov flattened her back against the wall and wondered how she was going to get past the man, who no doubt, was wearing an earpiece and had a radio attached to his belt, hidden under his jacket.

She knelt down, lifted her pant leg, and grabbed one of the knives from its sheath. She palmed the small handle, hiding the blade behind her wrist. With her left hand, she picked up her briefcase, stood, sucked in a deep breath, and backed up a couple of steps. With one last breath, she strolled around the corner. A businesswoman on a mission.

The man at the far end immediately saw her round the corner and lifted his wrist to his mouth.

Filipov heard the man say something in what sounded like Mandarin, but she couldn't make it out. However, she didn't need to. She knew what he said.

"Stop!" the man said in Mandarin. "Who are you? And where are you going?"

"My name is Elsa Gruber," Filipov said in her broken, Germanic Mandarin. "Here I am to see my associate business man, Hans Kilner. Do you learn him?"

"What?" The man's face appeared befuddled to Arina. It

seemed her fake language barrier was working. "I need to see your pass." He tapped his chest.

Filipov stopped about ten feet away from the man when another man of similar build rounded the corner and stood off to the first man's left side. She set her briefcase down, peeled off her ID with her left hand, and held it out.

The first man took one step closer. "What's in your other hand?"

Filipov wrinkled her brow. "I no understand words you use. Can you talk again?"

The man looked at his partner with a wary eye before taking another step.

Filipov noticed the second man slowly lift his right hand and sweep away his jacket from his right side, exposing a holstered weapon.

The first man, without saying a word, held out his right hand, fully open, and motioned to her right hand. He shrugged, as if his gesture made his request obvious.

Filipov flashed the knife before raising it high and throwing it at the second man reaching for his gun.

The knife pierced the second man in the neck, severing his windpipe.

The first man reached for his weapon while backing away.

Filipov yanked her gun from her waistband, beating him to the draw. She fired two shots, striking the man in the chest.

Gasping, with shock-filled eyes, the second man released the handle of his gun and pulled the knife out of his throat. Dropping the weapon on the floor, he, too, dropped to his knees and clutched his neck. A finalizing realization of his demise lodged its way into his expression.

Filipov bent over, secured the knife, and wiped the blade clean on the second man's suit jacket before putting it back in its sheath and grabbing each man's gun. She checked the ammo and stuck one of them inside her front waistband and the other in the small of her back, inside her waistband. She held on to her weapon with her right hand and picked up her briefcase with her left.

From down the hallway to her right, she could hear footfalls and keys jingling. She turned her head slightly and listened closely.

Three sets. Three men.

She backed up against the wall near the corner of the hallway and set her briefcase back down. She pulled the gun from her front waistband and continued to listen as the steps got closer. As they did, they slowed until only one could be heard running.

Filipov took in one deep breath, held it, and rotated her body, stepping out into the hallway in one adept motion. As she did, she fired both guns and instantly picked off the first two men with head shots.

The third man, seeing all of this unfold before him, dove for the floor, weapon drawn, and fired a round at Filipov.

She jumped to her right, trying to use the falling men as human shields.

The bullet sailed passed her left ear, nicking it on its way into the ceiling behind her.

Filipov aimed both of her guns and fired four, staccato-like rounds into the third man as she marched in his direction.

His weapon fired an errant shot across the hallway as he pulled the trigger in pain, falling sideways to the ground.

She stood over him, both guns pointed at his head, as he quickly succumbed to his injuries. Without wasting ammo, she examined the other men to make sure they, too, were dead.

Feeling secure enough, she unwound the scarf from her head and stuffed it inside her briefcase.

She then rummaged through the coat pockets of the three men until she found a set of keys. Checking each one, she found what she believed to be an elevator key.

Opening the briefcase, she placed all the dead men's guns inside, except one, and then jogged down to the next corner of the hallway. To her left, about halfway down, a set of elevator doors stood next to a doorway to a stairwell.

With her head down and her face aimed away from the cameras, she walked up to the elevator, inserted the key into the lock, and turned it.

As the elevator doors opened, she stood off to one side and checked to make sure it was empty.

She entered and allowed the door to close.

On the panel, two buttons with numbers, twenty-seven and twenty-eight, needed a key.

She smiled, inserted the key, and twisted it clockwise.

CHAPTER 23

Harrison Kelly and Agent John Mitchell had spent the better part of an hour listening to and examining one voice recording after another. Several voices had been identified, such as Sorensen, Murphy, and Klebnikov, and this new information energized Harrison.

Pushing Play, Harrison took a swig from his bottled water and leaned back in his chair, listening to a phone call between Markus Sorensen and a person named Vector.

"Markus, so glad to hear from you. I have good news. No, great news."

"I can always use good news, my friend."

"I have your Plan B contagion ready for deployment. The vials are almost ready. The only remaining step is to add a harmless blue dye to the vials so your men can tell they are full and ready to be used."

"That is good news, and it didn't take near as long as I had anticipated."

"I found a willing accomplice on my second phone call. I expected to have to go much deeper into my digital Rolodex. Nevertheless, they were able to mass produce the contagion in their lab from their stockpile."

"Their stockpile? Who keeps large quantities of contagions on hand? Besides our governments?"

"You'd be surprised, Markus, and you probably don't really want to know. But just so you do, and because you're in this business, it doesn't take much to do what you wanted. Fifty-plus vials? There are small terrorist groups in caves in the Middle East who have that much stored away somewhere. And they probably bought it from the United States. We did. Well, not us, but our shell corporation did."

"Don't they track these kinds of things?"

"They do. But if your corporation looks legitimate and there are no red flags with Interpol or Europol, then it's actually a quick and painless way to do this kind of business. A shell corporation in London with an A-plus rating on America's business listings doesn't even raise an eyebrow."

Markus Sorensen chuckled, but it sounded different to Harrison, like it wasn't genuine.

"I just need to know where you want me to send the vials once they are ready."

"I am in the process of lining up crews to help with the installation. I have several of my men recruiting as we speak, but we will not be ready to deploy the Plan-B devices until shortly before we are ready to launch our main attack, using the contagion in the air fresheners. I am told the battery life on these Plan-B devices doesn't last indefinitely, so we cannot install them too early.

"I am also having to coordinate each target separately. Because they

are all different, some targets will be easier to access than others. There-
fore, the plan is to have people in place, ready to act on a moment's
notice. They'll receive a phone call and be told where they can pick up
the device. Then, they will have forty-eight hours to get it installed and
another forty-eight hours to 'Get out of Dodge.'"

"All you have to do is call me or text me the location or locations,
and we will make sure you have the vials in time."

"I appreciate it. Oh, one last thing before you go. Do you know how
Murphy is coming along on the air fresheners?"

"We have the contagion ready to go. However, we have run into a
snag on the deployment aspect. When we place it in the containers and
then add all the components which make up real air fresheners, the
chemicals in the actual air freshening solution kill the plague
bacterium."

"Can't you just make them like the vials for the Plan B devices?
Make it all contagion with some color added for aesthetics?"

"We could, but Mr. Murphy has been very adamant from the beginning. He wants these air fresheners to be exactly like what can be bought
in the stores. He wants them to be, in his own words, 'camouflaged in
plain sight.' He believes this will prevent detection as long as possible. He
believes they will not suspect these devices until they have exhausted all
of their other angles on where the contagion originated and how people
are getting infected. By then—and I believe him to be right in this—the
contagion will have spread so far and so wide, even if they do figure it out
finally, it will be too late to make a difference. However, if the units did
not have a fragrance, people would start returning them to stores,
claiming they are defective, and the effects would not be nearly as severe."

"Of course. That aspect of the plan was what intrigued me and my
colleagues in the first place, but how do you plan to get around this
obstacle? My colleagues are growing more and more concerned as time
passes."

"We are hearing through back channels there is a promising young

Chinese scientist, a chemist, I think, who is working on the very solu-
tion we seek. I have a plane chartered to fly there next week to check out
his work. If he is doing what we hope he is doing, he may solve our
problem for us. Then, all we have to do is order whatever he's dreaming
up in his lab, add the contagion ourselves, package it, and ship it."

"Very well. Please contact me once you know more about this
Chinese scientist and his work."

"You are more than welcome to tag along. Your expertise may be
needed."

"I would love to, but I find it better for me to remain in the shadows
with this project."

"Suit yourself. Then, after I meet with this young scientist and get a
lay of the land, you'll be my second phone call."

"Right. And Murphy still doesn't know anything about our sidebar
working arrangement on the Plan-B devices, correct?"

"Correct. He suspects nothing."

"Good. Let's keep it that way."

"Oh, don't worry. Murphy is a powder keg. If he found out I was
working with you behind his back, I do not believe my death would be
quick and painless."

"Incentive. It always works when it is the right kind."

"In this case, it is mere intrinsic motivation to stay alive."

"Call me when you know something."

"I will."

Harrison heard the click. "We didn't get a name. Got anything
on the database?"

"Actually, no." Agent Mitchell let out a muffled expletive.
"There's no voice match."

"Really? You know what that means…"

"Yeah. There's a new kid in town. One without a criminal
history."

"There is one more audio file in the folder between these two. You ready?"

"Sure," Agent Mitchell said.

Harrison pushed Play, and they listened to a ten-minute conversation between Sorensen and Vector, dated August 1, 2012, about how the young Chinese scientist had some additional tests to run, but if they were successful, then his university would patent the formula, turn it over to one of the Chinese-owned companies, and mass produce the product for public consumption. Once that happened, which Vector believed to be by the year's end, they would order a shipment, have it sent to Klebnikov's lab in Novosibirsk, have the original contagion added, and then get the devices shipped to wherever they needed to go in the United States.

However, as Harrison and Agent Mitchell listened, not once did Markus Sorensen call Vector by his real name. He just kept referring to him as "my friend."

The call finally ended, and Harrison threw the empty water bottle across the room. "This guy is the brains behind all the contagions being used in this attack, and we can't even get a first name."

"And it's still coming up a 'No Match Found' in the database." Agent Mitchell grunted and sighed into the phone. "So, what can we deduce about this guy from the call? He sounds Indian to me, and I mean from the country of India. But not overly so. Sounds to me like he was either raised in the U.S. or has spent considerable time here."

"Okay, yeah, right. His accent is evident enough, but it is definitely Americanized."

"Educated in America, perhaps?"

"Perhaps." Harrison readjusted his headset and microphone. "And if so, it would probably be in some field revolving around making contagions, like immunology." He stood and walked over to pick up the bottle.

"Yes, or microbiology. I'm looking at some websites on this now. Seems there are a slew of specialty areas under these programs, like gene therapy....and are you ready for this? Infectious diseases."

Harrison bent over, picked the bottle up, and headed for the kitchen. "So, we have an Indian-born, Americanized, student from abroad who has probably worked on a degree in microbiology, probably specializing in infectious diseases, and possibly immunology. That should narrow things down a little." He tossed the bottle into the garbage can.

Agent Mitchell laughed. "Yeah, it's kind of like saying we have a suspect, wearing a hoodie, was driving a dark-colored sedan in New York City."

"Look, you guys captured Colin Murphy. Surely he had a phone on him? Did you dump it to see who he had been calling?"

"We did, but by the time we got to it, just about everyone he had contacted must have chucked their phones and gotten new ones."

"Of course, they did."

"Well, I guess the good news is—if you want to call it good news— we have a voiceprint of this man, code-named Vector. Therefore, if his voice pops up again, we can match it and maybe get lucky with an ID."

Harrison opened the refrigerator door and remembered he was out of bottled waters. He sighed and shut the door. "Tell me, does that get added to the FBI's database, thus making it available to anyone, or are you keeping it located locally on your server?"

"Well, I was going to download it into the system... What are you thinking?"

"I'm thinking we can't trust very many people. That's what I'm thinking."

"So, better to keep it close to the vest for now?"

"I would."

"Agreed."

"Good. It can always be uploaded later. But why show your enemy your hand when all the bets haven't been placed yet?"

"Indeed."

CHAPTER 24

OFFICES OF EMPEROR Pharmaceuticals
Beijing Central Business District
Beijing, China

Arina Filipov stood off to one side as the elevator car jerked once and ascended. She contemplated climbing through the hatch in the top and hiding above the elevator, just in case she was met with resistance. However, she also knew this elevator was separate from the general one everybody else used. For all she knew, it stopped at the twenty-eighth floor, thus leaving very little space between the top of the elevator car and the elevator shaft itself.

She decided, instead, to be ready for an all-out assault.

She knelt down and opened her briefcase. In the pockets under the lid itself, she retrieved two of the six specially made hand grenades, filled with flash-bang technology and a vial of concentrated, chloroform-based gas. One gasp of the gas after being disoriented by the loud noise and blinding light typically

178 C. KEVIN THOMPSON

rendered assailants disoriented in five seconds, unconscious within fifteen.

She pulled out the guns taken from the men two floors below and positioned them in her waistband. Use one, empty it, chuck it, and grab the next one was the plan.

She retrieved a specially made gas mask and slipped it on, tightening the seal quickly before closing the briefcase and hoisting it up.

Within seconds, the car dinged, and the doors opened to a barrage of gunfire. Bullets careened off the metal walls and railings, piercing other parts of the interior. Two ricocheting rounds grazed her back as she knelt down in the corner, using her steel-plated briefcase as a shield, waiting for the attack to subside.

She heard a voice shout for the gunmen to cease fire in Mandarin which became her cue. Holding the two grenades in one hand, she dropped the briefcase and pulled the pins. Then, with her right hand, she tossed the first one through the doorway to her right before grabbing the second one with her right hand and tossing it through the doorway to her left.

Immediately to the right, the loud bang and bright light sounded and flashed, followed by the second off to her left.

Filipov stood, yanked out the first weapon, and instantly saw one of the gunmen to her right. She fired one shot into the staggering man's chest.

Another man, stumbling in her direction and shouting for her to drop her weapon in his native language, fell against the wall and used it as a crutch just long enough to lift his weapon in her direction.

Filipov squeezed off two more rounds, causing the disoriented man to jerk the trigger and send a line of bullets from his AK-47 whizzing past her feet.

She immediately looked to her left, and on the floor, on his stomach, wiping his eyes, trying to see long enough to focus his eyes down his weapon's sight, was another gunman succumbing to the gas's effects.

His wavering hand fired his gun and struck Filipov in the right thigh.

She jumped to her left as another round blasted past her torso. She fell backwards into the wall, aimed her gun, and shot the man four times until his head dropped and the gun fell to the ground.

Filipov grabbed her thigh and winced. She looked down and saw blood ooze from between her fingers.

Not good.

She went back into the elevator car and grabbed her briefcase. She opened it again and snatched the scarf she had worn earlier and used it as a tourniquet while keeping an eye out for more trouble. Her back stung as well, and she knew it had to be bleeding, too, but her experience told her she could survive being grazed. However, it was the through-and-through of her thigh that concerned her. She would need to keep the tourniquet tight.

If the idiot hit an artery, I will see it bleeding through soon enough...

In the distance, she heard orders being given and more footsteps. Grabbing two more grenades, she held them in one hand while she stood and walked over to the man clutching the AK-47. She seized it from his grip and used the attached strap to sling it over her shoulder.

Now facing the elevator with her back against the wall, she limped...inching closer to the corner...listening for movement. She took one grenade in each hand and slid down the wall, using it to take weight off her right leg.

The sounds of guns being cocked and heavy breathing grew considerably louder.

They are running.

With a quick snatch with both index fingers, she pulled the pins and heaved one grenade after the other down the hallway.

She stepped out away from the wall and whipped the machine

gun around into position. As the grenades blew up and released their array of sound, flashes, and concentrated gas, she took two steps to the left and sprayed a stream of bullets from the left to the right and back again.

Two men, wearing ear pieces and suits, lead the charge of what Filipov immediately counted as five men. The two in front fell immediately, giving way to the next two as she continued her stream of bullets.

Another set of brief bursts from her gun mowed down the last man who had managed to fire in her direction. However, the bullet from his pistol sailed high, just missing her head.

Filipov jumped back behind the corner of the wall and listened. She waited for several seconds but didn't hear any additional commotion.

Surely they have more guards...

She checked the AK-47 for remaining ammunition and saw it was close to empty. Listening once more, she limped back to the elevator and retrieved her briefcase before stopping near the corner once more.

She set the briefcase down, slipped the machine gun over her shoulder, and checked her leg.

No substantial blood running down my leg. A very good sign.

With her right hand, she pulled one of the other men's guns from her waistband and prepared it for action. Picking up her briefcase, she held it in her left hand, pulling it up to cover her torso.

She peeked around the corner. All she saw were five dead men scattered across the hallway and a heavy fog that made visibility difficult.

With a deep breath, she angled across the hallway, around the dead guards, and turned her body so the briefcase would act as a shield for the front, and the wall became a shield for her back.

She inched her way down the hallway toward Zou's office,

which was around the next corner and about halfway down that hallway, if the computer geek's information was accurate.

Her thigh throbbed, and her blouse kept sticking to the two wounds on her back. Each time she moved enough, the material would pull away, reopening the wound, she surmised, causing pain.

You must focus on what is ahead...

Do not allow the wounds to distract you...

She angled back across the hallway, came to the corner, and stopped. Peering back to her left to make sure the coast was clear, she lifted the briefcase a little higher and pinned it against the wall, just inches from the corner. On a mental count of three, she slid the case to the left and peeked over it. To her amazement, there was nobody there.

She lowered the case a little and raised her weapon, ready to shoot anything that moved, and eased out into the middle of the hallway.

Feeling uneasy and wondering if she was being lured into a trap, she set the briefcase down against the wall and yanked another gun from her waistband. She lifted the strap from the AK-47 up and over her head, securing that weapon in an easy-access position. Now, she was ready. A gun in each hand, an AK-47, two additional pistols in her waistband, front and back, her throwing knives, and her twenty-two-caliber pistol...all within easy reach.

I will kill Zou or go down fighting...

She maneuvered her way down the hallway to the door leading to Zou's office. With one deep breath, she backed away from the wall and shot the door handle twice, obliterating the locking mechanism. She yanked off the mask and tossed it aside.

With her right leg injured, she couldn't kick the door in, so she stood against the wall and used her left hand to push it open with as much force as she could muster.

It banged against the wall, and she held it open while she stepped into the opening, weapons raised and ready.

And there, standing on the other side of the spacious office, his back against a wall of glass overlooking the city, was Ju-Long Zou. His arms hung by his side, and a fiendish glare fired back at her. A sterling-plated gun glistened in his right hand.

"Hello, Agent Filipov," Zou said in Russian. "We have been expecting you."

CHAPTER 25

LAZAR NICOLESCU'S Vacation Home
  Bystrovka, Russia

Karina Kuznetsova made sure she followed every traffic law on the way to Lazar's vacation home. She had heard too many stories of notorious criminals being caught because of some silly mistake they made long after their elaborate plans of stealing a famous diamond or committing multiple murders were completed. Being pulled over by police for a broken taillight or for speeding would be disastrous.

She also kept checking the rearview mirror, expecting a set of headlights to appear as a bright dot and slowly gain ground on them until one light became two.

But they never came.

Only once did a vehicle follow them, and even then, it was at a distance until it finally turned right and disappeared.

Two hours of non-stop driving had passed when Karina slowed down and peered in the direction of an older, two-story home positioned approximately one hundred meters from the road. Some faint lamps sat in the windows, illuminating the downstairs, and the front porch light was on as well.

The address on the sign nailed to the wooden fence matched the sticky note affixed to the dashboard. A long dirt driveway drew a straight line between the edge of the highway and the detached garage near the front of the house.

The "front lawn," on both sides of the driveway, was fenced off, and rows of potatoes trailed off into the darkness. Although she could not see it from the road at such an ungodly hour, Lazar had told her of the "backyard" and how it was a long strip, matching the width of the front parcel, stretching all the way to the road behind it, some three hundred meters. The plot of land behind the house was broken up into four quarters, he said. Strawberries, gooseberries, currants, and blackberries. Lazar said the small crop was then sold by the people who lived next door, Igor and Olga, at local markets as fresh produce. Between his property and theirs, it provided enough income so Olga, the elderly grandmother, could stay home and not have to find employment, while Igor, the budding grandson, could work at a nearby lumberyard. "And of course," Lazar said, "they never run out of jams, jellies, and wine during the fall and winter months due to Olga's propensity for canning and Igor's interest in distilling."

Karina smiled at the thought as she parked her vehicle. She reached over and patted Peter on the shoulder. "Stay here and let me go meet Olga and Igor first."

* * *

Peter nodded and didn't argue. Alert and troubled for the first thirty miles or so of their journey, he fought off his weariness and worked hard at getting his blood pressure to stabilize. He found breathing through the confounded mask to be anything but relaxing. "It is like lying flat on your back," he told Karina after they had escaped the Genforma compound, "trying to inhale while a small elephant dances on your chest. I can already tell sleeping will be next to impossible. Unless you want me to pass out from oxygen deprivation."

And he knew what he was talking about.

On the trip, he'd closed his eyes and tried to get some rest at the urging of Karina, once they both felt they were out of harm's way. He instantly felt a slow, smothering pressure being applied to his chest, which made the dizziness flare up and the sensation to vomit escalate. He had to concentrate at doing something as natural and autonomic as taking a breath. Drawing in each lungful became an exercise routine. Breathe in. Breathe out. Measured and steady. It kept the dizziness at bay, which was a good thing. However, it made sleeping impossible, and that worried him, because he knew rest would end this entire ordeal sooner than anything else.

He leaned against the passenger door with his head lifted up and watched Karina walk up to the house next door as a pale front porch light worked hard at covering all of the front stairs. He saw her knock and look back at him with a smile. She wiggled her fingers in a small wave and turned back toward the door as it opened.

An elderly woman in a dressing gown stepped out onto the stoop, and Karina said something to her. The woman smiled and called inside the house.

A few seconds later, a young man, a little older than Peter, opened the front door wide and stood beside the elderly woman, wearing a pair of blue jeans and a tight-fitting t-shirt.

Igor and Olga, I presume?

The three held a small conversation before Karina reached out and shook their hands. The elderly woman said something to the young man, and he went back inside.

Karina and the elderly woman walked together toward Lazar's house. Karina glanced at Peter and smiled, but turned her attention back to the elderly woman who was still talking.

They had almost reached the house when the young man suddenly appeared between the two houses, having exited his house from the back, heading for the back of Lazar's house, holding a flashlight.

Karina held up the key Lazar had given her and inserted it into the lock, opening the door. She stepped through the doorway, and the elderly woman followed behind.

Peter felt a twinge of concern when she disappeared into the house.

I wonder what Igor, if that is his name, is up to?

He tried to imagine why the young man would go out the back door and head for Lazar's backyard when Karina had a key.

He sat there for several minutes, imagining every horrible scenario.

All I know is this: If they hurt Karina and then come after me, I'll yank this mask off, jump them, and breathe into their faces until they start to show signs of infect—

He stopped. The aggressive thought instantly concerned him. It made him feel guilty. It appalled him, actually.

Has being a lab rat, after being falsely accused and injected with horrible things, turned me into one of them now?

Before all this happened, I wouldn't have hurt a fly...well, maybe a fly is not a good example, but I was not like this—

Just then, Karina came out of the house, followed by the elderly woman and the young man. She was smiling, and they seemed to be getting along splendidly.

Peter watched and felt even guiltier about his sudden, vengeful outburst.

God help me. I think this contagion has rearranged some grey matter.

* * *

Thirty minutes later, Karina and Peter were inside the house. Peter, quarantined to the master bedroom, sat in a comfy lounge chair in the corner with his feet propped up on an ottoman. A lamp next to him shed its necessary light.

Karina jotted down a quick grocery list for the young man next door named Igor. He had been tasked in Lazar's email with running to the store to pick up any items Karina and Peter may need. All items would be left on the back porch. Igor and Olga were not, under any circumstances, to enter the premises once Peter was inside.

Part of that list included a run to a medical supply store in Novosibirsk. Karina needed several bags of saline solution and electrolytes along with all the necessary tubing, tape, nitrile gloves, and needles, in order to hook up Peter to an IV feeding line. For the next two to three days, he would not be able to eat or drink anything orally because of their inability to create a Zone Three lab in Lazar's vacation home. Therefore, they had to improvise and use the mask as the Zone Three containment field. The filters, when removed and replaced, had to be burned in the fireplace after being soaked in kerosene.

Of course, those supplies would not arrive until mid-morning, Karina thought, so Peter would have to fend off hunger pangs until then. Therefore, she decided not to make the tea she desired, nor did she grab and eat any of the fresh, homemade bread Olga had made the evening before. At least, she would not eat any while Peter was awake.

She sat down at the computer she found in one of the spare bedrooms. Lazar used the room as an office, and he had given her the username and password before she left so she could access his email and send a missive to Vasily Yerzov.

She opened the program and crafted the email, informing

Vasily of how the vials of blood would be mailed in a few hours from Novosibirsk and sent the quickest way possible. He needed to be on the lookout for the package. She described the box, gave him the necessary information about the contents, explained how they would follow the package once Peter was asymptomatic, and how she would email him again right before they left so he would know when to expect them.

She closed with a request to treat Peter with the utmost respect, and to make him as comfortable as could possibly be afforded due to the nature of all the turmoil Peter had endured.

She also concluded her correspondence with a note about Lazar's plan, and how they would probably never see their friend again.

CHAPTER 26

OFFICES OF EMPEROR Pharmaceuticals
  Beijing Central Business District
  Beijing, China

Arina Filipov stood in the doorway of Ju-Long Zou's office. A small vestibule of sorts filled the first ten feet of the entrance. She recalled the plans of the building. To her right was a closet area with the door facing Zou's direction, as he stared her down, clutching a gun. To her left was a room labeled "telecommunications," which mirrored the closet on the other side.

Filipov's weapon was already aimed at Zou. "Drop it," she replied in Russian, "and I will allow you to live. For now."

Zou's lips curled up into a devilish grin. "I do not think so."

Filipov lowered her aim and fired.

Zou shrieked in pain and dropped the gun. He grabbed his shattered wrist and cradled it.

She marched forward. Her gun still raised. Her eyes pinned to Zou's. "Down on your—"

From her left, an object flew at her with amazing speed.

She spun around and ducked just as a knife glanced off her ear and tumbled by.

A man, six inches taller, average build, definitely Asian, and wearing a suit and tie, flew at her, spun his body around, lifted his right leg, and kicked at the gun in her right hand.

The blow pushed her arm across her chest, but she was able to hang on to the pistol.

The man landed on his feet, stopping on a dime. He bent his right leg at the knee, and swept his foot back against Filipov's face.

Filipov allowed the force of the kick's momentum to spin her around, using the motion to step away from her attacker and put some distance between them.

The man lunged at her, attempting to pounce on his faltering foe. He punched at her with his right hand, connecting with her nose.

Arina absorbed the blow, causing her to stagger more as she tried to put weight on her damaged leg. However, it buckled, and she collapsed onto her left knee. With the gun still in her hand, she lifted it up, but the attacker's left hand smacked it away while his right hand grabbed the barrel.

The attacker stopped for a split second and flashed her a confident grin before pushing the barrel upward and bending Filipov's wrist back, toward her body, in a contorted, painful angle.

Filipov gritted her teeth and growled at the sudden pain in her wrist. She grabbed the gun with her left hand and pushed against the barrel, trying to keep him from wrenching it from her grasp.

The attacker jerked her toward him and struck her in the left cheek with his right elbow.

Filipov pressed the lever and activated the safety before releasing the gun.

The man twisted the weapon around in his hands and stood

up straight. He looked down the sight into his adversary's eyes. "It is over, Agent Filipov."

Filipov, still on one knee, grabbed the AK-47 hanging by her side, aimed, and delivered a prolonged burst into the attacker's stomach as he tried pulling the trigger of the gun in his hand.

The man doubled over with a troubled look of surprise, and the gun he had taken from her instantly dangled from his fingers before falling to the ground.

Filipov groaned from the pain in her thigh as she stood and stepped sideways as her attacker fell to his knees.

She tossed the AK-47 on the ground and reached behind her, yanking out her own pistol. She aimed at her attacker and fired a single round into the side of his head.

Immediately, she turned and aimed her gun at Zou, who had bent over to pick up his gun with his left hand. She fired and put a hole in the floor next to Zou's feet. "I would not do that if I was you," she said.

Zou slowly stood erect, leaving the weapon on the floor.

Filipov closed the gap between her and Zou by half with her weapon still zeroed in on his forehead. "Now, you are going to tell me everything you know about The Consortium and the attack they are planning."

Zou cursed at her in Mandarin. "You must be drunk...or high... or just plain crazy. I am not telling you anything."

"Let me understand this, then. You would rather die and leave all of this behind, than tell me what you are planning and live?"

"By your hand, I might remain alive...if I give you what you want. But where would I end up? In prison. If I am lucky. And neither you nor I can predict which prison it would be. Could be here in China. Could be in the United States. Could be in Africa, Russia, or one of twenty other countries who will all surely want to extradite those of us who comprise The Consortium. So, forgive me if I reject your offer of life. Life in prison is really no life at all."

"Then, I will have to kill you."

Zou stood up as straight as he could and lifted his hands out, away from his side. "Be my guest."

"I will. But first," Filipov said, motioning toward the computer sitting on his desk, "you will gain me access to your computer."

"No. I will not."

Filipov fired a round, obliterating Zou's left kneecap.

Zou crumbled to the floor, grabbing his knee with his left hand and spouting something in a different language, not Mandarin.

Filipov walked over and kicked Zou's gun away from his reach. "If you are to die, and if your precious Consortium is to be found out, what difference does it make if you give me access to your computer or not?"

"I will not help you!" Zou winced as he tried to reposition his frame on the floor.

"All I want are the names of the Consortium members and the location of the contagion."

Zou crawled to the corner of his desk and used his right leg and left arm to push himself back to a standing position. "Are you sure that is *all* you want?"

"Yes."

"And if I give it to you, you will let me live?"

"Yes. You will be free to fend for yourself. Who knows, with all your money, maybe you could hide away on some remote island in the South Pacific."

Zou nodded and hobbled around his desk. He fell into the chair with a cry of pain and grabbed his knee. He glared at Filipov with menacing eyes, turned his chair toward the desk, and held up his right hand. "I cannot use the mouse, thanks to you."

Filipov walked around behind Zou. She shifted the gun to her left hand and jammed the end of it into the back of his head. She bent down, close enough to whisper in his ear. "If you try anything, then our deal of you living is off the table. Understood?"

Zou nodded.

She grabbed the mouse and pulled the wire as far as it would go to give her some distance between her and Zou. "Just point to the screen and tell me where to put the cursor."

"Here," he said. "I need to type in my password."

She clicked the mouse, and Zou used his left hand to type in the characters while his right index finger held down the Shift key when needed.

"Done. Click Login."

When Filipov did, a picture of a fingerprint reader appeared on the screen.

"It must read my right thumbprint." Zou slowly reached across the desk and grabbed a small, flat, square device attached to the computer by a wire.

He pulled the reader closer and turned it sideways so he didn't have to twist his broken wrist clockwise. He lifted his shoulder, wincing as he did, and pressed his right thumb against the two-inch-square pane of glass.

Instantly, a small beam of light scanned his thumb, and seconds later, the computer screen flashed to a picture of a fanciful paper dragon of red, purple, and yellow dancing along a street in the middle of what appeared to be a Chinese New Year festival.

Zou pointed at an icon in the upper, right-hand corner of the screen. "Click on this one."

Filipov did so, and a window opened, displaying a list of files.

"Scroll down. The file we need is toward the bottom."

Filipov clicked on the arrow to the right and caused the files to cycle upward.

"Okay, stop. It is the one called 'Consortium – Firewall.'" He tapped the screen, showing her which one.

She clicked on it, and a single file appeared.

"Click on the file. The information you seek is in there."

Filipov did so, and all the files displayed started deleting at a rapid clip. Seconds later, sparks shot out from under the computer. She jerked her hand away from the mouse and pressed the gun into Zou's neck with more force. "What have you done?"

Zou laughed. "I am preventing you from getting anything from me. Sorensen was a fool, allowing you into his hotel room. But I am not Sorensen."

Filipov scrunched her brow a little.

"Yes, Agent Filipov, we know all about your trip to Hong Kong. All about Sorensen's computer. All about how you staged the scene, making it look like Sorensen killed that other man. How you injected Sorensen with something lethal."

Filipov's brow knit together even more.

"Why do you think my associate was here? He knew you would show up eventually."

Smoke billowed out from under the computer, followed by tiny flames, licking their way around the edges of the computer tower. A foul smell of burning electronics filled the room.

Filipov withdrew the gun barrel from Zou's head, raised her left hand high, flipped the gun around, gripping the barrel, and slammed the handle against Zou's temple. She followed that blow immediately with a right cross to the same location.

Zou fell from his chair and braced himself as he tumbled to the floor. His right hand crumbled under his weight, and he yowled in pain, growling several obscenities at her.

She immediately jammed the gun into her waistband, snatched the computer off the desk, pulled all the cords loose, and threw it into Zou's private mini-bar sink. She jammed a nearby hand towel in the drain and turned on the water, allowing the sink to fill with water and extinguish the fire.

"There is too much smoke now," Zou said with an air of arrogance. "The fire alarm will go off soon, and you will not be able to get away."

Filipov contemplated his words and realized he was right. They would block all the entrances and exits. Sensors would tell them where the fire was, and when they arrived on the floor, all the dead bodies would cause a panic. Police officers would be summoned, and the building would be placed on lockdown.

She yanked the gun from her waistband with her right hand. Doing the only thing she could think of, she aimed at the expansive windows in the office and fired.

After four shots, one of the panes shattered and blew outward toward the river and street below. Some fragments fell inside on the lavish bamboo flooring.

Filipov fired at two more windows, opening up a sizeable hole and causing the smoke to race outside.

She then aimed her pistol at Zou's thigh and fired.

Zou howled in obvious pain and grabbed his leg with his left hand.

Filipov backed away, keeping the weapon pointed at his head.

Zou absorbed the attack and growled in defiance. "I am not afraid of you, Agent Filipov. I am a general. I have commanded thousands in battle. You are going to have to kill me, because if you do not, I will hunt you—"

Filipov fired three shots. Two into his chest. One into his head.

Zou's rage-filled expression froze before it eased into one of shock. His shoulders slumped, and his head rolled back against the floor.

Filipov raced around the desk and went through Zou's pockets. She found his wallet, a set of keys, a date book, and two smartphones.

She rummaged through his wallet, yanked out the wad of cash, and stuffed it into her pocket. She then snatched the phones and stood.

She got the screen of the first phone to illuminate, but to get inside, it required Zou's fingerprint. She knelt down again, wishing she didn't have to because of her leg, and used his right thumb to open the phone.

The home screen appeared, and she accessed his call history and saw several calls to various associates, one of them being to a "Li," who Filipov determined was the man lying on the floor behind her. There were other calls as well. Some to Sorensen. Some to Murphy. Some even to Liam Clarke.

This must be his personal phone...

She then accessed the second phone in the same manner and noticed how there were only two recent calls. Both were made to contacts with strange names.

Z-Detonator: Union Market.

Z-Detonator: Las Vegas.

She accessed the contacts section and saw over fifty numbers listed in the "Z" section with similar names.

These are the names of cities and places in the United States...

Is this how they planned to release the contagion?

She accessed the settings icon on both phones and attempted to change Zou's password to something she could remember, but a four-digit passcode screen popped up.

Frustrated, she stood and swore in Russian, realizing she needed more time than she had to determine Zou's secondary code. She limped over to the other side of the office and retrieved the knife Mr. Li had thrown in her direction at the beginning of their skirmish. She then walked back over to Zou, jamming her own pistol into her waistband again, and grabbed his right hand.

Flattening out his hand, she placed the sharpest edge of the double-sided blade against the second knuckle of Zou's thumb and pressed down with all her weight. With a few surgical moves, she severed the thumb so that she could continue to access the smartphone later. She found some napkins on Zou's mini-bar and wrapped the thumb before stuffing it in her left pants pocket.

She then wiped the knife down and placed it in Mr. Li's right hand, pressing his fingers into the handle. She wiped down the AK-47 and tossed it against the wall, right by the broken windows. She picked up the other pistol lying on the ground and stuck it in her waistband before wiping down the mouse on Zou's desk, the cords that were attached to hard drive, and the faucet handles of the sink.

Filipov wished she had more time, but there was one thing left to do before she vanished from this crime scene.

A message from The Blake Mist.

She walked around behind the desk and grabbed a pen. Then, she used another napkin to pick up an unopened envelope off Zou's desk:

For those who think killing innocent people with bioweapons, for the sake of personal and financial gain and the acquisition of power, is somehow acceptable, think again.

Signed,
　　The Black Mist

She threw the pen out the broken window and folded the envelope in half, using the napkin as a barrier for her fingerprints. She then bent down and stuffed the envelope into Zou's inner coat pocket.

She stood, took a deep breath and checked her thigh before dragging Zou's lifeless body by the arms to the line of broken windows, being careful not to step in any blood.

She kicked at the remnants of broken glass still sticking out of the frame, sending the fragments sailing down toward the road below.

She cleared a three-foot section until the edge was clean. Then, incrementally, she inched Zou's body into the opening until his arms dangled over the side. She sat down and pushed with her good leg until finally, the weight of Zou's torso pulled the remainder of his frame through the opening.

Filipov closed her eyes and inhaled deeply before allowing the breath to escape in a slow, measured manner.

She hated how her life had become one of destruction.

She truly despised the person she had become.

Zou, Sorensen, Miss Kim, and Baranovskaya had created her.

With each avenging death, Arina believed a little piece of her... of the little girl who was simply walking home from gymnastics practice that fateful evening so many years ago...of the little girl who was filled with hope and love...of the little girl who adored her family...a family simply desiring to enjoy life as best they could in their cramped home on the poorer side of town...was lost forever. In its place, cold, unfeeling bits of despair and hatred rushed in to take up residence where hope and love once lived.

She pinched her eyes together, trying to stop the tears from forming, but they did nevertheless.

Her damaged thigh suddenly ached and reminded her of how she needed to leave before the authorities arrived.

Like a wounded soldier who just fought an epic battle, she grimaced and groaned as she stood. *I need a way out and fast... walking two flights of stairs to get elevator access will take too long...and my leg will never manage the steps.*

She walked over to Zou's desk and used her knuckle to punch the speakerphone button and then pressed Zero.

"Front desk."

"Yes. Mr. Zou needs your assistance. His office is on the twenty-eighth floor. Emperor Pharmaceuticals. He has some large boxes which need to be shipped express mail. Can you help him get these to the lobby?"

"I am not supposed to leave the desk."

"It will only take a minute. And he says he will pay you handsomely for the trouble."

The front desk clerk mumbled something Filipov couldn't understand. "Okay, I am coming up now. We need to make this quick."

"The quicker the better. Thank you." Filipov tapped the speakerphone button and disconnected the call.

She walked to the door of Zou's office and peered in both directions before exiting and retrieving her briefcase.

She worked her way back to Zou's private elevator as the numbers above the elevator changed, counting down from twenty-eight.

Someone has recalled the elevator car...

Is it the clerk, or is it someone else?

Does Zou have reinforcements coming?

The numbers counted down all the way to one. The car remained there for a brief moment, and then the numbers counted upward again.

Filipov fled and rounded the nearest corner, waiting to see who got off the elevator. She pulled out her pistol, set her briefcase down, and checked the number of rounds.

Seconds later, the elevator stopped, and the doors opened.

Filipov picked up her briefcase and peeked around the corner.

The desk clerk took two steps out of the car and gasped. He immediately reached into his pocket and ran back inside the elevator.

Filipov ran toward the elevator as the doors closed and jammed the barrel of her gun into the remaining two-inch space, causing the door to reopen. She immediately shot the security camera in the corner of the car.

The desk clerk screamed and covered his head.

She aimed at the desk clerk and shook her head. "Turn the phone off and drop it on the floor."

The clerk instantly pulled the phone away from his ear and

ended the call. He manipulated the screen, shut down the phone, and showed Filipov. "See, it is shutting down."

Filipov gave it a quick glance. Before nodding at the clerk.

The clerk tossed it on the floor before raising both hands in surrender.

"I will not hurt you, if you do what I ask of you."

"Please! I have a pregnant wife... She is due any day now."

Filipov's finger pressed against the trigger and then eased back. "You are lying."

"No. I show you." The desk clerk stared back at her with questioning eyes as he reached into his back pocket.

"Filipov took a step toward the man. "Careful!"

Sweat broke out on the man's forehead. "I am just getting my wallet." He gently eased his hand out and pinched the leather case between two fingers. "May I?"

"Open it. Slowly."

The man nodded and did so and slid two pictures out of a plastic sleeve. He held them up for her to see. "See? One is an ultrasound picture of our baby. A girl. The other is my wife. See?" His voice squeaked in fear.

Filipov studied them before peering at the man. Her gun still pinpointed on his chest.

"I will not mention anything about you," the clerk said. I will tell them it was several big men who did all this." He motioned at the carnage behind her. "And I will erase all of the security camera footage. I have access. Besides, nobody is going to believe one woman could do all of this anyway." He shrugged.

She backed out of the elevator and motioned for him to follow her. "Lock the elevator door open, then get out. Face the far wall and get on your knees."

The clerk shuddered and did as he was told.

Filipov waited and set her briefcase down after he was on his knees. She stuck her gun back into her waistband, bent down, groaning as she did, and opened the case. She pulled out a syringe, filled it with a strong sedative, and grabbed a pair of metal handcuffs, tossing them at the man's knees. "Put those handcuffs on. Cuff yourself behind your back. When you feed the cuff through and hear it start to click, stop."

The clerk hesitantly picked them up, applied them to his right wrist, and then his left.

Filipov then closed the gap. "You are going to feel a stab in your neck. This shot will put you to sleep. However, you will eventually wake up."

The clerk bowed his head and began to whimper. "How can I erase the security cameras if I am restrained?"

"You let me worry about the cameras."

He nodded and became stone still. "Thank you."

"I do this for your wife. And your daughter. You must treat them well and protect them from men like Ju-Long Zou, or I will come back and do to you what I did to these other men. Do you understand?"

"Yes, yes. I understand. I love my wife. And I know I will love my daughter. They are my world. They are why I work this job. It is my second job. I do this so my wife can stay home."

Filipov nodded, thinking of how much he reminded her of her own father, and jammed the needle into the clerk's neck without saying another word.

She yanked the syringe out once the plunger was fully depressed, and within seconds, the clerk leaned to his left and collapsed beside one of the dead bodies.

She tossed the syringe into her briefcase and closed it. Picking it up, she turned, and walked into the elevator. She unlocked the doors and pressed the button labeled "One" before taking one last look at the clerk.

You are a lucky man.

Just make sure you keep your word.

CHAPTER 27

MANDALAY BAY CONDOMINIUMS and Resort
Jacksonville, Florida

Special Agents Gerard Ryker and John Sandburg turned right off Touchton Road into the Mandalay Bay Condominium Resort complex and pulled up to the guard shack. A sixty-something-year-old man with thinning salt-n-pepper hair and a thin moustache wore a pressed white uniform shirt and grey slacks. He stood by the door of the shack holding a clipboard with a small radio attached to his hip.

Agent Ryker chuckled as the vehicle edged closer.

"Great," Agent Sandburg said. "All the stuff we've been dealing with, and we get the poster boy for some rent-a-cop company."

"Now, now, Agent Sandburg. He's just doing his job."

"Probably failed the police academy."

"Or he could be retired military from up north who needs something to do." Ryker stopped their sedan and rolled down his window. "Good afternoon," he said, holding out his credentials in plain view. "My name is Supervisory Special Agent Gerard Ryker, and this is my partner, SSA John Sandburg. We're from the Jacksonville field office of the FBI. You have a tenant we need to speak with. His name is Joseph Ricatelli."

The guard, whose name tag said "Fred" in centered, bold letters, and "from Hoboken, New Jersey," in tiny letters along the bottom, took Ryker's credentials and examined them. He then dipped down enough to look at Sandburg in the passenger seat. He finally handed the credentials back. He flipped through the pages on his clipboard. "We don't have anybody by that name living here. At least, not going by what's on the leases."

"Not surprised," Ryker said. He grabbed the file from his partner, opened it, and pulled out a photo. "Ever seen this man?"

"Norman? Yeah. I've seen him. Norman, uh...uh, hold on." The guard wheeled around and went back into the shack.

Ryker could see Fred open a filing cabinet and riffle through some files until he found the one he wanted. He pulled the file out and walked back outside, thumbing through the few pages inside. "Here it is. Norman Gentry. That's the guy's name. Just moved in with a looker."

Ryker peered at his partner with a raised brow.

"She's a blonde dame, in her forties, I think, but looks like she's in her early thirties. Real hottie."

"Do you have an address?"

"Her place is 2-7-0-4. The building is toward the back of the property. If you take a right here," Fred said, pointing at the stop sign, "just follow the road around. It makes a big loop back to this intersection. Building twenty-seven is about halfway around on your right."

"Thank you, Fred. You've been very helpful."

"Sure thing. So, you think Norman knows this guy you're lookin' for?"

Ryker smiled. "I believe he might."

Fred shook his head with a look of sadness. "He's a nice guy. Always tips me, comin' or goin'. I'd hate to see him mixed up with somebody the feds are lookin' for, you know?"

"We do. Thank you, Fred. You have a good day."

"You as well."

Ryker pulled away and came up to the stop sign. "See, John?" He handed Sandburg the file on Joe Ricatelli. "Retiree from Hoboken working a part-time job, and gettin' some extra scratch along the way from thoughtful patrons like Norman Gentry. Gotta love America."

"Okay, so maybe Fred from Hoboken wasn't so bad after all." He took the file.

"You just have to know how to handle 'em, John. Give them some respect, especially from some 'feds,' and they bend over backwards to help."

"Yeah, yeah, whatever." Sandburg opened the file. "So, Old Joe has a new name? That's a...what's the word I'm looking for?"

Ryker rounded the corner and started looking for building numbers on his right. "'Convenient' is the word that comes to my mind. Uses an alias while living with 'a looker'? And I wonder who this 'blonde hottie' is?"

"It's sure piqued my interest."

"I'm sure it has, Casanova. If memory serves, you've never met a blonde you didn't like."

Sandburg pulled the visor down and checked his hair in the mirror. "You're forgetting my first wife."

"Oh yeah, right. But in my defense, your first divorce was before I knew you."

"True enough."

They continued to pass building after building, counting the numbers as they did, until they reached building twenty-seven. Ryker backed into a visitor's spot in front of the building but across the street, giving them a clear view.

"I don't see his car here," Sandburg said.

Ryker rubbed his chin. "If he's ditched his identity, he may have ditched his old car too."

"Let's go knock down a door then."

"You just want to meet the blonde."

"There aren't many perks to this job. So, when we get one, is it wrong for us to take advantage of it?"

"Just keep your head in the game, all right? With this Ricatelli guy trying to vamoose without a trace, it tells me he has inside information. He'd have no way of knowing we picked up Reese Thomas unless someone who knew we did let Joe know."

"You don't have to worry about me. Like I always say, 'Profession first. Confession afterwards.'"

Ryker rolled his eyes and shook his head. They were words he'd heard before from his partner. Too many times to count, actually.

Without responding, he opened his door, climbed out of the car, and scanned the surrounding area. Sandburg followed his lead.

* * *

They climbed up the stairs to the second floor. The condos in the buildings were done up in sets of eight per unit. Two per floor, four floors total. A stairwell ran up between each set of two giving access to the parking lot in the front and the property behind the building.

A quick examination of the building showed how each condo had a back porch which jutted out from the wall and was enclosed by a screen. An emergency door on each porch gave another point of egress, with the condos on the second floors having access to a metal ladder attached to the side of the building.

"I'll knock on the door," Agent Ryker said. "You go keep an eye on the emergency exit. If Old Joe is here, he's gonna rabbit as soon as I identify myself."

"Why do you get to knock?" Sandburg said.

"Because, I'll be able to look the blonde hottie in the eye when she answers the door."

Sandburg pursed his lips and nodded. "Good point. Okay, give me a second. I need to go back downstairs and grab a view of the exits."

"Make it quick."

Agent Ryker waited until he saw his partner wave his readiness to proceed. He shot Sandburg a thumbs-up and knocked on the door, standing off to the side. "Norman Gentry?" Ryker said. "FBI. We have a few questions we need to ask you."

He heard movement behind the door, like someone was startled from slumber and knocked over something. He could hear footsteps. One person, maybe, but it was difficult to be certain.

"Norman Gentry. This is the FBI. Open up!"

Seconds later, Ryker heard latches sliding before the door cracked open a couple of inches. A chain stretched across the opening and prevented the door from being opened any farther.

A blonde woman peeked out the opening. "May I help you?"

Ryker held out his credentials. "My name is Supervisory Special Agent Gerard Ryker. I'm here to speak with Norman Gentry. I understand he lives in this condo."

"Norman isn't here right now. He'll be back later, but it probably won't be until later this evening."

"And your name is?"

"Violet. Violet Epson. My friends call me Vy."

Ryker pulled out his smartphone and opened his picture gallery. He tapped on a picture and held it up for Violet to see. "Ma'am, do you recognize this man?"

"Yeah. Sure. That's Norman."

"And how long have you known Norman?"

"About two weeks? Maybe a little more."

"And ma'am, where did you meet Norman?"

"At my work?"

"Which is?"

"I work at a bar. Grendyll's Bar and Grill. I'm a waitress and part-time barkeep there."

"I see." Ryker scrolled to another picture. Joseph Ricatelli's latest mugshot. "Do you recognize this man, Miss Epson?"

She pinched her brow together. "Is this some kind of joke?"

"No, ma'am. This picture is of a man by the name of Joseph Ricatelli. This is his mugshot. We pulled it this morning off the Jacksonville Sheriff's Office website. There are two more mugshots in the system, but this is his latest, most recent picture."

"But...there must be some kind of mistake. He looks just like Norman."

Agent Ryker took a deep breath to keep from blurting out a guffaw. "Yes. Yes, he does. That's why it is imperative that we speak with Norman. It could be that someone is using his identity to do some bad things."

"I wish I could help you more, but like I said, he's not due back until later."

"Do you know where he went?"

"He said something about running some errands..." She paused and squinted just a smidgeon. "Now that I think about it, he did say he needed to get his address changed permanently now...since we've hit it off, you know what I'm saying?"

"Address changed to where? Here?"

Violet nodded. "I asked him last night if he wanted to move in with me."

"So, he hasn't officially moved in yet?"

She shook her head. "But now, I'm having second thoughts."

"I understand." Ryker pocketed his phone and reached inside his suit pocket and retrieved a business card. "Can you give this to Norman and have him give me a call?"

Violet took the card. "Sure."

"We just need to talk to him. Ask a few questions."

"I'll let him know."

"Thank you, Ma'am. And if you need to contact me about Norman, for any reason, you can use the card as well. Have a good day."

"Likewise," she said, and shut the door.

Ryker could hear the latches slide back into place as he walked away. Then, he heard a voice and stopped. He inched back toward the door and listened. The sound of an argument, made mostly with whispers and hushed tones, rose and fell inside. And an occasional "Shhh!" wafted through the door.

Ryker raced downstairs and flagged Sandburg to come join him.

"The blonde's name is Violet Epson. She says 'Norman' is gone and won't be back until later today. However, she never opened the door. Kept it chained. Then, when I left, I heard an argument inside."

"You think Old Joe is here?"

"I do. I showed her his mugshot and allowed her to see his real name. She wasn't too keen on him being an ex-con. I could see it in her eyes."

"Stakeout then?"

"I didn't mention you, so she doesn't know you're here. So, I'm going to go get in the car and leave. I'm sure Joe is watching the street and waiting for me to leave. I'll head for the front entrance and wait at the intersection. You hide and watch for him or her to leave the condo, then follow them. Find out which vehicle they get into, then call me and let me know which one to look out for."

"And you'll stop them at the intersection?"

"Actually, I'll wait at the intersection. Let me know which way they went, and I'll try to cut them off as close to this condo as I can. That way, you can follow on foot."

"Got it."

CHAPTER 28

ANFÄNGE BIOTECHNISCHE LABOTORIEN
Stuttgarter Straße 50
75159 Pforzheim, Germany

Vasily Yerzov had spent the last several hours making phone calls and sending emails.

He had the needed facility, compliments of a friend. The arrangement was simple. Vasily would use Lazar Nicolescu's work to develop an antidote and subsequent vaccine which would literally save the world. The man who owned the facility would be the one to profit greatly from Vasily's work, helping mass produce it for global distribution. He would have the exclusive rights and formula, and countries would pay whatever he charged to get their hands on it.

Vasily had the equipment necessary to do the job. The facility was first class in every regard, and if there was anything he lacked, one phone call would expedite the delivery of it.

However, what Vasily needed was manpower. Out-of-work

scientists were not the kind you wished to employ for such a project, and the good ones were already taken, working in various corners of the planet. Therefore, he had persuaded the owner of the facility to sweeten the pot so he could lure some scientists away.

Since the moment Vasily stepped foot in Pforzheim, this task took up the lion's share of his time. However, he was close to filling his team. Fortunately, he didn't need a large number of scientists. He needed strategic ones, skilled in certain areas of immunology and bacteriology. Once they produced the first vials of the necessary serum, the process from the lab to production facility would move quickly, and the man who owned the facility had plenty of those folks waiting in the wings, ready at a moment's notice to begin the final steps of the process.

Vasily took a break and made himself a cup of coffee. He walked across the small room he used as an office when he heard the familiar *Ding!* of an email arriving in his inbox. He had just corresponded with the two remaining scientists he was trying to persuade and thought maybe they had already given him their answers.

He sat down as a perplexed look spread across his face. An email from Lazar Nicolescu sat at the top on his unread list.

Weary, he leaned back into his chair and sipped his coffee.

This is not from his account in Novosibirsk. It's from his personal account.

He finally grabbed his mouse and clicked on it.

His concern was how this email was not encrypted like the others from Lazar. Hoping it was safe, he read as he sipped his drink.

Dr. Yerzov,

Lazar Nicolescu did not ask me to write you, but he has spoken highly of you in the past and has shared about how you two were dear friends. That is why I chose to write you on his behalf.

By the time you receive this, Dr. Nicolescu's plan will be well underway, and it is my understanding you are well-acquainted with Lazar's overall plan.

I have been tasked with bringing you the human subject. His name is Peter Zakayev. He is from St. Petersburg and was labeled a dissident by the Russian government so he could be used as a "lab rat." Vladimir Klebnikov and his people have conducted the human testing phase of their antidote on this young man. Peter is not a dissident. He is a young man who unfortunately knew the wrong people. When you and I are done creating the antidote, we must allow Peter to leave to go back to his family.

However, Peter is not completely asymptomatic yet. Therefore, he and I are hiding from Klebnikov's people and the Russian authorities until he is.

I will be mailing to you a box containing vials of Peter's blood. These were taken and packaged by Lazar. He said they would give you enough source material to begin testing until I could get Peter safely to your lab. The box should arrive by tomorrow night or the next morning at the latest. However, it will be several days before we arrive.

So, be on the lookout for a box addressed to you from Genforma Laboratories, Novosibirsk, Russia.

There is one more thing I thought you should know. As you probably already know, Dr. Nicolescu was in the advanced stages of a rare form of myeloid leukemia. He informed me, recently, it had reached stage M-7, but he claimed he was not seeing the symptoms typically associated with the disease at that stage. He joked about how his "clean" living in the lab for a year and a half had reversed the onslaught, ironically, while he worked with a disease that made this leukemia pale by comparison. I have come to know this about our friend. He can have a morbid sense of humor when he puts his mind to it.

In order to get Peter and me out of the lab, which was under tight security, we had to develop a plan. When we found out Klebnikov was coming much sooner than we thought, to personally take Peter and everything else he needed in order to produce the antidote, our original plan of escape changed dramatically. Klebnikov's accelerated plans left us with only one option. Get Peter and me out at any cost.

Peter and I did get out with the help of Dr. Nicolescu, however, I am sorry to inform you Lazar never intended to leave Genforma. He was going to capture Klebnikov and keep him there. I tried to get Lazar to elaborate on his plan, but he said it was better I did not know the details.

Therefore, I can only assume he was planning on releasing the contagion within the lab in some way. Otherwise, Klebnikov would eventually realize Peter was not there any longer, and a manhunt would commence. However, if Lazar was able to release the contagion and initiate a building-wide quarantine, then it would take days for Klebnikov to resurface, if he survived at all.

I do truly believe Lazar was on a kamikaze mission of sorts. He knew his days were few, and he wanted to make sure Klebnikov could not proceed, hence our escape and future arrival in Germany.

I concluded Lazar may not have time to sit down and write you, knowing his time was limited. Klebnikov and his team arrived just as Peter and I escaped.

I also concluded he would not tell you, because he would not want you to worry. But I thought you should know. He told me he counted you as one of his closest remaining friends.

I will email you again when we ready ourselves for departure.

Until then, wish Peter a full recovery and our safe passage to Germany.

Karina Kuznetsova

Vasily had set his cup down midway through the email. Karina's information about Lazar didn't surprise him at all. Lazar had told him on several occasions that he wished to correct a great many wrongs they had committed while working for the Ministry of Health all those years ago. He felt the same way. That's why he had been in Switzerland.

Karina's note, though, did one thing he was not expecting. The tears filling his eyes were expected. He knew he'd find out about Lazar's death eventually. He was a little shocked Lazar's illness had not claimed him years earlier. Instead, what this news produced, which caught him totally off guard, was how lonely it made him feel. It was as if his last and only true friend had passed away, or was about to. Even though he had other friends, they were more of the "business associate" variety. His true friends were the men who had early on devoted their lives to the cause of the Communist Party—not fully realizing its true intent—only to be followed by years of regret and separation as sides were chosen. His side, which was Lazar's as well in the end, fought against those who sold themselves out to the highest bidder for filthy lucre, like Klebnikov.

One by one, trusted friends who landed on the "good side" of the ledger passed away. Some from natural causes. Others were hunted down by the authorities on trumped up charges.

Lazar Nicolescu was the last decent friend left alive.

An era was coming to an end.

Vasily dropped his chin to his chest and offered up a prayer for his friend. Then, in a depth of sadness he had never experienced, he wept.

CHAPTER 29

MANDALAY BAY CONDOMINIUMS and Resort
  Jacksonville, Florida

Special Agent John Sandburg stood at the bottom of the stairwell in a small alcove where he could see everyone who walked down the stairs as well as the back of the building. Ten minutes after Agent Ryker left in their car, a person emerged from one of the condos upstairs. The individual appeared in a bit of a hurry and kept muttering to himself something Agent Sandburg couldn't understand. It was like the person was recounting a conversation or possibly practicing for an upcoming one. Either way, the resident immediately became a person of interest.

Sandburg watched as the person rounded the first landing and continued down the stairs. He eased back into the alcove and finally got a glimpse of the person's face.

Joseph Ricatelli.

Or Norman Gentry.

Or whoever he was at this moment.

Sandburg allowed him to descend all the way to the bottom floor while he pulled out his phone and readied his partner's number. As soon as Ricatelli angled to his left out of sight, Sandburg moved through the stairwell area, using the structure to block him from Ricatelli's view.

Ricatelli looked to his left and to his right as he crossed the street. He continued to angle over to the left until he reached a black BMW which happened to be parked two spaces over from where Ryker had backed in their sedan earlier.

Sandburg could hear the alarm beep as Ricatelli pointed his keys at the vehicle. He pressed the Send button on his phone and held it up to his ear.

"You see him?" Ryker said.

"You called it, Gerry. He was there all along. Just got into a black BMW. He went the opposite direction you did."

"So, he's taking the long way around?"

"Yes," Sandburg said, watching Ricatelli speed past him. "Probably thinks you'll be around the corner, so he's trying to slip out behind you."

"Gonna make a longer hike for you, but I'll head that direction and cut him off. Follow him, but don't let him see you. Catch up to us as quickly as you can. He's probably armed and dangerous."

"Should we call for back up?"

"No time."

"All right. I'm on my way."

"And if he backtracks, let me know."

"You got it."

* * *

Agent Ryker whipped the car around and whizzed through the intersection at the front of the complex. He slowed down and tried not to speed. He didn't want Ricatelli to see a speeding sedan racing toward him between the buildings. Instead, because he didn't know how far around Ricatelli had traveled, he got to a row of parking spots to his right and backed into a space next to a car similar in size. He eased back until his view of the road was good and most of his car would be blocked from Ricatelli's view.

Twenty seconds later, the black BMW rounded the curve, traveled over a speed bump, and accelerated.

Ryker threw his car into Drive and gave himself a silent countdown.

Five...four...three...two...one...

He slammed on the gas pedal and pulled out in front of the BMW. He veered the car to his right and blocked the road at a forty-five-degree angle.

Ricatelli slammed on his brakes and came within inches of plowing into the side of the FBI sedan.

Ryker opened his door and stood. With his gun drawn, he used the car and the car's door as a shield, aiming over the front window directly at Ricatelli.

Ricatelli shifted the BMW into reverse and started to back up erratically when another vehicle rounded the corner. He turned the wheel sharply and whipped the back end of the BMW into an open parking spot.

Ryker grabbed his phone and jumped into his car to pursue Ricatelli. "John, he saw me. He's coming back your way. Shoot out the tires."

* * *

Sandburg had tried to cut across the property, but a fence and some other structures had made it impossible. Now he was happy they were there. They had forced him back out to the road on the back end of the complex.

He hung up and walked out into the middle of the road, gun drawn, waiting for his prey to drive smack dab into his trap.

He heard an engine racing on the other side of the condo two buildings down, off to his left.

Suddenly, screeching around the corner was a black BMW, and it wasn't going to stop for anybody.

Sandburg took aim, and when Ricatelli zeroed in on him and accelerated to another gear, he fired at the left front tire.

The wheel instantly deflated, causing the car to swerve.

He fired at the other tire and missed as the car jerked back to its right. Sparks shot out from the car's undercarriage. One of the bullets punctured the grill and radiator.

Another shot, and the right tire instantly unraveled, ripping the tread loose from the sidewalls.

The car's front rims dug into the pavement and yanked the car to the left. Ricatelli slammed on the brakes, attempting to keep the car from swerving out of control.

Sandburg ran up to BMW just as Ryker rounded the corner and raced up to the now steaming car.

"Turn off the engine, and put your hands where I can see them!" Sandburg said.

Ricatelli dropped his chin to his chest and shut the car off. He then placed his hands on top of the dashboard.

Sandburg circled the front of the BMW with his weapon trained on Ricatelli.

Ryker jumped out of his car and drew his weapon as well. "I'll cover you."

Sandburg nodded and opened the driver's side door. "Get out, Ricatelli, and get up against the car."

Ricatelli got out and saw Ryker with his gun raised and huffed a breath of defeat. He turned around and slapped his palms on top of the BMW. "Look, fellas, this ain't what it seems, okay?"

Sandburg searched Ricatelli.

"So, Joseph, tell us what this really is," Ryker said. "Or should I call you 'Norman'?"

"Listen, there's a reason for me changing my name."

"He's clean," Sandburg said, securing a pair of handcuffs on Ricatelli. "Let me check the car."

Ryker holstered his weapon and yanked their suspect out of the way.

"Are we gonna find anything in your car, Norman?" Ryker said.

"Yeah. In the glove box."

"Did you hear that, Agent Sandburg?"

"Sure did." Sandburg opened the glove compartment and found a Ruger-57. He pulled a glove from his pouch and grabbed the gun with it. He stood and held it up. "Lookie what we have here, Agent Ryker."

"Oh, that's not good."

"Worse for Joseph, actually. He's the one with the felony record."

"That ain't true," Ricatelli said. "I don't have no record. If you don't believe me, check it out."

"Oh, we have, Joseph. And you're right. You don't. It seems every time you got busted for a crime, the witnesses who were scheduled to testify suddenly decided to recant."

"I can't help it if they were lying. All I know is, our justice system came through and kept an innocent man from being locked up."

"An innocent man?" Ryker said. "If you're so innocent, Joseph, why the name change? And why run? Innocent people don't have to do those things. Only guilty people do."

"I was leaving," Ricatelli said, "because I thought you were the guys who are after me, posing as FBI agents. That's why I changed my name. That's why I was on the run. The people I used to work for are after me."

Ryker peered at Ricatelli for a few seconds. "Sandburg, find anything else in there?"

"Nah. But I haven't searched the whole thing yet."

"Let's call this in. Have our forensic team pick up the car and take it back to the lab. If there's any truth to what this guy is telling us, then we'd probably be safer interrogating him back at the field office."

Sandburg stood and backed away from the vehicle. "Yeah, you're probably right." He plucked his phone from his pocket. "I'll call, and you can have the honor of putting Mr. Ricatelli—or is it Mr. Gentry?—in the car."

CHAPTER 30

BEIJING CENTRAL BUSINESS District
   Beijing, China

Arina Filipov exited the Wěidà de Guówáng Office Building in rough shape, but not before severing all the wires to the building's security cameras in the office behind the desk clerk's station. To save time, she just secured the hard drive under her arm and then found the server and shot it full of holes on her way out.

She had been at war. If the authorities watched the security camera footage, they would match her clothes entering over thirty minutes earlier to what she was wearing now. It would not take a great detective to deduce she was the one involved in the melee which took place on the floors above. She was just thankful she was not bleeding anymore, leading her enemies with a trail of red dots to her next location.

The more she thought about it, they would never match her DNA. It had been wiped from all Russian databases years ago. The computer geek had made sure any attempts to load it through

Interpol and Europol miraculously disappeared without a trace. However, in this particular instance, they wouldn't need to run it.

They had her note.

Her calling card, if you will.

The local authorities may not know who "The Black Mist" is, but those who need to know will.

They'll know Arina Filipov was here, but they will not have a great picture to share, thanks to the hard drive under her arm.

Therefore, even if they sent police to every hospital and clinic in China, they had no reliable photo to flash at every nurse and doctor, asking if they have seen this woman.

The Chinese authorities could broadcast the news of the atrocities all over the state-run media outlets. Monikers of "armed and dangerous" and "threat to our way of life" would no doubt be inserted into the copy read by every television personality, but again, no picture would be shown, even if this information was shared with other news agencies around the world.

Filipov suspected an international manhunt would ensue. She was sure of it, because she hadn't just killed some lowlife or middling mob boss who wouldn't be missed by most. Ju-Long Zou was a former Chinese general. He was connected. Sorensen's computer proved it. The knowledge of Zou's death would definitely send shockwaves to all who did business with him, legal and otherwise, and because he was so valued, those tied to Zou would probably quake in their swanky offices, wondering if The Black Mist would show up on their doorstep.

Therefore, she needed to exit the country as quickly as possible, but she couldn't do so in her current condition.

As she exited the Wěidà de Guówáng Office Building, she proceeded out the main doors, turning immediately to the right so as to stay in the shadows as long as possible while facing away from all the security cameras along the street.

She utilized a public restroom by a park and cleaned herself up as best she could before hailing a cab to take her to the airport. Once there, she retrieved her duffel bag from the locker, and contacted HK Jet Ltd., to see if they could fly her out of the country. They agreed, but the cost for the unscheduled flight would be considerable, especially since she wished to be flown to the Tivat Airport in Montenegro, not a usual destination for them and considerably farther away than Hong Kong and the southern part of the Pacific Rim.

She agreed to the cost without so much as a blink, accessed her bank account, under the name of one of her passports she never used for anything other than bank transactions, and transferred the funds on the spot.

When the company received the funds, they told her they would be ready to leave in three hours. She thanked them and hoped it would take three hours for the people of Zou's office building to find the carnage. By then, The Black Mist would have dissipated from China. However, tossing Zou's body out the window may have sped up her enemy's timeline. It simply depended on where Zou's body landed.

Filipov hailed a cab and traveled across town to the underground doctor she used when staying in Beijing. She had the cab drop her off a few blocks away from his home and waited until it vanished around a corner before walking the final two blocks to her destination.

She knew the doctor would help her. He was no friend of communism, having witnessed his father and mother being brutally beaten and taken into custody on fabricated charges when he was eight years old. He never saw them again. When he inquired about their location, he was told stories by government officials about their alleged treason to the Chinese government and subsequent imprisonment.

Filipov knew that when she answered his questions about what happened, her explanations would rekindle his anti-communist blood. Besides, she had over two hours to kill, and it would be best spent getting physically repaired.

Once she got settled in the doctor's basement on his surgical table, she called Blake Meyer.

"Agent Filipov?"

"Yes."

"I didn't expect to hear from you again."

"I have some additional information you will wish to act on immediately."

"I'm all ears. Go ahead."

Filipov grimaced as the doctor unwound the tourniquet and cut off her pant leg to expose the gunshot wound. "I just paid a visit to a man by the name of Ju-Long Zou. According to Sorensen's computer files, Zou was a major player in Sorensen's Consortium. I almost get the impression Sorensen worked for Zou, or owed him in some way. He seemed to be calling the shots toward the end, before I caught up to Sorensen. Zou also apparently knew what I had done to Sorensen, because when I arrived, he said they had been expecting me."

"They?"

"Yes. He and his fixer, Mr. Li."

"I take it this Zou and Li are no longer a threat?"

"You would be correct. However, the incident has placed me in considerable risk. Once the authorities find out what happened, you will hear news of every law enforcement agency on the planet searching for me."

"You left your calling card again?"

"Yes. Actually in two places recently—" Filipov stopped and grimaced at the pain as the doctor pulled the wound apart to ascertain the damage.

"You're injured?"

"Yes, but I am being treated as we speak. Hold on one minute."

"Sure."

Filipov pressed the smartphone against her chest. "Doctor, I am going to need something for the pain, and something for infection as well. I will not be able to go to a normal doctor or pharmacy to acquire the needed medications, if you know what I mean."

"Agent Filipov, you act as if I have only been doing this for a week. Trust me. You are not the only mercenary who traipses through my home. Looking at this wound, just know I have seen worse. The bullet is still lodged in your thigh. It is not a through-and-through as you suspected. Therefore, I will need to use some high-powered medications to numb your leg so I can remove the bullet before sewing you up. Will that be okay?"

"If they will make me drowsy and want to sleep, then no. I must be fully alert when I leave here."

The doctor lifted his brow and formed a pained frown. "Local anesthetic, it is."

"I can handle it, doctor. And when you are done, make sure it is wrapped so that it cannot bleed through."

"That will depend on how much you use your leg."

"I have a flight to catch once I leave here. It will keep me off my feet for several hours. Once I land, I have a hotel room booked. I can stay there as long as I wish."

The doctor shrugged. "You are the boss."

Filipov put the phone back to her ear. "Agent Meyer, are you still there?"

"Yes."

"I will need to lay low for a while," she said with a heavy sigh. "I will be changing my appearance and holing up in a series of hotels indefinitely."

"Understood."

Filipov motioned over to her bag. "Doctor, can you be a dear and get a smartphone out of my bag, please?"

The doctor eyed her as if she had lost her mind and then turned toward the bag. "You know you are bleeding right now."

"It will not take but a second."

He draped a towel over the wound, gave her an angry look, and walked over to the bag.

She offered a playful, yet fearful smile at him. "Please? I will pay you double."

The doctor shook his head and peeled off his gloves. He reached into the bag and found the smartphone. He inhaled and released a measured, calming breath before handing the item to Filipov. "Is there anything else?"

"No."

"Good. Now, I have to go wash my hands again. I will be right back. Do not move, and *do not* bleed out."

"Yes, sir," she said with a smile as she pinned her own phone between her ear and shoulder and turned on Zou's smartphone. She then set it down beside her, and while it booted up, she reached into her pants pocket and retrieved a wad of napkins. She unfolded the napkins, exposing Zou's severed thumb. "Please bear with me, Agent Meyer. I am accessing Zou's smartphone. The information I have for you is there."

"I'm on a plane back to the States, so I've got time."

Filipov picked up Zou's phone and used the thumb to gain access before putting it back inside the soiled napkins. "Now, for the reason why I called. I found a list of strange contacts on Zou's phone. There are over fifty of them. They are all at the end of the contacts list, and they all begin with 'Z-hyphen-Detonator-colon.' These contacts are then arranged alphabetically by what follows after each one. They are lists of cities in America, Agent Meyer. The first city listed is 'Albuquerque,' then 'Atlanta,' then 'Austin,' 'Baltimore,' 'Boston,' et cetera."

"Those are the same towns and cities on the list of targets we found on Sergei Botinkin. The six hundred families were residing in those places."

"It would appear they have planted devices in these cities, judging by the title of these phone numbers. I do not know what these devices do, but I can only imagine they are tied to the contagion in some way."

"Well, since you know about the devices..." Blake sighed into the phone. "Have you been able to see the news at all coming out of America?"

"No. I purposefully avoid the news whenever possible."

"It would appear Zou or one of his people have already activated the detonator in Las Vegas, Nevada. We have a hotel in Vegas on lockdown as we speak. Last report I heard on the news was over two hundred were infected with what appears to be bubonic plague. Most of the patients are starting with signs of pneumonia, indicating this contagion is a form of pneumonic plague."

Filipov mouthed the words "Thank you" to the doctor as he returned with a fresh pair of gloves on his hands and a syringe in his right hand.

The doctor gave her a thumbs-up and stabbed her thigh with the needle and injected a portion of the contents into her. Filipov pinched her eyes together but remained silent as she listened to Blake.

"They are countering the contagion with streptomycin and chloramphenicol," Blake continued, "as well as some other medications, but I've not heard any word yet on their effectiveness."

The doctor pulled the needle out and repeated the process around the circumference of the wound in Filipov's leg. With each stab, she winced a little more as the tenderness of the wound had apparently spread.

"Well then, we may have a bigger problem, Agent Meyer. Hold on a second."

The doctor got Filipov's attention. "Can you feel this?" he said, using the edge of the needle to prick her in the thigh.

"No."

"How about here?"

She shook her head.

"Here?"

"No."

"And how about here?"

"No. I can feel pressure, but is doesn't hurt."

"Good. Then, I will begin the surgical procedure. If you feel anything uncomfortable, let me know."

"Do not worry, doctor." She pulled the phone away from her ear and placed Blake on speakerphone. "Agent Meyer, can you hear me?"

"Yes, but is it okay for me to be on speakerphone?"

"No worries here. The good doctor is the only other person in the room, and I trust him with my life, so that is saying something." She glanced at the doctor while saying it, and he smiled under his face mask as he pulled a small table of surgical tools closer.

"I am accessing Zou's call history. According to his phone records, he called the number to Z-Detonator: Las Vegas at 4:16 p.m. Beijing time yesterday."

Blake paused. "That would have been 1:16 a.m., Las Vegas time."

"And when did the first victim get identified?"

"I distinctly remember talking to someone about it. We had just landed in Albania, and we were on our way to the embassy when I got the call. I had synched up my watch with local time in Tirana. It was 3:27 p.m. Albania is six hours ahead of the eastern seaboard of America, and Nevada is three hours behind."

"So," Filipov said, pausing to do the math, "it was 6:27 a.m. in

Las Vegas when you heard the news of first victims being identified?"

"And the first victims had already been identified by then... which means this contagion has a less than a five-hour incubation period."

"Then I think," Filipov said, "we have established that this bioweapon has been militarized. Bubonic plague typically takes days, not hours, to manifest."

"I need to make contact with my director and give him this information."

"Oh, there is more, Agent Meyer, so do not hang up just yet."

"More? More what?"

"According to Zou's phone records, he also made a call to the Z-Detonator in Union Market, Washington, D.C., at 12:13 a.m. this morning, Beijing time, which would have been almost a quarter past noon in your nation's capital."

Blake sighed heavily into the phone. "Around noon? At the Union Market? Do you know how many people will have traveled in and out of the Union Market area since then?"

"I had better let you go, yes? I suppose you have several calls to make."

"Did Zou call any of the other detonators?"

"Not that I can see. Not from this phone, at least."

"Okay. Thank you for the information."

"I am sure we will be in touch. This is not over yet."

CHAPTER 31

NATIONAL POLICE - CENTRAL Police Station of the 8th District
Paris, France

Sitting on the cot with his knees pulled up to his chest, Conrad Bowker leaned against the wall of his cell with his arms limply crossed. His left hand palmed his forehead, and nearly all his energy had been drained. He pled with his jailors on the way back from the phone call to Agent Scarfano, asking them to reconsider his case. He asked them where they had received their information. How did they know he was using a house in Gennevilliers? Who told them to sit on the house? How did the men driving the van—two men Conrad had never met face-to-face—end up with the same poison in their system as Major General Botinkin? Even if Conrad had poisoned Botinkin, why would he choose to do the same to the two men in the van? He had no beef with them. He didn't even know their last names? He didn't even know their nationalities!

Nothing from this case added up.

His line of reasoning seemed sound. However, the jailors didn't seem impressed, or at least they were good at hiding their thoughts, for they never said anything the entire way back to his cell.

"Please," Conrad said one last time as the door clanked shut. "Surely you understand what I am saying. You should not wish to keep an innocent man behind bars. Please, go speak with your superiors. Plead my case. Get a second look."

Officer Fabron waved the other men on, allowing them to go. He waited until they cleared the other door before speaking. "Agent Bowker, I fully understand your plight. We do not wish for innocent people to be wrongly imprisoned. However, your innocence is not for us to decide. As a matter of fact," he said, glancing to his left and then his right, "and you did not hear it from me, understood?"

"Understood."

"I overheard my superiors talking. You are to be extradited to your home country."

"I'm going to England? When?"

"Soon. It seems our government is willing to allow your government to conduct the trial and administer the punishment."

Bowker eyed the French officer. "What is that supposed to mean?"

"It would seem your government is not very happy with your actions."

Bowker chuckled. "Like they are innocent in all this."

"The two men in the van. You said you did not know their nationalities, yes?"

Bowker nodded.

"They were Slovakian hit men. Wanted for several crimes in both their country and elsewhere. Then, of course, the major general was Russian, correct?"

"Yes. But the Russians wanted him dead, so if anything, I should think killing him should earn me a Russian service medal."

"From what I am hearing, the Russians are viewing it quite differently, according to your country."

Bowker shook his head in disgust. "The Russians are accusing me of killing one of their own?"

"It would seem so."

"Unbelievable."

"Then there is an American, I understand. Something about him looking for you, and now he is missing."

Bowker could feel the blood drain from his head. He became at once dizzy and gripped his head with both hands. "So, they're going to try to pin his disappearance on me as well, eh?"

"Now, Agent Bowker," Officer Fabron said as he tapped his chest with his index finger, "do you see why we are staying quiet?"

* * *

Their conversation, which took place over thirty minutes earlier, was on a never-ending loop in Bowker's polonium-riddled mind as he sat on his bunk, when Officer Fabron, accompanied by three additional officers, entered the hallway in front of Bowker's cell.

"Blimey, they didn't waste any time." Bowker shook his head and stretched his legs before him. He massaged his thighs. "Don't I get a last meal or something before my flight over the channel?"

"Our orders are to secure the prisoner and ready him for transport," Officer Fabron said.

"Which airport? Charles de Gaulle?"

"Affirmative."

"The Roissy to Heathrow. Can't say I've never made the trek before."

"Please stand and insert your hands through the slot, please?"

"And if I refuse?"

Officer Fabron frowned. "We have been authorized to use any force necessary."

"You know good and well, Officer Fabron...if the French government sent a British intelligence agent back in pieces, it could ignite another one-hundred-day war."

"If the order had come from our superiors, I would agree, Agent Bowker," Fabron said. "However, the orders came directly from the British prime minister."

"You're lying."

Officer Fabron reached into his back pocket and pulled out a folded piece of paper. He slipped it through the bars.

Conrad spun his frame around on the bed and readied himself to stand. "I don't jump up as quickly as I used to."

"Neither do I," Fabron said with a slight smile.

Bowker stood, walked over to the cell door and took the paper from Fabron. He unfolded it and saw the photo-copied, black-and-white letterhead of the British SIS. He read down about half a paragraph until he saw the line Officer Fabron had referenced:

The prime minister wishes to have Agent Conrad Bowker extradited back to England to face numerous charges of international espionage and capital murder. Agent Bowker is wanted dead or alive.

Conrad shook his head and folded the paper back up. "What a way to thank a man for his years and years of service." He pinched his eyes together and inhaled deeply to keep his emotions in check. "Well, Officer Fabron," he said, sticking his hands out the slot in the door, "I prefer the latter as opposed to the former."

"I thought you might."

"When you're on borrowed time like I am, each day is a gift, right?"

Officer Fabron placed a pair of handcuffs on Conrad and locked the cuffs to prevent tightening. "I suppose so."

"And if I am to go down for all the crimes they assert, might as well go down pleading my innocence to the last."

CHAPTER 32

ABOARD A MILITARY HELICOPTER
En Route from the Atlanta Field Office

Strapped inside the Eurocopter AS365 Dauphin, Supervisory Special Agent-in-Charge Julee Scarfano watched as they lifted off the ground and rose high above the city of Atlanta. With Agent Williams sitting beside her, the chopper banked and headed southeast into a bright afternoon sun.

She marveled at how quickly a person could be in one location and then another. With jets and choppers and bullet trains, the only thing she could think of that would improve travel would be warp drive and transporter technology. Both of which were being worked on in laboratories around the world, she had heard.

She pointed out the window. "Check it out," she said, tapping Agent Williams on the shoulder.

Traffic going into the heart of Atlanta traveled along at a snail's pace. Every lane full. Backed up for what appeared to be miles and miles. The I-285 bypass also looked busy, but at least there was space between the cars, and they seemed to be motoring along at a much faster clip.

She continued to look down in thanks, aware of how long it would have taken to drive back to their field office. They'd be sitting in the logjam of vehicles, feeling the tension rise even higher, knowing they could be doing something productive, if it wasn't for all the summer vacationers and business travelers clogging the roads.

As they sped up a little, her cell phone rang. She looked at the screen.

Agent Meyer?

She pulled her headset off and pressed the green icon. "Agent Meyer," she said, having to raise her voice over the roar of the rotors. "I wasn't expecting any calls from you yet. Have you already landed?"

"No. We're close. But listen. I've got some information you're gonna want to relay to the president immediately."

"Oh, wow. Okay. What is it?"

"I just got off the phone with Agent Filipov. She's been following up on some leads she gleaned from Markus Sorensen's computer. It led her to a Chinese businessman by the name of Ju-Long Zou. According to Filipov, Zou was one of the leaders of Sorensen's Consortium group. She believes he may have been giving Sorensen orders."

"We suspected Sorensen was the money, not the one with all the plans. Is this Zou the mole we've been looking for?"

"No. Zou is not the mole."

Julee plugged her other ear with a finger. "How can you be so sure?"

"Trust me, Julee. Zou isn't the mole. However, he is the person who set off the device in Las Vegas. She has his call history. He remote detonated it from Beijing with his cell phone. The call was made at 1:16

a.m. Las Vegas time. And the first victim was identified around five hours later, which means this contagion must have released through the ventilation system. And because it has spread so quickly, it has to be pneumonic plague, and it has been militarized, because normal plague does not manifest itself in less than five hours after exposure."

"Blake, I'm not sure you've heard the news yet, but some of the very first victims have already died. They are treating everyone else with streptomycin and some other antibiotics. Because of how fast it's spreading, they are moving to implement all the medication intravenously now to get it into the patients quicker. However, because it has spread so fast and attacked the patients so viciously, by the time they determined what this contagion was, it was too late for the first victims. Also, the medical personnel on site are in need of additional medical supplies to convert to the intravenous method."

"How many victims do they have now?"

"Over four hundred. Ten deaths so far. To be safe, they are administering the streptomycin and other meds to everyone in the hotel, including the health officials. They told us it's 'a wait and see game' now. I am told bubonic plague and pneumonic plague can be beaten by those drugs. The question is whether or not the modifications made to this particular contagion will make the drugs ineffective."

"Well, we've got a bigger problem now. According to Filipov, Zou had another call on his cell phone to a detonator in Washington, D.C. Specifically, the Union Market."

"Oh, no."

"The call was made at 12:16 p.m., local time, Julee."

"Around lunchtime? Today?"

"Yes. And if this is the same contagion—and we have to work from that assumption—then you have about four hours before people start showing signs of infection. And because it is not in a closed environment you can lockdown, the spread of this device's contagion will be ridiculous."

"Okay, I need to hang up and call the president. He's going to have to declare a state of emergency in the surrounding area."

"You notify him and allow him to make that decision. While you're doing that, I'll call Director Jameson and fill him in so he's up to date. I'll also tell him you are calling the White House."

"Thanks."

"Godspeed, Julee."

"Yeah. You too."

Blake disconnected the call, and Julee just stared at her phone. It was starting. The thing they had worked so hard to stop over the last few days was in play. And to make matters worse, she had a cousin who lived thirty miles from Washington. And her cousin had a job that forced her to travel into the city at least once a week. Not on the weekends, thank God, but who knows how this thing would spread and where it would go, and for all Julee knew, her cousin might need to drive into the D.C. area tomorrow...

"What is it, Julee?" Agent Williams said.

"I've got a phone call to make. Just listen in to my side of the conversation, and then you can ask questions afterwards."

"Fair enough."

Julee scrolled through her contacts and brought up the line to the White House and dialed.

"Ben Jenkins."

"Mr. Jenkins, this is Agent Scarfano. I need to speak to the president immediately."

"You have more good news, I hope."

"Quite the contrary, actually."

"Seriously? Okay, stand by."

Julee waited for several seconds. She looked at Agent Williams and made a motion for the president's chief of staff to move faster.

"SAC Scarfano, this is President Gilmore. I understand you have some bad news?"

"Time sensitive bad news, sir. I have just received credible information from Agent Meyer. We believe another device, similar to the one released in Las Vegas has been activated in Washington, D.C. It's Union Market, sir."

"Please tell me you're joking. Union Market is less than three miles away from here."

"I wish I were, sir. And according to Agent Meyer, the call to activate the device was made at 12:16 p.m., local time, which means we have less than four hours before the first victims start showing signs of infection, if it is the same contagion."

"And how are you determining that?"

"Agent Meyer stated the call was made by a Chinese businessman named Ju-Long Zou. He remotely detonated the device in Las Vegas with the same phone, then made the call to another detonator labeled 'Union Market.' The timing of everything surrounding these events is all based on when the phone calls to activate the devices at the Bahama Bay Hotel and Casino, and now Union Market, were made. In Las Vegas, the first victims started showing signs a little less than five hours after the call was made."

Gilmore sighed and growled at the same time. "Are you sure it's Union Market? Do you realize how many people will have come and gone by now? And we just got the list of all the detonators from you an hour ago. Our teams have barely had time to mobilize."

"We know, sir. That's probably why it was done when it was and the way it was."

"Lord, help us all." The president paused. "Okay, thank you, SAC Scarfano. Good work. I've gotta go."

"Yes, sir."

* * *

President Gilmore ended the call and looked up at his chief of staff. "Ben, get all the top brass together in the Situation Room immediately."

"Yes, sir."

"I need to contact Patricia Williamson and have Homeland get a quarantine zone set up around Union Market and notify the CDC."

Ben Jenkins nodded and headed for the door.

President Gilmore pushed the button on his landline.

"Yes, Mr. President?"

"I need to speak with Director Williamson from Homeland Security immediately."

"Patch her through when I reach her?"

"Yes."

"Very good, Mr. President."

CHAPTER 33

Marfa Regional Medical Center
Marfa, TX

Captain Theodore "Harley" Harlan's phone rang as he and Detective John Forde sat in the cafeteria, eating hamburgers and fries for lunch.

"Dennis. You here?"

"Yeah. Did you get my text?"

"I did. Glad to see you could secure a chopper. Did you land on the helipad?"

"You're kidding, right?"

"Yes."

Dennis sighed. "We landed at the municipal airport. Then I had to bum a ride from one of the sheriff deputies."

"You could have called me. I could have had Forde pick you up."

"I was afraid to. The way you were talking on the phone, I

thought being seen together on security cameras at the airport wouldn't be good."

Harlan chuckled. "So, you thought being seen together at a hospital wouldn't get our mugs on any surveillance system?"

"Of course it will. Remember, I'm the tech guy in this relationship. I figured me showing up at a hospital would look more like a friend consoling a friend. Meetings at airports always look like spy movie material."

"Fair enough." Harlan picked up a fry off his plate. "Come in through the front doors and wait for me in the lobby. I'm on my way."

"Okay."

Harlan picked up two fries and jammed one of them in his mouth. He pointed at Forde with the other one. "I'll be right back. And Forde, don't touch my fries."

* * *

Captain Harlan ushered Dennis Morrison into the cafeteria.

"Dennis, this is Detective John Forde. He and his partner are the ones responsible for all those great pictures."

Dennis shook Forde's hand. "It's great to finally meet you. How's your partner?"

Forde finished chewing his food. "He's out of surgery and recuperating. Gonna be a while before he's back on the beat."

"At least he survived surgery. One step at a time, right?"

"Definitely," Forde said.

Harlan pointed at the buffet. "Are you hungry? Buy you some lunch? Food's not the best, but it's on me."

"I'm good. My stomach is in knots right now. I spent the entire flight here trying to think of why you would need to see me in person. My supervisor said it must be something really good or really bad. He wanted to send a field agent with me. Probably for my protection as much as anything else, but I told him I was okay. If I needed them, I'd call. Besides, I knew I'd be with you two."

Harlan smiled but didn't give away any clues. "Anything to drink, then?"

"Bottled water would be good. I doubt they have scotch here."

"Bottled water coming right up." Harlan stepped away and walked over to the cooler against the far wall.

Dennis sat down, peeled the leather computer bag from his shoulder, and set it on the table.

Harlan paid for the drink and strolled back to the table. "Here ya go."

"Thanks." Dennis took it and unscrewed the cap.

Harlan sat down. "Allow us to finish eating, and then we need to go somewhere a little more private." He grabbed another fry and stuffed it in his mouth.

"Sounds even more ominous, now." Dennis took a long draw from the bottle.

"Oh, you just wait," Harlan said, chewing as he spoke. "Ain't that right, John?"

"After we talk, I think 'ominous' may be an understatement."

Fifteen minutes later, the three men sat in a conference room typically used by hospital employees for staff meetings. Captain Harlan had requested a private place to meet for "official police business," and the office manager opened the room for them. "Nobody has this room booked today," she said. "There shouldn't be any interruptions."

With the door shut, Harlan sat on the far end of the table, facing the main door leading into a hallway, which happened to be on the other side of the room, to his left. Another door, connected to another smaller room containing a large copier stood closed to his immediate right. A large whiteboard, fastened to the wall, was behind him, and the conference table could easily seat ten people in an oval-shaped arrangement.

The head of the table, facing the door, was Captain Harlan's preferred seat. As a matter of fact, it was always his preferred seat, whether it be a conference room, a large hall, a restaurant, even his dining room at home. This gave him a clear line of sight for every angle and, in this case, both doors. It also made it easy to stand and reach for his pistol, should the need arise.

Old habits.

Detective Forde sat to his left. Dennis Morrison sat to his right, facing the only windows of the room, so his computer screen could not be seen by the security cameras or anyone outside the room, even if they peeked through the cracks of the now lowered blinds.

"Dennis, we have a major security breach, and we're trying to figure out where it is."

"We? You mean your sheriff's office?"

Harlan shook his head. "No. I'm talking about *your* office."

Dennis formed a confused look on his face. "*My* office? What are you talking about? DHS has one of the most sophisticated security systems and redundant group of protocols in the field of investigation. It's kind of a given, with the name, you know?"

"Dennis, Detective Willis was almost murdered this morning. Pedro Arroyo showed up dressed as a male nurse. Now, Dennis," Harlan said with his hands clasped, "how would Arroyo know Detective Willis was even here at this hospital? Even more puzzling to me is, why would Arroyo care? Detective Willis was injured at the abandoned town of Shafter after Castaneda and Arroyo left the area."

"Are you insinuating someone at my office is working with Castaneda?"

"Dennis, Arroyo got off two rounds before Forde was able to

subdue him. Had John not seen Arroyo in the parking lot prior to him entering the hospital, he never would have seen Arroyo coming. However, because he did, he was able to save Willis, keep the hospital staff safe, and subdue Arroyo."

Dennis smiled. "By the way, good work, Detective Forde."

"I appreciate it," John said.

Harlan looked at his watch. "Arroyo just got out of surgery a little bit ago, so he's not going to be able to answer any questions, even though I don't expect him to anyway. He'll clam up and demand a lawyer, and knowing what I know right now, I would not be surprised if one is already on the way here. And if it ain't a lawyer, it's gonna be one of Castaneda's men sent to finish Arroyo and his original mission."

"I...I don't know what to say, Harley," Dennis said. "I can't think of anyone at our Dallas office who would side with the enemy."

"All I know is this," Captain Harlan said. "Arroyo has four Marfa police officers standing guard. Two in his room and two outside the door. The local Sheriff's office also has deputies monitoring the parking lot outside and the interior hallways. We're as prepared as we can be for all scenarios.

"Send a lawyer or send a hitman. Either way, the cartel will look at this mess as Arroyo botching his mission. It's only a matter of time. If the lawyer gets him released, he's toast. If they send a fixer, he's toast—"

"And if I may interject something here," Detective Forde said with a slightly raised hand, acting like a student before his teacher. "Because they tried to take out Willis, I can only assume they now know I'm his partner. Once they learn I was the one who shot Arroyo, then I'm sure they'll have a price on my head too. Both Willis and I will be targets."

Harlan pointed at Forde but stared at Dennis. "And there's that. Which raises another question? Even if Castaneda and Arroyo found out Forde and Willis were following those two INS agents, they wouldn't care. Even if they thought Forde and Willis watched the bomb go off, killing the INS agents, they still probably wouldn't care, because pinning the bomb on Castaneda and Arroyo would be next to impossible, unless—"

"They found out about the pictures," Dennis said with closed eyes and a sudden understanding of why Captain Harlan called him there.

Harlan lifted one eyebrow and nodded. "According to you when we talked on the phone initially, nobody knew much about Castaneda and Arroyo until you received those photographs. You didn't even have a good picture of Castaneda. And you told me when I called you earlier this morning that you showed those pictures to Larry Montrose and the DHS director, correct?"

"Yeah. When Larry saw them, he immediately told me to send them to the director."

"Why?"

"He thought she should know."

"But why immediately?"

Dennis paused, as if trying to recall the exact conversation. "He asked me when the photographs were taken. When I told him, he said, 'Castaneda will be back in Mexico by now. And those Hands of Allah guys will be too.' However, he did mention something about wondering if the Mexican government would help us find Castaneda and possibly the two guys in the box truck for extradition purposes."

Harlan smirked. "And that's when he told you to send them to the director."

Dennis nodded.

"How well do you trust this Larry Montrose?"

"With my life. He's a stand-up guy." Dennis stared at Harlan. "I just don't know how much I can divulge about my colleagues at Homeland. I mean, I've known you for years, so I can trust you with my life as well..."

Harlan lifted an eyebrow. "If you're wondering about Forde...or Willis, for that matter, I feel the same way about them as you do about your supervisor and me. Whatever you can 'divulge' about your Homeland colleagues, you can say it with Forde in this room. Besides, he was the one dodging bullets this morning. I think he's earned the right, don't you?"

Dennis slowly considered Harlan's words. "One of the tasks assigned to me, one I have to perform each day, is to check into our employees."

"Which ones?"

"No. I mean, one to two employees *per day*. I had to develop a protocol, which had to be approved by Larry. I use a random generator to select the names each day, so no one can say I am targeting anybody."

Harlan chuckled until it grew into a hearty laugh. "The spies spy on their own too."

"It's the nature of the beast. And as you have found out first hand, when you're investigating people with money and connections, it can be easy to either switch allegiances or decide to play for both teams. The scales of risk versus reward becomes something one is willing to consider, if not act on, if the price is right, and especially if the one asking has connections ready to hand out 'get out of jail free' cards on a moment's notice.

"Therefore," Dennis continued, "I have permission, off the books, mind you, to dig into our employees personal lives. I check into everything. However, since I have other official duties, too, such as the job I was originally hired to do, I use my spare time for this other task."

"Spare time?" Harlan said with his brow wrinkled completely. "You have spare time?"

"If I get a lull in the action, then I'll work on it some. However, I'm often working past my salaried hours. That's when I get the majority of it done."

"It should be easy then to find whoever is leaking the information, right?" John said. "I mean, can't you manipulate your random generator to choose specific people you need to examine now?"

"Yes, but that's my point. I've been monitoring those things for literally months now. I have programs that scour emails, phone records, bank records, travel history, everything. We even have trackers on all our vehicles now. Nothing has popped that would lead me to believe we have anyone in our Dallas office who is involved in this."

Harlan cleared his throat. "Maybe you're looking in the wrong places."

"Meaning?"

"When we sent you those photos, you said you showed them to Larry Montrose, correct?"

"Yes."

"Who else in your office saw them?"

"Nobody."

"And how are you so sure?"

"Because I was in my office when you contacted me and sent them. Once I figured out who was in the pictures, I called Larry and asked him to come to my office. He showed up alone, I showed him the photos, we talked about them, and then he directed me to send them to the director over one of our secure channels. We bypassed everyone else at our office."

"Montrose didn't call the director to inform her of what was being sent and why?"

"Of course he did."

"And from where did he make the call?"

"My office. Once she heard we had Castaneda on film, she wanted the pictures sent to her immediately."

Harlan rubbed his face as if he was about three thousand hours behind on his sleep. "Then, Dennis, it would seem that once the photos left your office, whoever received them shared them with someone who had ties to the Sinaloa Cartel. Somebody informed Castaneda, because his little lap dog would never have shown up at this hospital unless they knew about the pictures, and more importantly, *who* took them. All of this makes me wonder about Larry Montrose since he and you were the only two other people who knew about the photos besides, me, Detective Forde, and Detective Willis."

"And Willis had no idea who those men were," Forde said. "He was unconscious when you identified Castaneda and Arroyo from the pics I sent you."

Dennis closed his eyes and winced. He sighed in frustration. "Uh, I just remembered something. When the director asked us to send the pictures, she also asked Larry how we obtained them."

"And he told her?"

Dennis nodded and pressed two fingers against his forehead. "That means the director's office has a leak."

"It would seem so, since your office seems to be so squeaky clean."

"I don't know if I would say that."

"What do you mean?" Harlan said. "You just said you check all the people from your office."

"We've had some bad eggs in the past. Now that I know what I am looking for specifically, I'll do another sweep to see if I can find anything."

"And if you don't?"

"Then, I'll have to speak with Larry about where we go from there."

"I'm not so sure that's a good idea, Dennis. You're gonna have to employ those program-writing skills of yours and investigate everyone on your own dime."

"What do you..." Dennis paused. His befuddled look shifted to one of increasing enlightenment. "No. You're not suggesting..." He continued to eye Harlan.

Harlan didn't respond except to tilt his head ever so slightly.

"And how am I supposed to do that without being discovered?"

Detective Forde watched this conversation volley back and forth between his boss and Dennis with a growing look of puzzlement of his own. "Excuse me? Do what exactly?"

Dennis huffed. "Your boss wants me to investigate everyone, even the director and everyone at our D.C. office."

Forde lifted his chin. "That sounds risky."

"No, it sounds like espionage, because if I was found out, that's exactly what they would charge me with. They'd want to know who I was working for."

"Tell them you were investigating for me and following up leads," Harlan said. "I'm not afraid of those Beltway blowhards. They have to obey the laws of the land just like everybody else."

Dennis blurted a nervous guffaw. "You do know we have a two-tier justice system in this country, right?"

"No, we don't. We have people who think they are above the law, but last time I checked, everyone who breaks the law is subject to punishment under our penal codes. There are no caveats or asterisks, giving certain people passes."

"Well, may I say, Captain Harlan, of a sheriff's office in a small county of a big state, the law in Texas is a little different than the law in the nation's capital. Trust me. I see it all the time."

"I'm sure you do, Dennis, but I paid attention in history class when I was a kid growing up. Did even more so in college. As the Constitution says, we formed a more perfect union to abolish the reign of monarchs and dictators. We also formed it the way we did to prevent a group of thugs from taking power and doing exactly the same thing one monarch could accomplish with an army behind him." Harlan leaned a little closer to Dennis. "'Which is better—to be ruled by one tyrant three thousand miles away or by three thousand tyrants one mile away?'"

Dennis shot Captain Harlan a pained smile. "I don't know

professor. But I have a feeling you're going to enlighten me, nevertheless."

"Those words, spoken by a New England minister, Dennis, came from a man who was actually on England's side. Those comments were directed at an American group called the Sons of Liberty. They were a radical group who wanted to overthrow English rule." Harlan leaned back again and interlaced his fingers. "I've always thought those words were interesting. He believed a king three thousand miles away was better. Back then, I would have been on the side of the Sons of Liberty. But now, having worked law enforcement for as long as I have, I see that both sides were wrong. It was never about who rules. It's about justice. All we did was trade one tyrant for 537 in Washington, D.C., if we allow this corruption to go unchecked. And from what you are telling me, if you and I rise up against these tyrants and find one or more of them guilty of crimes against our American citizens, we'll be the bad guys?" Harlan peered at Dennis. "Does that sound like liberty and justice to you?"

"No, it sounds like death by lethal injection. Yours and mine."

"Then, my friend, it appears you have a choice to make, because if my take on all of this is correct, then some of our 537 tyrants have made an allegiance with a deadly cartel. If they get away with it, you, me, Detective Forde, and Detective Willis will probably be dead in a few days anyway. So, do we allow Arroyo and his people to finish the job, or do we stand up and fight?"

Dennis closed his eyes and rubbed his head with both hands for a few moments. An occasional sigh blurted out, more in frustration than exasperation.

Harlan could see the internal struggle.

"Who do you want me to investigate first?" Dennis said. His eyes were still closed.

"I'd follow the photographs, if it were me. They are the only link between Arroyo and Detective Willis."

Dennis dropped his hands to the table. "So, you want me to investigate my boss, and then the director of Homeland?"

Harlan smiled. "The way I look at it, the last thing we need are more corrupt tyrants. And if your boss and his boss are as squeaky clean as you think and hope, then I'm sure they'd love to know if they are being used or their systems are being hacked for information."

"Okay. I'll look into it."

"And you can be discreet. I have faith in you, Dennis. Make it part of your mandate to check into everybody's lives. Like John said, spin the random generator to your advantage, if necessary."

"If the water gets hot, Harley, you're gonna have to come to my aid."

"Dennis, if I have to, I'll ride into the Capitol Rotunda on my hog, full guns a-blazin'." Harlan straightened his back with a broad smile. "I ain't skeered. I've been doin' this job a long time. I know how to work the press and which buttons to push, just like they do."

Dennis peered at his friend. "Let's hope it doesn't come to that."

CHAPTER 34

THE SITUATION ROOM
  West Wing
  White House

President Gilmore entered the Situation Room with a little more urgency than in previous meetings. It caught several of the ranking officials sitting around the table off guard, and they scrambled to their feet as he passed them to get to the other side of the room.

"You may be seated," the president said. "We have a problem... well, actually two problems. However, one of them can wait.

"I just got off the phone a few minutes ago with Supervisory Special Agent-in-Charge Julee Scarfano from our FBI field office in Jacksonville. She was contacted by SSA Blake Meyer. He informed her another device—similar to the one used in Las Vegas at the Bahama Bay Hotel and Casino—has been activated somewhere close to, if not directly at, the Union Market here in D.C."

"What?" General Hoskins said. "When?"

"They believe it was activated around 12:15 p.m., local time. According to Agent Meyer, he has reason to believe the device in Las Vegas was activated a little less than *five* hours before the first victim fell ill, which means that if this most recent device contains the same contagion and was rigged to release its contagion in the same manner, then based on when his intel says the device at Union Market was activated, we have less than four hours before the first victims will display symptoms."

"Mr. President," Director Randall Lange of the NSA said, "I can state almost unequivocally—and I will check my sources again, but there has been no chatter on this at all. Trust me, if there had been, I would have been notified, then you would have been notified."

"Director Lange, thank you for the nice segue to the rest of the information Agent Meyer delivered to Agent Scarfano. They found this evidence on a cell phone belonging to a Chinese businessman named Ju-Long Zou. Apparently, this man had these devices rigged with cell phones or some such device. We are assuming all he has to do is pull up the phone number of any device and dial it, activating the device to release the contagion." The president looked each member in the eye. "Ladies and gentlemen, according to intel SAC Scarfano shared with Director Jameson, they found over fifty phone numbers on his cell phone with the same designation: Z-hyphen-detonator-colon, and then the name of the location, including one for Las Vegas and one for Union Market. It appears each detonator is tied to the same cities used to plant those six hundred families we currently have in custody."

"The top one hundred most-populated cities?" a joint chief said. "That list?"

"Yes."

"Mr. President," General Hoskins said, "how reliable is this intel provided to us by Agent Meyer? And do we know the name of his source?"

"General, if there is one thing I have learned throughout this entire ordeal, if Agent Meyer says something, you had better believe it. Or at least listen to it. He's been right about everything so far. Had we listened to him at the beginning, we might have been able to stop these people from getting this far."

"It does makes sense," another joint chief said. "These Hands of Allah fools said they had multiple devices. In the recording they sent us, they stated how they were going to release the first one at noon today, if we hadn't met all their demands. This last one *was* around noon local time."

"But not the first one, Admiral," Congressman Bill Waldegon said. "Based on that recorded message, the one in Las Vegas was released early. They broke their end of the bargain. Instead, they have committed an act of terrorism that can only be answered with a declaration of war."

Several of the members around the table laughed.

"A declaration of war, Mr. Waldegon?" General Hoskins said, "And who exactly would you like us to strike first? The Saudis? The Iranians? The Russians? The Chinese—"

"Gentlemen, please," President Gilmore said. "Regardless of when or who or how many, we don't have time for this. We need a response plan for Union Market. And we need it now."

"How much information do you want to release?" Ben Jenkins said. "I mean, we don't have official confirmation one was actually set off at Union Market or not."

"And how much area do you want to quarantine around Union Market?" FBI Director Sam Jameson said. "I think Mr. Jenkins brings up a good point. If we center on Union Market, lock down a five-block area around the building, and then find out it was released in the 'Union Market area' and our quarantine zone isn't big enough, we will have wasted valuable time and assets."

"I believe this Zou and whoever else is working with him are being specific for a reason. The *location* of their targets has as much to do with their release as anything else. For example," Gilmore said, glancing at his notes, "one of the detonator's names on Zou's phone is 'Washington, D.C. – T-Building.' Care to guess what building that may be?"

"The Treasury Building," General Hoskins said.

"So, they wish to strike us right in our monetary gut, figuratively speaking," another joint chief said.

The president glanced at his notes again. "Another one was Washington, D.C. – Capitol Hill."

"Dear God," another joint chief blurted out.

The president dropped his notes on the table. "So, ladies and gentlemen, what is our plan for Union Market?"

"The biggest issue I see, Mr. President," Director Jameson said, "is if it has been about an hour since this device has been released, then by now, people exposed to it will have surely gone home, gone shopping, gone to the airport, taken flights out of the city, ridden on buses and in taxis...Sir, simply put, it's too late to contain the spread of this one like we were able to do in Las Vegas. The timing of the release and the location is entirely different."

"He's right," an admiral chief said. "The window for containment has passed, sir. Now, we must lock down Union Market to see if indeed Agent Meyer's intel is correct. If we find the device, and it has been detonated, then we have to inform the public of what has happened and instruct anyone who was at the Union Market between noon and the time of the lockdown, to report to the nearest hospital immediately. Sir, we already know what contagion they are using, if it's the same one as in Las Vegas. At least we have a leg up there. Medical personnel can create quarantined wings in the hospital and start the intravenous antibiotic injections immediately."

"This sounds like a good time to bring in Doctor Andrew

Turner, head of the CDC, to join us via video. I've asked the good doctor to be here so we have an expert on our panel with intricate knowledge of these things." The president turned to the flat screen mounted on the wall. "Doctor Turner, what's the latest news on Las Vegas?"

"We actually have some good news. As most of you probably already know, we lost our first few victims in Las Vegas because we simply didn't have enough time to figure out what we were dealing with and then start treating patients accordingly. Simply put, the initial antibiotics didn't have enough time to work. And that's how this particular strain was designed, by the way. It attacks through acceleration. The people who militarized this version of bubonic plague were hoping it would spread and infect people so quickly, by the time we identified the illness, it would be too late for those first victims. Then, even if we did administer appropriate antibiotics to combat it, it would spread too quickly to allow enough time for the drugs to work, thus making the disease extremely lethal.

"However, we have ten patients right now, I am told, who were given streptomycin intravenously in the highest doses we can administer at the very beginning of the patient showing signs of infection. They are starting to show signs of improvement. The disease is not progressing in these patients. Therefore, as we continue to administer more of the drug into their system, our hope is we'll get the upper hand and eventually cure the patient."

"But I thought we were told this contagion had no known cure?" Congressman Waldegon said.

"That was the intel Agent Meyer provided," President Gilmore said. "However, let me remind everyone. He stated the particular strain you are referring to was to be administered via air fresheners, the kind that plug into electrical outlets or are battery-powered. These detonators are something different, so maybe they used a different contagion in these."

"If I may, I believe the admiral's suggestion of how to handle Union Market," Doctor Turner said, "is sound. You need to lock down the market and the surrounding blocks. You find the device so we can test it to make sure it is the same thing as in Las Vegas. And while all of that is happening, you put out over the airwaves that if a person was at the Union Market between those times... noon to whenever it is locked down, have them report to the nearest hospital or urgent care center. We will contact the area hospitals and UCCs and coordinate with them proper response protocols and development of quarantine zones. And please, make sure you urge people to go, even if they are not feeling ill. Timeliness with this contagion is key. If it gets too far along, we are finding the drugs are having a hard time preventing the progression of the bacterium."

"How many patients do you have now in Las Vegas?" General Hoskins said.

"We just topped five hundred, general. That's half of the people who were in the hotel at the time of the attack."

"Wow. Pretty potent stuff."

"All right, everyone," the president said, "Let me know if you need anything from me. Otherwise, let's coordinate with each other and get Union Market locked down and a message crafted for immediate release. I had a press conference scheduled to address the situation in Las Vegas. We'll address this situation as well."

"Sir," Director Jameson said, as if looking over a pair of glasses. "Were you going to mention the other issue?"

"Oh, yes, yes, I forgot," the president said. "Before everyone leaves, there is one more thing which may factor into one or more of your investigations. You may have noticed the absence of Congresswoman Merina Parker at this meeting, and you may already know why. However, in case you have not heard yet, she has been arrested. Apparently, her phone number was somehow tied to the release of the contagion in Las Vegas. Now with the new intel Agent Meyer has provided about Ju-Long Zou and his cell phone, it definitely muddies the water as to her connection to Zou, if there is one. Director Jameson and his department are investigating this case as we speak, so for now, as we would hope would be the case for any of us, she is innocent until proven guilty. Until this mess sorts itself out, however, she obviously will not be joining us here nor have any part of the decision-making process of this body. And I would appreciate it if you didn't share this information about her to anyone not directly tied to her investigation. The news networks know about it now, thanks to her lawyer, so we'll get enough interference and conflicting reports from them. No need to add any tidbits to their myriad stories. Agreed?"

Several members nodded. A couple verbalized their understanding.

"Very well. Let's get started then."

CHAPTER 35

Gerard Ryker and John Sandburg escorted Joseph Ricatelli into the empty interrogation room, sat him down in a chair, and cuffed him to the table. Ironically, it was the same room Sergei Botinkin had occupied just a couple of days ago. Ryker remembered being stationed outside the room, acting as one of the gatekeepers while Agent Meyer was inside, getting Botinkin to sing.

That seems so long ago now...

"Hey, what's with the cuffs in here?" Ricatelli said. "It ain't like I'm gonna escape from an FBI joint."

"Well, Mr. Ricatelli, or may we call you Joseph? Or would you prefer Norman?" Ryker said.

"I prefer Joe."

"You see, Joe, you tried to run from us at the condominium complex. You even tried to run *over* my partner here," Ryker said, thumbing at Sandburg.

Joe lifted his hands in supplication until the cuffs jerked them back down. "I wasn't trying to hit him. He jumped out in front of my car."

"Well, that's not how we saw it."

"I ain't never hurt nobody."

"Maybe not directly," Ryker said, walking toward the door. "But as an accomplice, well, now, that's another story entirely. But, I'm getting ahead of myself. We'll be right back, Joe. Would you like anything to drink? Water? A cup of 'Joe'?"

"No."

"All right then. We'll be right back."

* * *

Ryker and Sandburg stepped out into the hallway and faced each other.

"I'll call Julee, fill her in, and see if she wants to be here for the interrogation," Ryker said. "Why don't you go get all the info we have on this slime ball as well as an update on the people injured in the InterHealth bombing. Then, we'll reconvene here."

"You got it," Sandburg said. "Coffee? I'm gonna grab some."

"Yes, please."

Sandburg gave him a thumbs-up and walked away.

Ryker plucked his cell phone from his pocket and dialed.

"Agent Ryker? Everything okay?" Julee Scarfano said.

"Uh, yeah. I was just calling to let you know we have Joseph Ricatelli in custody. We're back at the office," Ryker said, squinting a little. "Are you on your way back? Sounds like you're either on a helicopter or you borrowed some biker's tricked-out Harley-Davidson."

Julee laughed. "We're on our way back...*in* a chopper...not on one. Did Ricatelli give you guys any trouble?"

"Besides trying to evade us and attempting to run over Sandburg with his Beamer, Nah."

"Are you serious?"

"As a heart attack."

"Then, go ahead and question him. Nail him to the wall, Ryker. And if you run across anything earth-shattering, let me know. Otherwise, I'll see you when we get there and get up to speed then."

"You got it."

"Oh, and one more thing. Just to let you know, another device has been released. This one was in Washington, D.C. at the Union Market, apparently. You'll probably hear more about it soon, but I wanted to let you know in case anything from your interrogation of Ricatelli ties in."

"Not good news, but thanks for letting me know. Is it okay to let Sandburg know?"

"Of course. There will probably be a memo coming out from the director's office in the not-so-distant future."

"All right. Stay safe, and we'll see you when you return."

"Oh, and one more thing. Make sure Ricatelli knows we have Reese Thomas in custody. Use that to your advantage."

"Don't worry. We plan on it."

* * *

Fifteen minutes later, Ryker and Sandburg reentered the interrogation room with coffee in their hands. Ryker held a brown folder in his other hand. They both sat down across from Joe, who looked bedraggled and sweaty, as if the realization of why he was there was closing in on him like a rabbit in the snow watching a pack of Timberwolves inch closer and closer.

Problem was, Joe couldn't "rabbit" now, and Ryker used Ricatelli's anticipation of impending doom to his advantage as he took a sip from his coffee and then set it down in front of him.

"Joe, I'm gonna give it to you straight. In the long run, it'll save us a bunch of time, which is good, actually, because we don't have a lot of it these days." He opened the file. "Are you aware of what happened at the InterHealth Medical Center a few hours ago?"

Joe inhaled but held it. "No. Should I?"

"There was a bomb planted in one of the rooms. It exploded and nearly killed three FBI agents. It took out the power to half the hospital, and a bunch of patients who were in no condition to be moved had to be transported to other facilities. It's a real mess over there."

"What's that got to do with me?"

"In conjunction with the bombing—which, by the way, is being considered an act of terrorism—we caught a young man who we have now linked to it. His name is Reese Thomas."

Ryker paused and watched the color of Joe's face change from bright red to pale tan.

Joe stared at Agent Ryker for a couple of awkward seconds before looking down at the table.

"I take it you know him?"

Joe puckered his lips and extended the bottom one a little further. "We've met a couple of times. Don't really know him, though. We're just, uh,...what do you call them kind of relationships?"

"Acquaintances?" Sandburg said.

"Yeah," Joe said, pointing at Agent Sandburg. "One of those."

"Interesting," Ryker said, pulling out a sheet of paper from the folder. "According to the phone records we have from Mr. Thomas, he's called you numerous times over the last few years. Last couple of weeks, actually. Even within the last couple of days. And according to Mr. Thomas's bank records, which I have right here," he said, pulling out another sheet of paper, "as well as Mr.

Thomas's own witness statement, there were some sizable payments received a few years ago from you...payments he used to pay off his student loan and purchase a really nice sports car. When we asked him why you would be so generous, he said he worked for you on a kind of freelance basis. Odd jobs, like making signs for law-abiding protests, picking up packages, delivering said packages, that sort of thing."

Joe nodded. "Oh, yeah, I had forgotten about that. It's true. He was doing all sorts of odd little jobs for me. It really freed me up. It was worth it. Besides, I was helping out a fellow human being, you know? It felt good."

Ryker squinted at Joe like he'd just spoken some alien language. "Over a hundred dollars a sign is a lot of scratch, Joe. And delivering a package for five hundred dollars a pop? Must have been some package. Fed-Ex or UPS would have been a lot cheaper, I bet."

Joe shrugged with a smile. "What can I say? I'm a softie."

"And how much did you pay Guy Chevalier?"

"Who?"

"The plumber who had been in contact with Reese Thomas, almost right up to the moment he entered the medical center, carrying the bomb materials with him. Thomas said all that had been arranged by someone else." Ryker smiled.

"Who?"

Ryker chuckled. "You, Joe." He pulled out another sheet of paper from the folder. "Reese Thomas said in his formal statement, and I quote, 'Joe was some kind of community organizer and knew how to get people together to make things happen.' End quote. When he was asked what he meant exactly, he said, and I quote, 'Joe has ties to the mob, among other people. They always supply him with work, and when Joe gets in a pinch, they find a way to get him out of it.' End quote." Ryker eased the sheet of paper back into the folder. "Joe, I'd say his feelings about you are *not* reciprocal."

"Listen, I don't know what he's talkin' about. I ain't no mobster. And I ain't had no dealings with a plumber."

"Coulda fooled us, Joe." Ryker pulled out another sheet of paper from the folder. "You've been arrested three times for assault and battery. In each case, the victim had at least one body part broken...according to the reports, seems you fancy the fingers, but are not exclusively tied to digits," Ryker said, flipping a picture around for Joe to see, and then another. "And in each case, Joe, the person with the broken body parts owed money of a sizeable amount, according to the court documents. But strangely, before each case went to trial, the charges got dropped." Ryker peered at Joe. "How does that happen, Joe?"

"Look, do I know people? Yes. Do they pay me well? Yes. When I get in a pinch, do they help me out? Yes. But I ain't no mobster. I don't kill nobody." Joe pointed at the photo. "I wasn't even the one who did those things." He repositioned himself in his seat. "Look, Reese Thomas was right. I get people together. And yes, I have set up other deals and hired people to do jobs...like Reese Thomas, but I have never set up any hits, never set up any bank robberies, nothin' like that. The stuff I set up is legitimate business. Get a package from Point A to Point B, hire some people for a protest, find people who don't want to be found, et cetera and so forth— which was what all the finger-breakin' business was about, by the way."

Ryker tapped the photo on the table. "These people were runnin' from the mob? Is that what you're tellin' us?"

"I don't know who they were runnin' from. I just make the calls, find out where they live, then escort the person payin' me the cash to the location...and if we don't find them, I gotta make more calls."

"What about your other calls? Like the ones between Reese and the plumber?"

"It's true—sometimes—I get calls for other things too. Somebody calls and asks if I know somebody who can do this and that. If I do, then I look into setting up the meet. What they decide to do once I set it up is on them. I don't ask too many questions, and I tell them I ain't wantin' too many answers. Just the particulars so I know what or who the client needs, you know?"

"The client," Ryker said with a big smile on his face. He turned and looked at his partner, pointing at Joe as he did. "The client. He sounds like a regular businessman, Agent Sandburg."

"Crooks 'R Us?" Sandburg said.

"Well, we know it ain't Trader Joe's." Ryker blurted out a fake belly laugh, and Sandburg joined him.

Joe Ricatelli smirked. "Very funny. You guys seem to be enjoying this."

Sandburg gave an emphatic nod. "We are. Helps cut down on the stress."

Ryker nodded, too, and continued the interrogation. "All kidding aside, if a person comes up to you and says, 'Hey, I need a guy who can sneak into a hospital and light it up with some bombs,' you say what?"

"'No can do.' That's what I say." Joe rubbed his wrists, readjusting the handcuffs. "I don't want that blowback on me, you know what I'm sayin'?"

"I do," Ryker said. "But then that makes me wonder why you were running from us. I mean, if you are a straight up businessman, why did you change your name? And why did you feel the need to have your new girlfriend lie for you and say you weren't home? And why did you try to flee once I left your parking lot?" Ryker shrugged his shoulders.

"She told me you were from the FBI, but you and I both know those credentials can be forged."

Ryker pinched his brow together and looked at his partner for a long second. "Why would you think my credentials aren't real?"

"Because the people who hired me...to put Reese Thomas in touch with someone who could build a bomb...they're after me. They want my head on a platter, so I'm told."

"But I thought you said you didn't know anything about any bombs, Joe?"

Joe cursed under his breath. "Okay, so I knew about the bombs. But I had no idea they were going to use them against youz guys. I never would have signed on, if I did."

"So, Joe...those who want your head on a platter...we need names."

"I don't know their names. They call me and give me specific information, so I know they are legit. Then they give me the job. I either accept it or decline it."

"And did one of those jobs have something to do with the InterHealth Medical Center?"

Joe shrugged. "They didn't say."

"Okay, so let's talk about your last call. How did it go down?"

"I get a call from my usual contact. Calls himself 'Mr. X,' like he's from some James Bond movie or somethin'. He tells me to contact Reese Thomas and put him in touch with a guy I know. A friend of a friend of a bomb maker."

"Does this bomb maker have a name?"

Joe nodded. "Rico Sandoval."

Ryker scribbled down the name. "Continue."

"He said all I had to do was call my guy and have him get in touch with Rico. My guy would give Rico Reese Thomas's phone number, they would arrange a meeting, and I would be done."

"And just like that, you made the call, even though you knew one of the men in this particular chain of calls builds bombs?"

"Bombs ain't all Rico does, so I had no idea of knowing exactly what they wanted Rico to do. All I had to do was make a call." Joe turned his palms up and sneered. "I thought it would be easy money, but look at me now."

"I can tell you didn't feel comfortable with this particular job, Joe, so why didn't you decline it?"

Joe repositioned himself in his seat again. "I tried to decline it because of Rico, but Mr. X said I didn't have a choice with this one. He said it was a time-sensitive job, and he didn't have time to find someone else. Offered to pay me double, if I got my part of the job done inside of thirty minutes."

Ryker leaned back in his chair. "Well, Joe, it would appear you delivered. A bomb did go off at the medical center, and Reese Thomas was involved in it. However, I'm still a little fuzzy as to why Mr. X would come after you. Especially since it looks like you delivered. I mean, they got their bomb on short notice, just like they wanted."

Joe cleared his throat. "But didn't you say those agents were alive?"

"They are, thankfully."

"Then, it's my guess things didn't go according to the plan. They obviously wanted those agents dead. And because they survived, it would seem Mr. X is holding me at least partially responsible."

Ryker turned to face Sandburg. "Which means they will be after Thomas too. And Guy Chevalier."

Sandburg stood. "I'll make the calls. Have Chevalier picked up."

"Who is after you, Joe? Do you have a name other than Mr. X?"

Joe shrugged and shook his head like their efforts were not going to help him. "Some Muslim group, I think. Probably a bogus name anyway."

"Indulge me."

Joe inhaled and blew the breath out in exasperation. "They

call themselves some mumbo-jumbo religious name…The Hands of—"

"Allah?"

Joe cocked his head almost sideways. "Yeah. How did you know?"

Ryker looked at Sandburg as he was about to open the door. "What makes you think The Hands of Allah are looking for you?"

"They accosted one of my contacts, asking where they could find me. That's why I got spooked when you showed up. I had no idea the FBI was looking for me too. I thought you were them. Then, when I call Mr. X back for more details, it goes to voicemail. I called eight times. Still ain't got a call back."

Sandburg and Ryker eyed each other again. Sandburg held up his phone. "Gonna make those calls now," he said as he exited the room.

Ryker pulled Joe's phone records from the folder. "What number did Mr. X use to call you?"

"I don't remember, but if I could have my phone, I could look it up. I know when he called."

Ryker pushed his chair out from the table, reached behind him, and grabbed a manila envelope holding Joe's personal effects. He reached inside, found the phone, and handed it to Joe. "Just pull up your most recent contacts and tell me which phone number it was."

"Sure." Joe entered the password and opened his call log. He scrolled down a few seconds and then stopped. "Here it is. Number at the top."

Ryker picked up the phone and turned it so he could read the screen.

773-555-4532.

"It was this number?"

"Yeah."

"And it was Mr. X on the other end every time?"

"Yeah."

"And what does he sound like?"

"His voice is always altered. Sounds like a teenage robot from a bad sci-fi movie."

"Has this Mr. X ever given you details about himself, like where he lives, or who he works for?"

"Nope."

"How long have you been 'doin' business' with Mr. X?"

Joe twisted up his face. "Goin' on...twelve years? Yeah, twelve. Will be thirteen in December."

"And how many times a year does he call you?"

"Depends. Some years, maybe four times a year. Some years, it's twice a month. But in each case, he's never steered me wrong, and he always had my back when things got sticky."

"Did this Mr. X ever threaten you? Say he was going to hurt you, if you didn't carry out a job?"

"He never came right out and said it, but it was always implied."

Ryker pulled out his phone and took a picture of the screen displayed on Joe's phone. He then powered down Joe's phone, stuck it back inside the envelope, and stood. "I'll be right back."

* * *

Agent Ryker walked outside the interrogation room and called Agent Scarfano.

"That was quick," Scarfano said.

"Yeah. We have a problem."

"What kind of problem?"

"Do you remember a phone number you shared with me and Sandburg a while back? Had a Chicago prefix? You told us Agent Meyer found it when he searched Sergei Botinkin's communications?"

"Yeah. I told you to keep an eye out for it....and call me if you ever ran across it..." Julee paused. "You ran across it?"

"We did."

"Ricatelli?"

"Yep." Ryker explained how a mysterious Mr. X calls Joe and gives him assignments.

"But we don't know anything about this Mr. X? Other than the phone number he used, and that it's a man?"

"Well, Joe has been assuming it's a man, but he admitted the voice is altered by some software. He said the person sounds like a robot. A teenage robot, specifically."

"So, it could be a woman for all we know."

"It's a possibility."

"I'll be back in Jacksonville in about thirty minutes. I'll need a list of every call to Ricatelli by that number."

"Already have it."

"Good. Then, go ahead and officially arrest Ricatelli and charge him with the same crimes as Reese Thomas. And when you find the plumber, Guy Chevalier, do the same to him. We're gonna round up every one of these clowns, and maybe they'll become just the bait we need to nail this Mr. X."

"Will do."

CHAPTER 36

President Walter Gilmore strode to the podium with a folder in his hand. He nodded and smiled at his press secretary, Jonas McCormick, for the brief introduction as they passed each other on the platform.

He turned and faced the crowded room as flashbulbs "popped" in a staccato-like manner. It seemed as if he'd gone through this same scenario at least a hundred times since taking over the office of the presidency. He wasn't counting, but he was sure some staff member had the stats tucked away somewhere. They had stats for everything these days.

Some of those hundred-plus pressers were easy. Some not so much. But for the monumental ones, the president thought, as he set his folder down, no amount of practice, no amount of preparedness, no amount of running the scenarios through your head, trying to anticipate each and every conceivable question which might be asked, equipped you, as the commander-in-chief, for what lay ahead.

"Thank you, everyone, for coming on such short notice," he said, scanning the room, trying to make eye contact with each individual in the midst of flashing bulbs and multiple cameras, large and small, aimed at him. "As many of you know, we have a situation in Las Vegas. Many of you have already reported on it, and if I may say, you've done a good job at reporting the facts as they have been revealed to you. Now, I would like to get everyone up to speed on the government's response.

"It has been confirmed. The incident in Las Vegas at the Bahama Bay Hotel and Casino was an act of terrorism. A group, calling themselves The Hands of Allah, is claiming responsibility. Our government agencies are already familiar with this group. They are a radical Jihadist group, similar to Al Qaeda. They have two arms or branches, if you will. One part of their organization is designed to be benevolent. They go into countries, much like the Peace Corps or other similar groups, and help build homes, dig wells, fund locals with small loans to start businesses, and otherwise attempt to help poor and impoverished areas of the world.

"However, the other branch of their organization is designed to carry out terrorist activity right under everyone's nose. Until a couple of days ago, we had suspicions The Hands of Allah was operating in this way, but we never had any hard evidence to prove it until we captured two of their operatives smuggling illegal aliens over the border for the purpose of carrying out a much larger planned attack than what has occurred in Las Vegas.

"It would seem our efforts at finding the people responsible have created some issues for this group and those working with them. We believe the attack in Las Vegas was a backup plan they had in place should their original plan fail or get delayed.

"We have received credible evidence that the device carrying the contagion was activated at approximately one o'clock in the morning, Las Vegas time.

"There were a little over a thousand people staying at the Bahama Bay Hotel and Casino when the contagion was released into the ventilation system. The first people to show signs did so about five hours later. Medical officials have determined we are dealing with an altered version of bubonic plague, designed to be a fast-acting contagion. The CDC and other health officials are on site, assessing and handling the situation as we speak.

"In regards to those who have been infected and subsequently treated by the CDC, we just received some encouraging news a few minutes ago. Some of the people who began showing signs of infection and were diagnosed early are responding well to the antibiotic treatments they are receiving. Right before this press conference began, I received word concerning one patient who is already seeing the infection decrease, and the patient's vital signs are trending in the right direction. So, we can hope and pray this will be the trend among all the remaining patients and those who come down with it.

"I am sorry to report, however, there have been some fatalities in Las Vegas. So far, ten of the very first victims who showed signs have passed away from the contagion. We believe it was due to the nature of how this contagion was engineered. We just didn't know what we were dealing with at the beginning of this attack. By the time the disease was identified, and proper medical treatment was administered, it was too late. I have already reached out to the next of kin and expressed our heartfelt condolences."

The president paused, and several hands went up, and numerous reporters blurted out questions. He held his hands up shoulder high. "Please, I'm not finished yet, and I think you're going to want to hear this next bit of information I am about to relay." He waited for the room to get quiet. "Thank you. Now that we know what we are dealing with, we feel confident we can beat this attack with minimal casualties. Unfortunately, The Hands of Allah and those helping them were diligent in their planning. We just received word approximately an hour ago about more of these devices, similar to the one activated in Las Vegas, scattered around the United States. We also have received intel as to their locations. We believe these locations were chosen to be high profile areas for the purpose of maximizing their impact and effect. The good news is we know where these devices are, and we are in the process of seizing these devices and disarming them.

"However," the president said with a frown, "we have been told, and are in the process of confirming it as we speak, that another device, like the one in Las Vegas, has been activated by these Hands of Allah operatives. The location of this second device was said to be at the Union Market here in Washington, D.C. Therefore, we are asking that anyone who has been at the Union Market today from 11:30 this morning, Eastern Time, until right up to this very moment, to please report to the nearest local hospital or urgent care center to be tested immediately. This contagion does not take long to begin showing symptoms, so getting to a hospital or urgent care facility as soon as possible is crucial to stopping the spread. We have already notified all area medical facilities to make them aware of what they will be dealing with should someone become infected. They are all designating quarantine areas in their facilities, and if they do not have the capacity to have a quarantine zone, then the facility will divert you to the nearest quarantine zone.

"We are also asking those who were in the Union Market area, within a two-block radius, between the times of 11:30 this morning, Eastern Time, and now, to report to a local hospital or urgent care center as well.

"We are strongly urging anyone who was at the Union Market and has since boarded a plane or a boat that has left the Washington, D.C. area *or* the United States to report themselves to the pilot of the plane or the captain of the ship so they can be quarantined and proper protocols can be put into place. And yes, we have notified the airlines and cruise lines and made them aware as well.

"If you were at Union Market during those designated times and have since traveled home, visited a friend, been to the super market, or whatever, you not only need to report to a local hospital or urgent care center, you also need to notify those family members and friends so they, too, can protect themselves and get tested. And if you went to another public place, then let the medical officials know so they can notify necessary personnel."

The president paused and lifted his hands. "This is not a time to panic. I repeat, this is not a time to panic. It is a time for level heads to be diligent and respond properly. Signs at the Las Vegas site are showing we have the means to combat these attacks, but we must be smart. We must be calm. We must be diligent and responsible for our own actions.

"The sooner a patient is identified, the better. If you start to show signs of a fever, light-headedness, a rash, or have swelling or lumps in the armpit or groin areas, you need to report to the hospital immediately. We also strongly urge you to wear a mask or some covering over your mouth and nose as this contagion can become airborne once a patient becomes infected, especially if the patient starts coughing uncontrollably. And if you feel traveling to a healthcare facility is not something you *can* do our *should* do, then you can call the local number below on your screen, if you live in the Washington D.C. area, and it will direct you to a special hotline where emergency operators are set up to take calls and direct first responders to your home.

"Since this contagion starts to show signs in a matter of just four to five hours, we cannot stress enough the urgency of having people who were physically at the Union Market during the times listed on the screen to report to the hospital or an urgent care center and not wait until signs become apparent. These facilities have designated areas now to handle the volume of patients. They also have transports ready, should one of them get too busy and need patients taken to another facility."

The president paused and closed his folder. "Okay, I believe we are ready for questions."

A cacophony of inquiries slammed the president's ears. He listened and sorted out what amounted to three questions being asked in various ways.

He lifted his hands again. "By hearing your questions, it seems that if I answer about two or three of them, I'll take care of the majority of you all at once. For those wondering about the locations of the other devices, let me say this: We know where they are, but I am not going to list them for you at this time. For some, we know specifically where they are and have military and health officials in route as we speak to locate and destroy these devices. In those cases, we know exactly which building it is, and it's a matter of evacuating that building and locking it down until the device is found and eradicated. And because the one in Las Vegas was found in the ventilation system—which makes sense if you are trying to impact as many people as possible—then we know where to start looking.

"The others on the list are a little more general in location, meaning we know it's in a specific city, but it's an area bigger than one building. Therefore, we are in the process of notifying the people who control those areas so a search can commence. We are not going to rest until we find all of these devices and destroy them.

"The second question I heard many of you ask was, are we going to raise the threat level? It is our belief that raising the threat level may cause undue panic at this time. We feel we are gaining the upper hand in this situation. So long as we can continue to do so, then we will not raise it. However, we have benchmarks in place. If we start to cross those benchmarks, then the level will be raised to prevent certain things, like air travel, border crossings, et cetera, in an effort to contain this contagion and defeat it.

"Also, some of you were asking about shutting down the Washington, D.C. area to prevent the spread. After talking with my cabinet, CDC officials, and others, such actions were believed to be ill-advised. Simply put, we are not sure even if a device was released at the Union Market or not. It could be a hoax to cause widespread hysteria, so we are alerting people to the possibility. If our hospitals and urgent care centers start to get overrun, then enacting some form of martial law until we can get things under control may be an option. However, for right this moment, everyone agreed such actions would be unwarranted and cause more harm than good."

The reporters jumped on the pause and talked over one another like a bunch of yapping Chihuahuas.

The president pointed at one of the familiar reporters from a prominent cable news network, cupping his ear with his other hand at the same time. "Yes, Frank, what's your question?"

"Thank you, Mr. President. You stated a few minutes ago that two of these operatives from this group called The Hands of Allah were caught smuggling illegal aliens into the United States. My sources tell me the accident you referenced happened in Texas, and the border crossing took place somewhere in New Mexico. Apparently, the family being smuggled inside the country was on their way to Orlando, Florida—"

"I haven't heard a question yet, Frank," the president said.

"My sources are also telling me this family being smuggled was part of a larger operation wherein over six hundred families had already been smuggled into America to be used as cannon fodder, if you will, to launch a more massive attack on America. Can you confirm for us, Mr. President, that this information is true, and if so, does it alter your stance in illegal immigration?"

The president stood and smiled at the reporter. "Frank, I

cannot confirm or deny your sources' information at this time. I'm sure I'll be able to elaborate on it at some later date. However, as for my stance on illegal immigration, nothing has changed. Just because a group of people have found a loophole to exploit doesn't warrant an entire shutdown of our country nor does it warrant rewriting immigration law. And can I say, unequivocally, in light of what we are currently facing, my views on this subject, or the views of any member of my cabinet, for that matter, don't really matter right now. All that matters is that we catch those responsible for these attacks. We can discuss policy later. And as a matter of fact, I told them this very thing in a meeting a day or so ago when this topic came up. If you don't believe me, ask them."

The president looked out across the raucous group and saw a newspaper reporter who was not blurting out questions, trying to monopolize his time. Instead, she had her hand up and made eye contact with him. He didn't recognize the woman, which was refreshing, and pointed at her. "Yes...the lady in the green dress."

"Yes, Mr. President. Thank you for taking my question. Janice Watterston, the Chicago Advocate. My question is a nice segue, actually. As we know and it has been reported, Congresswoman Merina Parker has been arrested in conjunction with this terrorist attack in Las Vegas. Can you confirm for us the validity of this claim? And if so, what role did she play, if any, in this incident?"

The president stared at the reporter, wondering if she was a personal friend, perhaps, of Merina Parker. "I cannot confirm or deny the validity of your information at this time. You would have to contact her lawyer."

"So, Mr. President," Janice Watterston said, "it is true she is still being detained? And if so, is she considered a flight risk?"

"Again, you will have to contact her lawyer, who I understand, has already held a press conference on the matter."

The president peeled his eyes away from the reporter and looked down at the front row. "Next question."

CHAPTER 37

LAW OFFICES OF TEMPLETON DRAKE & Associates
  1199 G St. NW, Washington, D.C.

A large, spacious office with floor to ceiling windows overlooking G Street, genuine hardwood floors, a teakwood wainscot with marble-colored wallpaper above, and a mammoth, twelve-foot-long cherry desk—to accent the space—created the home away from home for Congresswoman Merina Parker's personal and professional lawyer, Templeton Drake. He stood off center of the room, near the edge of a Persian rug, given to him as a gift by a former CEO of a Maryland-based company, whose behind Templeton had saved many years ago from certain prison time.

With a remote in his right hand and his left hand in his pants pocket, he watched President Gilmore's press conference with interest on the flat screen television hanging on the wall.

He listened as the president explained the tragedy in Las Vegas concerning the Bahama Bay Hotel and Casino. It was ironic, he thought, as he watched. He and his wife had just been at that very hotel the week after Christmas. A gift from all the associates in his law firm. A "thank you" for giving them such wonderful jobs, they said.

And a kiss of my posterior, if you ask me.

Trying to butter me up for larger bonuses...

He listened as the president announced how they had learned in which cities the other devices were, and how they were working in real time to pinpoint the exact location of each and every one of the devices still out there.

The president appeared haggard to Templeton. Tired beyond the physical variety.

I sure wouldn't want his job.

Templeton's ears perked when President Gilmore stated that a second device had been activated. His heart sank when he learned of the location. He knew many people who ate and shopped and met there on a regular basis. And it wasn't that far from his office.

A few miles as the crow flies...

He walked over to pick up his cell phone from his desk. He thought he had better contact his wife and let her know, just in case she hadn't heard the news.

He opened his phone, found her number, and dialed just as President Gilmore began taking questions from one of the reporters.

Eh, Frank Spotchnik...or Sputnik...or whatever his name is...such a liberal putz—

"Hi, darling. Are you still at the office?" his wife said.

"Afraid so."

"What did Merina want when she called this morning?"

"It's a long story. I'll fill you in when I get home. The reason why I called was to tell you to turn on the news. Apparently, there has been an attack at or near Union Market today. You haven't gone out today, have you?"

"No, thank goodness. That's terrible news. Do they have any idea what happened?"

"According to the president, it's a similar attack to the one in Las Vegas."

"Oh, my. Then, sweetheart, you need to get home before they lock the city down and prevent you from doing so."

"I'll be leaving in a few minutes," he said. "Hey, can you call the kids and let them know? I'd hate it if they went out for lunch or dinner in that area and didn't know."

"Sure. What are we to do if we get infected?"

Templeton tried to pay attention to his wife but couldn't help but catch some of the words of the press conference. "He...uh, he said, uh—"

"Drake, stop doing what you're doing and focus," his wife said.

"Sorry. Let me pause this so I can focus on it in a minute." He pressed the button, stopping the president mid-sentence. "Okay, uh, he said that if anyone was in the Union Market area around lunchtime, they needed to seek medical attention immediately and tell the doctors and nurses they were in the area allegedly infected so the medical staff can test them and go from there."

"Sounds serious."

"It is. Hey, I hate to run, but I have a couple of things to wrap up here, then I must stop and see Merina before I come home."

"Please hurry, honey."

"I will. I'll call you after my visit with her. Love you."

"Love you too."

Templeton hung up and rewound the press conference back to the section where the president started taking questions. He pressed play and listened to Frank what's-his-name ask his usual "gotcha" questions and the president's subsequent responses.

He then turned up the volume a little when Gilmore pointed to the woman in the green dress.

"Yes, Mr. President. Thank you for taking my question. Janice Watterston, the Chicago Advocate. My question is a nice segue, actually. As we know and it has been reported, Congresswoman Merina Parker has been arrested in conjunction with this terrorist attack in Las Vegas. Can you confirm for us the validity of this claim? And if so, what role did she play, if any, in this incident?"

Templeton paused the video. "The president said the attack in Las Vegas took place around one o'clock in the morning, Vegas time," he said out loud. "That would've been around four o'clock here...Merina said she was arrested around six...six-twenty, somewhere around then...And he said earlier the first victims didn't start showing signs of infection until about five hours after the contagion was released."

He walked over to his desk, grabbed a notepad and pen, and quickly jotted down his thoughts. "And Merina was arrested about what? Six hours before the president received this information about the devices?" He scribbled more notes and questions before standing erect. He turned back to the television and stared at President Gilmore, frozen in time. "She was arrested before they had victims." Drake jotted down more notes and smiled to himself. "Yet, it was the report of victims which alerted authorities there was a problem in Las Vegas." He scribbled more notes. "It would appear someone jumped the gun, Mr. President. Someone issued the warrant to arrest Merina a little too soon." He wrote down two more questions: Which judge granted the warrant to arrest Merina? And who requested it?"

He tossed his pen on the pad of paper and pressed play.

He watched as the president basically dodged Janice Watterston's questions and said to make contact with "her lawyer," if they wanted any answers.

The classic Potomac Two-Step...

He shut the TV off and gathered his things.

I need to speak with the judge who issued the warrant...

The charges against Merina need to be dismissed based on this new information...

And I need to get moving so I can get home...

He smiled at the thought.

Happy wife, happy life, as they say.

CHAPTER 38

MARFA REGIONAL MEDICAL Center
Marfa, TX

Dennis Morrison tapped away at his computer, attempting to find answers to the questions his gut didn't want to ask.

Detective Forde had exited the room to go find some coffee for the three of them, and Captain Harlan sat quietly, checking his email on his phone.

"This doesn't make any sense," Dennis Morrison said, breaking the silence and leaning away from his computer screen with a puzzled expression. "I was just looking at this two weeks ago."

Captain Harlan tapped the screen on his phone one last time and set it down on the table. "Looking at what?"

"This file logs every person in DHS's system. It tracks their movements within the building. Records every time they swipe their key card."

"Every DHS office?"

"Yes."

"Including Washington?"

"Yes."

"And how many employees is that?"

"Last time I checked, it was 230,000."

Harlan's jaw dropped. "You have 230,000 people...in DHS alone,...not to mention the FBI, CIA, NSA and the rest of the alphabet society, and we still can't get the job done right." He rolled his eyes. "Too many cooks in the kitchen, if you ask me."

"What does that make me?" Dennis said.

"A bottle washer, Dennis. An expensive, expendable bottle washer."

"Thanks a lot."

Harlan laughed and patted Dennis on the shoulder. "Hey, at least you're on the inside. I just sweep up the trash in the parking lot."

They both allowed a strained chuckle to escape when Detective Forde opened the door.

"Did I miss something?" Forde asked as he handed the cups to his friends.

"I'm not sure," Harlan said. "Dennis was noticing some kind of irregularity, but he hasn't divulged the issue yet."

"And you both find it funny?"

"No. We were laughing at something else." Dennis clicked on a couple of other logs. "See, here it is again. Two weeks ago, I could see these logs. These particular ones, specifically. Now, today, I can't."

"Well," Harlan said, "it would appear someone doesn't want people like you snooping into their business. Which makes me believe your beloved Washington office is more corrupt than you thought."

"In light of everything that's happening," Detective Forde said, "maybe they're just taking extra precautions. Maybe they've had trouble with hackers during this whole contagion crisis I keep hearing about every time I walk past a TV in this place."

Dennis gave Forde's words some thought. "We already have firewalls set up to prevent outside entities from hacking in. This is different. It's like there is a firewall inside the firewalls. Designed to keep people who work for DHS out. Every employee with my clearance level or higher should have access to this log. And there aren't very many who are higher up the food chain than this expendable bottle washer, by the way, Harley." He paused and stared at his computer screen. "I mean, it's not like people can be very clandestine in these buildings, even if they were having an affair and were just looking for a safe place to...you know. It would be difficult to do something 'clandestine' without people like me knowing who was in what room at what time. Then, all I'd have to do is match the log to the security camera feeds in the hallways, and the rest would be easy to assume."

Captain Harlan slowly wheeled his chair in Dennis's direction. "Maybe they aren't trying to keep you from seeing who was *inside* the building and where. Maybe they are trying to keep you from seeing who *entered* or who *left* the building and when."

"But why? People come and go all the time."

"Yeah, but if they entered the building and were not supposed to be there..."

"Then, they wouldn't have a key card, so this log would not track them anyway. Besides, getting inside undetected would be next to impossible. They would have to enter as a guest with an employee who did have a card."

"So, through the process of elimination," Forde said, "whoever had this additional firewall set up obviously doesn't want you to know when they either entered or left the building."

"This firewall does make it harder to track. And even if they did leave, unless we knew it ahead of time and could follow them, their exit would look normal."

Harlan eyed Dennis with a look he used to get from his father when he was trying to teach his son something without spelling it out.

Forde turned his palms up. "The security cameras wouldn't catch anything suspicious then?"

Harlan lifted an eyebrow. "Unless they left with someone or something they shouldn't have."

"But, Harley,...everyone in the building would have a key card..."

"That's your assumption. When was this new firewall put in place?"

"Sometime between now and when I accessed this log two weeks ago."

"So, Dennis, you've had up to two weeks of people coming and going from DHS buildings, including HQ in Washington, and nobody has been able to access this log to see when they came and went?" Harlan held his hands out as if the answer should be obvious. "That's a great deal of unexamined foot traffic, wouldn't you say? And you would think DHS would want those movements documented even more now, not suppressed, in light of everything that's going on right now in Las Vegas, and allegedly now, at the Union Market in D.C."

"He's right," Forde said. "The longer investigations go on, the larger the suspect pool grows until you get more specific clues or information which helps to narrow down the field. So, in other words, depending on the stages of DHS's current investigations, their suspect pool is either widening—meaning they would want eyes on every door twenty-four-seven to gather more intel, or they have already narrowed down the suspect pool considerably— meaning setting up a firewall now would have only one purpose."

Dennis squinted just a little as he contemplated their words. "So, you're telling me this new firewall is part of a cover up?"

"We're just saying it's a real possibility, Dennis," Harlan said.

"Why would they throw up such a roadblock at people like you—who work for Homeland, no less!—without giving you the access codes to get around it?"

"Or, at least, send you a memo, informing you of it, explaining why it's there?" Forde said.

Dennis scratched his head. "This isn't good, guys."

Just then, Dennis's cell phone rang.

He picked it up and scrunched his brow. With a quick glance at Harlan and Forde, he swiped the red icon and allowed it to go to voicemail. "I don't answer restricted numbers."

Harlan shook his head. "Neither do I. If it's important enough, they'll leave a message."

Dennis's phone rang again. Same number.

"They're persistent," Harlan said.

"Yeah." Dennis swiped the red icon again.

Seconds later, the phone rang a third time.

Dennis held it in his hand and stared at it.

"Maybe you should answer it," Harlan said. "Put it on speaker."

Dennis nodded and did so. "Hello?"

"My name is John Mitchell. I am a federal agent for the FBI. I work out of the Jacksonville field office. Your phone number was given to me by a trusted colleague. He is the field agent who is in charge of the investigation into the recent terrorist attacks. Is this Dennis Morrison?"

"It is."

"Are you on a secure line?"

"I am, but I have you on speakerphone. I am here with the sheriff of Wichita County, Texas, and one of his detectives."

Dennis could hear some tapping in the background. He leaned forward, placed his arms on the table, and turned his head slightly.

"Is the sheriff's name Captain Theodore Harlan?"

"Yes."

"And the detective is John Forde?"

"Yes...How did you know this?"

"We have been monitoring your situation. We understand Forde's partner was injured and hospitalized, is this correct?"

"Yes."

"And according to recent police reports just filed, he was attacked. Is this also correct?"

"Okay, now this is getting a little spooky."

"Mr. Morrison, do you know a man by the name of Blake Meyer?"

Suddenly, Dennis' eyes widened, and he lifted his chin as his mouth fell agape. "I do. Is he involved in this investigation?"

"He was the person who told me to contact you. He said you were a straight shooter and could be trusted."

"Just know, Agent Mitchell, that I'd trust Agent Meyer with my life. But I thought he retired?"

"He was planning to soon. However, it would seem the events of the last few days has postponed those plans."

"I'm sure they have."

"Can you trust Captain Harlan and Detective Forde as much as you do Agent Meyer?"

"Yes." Dennis faced the other two men. "Absolutely."

"The information we are about to discuss cannot be heard by anyone else, so I need you to make sure the room is secure."

"We're at the hospital, Agent Mitchell. We are in a conference room. Door is closed. Windows have the blinds pulled, but we have no way of knowing if it is completely secure or not."

"Then, may I suggest you step outside and get into one of your vehicles?"

"You do know it's midday in July in southwest Texas, right? It's gotta be five hundred degrees right now inside our cars."

"Can you think of another secure location close to where you are?"

Dennis looked at the other two men. They both had looks on their faces that were not promising.

"The only vehicle we have is mine," Forde said. "Cap came in a chopper, and Dennis was transported here by local police."

"I'm sorry, gentlemen, but what I have to share with you will blow the doors of your conference room wide open, if it gets into the wrong hands."

"It'll take us a few minutes," Harlan said. "I need to make sure the officers watching Willis's room have explicit instructions. If these people sent Arroyo, they surely have others they can send to finish the job."

"Look," Agent Mitchell said, "call me back when you're set up and ready. And Dennis? You'll need to be able to access your secure email by computer."

"You don't want to make this easy, do you?"

"Once I share this with you, then you'll understand."

CHAPTER 39

MARFA POLICE DEPARTMENT
Marfa, TX

Thirty minutes later, Dennis Morrison sat down in a small interrogation room at the Marfa Police Department. Captain Harlan had worked out the arrangement with the police chief, and believed it to be the safest location available.

Dennis called the number Agent Mitchell provided as Harlan and Detective Forde settled into the chairs across from him.

"FBI, Jacksonville field office. How may I direct your call?"

"Agent John Mitchell, please?"

"Can I ask who's calling?"

"Dennis Morrison, Department of Homeland Security."

"Please hold."

Dennis put the phone on speaker and set it down on the table. "Well, at least we know Agent Mitchell was legit."

"Number could have been spoofed," Harlan said.

"I looked it up." Dennis spun his computer around for Harlan to see. "Matches the number on the FBI's website at least. Doesn't mean much, I know, but his information should prove who he is."

The phone clicked out of its silence. "Dennis? Are you there?"

"I'm here. Captain Harlan and Detective Forde are here too. We moved to the local police department. We're using their interrogation room."

"No cameras or speakers?"

Dennis took a quick peek at the camera in the corner of the room. "All turned off."

"Okay. Good. Now, I'm going to send you an email. In this email, there will be a link. When you click on the link, there will be a login screen. Let me know when you get to it."

"Okay. Shoot."

"Email's already been sent."

Dennis waited a few seconds before it arrived. He opened the link, and immediately, a nondescript login screen appeared. "This doesn't look very official."

"Technically, it isn't. Another IT guy and I rigged this so only we could access it. We could not chance putting it on the FBI servers."

Dennis looked at his two partners. "Why, may I ask, can you *not* use your own servers?"

"Just log in. The info will speak for itself. The username is 'diabolos.'" Mitchell spelled it for him. "And the password is three letters, followed by seven numbers. The letters are R-E-V, all capitals, followed by the numbers one, seven, one, two, three, four, five."

Dennis drew in a deep breath. "Got it." He hit Submit, and instantly, a screen appeared with a list of hyperlinks to the left. A window, filling three-quarters of the screen, occupied the right side. "Okay, I see a bunch of hyperlinks with a blank video screen."

"Good. Those links will open files. Each file contains information pertaining to the Department of Homeland Security, Dennis.

The first three links are audio conversations between Director Williamson and Markus Sorensen. We have linked Sorensen to the terrorist attacks in Las Vegas and Washington, D.C. He apparently had a group called The Consortium, which was made up of a slew of politicians and business leaders from around the world.

"As it turns out, Sorensen saved everything. All the phone conversations. All the video evidence. Even invoices and who got paid and how much. We believe these files were his version of 'insurance policies' to keep himself safe against anyone who had thoughts of being a turncoat. He saved everything in two distinct locations. One of the servers he used was in China. The other was in Bluffdale."

"Bluffdale?"

"Yes. We've been able to confirm it."

"What's so significant about Bluffdale?" Harlan said.

Dennis eyed Harlan with a frustrated expression. "Bluffdale is where we have our military servers housed. A civilian should not be using those servers...well, not unless someone in the government gave him access."

Harlan lifted his chin and raised his eyebrows. "You mean we have dirty folk in the U.S. government?"

"'Dirty' is a kind term," Mitchell said. "We were able to identify everyone in both the audio and video files except one voice and one person in a video clip. One of those files before you lists all the members of The Consortium we have identified. There are two high-ranking officials within the U.S. Government acting as members of this group." Mitchell cleared his throat. "Dennis, Williamson is one of them."

"You have her voice on tape? That's it?"

"It's a 99.7% match, Dennis."

"But she could easily deny it's her."

"True, but that's not all. Uh...click on the seventh link down, the one titled 'Mexico.'"

Dennis did so, and a video appeared in the screen to the right. It was a surveillance camera feed. At the top of the screen was an airplane. A Gulfstream to be exact. It was parked on the edge of a tarmac designed for smaller aircraft, and its stairwell was extended. "Okay, what am I looking at?"

Harlan and Forde stood, walked around the table, and peered over Dennis's shoulder.

"Play it, and I'll walk you through it."

"So, you're watching me access these files?"

"Yes."

Dennis frowned but double-clicked on the little triangle anyway, and the video lurched forward.

"As you can see," Mitchell said, "this plane is parked and waiting. In about five seconds, you're going to see a limousine pull up, and a man is going to exit the plane and enter the limo. Please pause it when the man is facing the camera."

Dennis did so as the man stepped out of the plane and looked toward the camera, scanning the area before venturing down the stairs. Dennis paused it.

"That's Castaneda," Harlan said.

"Castaneda? Are you talking about *the* Castaneda? The one on the FBI's Most Wanted List?" Mitchell said.

"Yes, Agent Mitchell," Harlan said. "Detective Forde and his partner were able to catch him and his little loyal, lap dog, Pedro Arroyo on film. Dennis took those photos and sent them to his supervisor, Larry Montrose, who in turn had them forwarded to Williamson per her request."

"And when were those pictures sent?"

Dennis peeked at his watch. "Approximately twelve hours ago."

Mitchell grunted. "Well, gentlemen, this video was shot at an airport in Tijuana. Our best guess is the meeting took place approximately six days ago. Now, make note of the license plate on the limo. Jot down the plate number for me."

Harlan motioned at Forde who pulled out his little notebook and scribbled it.

"Okay, we have it," Dennis said.

"If you watch the rest of this video, Castaneda is going to enter the limo and stay inside for about twelve minutes. Then, he exits the limo. As he reenters the plane, the limo remains in place. We won't take the time to watch it now, but you can look at it later." Agent Mitchell paused. "Now, click on the link at the bottom. You're going to see that same limo, identified by the license plate, drive away and eventually disappear off camera."

"We're seeing it," Dennis said.

"The video will then cut to a satellite feed of the Manuel Marquez de Leon International Airport. You will see the same limo arrive and park beside a smaller plane. The license plate will match. The time elapsed between feeds fits the travel time from the smaller Tijuana airport to Manuel Marquez de Leon International. Now, watch who gets out of the limo."

Dennis, Harlan, and Forde all watched as the limo came to a stop. Seconds later, the driver got out and opened the back door on his side of the vehicle. A woman with long, spindly legs emerged, wearing a tight-fitting dress and high heels, carrying a briefcase.

"There's your leak, Dennis," Harlan said, pointing at the computer screen. He stood and kicked the chair next to him. "We wanted to know how Arroyo knew where to find Willis? This is how. Your director is playing footsies with one of the FBI's Ten Most Wanted."

Dennis shook his head in disbelief. "This would explain why the firewall was put up to block my access to the logs we talked about earlier. I was the one who sent those photos to Larry. And he had me forward them to her. I painted a target on my own back without realizing it."

"As well as my back and Detective Willis's back, I might add," Forde said.

Dennis turned to Forde. "I am so sorry. I had no idea."

Harlan patted Dennis on the shoulder. "It would seem Director Williamson didn't want prying eyes—yours or anyone else's—to have the ability to time stamp her departure from HQ. If you could, then you could tie it to the time stamp of her hopping a plane, flying to Mexico, and meeting up with Castaneda. Block the initial time stamp of the departure from HQ, and nobody can witness her leaving. Thus, they'd have no starting point from which to formulate a timeline."

"Which means...," Dennis said, contemplating the situation, "she must have known about my clandestine job of screening everyone. The logs. Everything. Otherwise, she'd have no reason to do what she did."

"Maybe she was just being extremely careful," Forde said. "You know. No honor among spies, right? Trust no one?"

"Who else knew about your clandestine job of checking those logs," Harlan said, "besides you and Montrose?"

"Nobody, as far as I know." Dennis shrugged. "That was the point. If too many people knew, it would defeat the purpose of the job itself. Everybody would pretend while at work and not be natural, because they would know I was logging everything."

Harlan ran his hand through his hair. "Or maybe Montrose was using your logs to keep tabs on others as well, including you?"

"I can't believe Larry is involved in all this."

"But Dennis, you can't rule him out either."

"Gentlemen, before we start implicating everybody," Mitchell interrupted, "let's stick to what we do know. We tracked the limo Director Williamson used back to its owner. It's owned by a company called DSF, Ltd., which stands for 'Domestic Shipping and Freight.' It's a shell corporation for the Sinaloa Cartel. The CIA has been tracking their financials for months now."

"So, Agent Mitchell," Dennis said, "why send these files to me? What am I supposed to do with all this?"

"When Blake Meyer was made aware of this information, he wanted you to be aware. He knew you'd be investigating things, based on what he knew of your job. He also knew that because of the arrest of the two Jihadists in Texas, who were trying to smuggle illegals into Florida, your office would be all over it. As a result, he felt it best to warn you."

"Yeah, we already got a warning shot. Literally," Forde said.

"What does that mean?" Mitchell said.

"Castaneda sent his right hand man to the hospital here in Marfa to kill one of my detectives, Agent Mitchell. That's what it means," Harlan said. "Nearly pulled it off too."

"Does the FBI and Homeland know about this?"

"They do now," Harlan said. "Marfa police notified the FBI when they realized what happened. Detective Forde tried to get them to not do it, but they said it was procedure, especially when it involved a member of the Sinaloa Cartel."

Agent Mitchell sighed heavily into the phone. "Gentlemen, here's the dilemma. We don't know who we can trust right now. The voiceprints we identified from Sorensen's computer files are a literal Who's Who. And there are at least two very high-ranking U.S. government officials who we know are involved, whose voices do not appear in any of the voiceprints we have uncovered so far. One of the voiceprints we do have is an FBI Agent-in-Charge, and another is Director Williamson's, so we know the mole has inroads in both agencies, not to mention the NSA, the CIA, and about half a dozen other agencies."

"It's a sad day in America when the bad guys and the good guys are playing on the same team," Harlan said.

Forde scoffed. "Especially when you find yourself on the opposing team."

"You got that right." Harlan slammed his fist down on the table. "Now, I want to nail these scumbags more than ever...but how can you when the system is rigged to protect 'em?"

"Agent Meyer is working on that as we speak. According to some information I just learned a few hours ago, Agent Meyer has been working on this case for over ten years off and on. Therefore, I believe that may be the reason why he wanted me to show you all this. First, so you wouldn't get in the way by doing your job unaware of his investigation. Second, so you could watch your back and be on the lookout. And third, so you could be thinking about what to do when the time is right. He can't arrest everybody when it all breaks. He'll need help."

"Okay, okay," Harlan said, "now things are starting to make a little more sense."

"There is another piece of evidence Blake wanted you to see," Mitchell said. "It's the file titled 'FTMW Home.' Open it, and you'll see where Castaneda is hiding out. The video shows him getting out of the plane and getting into a limo. It takes him to a warehouse in Mexico. It was Blake's hope that you could examine this video and determine exactly, by the landmarks, street signs, etc., where the warehouse is located. He said if you could, then he had a name of a *federale* he trusts who you could contact."

"I'm starting to like this Agent Meyer," Harlan said.

"Blake did emphasize you should wait until he was done with his investigation. Arresting Castaneda before his investigation is completed would definitely tip off those he is trying to catch."

"Understood, Agent Mitchell." Dennis looked at Harlan. "But how did you get all of these satellite videos and images on Castaneda? He's been a ghost for years now."

"One of Sorensen's men. An IT whiz who apparently didn't trust Sorensen very much. He had copied what he deemed as

Sorensen's pertinent files, stored on those two servers I mentioned earlier. Of course, he had his own server as well..." Mitchell harrumphed. "And who says crime doesn't pay...but I digress...

"We suspect this IT guy intended these files to be his insurance policies as well. When we arrested him, his computers became a treasure chest."

Harlan eyed Dennis with a smile on his face. "It would seem so."

"Okay, gentlemen," Mitchell said. "Stay alert. I'm told big news is coming. And in our line of work, it could end in a series of arrests or a barrage of gunfire."

Forde smirked and ran his hand through his hair. "You don't have to tell me twice."

CHAPTER 40

NORTHEAST KINGDOM INTERNATIONAL Airport
 Newport, Vermont

The plane came to a halt after taxiing back to the small hangar area at the Northeast Kingdom International Airport. Blake Meyer stood and watched as Captain Davis opened the doorway, allowing the staircase to unfold and slowly fall to the ground. He scanned the area and stepped back inside and gave Blake a quick nod.

"Gentlemen, we need to make this transition quick. I need to get back in the air."

"You got it, Cap," Davis said.

Master Sergeant Alwin Nefarje led two of the other men, Corporal James and Corporal Reynolds, off the plane. He walked out far enough to be able to see all the hangars and the surrounding area. The two corporals went to the front and back of the plane and spied the area out across the landing strip. Each man gave Nefarje a nod.

Nefarje, in turn, motioned for Blake to come out. With Little Sara in his arms and Jacob holding his right hand, he descended the stairs, looking in the direction of the small building acting as a terminal. He could see his wife, Sara, peering out the series of windows. Her hand was over her mouth, and her other hand covered it, as if the first hand didn't have the strength to press against her face on its own.

The other two men, Sergeant Spanarkle and Captain Davis brought up the rear, and the other men came back, forming a circle of protection around Blake and his children.

As the procession cut the distance in half, Sara burst out of the back door of the terminal and ran toward her family.

"It's okay, gentlemen. That's my Sara," Blake said. "And those are her parents."

Nefarje stopped and stepped aside, allowing Sara to fly past him.

Blake released Jacob's hand and set Little Sara down. Both children ran to their mother.

Sara knelt down and embraced her children as they clasped their arms around her neck. Her sobs of joy caused each of the soldiers to look at the others and smile.

Blake slowed his gait and allowed Sara to enjoy the reunion. He finally came to within a couple of feet and stopped. A tear dribbled down his cheek as he watched.

He glanced up at Sara's parents and waved. Both arm-in-arm with one another, they, too, were crying. They waved back, and Sara's mother mouthed the words "Thank you" to Blake.

He smiled at her. There was really nothing else to say or do. He knew the moment would wear off, and the reality of his past and the pain it had caused them would be a subject of discussion. But not yet. Not now. He didn't want to interrupt this victory cele-bration.

Sara kissed her children and hugged them until Jacob began to protest a little. He wanted to go hug his grandparents, and Sara finally granted his wish. Little Sara, not wanting to be outdone by her brother, asked if she could also go see her grandparents. Sara kissed her forehead and patted her on the behind. "Go."

Little Sara screamed in delight as she ran toward them.

Sara watched her children interact with her parents before turning to face Blake, who stood a few feet away.

She gazed at him with a tired, but relieved smile. She took one step, and then another, and before he knew it, she and Blake were hugging each other.

"Thank you," Sara said.

"They are safe now," he said. "And these men will make sure of it until I return."

"Are you sure you have to leave? Don't you want to come back to the house and get some rest?"

"I have to end this, Sara."

"Why you? We've got an entire government. Let them handle it. You have a family to protect."

Blake closed his eyes for a brief moment. He knew what her words really meant. He understood her heart. But she didn't understand his dilemma. He opened his eyes and peered into hers. He held her head in his hands and rubbed his thumb against her cheek, wiping the tear away. "That's exactly what I am doing. These people are after me. If I don't put an end to it, then none of us are safe."

Sara gripped his hands with hers and slid them down, off her face. She held them with hers and swallowed. Blake could tell she was tamping down her emotions with every ounce of energy she had left. "Will it ever end, Blake? If these people are stopped, won't others just take their place?"

"Maybe. But at least they won't have a vendetta against me."

304 C. KEVIN THOMPSON

"How can you be so sure?"

"Truthfully, I can't. Not one hundred percent. But I can follow this through and get as close as I possibly can to it."

"I wish I understood the world you lived in...live in..."

"No, you really don't. But when this is over, I will answer any questions you have. I'll tell you about every mission and case I was ever involved in, if it means repairing our marriage and our relationship." He pushed their hands together and used his thumbs to lift her chin just a smidge. "I do not want to lose you, Sara. You changed my life. Our children changed my life. And I want to get that life back." He motioned to the soldiers around them. "I left this life for a reason. I never wanted to go back. I never wanted all this to happen. And if I could, I would go back in time and make sure what we are going through now would never happen. But I can't. Instead, I have to deal with what's happening now and put an end to it. And trust me when I say this: I'm close. Real close. We're about the blow the lid off this thing, and when we do, you're gonna hear things in the news you never thought possible. Then, maybe, you'll begin to understand why and how all this happened."

"I just want it to end. I want them to leave us alone."

"So do I." With those words, Blake leaned forward and kissed her.

He was surprised by the force of the kiss she returned with a fervor he had hoped for but didn't expect.

"Eww," Little Sara said. "Can you not do dat here? That's gwoss."

Sara smiled and chuckled with her lips still pressed against Blake's.

Blake laughed, too, and allowed the kiss to end with their foreheads pressed together.

Their eyes were locked on one another, and Blake could feel a sense of hope in the moment.

Suddenly, the others standing around broke out into laughter as well.

"Yeah, you might want to get a room, Cap," Corporal James said.

CHAPTER 41

Templeton Drake sat in an interrogation room, waiting for U.S. Congresswoman Merina Parker to be brought to him. It was several minutes before the door opened and Parker shuffled in with her hands cuffed, secured to a belly chain. Another long chain connected the belly chain to the shackles around her ankles.

Drake stood in protest. "Are all these restraints necessary? She's a fifty-something-year-old woman who could be broken in two like a toothpick by any one of you. Show some respect."

"She's being accused of domestic terrorism," the first agent said. "Unless she's found innocent by a jury of her peers, then we will treat her like any other person accused of the same. If you have a problem with it, then I suggest you take it up with the director."

"You can count on it," Drake said, still standing with his hands on his hips. He turned to his client. "Are they treating you okay?"

"Yeah," Parker said. She lifted her hands as much as she could. "They only put these on me to bring me here." She sat down in the chair pulled out for her.

Drake continued to stand until the two agents stepped out of the room and closed the door. "Well, you're not going to be in this place much longer," he said as he sat down again.

"How much longer is 'not much longer'?"

"I wanted to stop by and tell you my plans before I set them in motion so you wouldn't be blindsided." Drake pulled out a notepad from his briefcase. "When I leave here, I'm going to see the judge who issued the warrant for your arrest. I want to know who requested it. I also am going to ask him to rescind it."

"Based on what?"

"Based on two things. First, there's been another attack. Right here in D.C. Union Market. It occurred around noon."

"Which means I couldn't have had anything to do with it, because I was in here."

"Well, not exactly. They could argue your associates pulled it off as an attempt to make you look innocent."

Parker huffed. "Templeton, you're sounding like the prosecuting attorney again."

"I know. It's my job. It's also my job to poke holes in their case. Yes, you were arrested after the terrorists released the contagion in Las Vegas, but you were also arrested *before* anyone started showing signs of infection. A couple of hours before, actually. And several hours before the president was made aware of the specific contagion being used. In other words—"

"How could they know to arrest me when they didn't even know they had an incident yet?"

Drake nodded with his lips pursed. "Precisely. It would seem whoever set out to frame you jumped the gun."

"They made a mistake."

Templeton smiled. "Didn't I tell ya?"

"This is great news, Templeton. So, when can I expect to be released?"

"However long it takes the judge to revoke the warrant and order your release."

"I want Samantha released as well."

"Oh, don't worry. I'm requesting her release as well."

"And when you get the name of the person who requested the warrant, I want to be the first to know."

"That was my plan."

Parker stood and glared at her friend. "There's gonna be more than hell to pay when I'm finished."

CHAPTER 42

OVER NEW YORK STATE
En Route to Chicago, Illinois

Blake Meyer sat alone on the Gulfstream. The precious voices of his children and the casual conversation of his trusted friends were a memory now.

He stared out the window, but all his mind could do was relive the scene at the airport in Vermont.

The smiles of Jacob and Little Sara.

The ferocious hugs they gave their mother.

She, in turn, smothering her children with a barrage of kisses.

Yet, it was his exchange with Sara which replayed the most.

Despite her pleas for him to stay and allow someone else to end this nightmare, Sara's embrace lifted his spirit. The kiss which followed strengthened his damaged heart. The comments and the recommendation from his colleagues to "get a room," offered him hope. It forced the sorrowful recollection of their previous encounter on the ship to fade into the background.

However, now, in this moment, there was optimism, and it fueled his desire to catch those responsible, once and for all, and end this madness.

He simply wanted his life back, so they could begin healing.

Together.

As a couple.

As a family.

He left his five fellow soldiers behind to help with the process. To guard Sara and the kids in his absence.

He gave them strict instructions on the tarmac: "Protect my family at all costs. Call every law enforcement agency nearby for back up at the beginning, should someone attempt to strike. Don't wait. Don't try to be heroes. And keep me posted via text at the top and bottom of every hour. I won't be able to function properly, not knowing if they are okay or not," Blake said as he watched Sara and the children walk towards the grandparents' car. "Promise me, gentlemen."

Captain Davis stepped forward and placed his hands on Blake's shoulders, "Blake, everything is going to be fine. You have my word." He nodded in the direction of his fellow soldiers. "You have *our* word."

The other four men voiced their agreement.

"Now, before you change your mind, get on the plane and bring this to an end, sir." Captain Davis took a step back, stood at attention, and saluted his friend. The other men did the same.

Blake inhaled deeply, straightened his stance, and returned the respect.

With quick nods, all five soldiers turned and followed Sara and the kids toward the car.

"Oh, hey, I almost forgot," Blake said.

The five men stopped and faced Blake.

"The rental company has another car waiting. It's all ready to go. Give them my name, and all the paperwork should already be taken care of."

"I was wondering how all ten of us were going to fit in one vehicle," Alwin Nefarje said. "But I should have known. Captain Meyer thinks of everything."

Blake shook his head and waved them off. "Tell Sara to wait until you get the other car."

Captain Davis pointed at the plane. "Get on it! Now! I think we can handle a rental car."

* * *

It was thirty minutes later now, and staring out the window, Blake continued to replay the images, using their joy to replenish his strength. He leaned back in his seat and closed his eyes.

I'm exhausted. But I'll never be able to sleep with so much at—

His satellite phone rang.

Blake picked it up answered in a low voice, closing his eyes again. "Meyer."

"Blake, this is Julee. How are you doing?"

"Better. Sara and the kids are reunited. Now, I'm on my way to Chicago. I should be there in an hour or so."

"That is such good news. It must be a huge relief for you to have them back with their mom."

"You can't imagine. Unless you've been through it...there are no words."

"Well, listen, I may have more good news."

"I'm all ears."

"There are two things, actually. First, you know about the release of the contagion in Las Vegas. Well, Harrison found a list on Sorensen's computer, showing where every device like the one used in Las Vegas is currently located. As we speak, these devices are being located, deactivated, and removed. They were planted in the same cities found on the flash drive you got from Sergei Botinkin."

"Sergei's list was used for many things, apparently."

"The devices are believed to be in those locations. The same locations where the 605 smuggled families were transplanted. I have to think the contagion was supposed to be there as well."

"Probably so. Makes sense." Blake grunted. "Seems like eons ago since I had my little tussle with Sergei."

"Also, I just got off the phone with the director for the CDC. They have finished testing the strain of plague used at the hotel in Las Vegas. It's been verified by forty-seven different samples taken from forty-seven different patients. They have confirmed it, Blake. This variant of bubonic plague has been modified and militarized, as they suspected, to speed up the rate of transmission, from one host to another. *However*, it is just the plague. *It is not* an antibiotic-resistant form. It can be treated successfully with the medications we have on hand. As a matter of fact, almost all the patients being treated are beginning to show signs of improvement."

"Great news."

"It sure is. We've lost a few people, mainly because we just didn't know what we were dealing with in the beginning. By the time the CDC figured it out, it was too late for the people infected first."

"I'm sorry to hear that. I know their families will be devastated."

"Of course." Julee cleared her throat. "Blake,...are you okay? You're not your usual, talkative self."

"I'm fine. I'm just....beyond tired. You know? The kind you can't sleep off?" Blake switched the phone to his other ear and wondered when the throbbing headache would go away. "And ...I was thinking, too...about what you just said."

"About what exactly?"

"Does it make sense to you, Julee, for groups, like The Hands

DEVIL OF A CRIME 313

of Allah, or The Consortium...or whoever they are...groups who have spent all this time and effort to bring our country to its knees,...does it make sense for them to use a strain of the plague that can be easily cured? Knowing there are strains out there of the same contagion that cannot? We were told they had the antibiotic-resistant version at their disposal. Or at least we suspected they did. Even Sergei Botinkin alluded to it. Remember? He told me to go home and enjoy my family, because first, he knew they were going to be abducted, and second, he knew an antibiotic-resistant form of the plague would decimate the population, which was the reason why he was leaving the country. He'd been recalled before its release to save him from becoming infected."

"I remember."

"And why have The Hands of Allah send the message to the president, threatening the release of the contagion—if he didn't meet all their demands—only to then release a less-lethal version doctors can treat with normal antibiotics, ultimately healing just about everyone?"

"A couple of hours ago, I would have had no answer for you," Julee said with a slight chortle. "However, our raid in Atlanta has shed some light on your inquiries.

"According to Kurt Bowker, they were planning to release several versions of the plague all at once for the purpose of causing confusion amongst the medical professionals."

Blake checked his bag for the pain medication the doctor in Tbilisi had supplied him. "Interesting. It would've worked. CDC officials wouldn't have had to spend additional time attempting to ascertain which strain they were fighting, so they'd be unsure what medicines to administer until they did. It would have bought The Consortium valuable time."

"But now that you mention it," Julee said, "why release the lesser of the strains in an environment where it can be contained and studied until it can be identified? Had they released the killer version, with no known cure, then it wouldn't have mattered where it was used."

Blake glanced out the window at the passing clouds. "The president's decision to recall all the air fresheners must have really crippled their plan...more than we thought. It forced them to improvise in ways they had not considered. I don't think they ever imagined us figuring out that part of their plan, and had those two agents not captured the image of the air freshener on Colin Murphy's computer, and had not Harrison been able to identify it and subsequently put two and two together, we *never* would have figured it out."

"So, you know where all of this is pointing?"

"Yeah. The antibiotic-resistant strain is still out there. And it must be in that warehouse in Chicago, Julee. Packaged in air fresheners." Blake sat up straight. "Now, can you guess their next steps, if this is true?"

Julee cleared her throat. "I think they'll pretend they attacked us the way they had planned all along...and allow us to take our victory laps for allegedly stopping them."

"Good. And...?"

"Then, when things calm down, and the president lifts the ban on air fresheners, they will go back to their original plan and release it without any forewarning."

"It's what I'd do, if I was in their shoes."

"Me too. So, we're not out of the woods yet."

"Not by a long shot." Blake finally retrieved the bottle of pills. "Who are the agents meeting me at the airport?"

"Agents Forsythe and Bradley. They said they could have a team ready when you arrive so you could go straight to the warehouse."

"Okay, but if my gut is correct, and if this warehouse does contain the antibiotic-resistant strain, we're gonna need CDC officials and National Guard personnel staged nearby. We'll need the area quarantined and the strain tested as soon as possible. We won't have time to wait for them to gather their resources and make the trek. It would take hours we don't have, so please confirm we'll have those teams ready to go."

"I'm on it."

"Good work, Julee. You've done good work throughout all this. And if there's anybody left in power I can sway, you'll have your pick of field offices, if you still want your own."

Blake could hear Julee clear her throat again as he popped a tablet into his mouth and washed it down with a swig of water.

"I appreciate it, Blake. Means a lot coming from you, but what did you mean when you said, 'If there is anybody left in power...?'"

Blake chuckled. "Let's just say the warehouse is the least of our worries."

CHAPTER 43

Nathansen Holdings Distribution Center
Chicago, Illinois

A warehouse, abandoned by a burgeoning company which chose to move its operations out of the country, was teeming with life. Two weeks prior, its lifeless shell was surrounded by empty parking lots and loading docks, a couple of left behind shipping containers, and plenty of loose trash, blowing across the property in the constant gales of the windy city. For sale signs, with the word "Sold" slapped across their midsections, lined South Torrence Avenue, pointing down the road toward the complex.

Now, seventeen cars and trucks were scattered around the building. Five more shipping containers had been added to the ones already there.

Four men, decked out in gear fit for a small incursion into hostile territory, strolled back and forth, in sight of at least two other comrades at all times. They arrived and started their shifts as watchmen forty-eight hours ago. Each man was positioned off the corner of the warehouse, giving him the ability to monitor two sides of the warehouse at all times. The headsets made it possible to communicate with the other three guards all at once.

* * *

Blake Meyer met up at the airport with the agents Julee had secured for this mission, SSAs Waylon Forsythe and Kenzlee Bradley. On the ride to the warehouse, they briefed him on where the situation currently stood.

The warehouse was being monitored from the marina, where the Little Calumet River and the Grand Calumet River meet. Several undercover FBI agents, pretending to be marina workers, had ready access to three boats moored along the marina's dock. Additional agents played the part of employees outside the Hercules Tire complex to the northeast. They often stood outside on "smoke breaks" and used small, hand-held binoculars to give updates to the central command post.

Another group of agents stationed themselves inside the warehouses on the next block south. Through a couple of conveniently placed windows, they were able to use high-powered binoculars to view the scene and give additional updates.

A National Guard unit was staged less than a mile away to the north and the south along South Torrence Avenue, out of sight of the targeted warehouse but ready to block the avenue and use it as an entry point for what Blake hoped would be a peaceful surrender by the mercenaries.

"And what about the CDC?" Blake asked as they turned onto South Torrence Avenue.

"We were told the CDC officials would arrive shortly after you arrived," Agent Bradley said. "They have been instructed to be ready to test the contagion, using the particulars from the Las Vegas attack as a reference point."

The Ford Expedition slowed and turned left onto East 136th Street and eventually pulled into the parking lot of Hercules Tire.

"We're here," Agent Forsythe said, pulling into a parking spot facing east, so the target would not be able to read any license plates, if they were attempting to do so. "Our agents are over there, sitting at the picnic table, pretending to be on a break."

Blake hopped out of the vehicle and strode directly to the agents. "Ladies and gentlemen, don't get up. Don't salute. Don't reach out to shake hands. Treat me like a supervisor you already know and who is wondering why you all are out here. My name is Blake Meyer, and I am heading up this operation."

Agents Forsythe and Bradley caught up with Blake and stood on each side of him. "He's legit. We just picked him up from the airport."

Blake smiled. "Now that my credentials have been verified, I need an update. What are we facing?"

One of the agents sitting down, motioned at the others, and they all nodded and waved at him to do the honors. "I'm SSA Hugh Fielding. We've been here over an hour now. From what we can see—and it's been confirmed by our other surveillance teams at the marina and the warehouse south of the target—there are four armed guards outside the warehouse. They have the entire perimeter covered. We believe there are others inside, and judging by the weaponry the four guards are carrying, these guys are top of the line mercenaries. They probably invade small countries in their spare time."

"You haven't seen any others?" Blake said.

"We've seen two others so far. They came out, gave each of the four a break, then they went back inside."

"So, a minimum of six verified." Blake pulled out his phone. "How many vehicles? And were they here when you arrived?"

"We've counted seventeen so far. However, we cannot confirm they all belong to these guys, and they were all here when we arrived. None have left, and no one else has entered the premises. We have run plates on seven of the seventeen. All rented by the same company who purchased the warehouse, Nathansen Holdings, LLC."

Blake dialed and held up his hand for the agent to pause.

"Blakey Meyer, my old friend. I was expecting you to call soon. Sara told me you wouldn't stay with them, so I just put two and two together, figuring you would need my assistance sooner or later."

"How did she get your number?"

"From one of the men you left behind. Captain Davis, I think."

"Why did she call?"

"She wanted updates on you. I assume you asked for updates on her and the kiddos. Apparently, she's learned from the best and is applying those skills in her favor."

"Clearly."

"The good sign is, Blakey, she obviously cares about you still, despite what's happened. She wants to know you're safe. I am to give her an update every hour on the hour. And I am to let her know when you will be coming home. Those were my orders."

Blake scratched the back of his head and smiled again. "Good to know. I suggest you obey them."

"Oh, don't worry, mate. You know, a woman's scorn...but enough with the orders from Mrs. Blakey. What do *you* need me to do for you now, Mr. Blakey? And you are familiar with my fees, so you are also aware your bill is getting pretty hefty, right?"

"Yeah, I do owe you big time, and this one may be one of the biggest yet."

"I suppose you'll be wanting mate's rates then?"

"I'm not sure if I fully understand the meaning behind that phrase, but if it can be taken at face value, then, yes. Most definitely."

"For you, mate, since you're shattered, I'll cut you some slack."

"I appreciate it...I think."

Harrison laughed. "What's on your list of things to do, Blako?"

"I sent you a code via our D-Mail account. It will get you access to a satellite hovering over our position as we speak."

"This has been authorized by all the right people...right? They typically do not take too kindly to outside computer geeks invading their playgrounds. They have systems in place to track said geeks, then the said geeks have FBI agents storming their homes." Harrison grunted as he tapped away at his keyboard. "I've already played that game. Not a fan, by the way."

Blake listened to his friend manipulate his keyboard. Harrison's little diatribes always accompanied his efforts. Blake viewed them as his mind's way of having something to do while his fingers did all the dirty work and heavy lifting. "I understand why you would think such things. And I'll make sure the bureau reimburses you for any losses when this is all said and done."

"They will pay for my fried computers in Maryland?"

"Yes, and anything else."

"Not sure they can repair my frazzled nerves...Okay, I have the D-Mail open, the satellite has been located, and the code has been entered. South side of Chicago, eh? Are you there?"

"Yes. Corner of South Torrence Avenue and East 136th Street."

"Got it. Zooming in now...scanning...scanning...are you inside or outside?"

"Outside. We're—"

"Sitting around a picnic table, perhaps? Well, all but three of you. And it appears the man in the middle of those standing is on his cell phone, talking to the best computer geek ever, possibly in the world, or even the galaxy."

Blake wanted to look up and wave, but thought better of it. "It would appear you're in and ready to go."

"These toys the government has are amazing. Did you know

the guy sitting at the table, with the blue hoodie, is wearing black Converses? I can actually read the label on the side."

Blake stepped to his left and saw exactly what Harrison was referencing. "That is impressive."

The agents sitting at the table gave Blake befuddled expressions.

Blake pointed at the man's shoes. "He can read the label on your tennis shoes. So, it would seem we are ready."

The agent looked down at his sneakers and then lifted his eyes toward the sky, shielding them as he did.

"Don't look up!" Blake said. "Our target could be surveilling us just as easy as we are about to do to them. Trust me."

The agent straightened his posture and lifted his hands in surrender without raising his arms.

"What am I supposed to be spying on, Blakey?" Harrison said.

"There is a warehouse on the other side of the river. Rectangular in shape. White. There are four guards standing off each corner. I need you to zoom in and get some really good pictures of their faces. Then have Agent Mitchell run them through facial recognition. We need them identified. It might help us to know who we are dealing with."

"Dead easy."

"Also, screen grab all the license plates you can see in the parking lots surrounding the warehouse. I'm told there are seventeen vehicles total. Some of the plates have already been run. Maybe we'll get lucky and gather some additional intel by running the remaining plates."

"Done."

"One last thing. I'm hoping this satellite was positioned when they said it was, because I need you to go back in time. There are seven shipping containers in the parking lot to the east. Start two days ago, and see if you can find out when they arrived, which transport company delivered them, the works. You should also be able to get pictures of everyone who entered the building too."

"Okay, but you know that one will take a little longer."

"You have one hour tops. And if we start seeing any movement in or around the warehouse in question, then we will need it sooner."

Harrison harrumphed. "Then I suggest you let me go."

"Call me as soon as you have anything."

"Hooroo."

Blake hung up and looked at his new team. "Now, we wait. Keep surveilling them. We can't let anyone leave the warehouse area. If someone jumps in a vehicle and leaves, they must be intercepted and quarantined."

"Is it that bad? The contagion, I mean?" Agent Bradley said. She waved her arm around at her fellow agents. "We all have family in the city."

"As you may have heard through memos and briefings, the contagion in Las Vegas has been identified. It's a much milder version of the contagion than the one we were told would be used. So, for most of the people in Las Vegas, it's good news. However, we still have reason to believe a much deadlier version is still in the possession of the enemy. We have narrowed it down to that warehouse."

"Not good." Agent Bradley said.

"Until we know what we are dealing with, we must treat it as if our lives and the lives of sixty percent of the planet hangs in the balance."

"And with this being *The Windy City*..." Agent Forsythe said.

"Right," Blake said. "Knowing our adversaries the way I do, shipping it here may have been done because of this city's characteristics. What better way to spread an airborne contagion than to have it breached in one of the windiest cities in the States, not to mention one of the largest by population?"

CHAPTER 44

NATHANSEN HOLDINGS DISTRIBUTION Center
  Chicago, Illinois

For over thirty minutes, Blake sat inside the Ford Expedition with the air conditioning running. He watched the agents from the Chicago field office sit around the picnic table, pretending to be workers for the huge Hercules Tire plant facility behind them.

Blake memorized each agent by name as he scrolled through their dossiers, provided by Agent John Mitchell, once Julee Scarfano provided John with the names—all approved and actually ordered by the director himself. Blake trusted very few people at this stage in the operation, and with the bombshell information Harrison uncovered just hours earlier, nobody got a pass.

As he read through the last agent's file, his phone rang.

"It's about time. I was running out of reading material."

"Been a little busy, you know?" Harrison said, with a pound of snark thrown in for good measure. "This bloke from the Bureau keeps piling work on me. I can manage it, mind you, but he keeps doubting my abilities...it's annoying, actually...as many times as I have come through for him...but because he's my friend, I cut him serious slack."

"Good to know you are so forgiving."

"The new me is much more so than the old me."

"I've noticed."

"Enjoying those files Agent Mitchell sent you?"

"Yes. Very informative."

"Well, I would have gotten back to you sooner, but apparently there has been some additional exploits taking place since we spoke last. Frankly, it's uncanny how you know these things."

"It's years of experience talking, Harrison. Knowing what to look for...knowing how things work. Or don't. Knowing people. Predilections. Tendencies. Or in this case, it was the person's will-ingness—no, *eagerness*—to join the group that threw up red flags for me." Blake blew out a huge sigh. "And trust me, I hate it when I'm right, because it means somebody is dirty."

"Well, you're right. As usual. Absolutely right. My computer screen to the far left has been very active."

"In what way?"

"Mostly texting. There was one image sent. You'll never guess what the image was?"

Blake lifted his eyes from the screen and watched the agents sitting around the table. Half of them were on their smartphones. The others were talking and laughing. One held a cigarette. "I hope it's a profile picture."

"Sorry, but it's a full-on frontal with all the scars and warts."

Blake chuckled. "Nice."

"I placed everything I found in our D-mail, just in case you needed to access it later, but if you access it now, I can walk you through it."

Blake manipulated the mousepad and opened the email account. "I'll tell you what. Let me pull this up, and then I'm going to walk out to the group of agents and have you explain it to me while they listen in."

"Oh, you're a sly one, Mr. Grinch."

"Nope. Wrong analogy. I'm not stealing anything." Blake reached over and shut the vehicle off. "I'm done crawling through the air ducts of Nakatomi Plaza. It's time to flush out Hans and his henchmen. But to do this, I need you to lose the Aussie accent."

"No worries, mate—I mean, no problem, bro."

"Uh, maybe just talk normal without having your grammar do a walkabout."

"Oh, I like that. *'Have my grammar do a walkabout.'* I'm gonna steal it."

"Whatever, just as long as I don't call you by name, or they may relay that information too. So, what do you want me to call you?"

"Probably not smart to use any of my old aliases either. No telling what files still contain those."

Blake opened the door. "How about I call you 'Al'? Sgt. Powell doesn't fit in this context. And you're not a Dwayne T. Robinson."

"Al...yeah, Al works."

"Then, it's showtime, Al. I'm going to put you on speakerphone."

Blake hopped out of the SUV and slammed the door shut. "Ladies and gentlemen," he said as he closed the gap between him and the now quiet agents. "I have one of the FBI's finest on the line. He's got pertinent information for us, concerning our operation." He walked up to the picnic table and set his phone down with the volume as loud as it would go. "Okay, Al, you're on."

"All righty, then," Harrison said. "First, you asked me to run facial recognition on the guards standing outside the warehouse. They have been identified as part of a group we now know is responsible for orchestrating the release of a contagion in Africa, Bunia to be exact. That's in in the Republic of Congo, by the way.

The contagion released there in 2010 was similar to the one released in Las Vegas.

"This group, which doesn't have a name, but is run by a German ex-military commander, worked for Colin Murphy and were paid by Markus Sorensen. All of this information has been verified by Sorensen's own computer files."

"So, these four men are the 'guns-for-hire' variety?" Agent Forsythe said.

"Not them alone, no," Harrison said. "They work with a larger band of brothers usually numbering around fifteen men. However, the larger group is always employed to the highest bidder, our intelligence shows."

"And what about the vehicles surrounding the warehouse, Al?" Blake said.

"Besides the ones linked to Nathansen Holdings, LLC., half of the remaining vehicles are stolen. The other half are either bogus plates or are rentals under bogus names, so no real help there."

"What about the satellite footage?" Blake said as he scanned the other agents with his eyes.

"That proved to be the most helpful," Harrison said. "I ran it back until the parking lot was empty, roughly seventy-two hours ago. Then, two of the vehicles still present showed up, and the drivers went inside. They were on the premises for over a day before the remaining vehicles showed up, escorting five tractor trailers. Each semi carried a shipping container. One-by-one, a semi backed into one of the bays, stayed in position for about twenty minutes, then it pulled out and had the container offloaded. They handled all five shipping containers in the same way, and the containers haven't moved since they were offloaded.

"I ran facial recognition on all the other personnel present, and they match all the mercenaries who worked in Bunia in 2010. It would seem Colin Murphy and Markus Sorensen liked keeping the inner circle as small as possible."

"And if memory serves," Blake said, "these men are believed to be responsible for smuggling the needed materials into Pakistan which were eventually used in the Peshawar bombing on June 11, 2011."

"Your memory is good, Agent Meyer," Harrison said. "This group was believed to be a responsible player in the Peshawar attack. However, they are not affiliated with any other group, per se. They are an independent entity. They could care less about political alliances. They also don't do anything to get their hands dirty. They supply weapons. They deliver people into the hands of others. They guard warehouses, et cetera, et cetera, but they never pull the trigger, so to speak."

Blake watched as one of the agents, Edgerrin Felder, continued to type something on his phone. "So, we know who these men are and what they are capable of. And we now have enough evidence to tie them to multiple terrorist acts around the world, all thanks to Markus Sorensen's breached computer. But their arrests are secondary to securing what they are guarding."

Edgerrin Felder continued to type, looking up now and then.

"According to those same files," Blake continued, "this group is guarding an antibiotic-resistant form of bubonic plague. It has been militarized, meaning, it has been modified for warfare. It is pneumonic, and when it jumps from host to host, the incubation time accelerates. So, for example, if I caught it by breathing it in and became symptomatic inside of six hours, then when I breathe out and say...you, agent...?"

"Uh, me? Uh, Edgerrin Felder, sir."

"When I breathe out, after showing symptoms," Blake said, pointing at Agent Felder, "and he breathes it in, then his incubation period speeds up. Instead of six hours, it becomes five or four hours, depending on the health of his immune system. Then, when he becomes symptomatic and spreads it to the rest of you, you all would show signs in even less time.

"The point is," Blake said, looking at each agent in the eye, "by the time the contagion spreads to the fourth and fifth hosts, the incubation time will have been cut so short, the people will start dying before they even know what they have. And with the contagion being resistant to normal antibiotics used to treat bubonic plague, all those worthless efforts by health officials will only buy the contagion time to spread even more and kill the already-infected victims, not to mention take out health care officials along the way."

"So, let me get this straight, Agent Meyer," Agent Felder said. "That warehouse over there—the one surrounded by these mercenaries for hire—is filled with the contagion you just described?"

"That's what Markus Sorensen's computer files indicate. The contagion's creation originated somewhere in Russia. Then it was shipped across the Pacific, made landfall in Los Angeles, and was subsequently shipped here." Blake inhaled deeply and sighed just as heavily for effect. "My guess is, those mercenaries have no idea what they are guarding. The plague bacterium released in the Congo back in 2010—the one they assisted with—killed about one hundred and fifty people total. Most of them could have been saved had they not lived so far out in the bush. Doctors Without Borders happened to be nearby, and they identified it as quickly as they could. No doubt, they saved many more lives by just being there."

Blake pointed in the direction of the warehouse. "Now you know why I don't want to storm that warehouse with guns blazing. We were told the contagion was packaged to be shipped to stores across the United States. They allegedly put it in air fresheners... you know, the kind you plug into a wall outlet? Or the battery-powered kind? These people were planning on having those units sold in stores. If they had succeeded with those plans, innocent people would have bought the air fresheners, thinking their house was going to smell good, only to infect every living thing in their home, including their pets."

"That's sick," Agent Bradley said.

Blake nodded in agreement. "If we force our way into the warehouse and a gun battle ensues, some of the containers could be damaged. If they are, and some of the contagion gets released, then all bets are off when it comes to containment."

"Our people could go in wearing masks," one of the other agents said. "As for the mercenaries, they'd be toast, but at least it would protect us."

"True," Blake said, "but what if it spreads across the river to those buildings over there? Or the marina where your other fellow agents are stationed?"

"Good point," the other agent said.

"Let's cordon off however big of an area we need to block off," Agent Felder said. "That would help protect all of those people."

"Yes, it would, Agent Felder. But as we start doing so, our mercenary friends will see it, and they will know their cover is blown. Knowing this group the way we do, they have contingency plans. And I'm sure having the contagion loaded back into the shipping containers or into smaller box trucks for a quicker exit strategy would be their next move. So, Agent Felder, are you simply going to allow them to slip it out of here?"

"Yes. Then, we'll just wait for them to come to us. Set up road blocks. Bag 'em and tag 'em."

"And if they decide to set off an incendiary device and blow up some or all of the air fresheners, sending the contagion into the air, then what, Agent Felder? Are you willing to take that chance?"

Agent Felder set his phone down on the table. "So? What's your plan? As you seem to have all the answers."

Blake smiled, although he didn't appreciate the agent's tone, but he kept his eyes pinned to Agent Felder's, nevertheless. "Al, you want to tell him?"

"It would be my honor, sir." Harrison cleared his throat with a dramatic flair. "It would seem Markus Sorensen had it rigged through his bank to send payments to these mercenaries each time a crucial step in the process was completed. Get the contagion from Russia to L.A., *cha-ching*. Get the contagion from L.A. to Chicago, *cha-ching*. However, what the mercenaries are not aware of is how the federal government of the United States has been in the process of seizing the funds of one Markus Sorensen over the last several hours. Not only has all of his money been frozen, but every entity who has received funds from Sorensen is also having their funds frozen. If their monies were transferred through third party companies or transferred into something like cryptocurrency or gold and silver, then those companies are being asked 'politely' to surrender those funds, or they will be charged with conspiracy to commit acts of terrorism." Harrison cleared his throat again. "As you can imagine, those contacted thus far are gladly cooperating with federal authorities."

Blake watched as Agent Felder's face slowly morphed from an air of arrogance to one of dreadful concern.

Felder slowly picked up his phone, checked the screen, and then acted surprised. He pointed at his phone. "Excuse me, I need to take this. It's the boss...my wife."

Blake waved him on and picked up his phone. "Is there anything else we need to know, Al?"

"Nope. But I will keep monitoring everything from here and will continue to watch the satellite feed."

"Yes, please monitor *everything, Al*," Blake said. "I suspect activity will pick up on *all your computer screens* once the news on Sorensen's funds gets out."

"Yeah, I was thinking the same thing. On it."

"Call me, if you gather any information you think I need to know about right away."

"Hoo—uh, I mean, will do, sir," Harrison with a grimace.

Blake ended the call before Harrison made another slip of the tongue.

CHAPTER 45

NATHANSEN HOLDINGS DISTRIBUTION Center
Chicago, Illinois

Fifteen minutes had passed when Agent Bradley, using a camera with a telephoto lens to zoom in and get a look at the guards surrounding the warehouse, saw additional men come out and speak to one of the guards. She reached up and pressed in on her earpiece. "Hey, you guys, are you seeing this?"

"We have activity, people," one of the agents at the marina said. "And this doesn't look like one of the routine bathroom breaks."

Agent Forsythe, noting the conversation, walked over to their SUV and knocked on the window. Agent Bradley, close behind, was cycling through the images she took.

Blake Meyer opened the window. "What is it?"

"We've got activity at the warehouse, sir," Bradley said.

Blake snatched his smartphone off the dashboard, dialed, then set it back down before grabbing a pair of high-powered binoculars from the seat beside him. He scanned the area. "Ah, we've gone from four guards to seven...no, wait. Eight. Now nine..."

"You called?" Harrison said.

"Yes, *Al*. I have you on *speakerphone*. Agents Forsythe and Bradley are with me. We have something brewing here. Over at the warehouse. What are you seeing on the satellite feed?"

Blake could hear Harrison tap away at his keyboard. Then he heard some clicks of a mouse.

"There is definitely some activity. I'm counting...one, two, three, four...six...ten...twelve men. All armed. All standing on the west side of the building. The guards on the east side have either gone inside the building or they are part of the group...and judging by the body language, they seem to be having a heated discussion about something."

"Hold on, Al." Blake lowered his binoculars and picked up his smartphone. "Agent Forsythe, you and Agent Bradley need to notify the commanders of the National Guard units, and fill them in on what's happening. They still need to wait for my signal. Understood?"

"Got it."

Blake shut off the speakerphone feature to his phone. "Okay, 'Al,' I took you off speaker. How is the 'screening process' going?"

"I was about to contact you, but I was waiting for one last shoe to drop."

"Meaning?"

"Your FBI agent buddy, Felder, is it?"

"Yes."

"He's been busy. He texted the guards and told them what you said about the money. I've been monitoring Sorensen's accounts, and there was someone trying to access his account shortly thereafter. I had the pleasure of blocking said bloke and sending a message, informing said someone about how this account was no longer active. I followed the message, and it pinged to an IP address from inside the warehouse."

"So, they are arguing about the money." Blake put the binoculars back up to his eyes. "Good."

"Like you always say, 'Follow the money.'"

"And what did our buddy say when the guards discovered they weren't getting paid?"

"It's been a fun convo, actually. They didn't believe him at first. But when he also told them they were under surveillance—pointing out the agents at the marina and giving them the location of where the National Guard is staged—they started to listen."

"And no doubt, they have their own surveillance in place to verify."

"They do. They admitted to our buddy they could see the National Guard troops, and they are now watching your group by the tire company. And to put it mildly, they're ticked."

Blake kept his eyes on the warehouse. "I'll bet. Desperate times make desperate people act desperately."

"You ain't jokin'. They made threats against Felder. Said they would hunt him down, if they didn't get paid. He said it wasn't his fault. He had nothing to do with the money, and instead, they should be thanking him for giving them a heads up before the Feds arrived."

Blake scanned the area for any additional movement, but didn't see any. "When you make a pact with the devil, expect to get burned, right?"

"In more ways than one, my friend. Trust me on this. It's never just physical with *diabolos*. He always has your soul in his sights."

Blake pulled the binoculars away and stared down at his computer. He wasn't sure what hell was like, but if any of this ordeal he'd been facing for several days now was anything like it, then he really didn't want any part of it. "You said you were waiting to call me. What else were you waiting for?"

"When they tried to access Sorensen's account and failed, they texted our buddy, Felder, for a few minutes, going back and forth. Then another transaction occurred from the same IP address. An encrypted message was sent to our infamous 773 area code phone number. I was waiting for a response from the notorious number. I am all set to intercept it, but no one has answered back yet."

"Do you think the lack of a response is what they are discussing now?"

"Judging by our buddy's recent text messages, they have narrowed down to two options. Either, they use our buddy to surrender, or they wait to see if the person on the other end of the 773 number has any better ideas."

Blake closed his laptop and set it on the dashboard. "The person on the other end of the encrypted message isn't going to help. If these mercenaries are exposed and being watched, and the funding has been seized, the 773 number will abandon them. It's too risky to attempt a rescue mission to get them and the contagion out."

"Maybe the 773 number can supply the money instead. I'm mean, it would be worth it, right? Losing the contagion in the warehouse would be a huge blow to their overall plans," Harrison said.

"Yes, but they can always make more contagion. But it will be infinitely more difficult to do so from prison. Better to punt than risk turning the ball over deep in your own territory. Besides, these mercenaries are fodder. Those running this operation can always get new mercenaries, and these mercenaries know it. These guards only have one real choice here. Turn themselves in. And because they think they have our buddy on their side, they probably think they have the upper hand. They may even have an escape plan in the works already."

Harrison grunted. "Attack the transport while they are being moved from one facility to another, perhaps? And use the inside man to help carry it out."

"That's what I'd do. Lucky for us, though, we know the inside man—" Blake pulled his phone away and saw another call coming through. "Hey, I've gotta go. The Chicago AIC is calling."

"Laters."

Blake pressed the green icon. "Agent Meyer."

"Agent Meyer, this is Supervisory Special Agent-in-Charge Mark Rumford of the Chicago field office. I trust my agents have been helpful in your efforts."

"Very helpful, sir. How can I help you?"

"I just received a very strange phone call. The call came from a burner phone, but the person on the other end claimed to be the head of the group you are currently surveilling. His name is Johannes Schreiber. Have you ever heard of him?"

"Yes, as a matter of fact. He's been on our radar for years." Blake grabbed his laptop and opened it again. "The man is a bit of a ghost these days. He's an old man now. Has to be in his seventies, at least. It has been rumored he runs things from the basements of his multiple houses spread across Europe, but nobody knows for sure. However, he has all the contacts and all the money, so it's easy for him to find loyal mercenaries to do his bidding. He supplies them with everything they need, and they get the jobs done." He logged back in and accessed the needed files.

"Well, it would seem he's conceded this fight to you, Agent Meyer. He told me, and I quote, '...to let whoever is in charge of our operation know his men at the warehouse have agreed to hand over their weapons and go peacefully into custody.' End quote."

"Sounds easy enough. Almost too easy."

Rumford laughed. "I told you it was a strange call."

"And what assurances do we have we won't be walking into a trap?"

"He gave me another phone number. He said to call it. It supposedly belongs to the leader of the group at the warehouse. You are to tell him what to do, and he will have his men do it without any questions. He only had one request. To treat these men well, since they are surrendering peacefully."

"And what about the warehouse?"

"He said the warehouse wasn't his nor anything in it, so you could do with the contents as you see fit."

Blake smiled and opened Schreiber's file. "Very good, sir. Was there anything else?"

"No, but I am on my way to you as we speak."

"Excellent, because there are some things you're gonna want to see with your own eyes."

CHAPTER 46

FBI FIELD OFFICE
Washington, DC

Merina Parker heard someone outside the door to her holding room. Voices added to the commotion, and within seconds, she heard an electronic *Beep!* The door opened, and one federal agent stepped inside as Templeton Drake darkened the doorway with his patented victory smile.

"Congresswoman Parker," the agent said, "your attorney is here to give you a ride home. I have been instructed to release you. You're free to go."

Merina's face lit up with hope. She peered past the agent and eyed Mr. Drake. "Templeton, you did it?"

"It wasn't hard. Once I showed the judge the timeline—verified by the FBI itself—he didn't even need to have you arraigned. He dismissed the charges forthwith, and the prosecution agreed. You can go home now."

Merina let out a celebratory shout. "And Samantha?"

"She's being released as well. If you'd like, I can give you both a ride home. But we must hurry. Due to certain circumstances we can discuss later, my wife expected me to be home about fifteen minutes ago. But I called her and got a short reprieve."

"Thank you." Merina closed her eyes and inhaled deeply. She opened her eyes, and they welled up. "And I'm sorry if my life is getting in the way of yours."

Templeton gave Merina a tip of his flat cap. "This is why you pay me the big bucks."

"Well, in light of everything you've done, they can be a little bigger this time around. Tell you wife it's a 'thank you' for sharing your time with Samantha and me."

"Done and done."

* * *

Twenty minutes later, Templeton Drake, Merina Parker, and Samantha Springer exited the FBI field office, and Templeton led them to his car.

"Heads are gonna roll, Templeton. Have you seen the headlines? The agent who originally escorted me to the holding room when I first arrived showed me an article on her phone shortly before you showed up." Merina raised her hand in front of her and pretended the headline was written across the sky. "**CONGRESSWOMAN MERINA PARKER ARRESTED: FBI LINKS ELECTED OFFICIAL TO LAS VEGAS TERRORIST ATTACK.**"

"Merina," Templeton said, "Please. Wait until we get in the car to discuss this. D.C. has eyes and ears everywhere."

Merina glanced at Samantha and pursed her lips. "Oh, I'm gonna stab the eyes and blow the eardrums of D.C. by the time I'm done. Nobody locks me up on false accusations and gets away with it."

Templeton unlocked the vehicle, and Merina got into the front passenger seat. Samantha gladly piled into the back seat and slinked down as far as she could.

He started the engine, locked all the doors, and checked his mirrors.

"Now, can I talk?" Merina said.

"Listen, I fully understand your frustration. And yes, I saw the headline as well. They will have to retract it. Obviously."

"But you know how these things work, Templeton. I'm now guilty until proven innocent. People will say, 'It was in the newspaper, so it must be true.' And yeah, I got out, and we can hold press conferences and post on social media all about my innocence, backing it with proof. But there is always a lunatic fringe out there who will keep it alive. They'll say I'm a poster child for why our government cannot be trusted. If I was falsely accused, then there's a big problem. If I'm actually guilty, then there's a bigger problem—"

"And they would be right, Merina," Samantha said.

Merina spun around in her seat, adjusting the buckle as she did. "Yes, we know D.C. has its issues, but what government doesn't?"

"And isn't that the point?" Samantha lifted her hands as if her statement was the truest one ever made. "Governments, on the whole, cannot be trusted. If they are not dictatorial or militaristic in nature, then they are filled with greedy people who have their own agendas. They vote, pass bills, work backroom deals, all so they can take advantage of the system, gain more financial assets, more power, and more notoriety for themselves and those who support them. You're just as guilty as the rest, if we're being honest, Merina. Every last person in congress comes out richer than when he or she got into office. How does that happen, if corruption isn't center stage? You can't get rich off a salary of less than $200,000 while living in two places. You all walk out millionaires. You know it's true."

"That's why we are there, Samantha. To take a stand, especially for those who are not in power and have to live with the decisions of those who are. It's people like us who keep those folks in check. Without us, it becomes a dictatorship or a military regime, with no one to stop it. And that's why men like Templeton exist, to defend people like us who stand up for what is right and are blackballed in an attempt to get us out of the way."

Samantha listened to Merina, but stared at the back of her seat the entire time. "I hear what you are saying, Merina. I do. Those ideals are what motivated me to go to college and pursue my poli-sci degree. But, being locked up in there...being the no-name aide and not the high-powered congresswoman...it's changed my perspective." She paused and ran her fingers through her hair. "All I'm saying is, I've got some serious thinking to do about my career choices."

"It's understandable," Templeton said. "Being arrested, under false allegations, too, is never a pleasant experience. But let me give you something else to consider, Samantha. You and Merina must have hit a nerve. Notice, they didn't have any of the other members of the president's cabinet arrested. They manipulated a judge and a bunch of paperwork. They wasted the man hours of those FBI agents, and lied to them in the process to have you arrested the way they did. Somebody had been making plans. They didn't pull your arrests off on a whim. Things were already in motion. They simply were waiting for the right time to pounce. Luckily for us, they jumped too quickly. And now, we have a paper trail, provided by the perpetrators themselves, and I am going to trace all the way back to the source." Templeton checked his mirrors and pulled out from the curb. "Without knowing it at the time, your combined beliefs for what you deemed as right, coupled with your political stances based on those beliefs, forced your enemy's hand. You forced him or her to act, probably against their will, so they arrested you both out of necessity. Now, *they* are going to have to live with *their* decisions."

"If they are caught," Samantha said.

Merina gave an angry chuckle. "Oh, they will be, honey. You can take it to the bank. Templeton and his team are going to back trace our arrest warrants to the source, and I am going to fry whoever ordered it, whoever knowingly carried it out. Everybody is going down." She paused in an attempt to gain some composure. "And this is why you are no longer going to play the plucky sidekick. I've told you before there are seats needing to be filled by young, idealistic women like you. Local seats to start...to get your feet wet. But with my backing and support, it won't take long before you're sitting next to me on some congressional committee, fighting for justice."

"I'll take all of this under advisement," Samantha said, staring out the window as one building after another whizzed past. "But I have some soul-searching to do first."

"Well, don't wait long." Merina turned around and faced forward. "We need to strike while the iron's hot. And when we cause our enemy's castle to come tumbling down, we'll have all the momentum we need. However, in the meantime, you're still under my employ, right? As my plucky sidekick, so to speak. We'll go home and get some rest. Then tomorrow, we fight."

CHAPTER 47

NATHANSEN HOLDINGS DISTRIBUTION Center
Chicago, Illinois

While Blake Meyer waited for the AIC of the Chicago field office to arrive, he called the phone number provided to him by the AIC, via the man responsible for the guards around the warehouse.

"Hello?"

"This is Supervisory Special Agent Blake Meyer. To whom am I speaking?"

"Aldous Silva. I am the leader of this group of men."

"Mr. Silva, a man by the name of Johannes Schreiber gave a colleague of mine this number and said I could use it to work out the terms of your surrender. Is this your understanding as well?"

"Yes."

"Very well, then. This is what I need you to do. I need all of your men to remove all of their outer clothing. Vests, jackets, coats, hats, everything, and throw those items into the dumpster on the northeast side of the property along with all of their weapons and

344   C. KEVIN THOMPSON

communication devices. Once all of you have complied, then I need you to walk, single file, two minutes apart, to the west until you get to South Torrence Avenue. Then, turn north and walk across the bridge. We will have FBI agents on the other side of the bridge waiting. We will be taking each man alone, placing him into a transport vehicle, and then taking him to an undisclosed location for further interrogation."

Silva grunted. "I was told my men would be treated well. How can I assure this, if we are separated?"

"Mr. Silva, we want information. If your men cooperate and answer all of our questions to the best of their ability, then we have no reason to hurt them physically."

"It will take us a few minutes to comply with your demands. I will call you from this number when we have."

"Understood. And please inform your men to make sure all weapons and communication devices get placed into the dumpster along with your outer clothing. If we find so much as a pocket knife, then this deal is null and void. Do I make myself clear?"

"Crystal."

"Good. And do not be alarmed when the National Guard units arrive. They will simply assist us with the transportation and the securing of the warehouse."

* * *

Forty minutes had transpired. Blake had received the call from Aldous Silva, and approximately half of his men had been searched and hauled off to the Chicago field office by the time the AIC arrived.

"How's it going, Agent Meyer?" AIC Mark Rumford said. "Did the men surrender peaceably as their illustrious leader promised?"

"Yes, sir. They have complied with every directive. Now, we are in the process of transporting each man separately to the field office for interrogation."

Rumford shot Blake a puzzled look. "Why transport them separately? They have promised to work with us, and it seems they are holding up their end of the bargain."

"We are taking extra precautions, sir, because we believe they could have a backup plan."

Rumford straightened his stance and faced Blake more directly. "What sort of backup plan?"

"I believe they had two plans, actually. One of which they may have already ditched because of the current process of transporting them one at a time. The other will probably be enacted once we officially start asking questions, especially when those inquiries dig into their employer's affairs and whereabouts."

Rumford bit the inside of his cheek. "You think they'll lawyer up?"

"No. I think they will have some provided to them by Schreiber. Probably on their way as we speak."

"But if you are moving them one by one," Rumford said, scratching the back of his head, "then how will Schreiber know how many lawyers to send, and where to send them? And do those men even know they are going to the FO?"

"No, sir. I told their leader, Aldous Silva, that they would be taken to undisclosed locations."

Rumford looked around at all the activity and then back at Blake. "Okay, you're not making any sense, so you must know something I don't. Therefore, as the AIC, I suggest you inform me before we proceed much further. I run a tight ship, Agent Meyer, and I don't like being kept in the dark."

"Sir," Blake said, motioning toward the SUV. "Come into my office. There are some things I need to show you."

CHAPTER 48

NATHANSEN HOLDINGS DISTRIBUTION Center
Chicago, Illinois

Blake sat behind the wheel of the Ford Expedition and opened his laptop. He accessed his D-mail account and opened the files Harrison had supplied him.

"Sir, because of the nature of this investigation, which has taken me literally halfway around the world and back again, my inner circle of people I can trust has shrunk considerably. We have caught a bunch of bad actors, whose names will come out on the nightly news sooner or later, but unfortunately, we are not done yet."

"You found someone within my FO?" AIC Mark Rumford said.

Blake nodded. "Agent Edgerrin Felder."

"Felder? He's been with me for years...I actually requested and approved his transfer from Los Angeles. I used to work with him there and felt I needed people I knew when I was promoted to

AIC. He's literally followed me from Los Angeles, to Seattle, to Chicago."

"We have irrefutable evidence implicating him. I literally watched him text in real time when we fed him information, believing he would send it to Schreiber's men. We fed them some specific info, and Schreiber's men acted on it."

"What information did you feed Felder?"

"Well, we told all of the agents at the Hercules Tire location about how the packages being guarded in the warehouse under surveillance contained the contagion we had been looking for, and it was an antibiotic-resistant version of the bubonic plague. If we got into a gun battle with those guards, and some of those packages were damaged, and some of the contagion was released, the guards would die, because they were not wearing any biohazard gear, and a lot of other people would die as well, once the wind got ahold of this airborne contagion.

"Even more incriminating was the information we gave the agents about the money promised to those guards and how it had dried up. A colleague of mine was able to breach a computer owned by a man who was sourcing much of the operation to release the contagion. When his computer was breached, a wealth of information was unearthed, including the banks and accounts he had been using to fund it all. We seized those funds and shut down the accounts. When those guards finally realized they weren't getting paid, and they were courting disaster, they became very...*peaceable*."

Rumford peered out the window and saw Agent Felder, giving orders, acting like nothing was wrong. "I'm going to need to see your evidence."

"It's all here." Blake pulled up the text thread and turned the computer so Rumford could see. "He's been texting these mercenaries for several days, but there's another number he's been texting for longer than that. Unfortunately, because of my overall investigation, I cannot divulge the other number just yet, so you will notice it has been blacked out."

Rumford stared at Blake. Disbelief written all over his face. He turned the computer a little more and began reading.

Several minutes passed as he kept reading and reading.

"This other number that keeps popping up...not the blacked out one, but this one," Rumford said, pointing at the screen. "Is this the Silva guy?"

Blake accessed his phone, pulled up his most recent calls, and held the phone out for Rumford to see. "According to my list of calls made, it would seem so. Once we match the communication devices thrown into the dumpster with the guards' fingerprints, then we'll know."

Rumford shook his head and continued reading a little further before leaning into the chair back and gripping his chin. "Now I know why you transported the men like you did...one at a time. Felder was going to help them escape."

"Yes, sir. Felder knew there wasn't enough time to orchestrate any plan before they arrived at the FO, but he was formulating plans for when they were taken from the FO to their next destination. My plan to separate the men on the way to the FO and not tell them where they were going was done for two reasons. First, I simply wanted to be extra cautious, not knowing who else Felder may be working with. And secondly, this process slowed down the transport time and did not give Felder any information on where the men were being taken. I was buying *us* time until you arrived and decided what to do next."

Rumford gazed out the window at Felder. He watched Felder tap away at his phone and look more and more distraught. "He's nervous."

"And as you can see, he's still texting with someone. Yet, Aldous Silva has been in our custody for almost thirty minutes now."

Blake minimized the window on his computer screen and opened another. A program monitoring Felder's phone in real time was displaying the very texts Felder was typing right in front of them, with a ten-second delay, of course. "I can't allow you to see this, because Felder is texting the blacked-out number again... which is not blacked-out yet on my screen." Blake opened another file. "However, this is what he has been texting to the blacked-out number today." Blake cleared his throat and began to read:

Blacked-Out Number: "Update?"

Felder: "All the mercenaries are being rounded up as we speak. Why didn't you respond earlier?"

Blacked-Out Number: "Too many irons in the fire. Can't keep up right now."

Felder: "So, now what?"

Blacked-Out Number: "Play along. You should be safe. Silva's men, not so much."

Felder: "And the money?"

Blacked-Out Number: "Is the money all you care about? If so, then maybe you are not the man for the job after all."

Felder: "No need to get nasty. But I ain't doin' all of this for free either."

Blacked-Out Number: "Relax. You'll be compensated. Just do your job and get out of there ASAP. I need eyes and ears on your boss. We need to know what his next move is so we can make plans on our end."

Felder: "No worries. He's here on site right now. Meeting with Meyer."

Blacked-Out Number: "Ugh. That's not good. Keep a close eye on them both. Meyer has been a thorn in our side for days now."

Felder: "Understood."

Blacked-Out Number: "And since Silva and his men have been compromised, we can't take any chances. Ditch this phone ASAP and pick up another one. Text me the number. You know the drill."

Felder: "Understood."

Rumford sat motionless for several seconds. "Conspiracy to commit acts of terrorism, cyber terrorism, conspiracy to traffic biological weapons onto American soil, bribery, treason..." He shook his head. "Do you know how much paperwork is going to be involved?"

Blake smiled a little. *You don't know the half of it.*

Rumford placed his hand on the door handle. "So what are we waiting for?"

"I was waiting for you, sir." Blake offered a sorrowful grin. "He's your agent. I thought you should do the honors."

"*Honors?* It's never an honor to arrest a traitor, Agent Meyer. It's always a sad day for the Bureau when we have to arrest one of our own who has broken his or her oath."

"Agreed."

Both gentlemen exited the vehicle without another word. AIC Rumford called Agents Forsythe and Bradley over to him. "Agents, come with me." The three of them started to walk away from the vehicle, and Rumford turned around. "Agent Meyer, I would like you to join us."

Blake nodded and followed behind.

"Agent Felder!" Rumford waved him down.

Blake watched as Felder quickly tapped away at his phone and slipped it into his pocket.

"Yes, sir," Felder said, walking in their direction.

"Agent Felder," AIC Rumford said, "you are under arrest. Hand me your weapon, your credentials, and your phone."

"I'm what?" Felder laughed and peered at his supervisor. "Is this a joke?"

"Do I look like I'm joking, Agent Felder?" Rumford said, with his hand out.

Felder looked at Forsythe, then at Bradley. "What is he talking about?"

"You had just better do what he asks, Ed," Forsythe said. "You can get it all sorted later."

Felder turned to face Blake. "This was all you, wasn't it?"

Blake didn't respond. He simply stared back at the agent.

Felder unzipped his blue hoodie, lifted his shirt in frustration, reached around, and pulled his weapon from his waistband at the small of his back.

"Easy, Ed," Rumford said. "Just look around. You don't want to do anything brash."

Felder eased the weapon out and held his arm straight out from his side. He spun the weapon around in his hand, gripping the gun with his index finger and thumb.

Rumford took it and held out his hand again. "Your credentials and your phone. As a matter of fact, just empty all your pockets and give those items to these agents." Rumford turned to Bradley. "Go get some evidence bags, and bring Salazar and Guidry too."

Felder's frustrated expression turned to anger. "Why do you need those two?"

"Because, if you weren't guilty, you'd be acting differently. And I don't take too kindly to agents who break their oath."

"I have no idea what you're talking about."

"Oh, you will, Agent Felder. You will."

Bradley arrived with the other two agents. Once his possessions were placed in bags, Rumford motioned for Forsythe to place him in handcuffs and read the wayward agent his rights as they walked toward the AIC's vehicle.

CHAPTER 49

MARFA REGIONAL HOSPITAL
  Marfa, TX

Detective John Forde sat in a chair in the corner of Room 229. The room was under heavy guard, courtesy of Captain Theodore "Harley" Harlan and the local sheriff's office, as well as the Marfa Police Department.

Forde felt like he could relax a bit, knowing how many layers of security stood between Willis's new room and the outside world. Even good, loyal nurses and doctors who had worked at Marfa Regional for years were vetted, scrutinized, and escorted into the room by law enforcement. No one, not even Forde himself, was allowed in without having a background check run.

When you have one of the FBI's Top Ten Most Wanted villains after you, Forde thought, it can cause some paranoia to overtake the entire process of patient visitation.

Forde watched his partner breathe freely with the oxygen tube still positioned under his nose and draped over his ears.

Especially when you're still in a coma and can't defend yourself.

It had been a whirlwind case, for sure, Forde thought, as he replayed in his head the last four days. They went from investigating an elderly woman's missing diamond necklace the day before—which had been hocked at a pawn shop by the new playboy "boyfriend" she had met on a cruise—to investigating the survivors of a crash on Highway 287.

Those survivors, identified as illegal immigrants from Mexico, Hector and Elena Jimenez, identified a group called The Hands of Allah as the means by which they had entered the country. *Coyotes* smuggled them to the border, The Hands of Allah got them over it, and they were on their way to Orlando, Florida, when the tire on the SUV blew.

However, it wasn't a mere tale of seeking a better life in another place. Forde and Willis had surmised Hector was running from someone, and when the Sinaloa Cartel's top fixer showed up, it became more obvious. What Hector failed to realize, though, was how he could never travel far enough to extend past the cartel's reach.

Forde and Willis also knew The Hands of Allah drivers in the SUV were slimy too. And when they heard these "Egyptian diplomats" worked for an organization with Saudi Arabian ties, their "Spidey senses" went off.

And for good reason.

Now, here they were, four days later.

Hector Jimenez's body would be dug up soon, evidence against those responsible.

Pictures of Elena Jimenez and her three children had been circulated through Interpol and Europol, along with the very clear photos of who they now knew to be Pedro Arroyo and Guillermo Castaneda. Of course, Arroyo was healing in another room in the hospital, under even heavier guard, waiting to be transported to a federal facility in San Antonio.

If I had my way, Forde thought hours earlier, I'd walk into Arroyo's room and finish what he started in Willis's old hospital room. Because of all the corruption Captain Harlan, Dennis Morrison, and I uncovered, I'm not certain justice will ever be served.

Yet, Forde knew. As soon as he did whatever he would do to end Arroyo, at that moment, he'd become Arroyo. And this was a line he could not cross, which was why he sat next to Russell's bed. He was safe from himself, if he remained there, and Captain Harlan had granted him however long he needed in order to be there when Willis woke up and eventually could be discharged.

Castaneda, on the other hand, was still a ghost...of sorts. Video footage of him sharing a moment with the Director of Homeland Security and supplying her with a limo to and from the airport so they could meet privately was gold. And the photos released to Interpol and Europol, Forde learned, were going to be circulated to every news agency in the known world, once all of his crooked contacts in the States were rounded up and read their rights.

The FBI, CIA, and trusted people like Dennis Morrison within DHS all believed once Castaneda's face was shown all over the globe, his associates in the Sinaloa Cartel would decide he had become too much of a liability and take care of the problem of "the ghost who is Guillermo Castaneda" for them.

I'd love to be a fly on the wall when that happ—

Russell Willis's fingers moved suddenly, causing Forde to jump.

"Man, you scared me, Russell. I'm sitting here, reliving all this madness we've been through, and you move your fingers like they're trying to break free or something." Forde watched him intently for a few additional seconds. "Next time, warn a guy, will ya?"

"Okay," Willis said.

Forde immediately stood.

Willis's face was facing away from Forde, so he stepped around to the other side of the bed. "Russell. You awake?"

Forde noticed a change in Willis's vitals on the monitor. Everything appeared to rise, and as he glanced down at Willis and then back at the monitor, he could see Willis's eyes moving, like he was in some kind of deep REM sleep.

Forde pushed the call button.

"How can I help you?" came the voice a half-minute later.

"I think you all need to come check on Mr. Willis. His vitals have shot up."

"We're on our way."

Seconds later, a nurse and the shift physician arrived and entered the room with a deputy sheriff.

"What happened?" the doctor said.

Forde pointed at the chair. "I was sitting over there, and he moved his fingers, like this." Forde demonstrated what he saw. "It freaked me out, so I told him he needed to warn me before he did that again...you know, joking around with him? I've always heard how people in comas can still hear you, right? And when I said what I said, he replied to me. Said the word 'okay.' When he did that, I got up, walked over to this side of the bed, asked him if he was awake, and his vitals jumped up. They're even higher now."

The doctor, already with his stethoscope removed from around his neck, positioned the earpieces into place, pulled down the sheet to Willis's waist, and slid the bell and diaphragm inside Willis's gown until it was resting on Willis's chest. He pressed on it.

"That's cold," Willis said.

The doctor yanked the earpieces out and peered at the nurse. "Did he say, 'That's cold?'"

The nurse nodded as did Forde.

"Detective Willis, this is Doctor Reynaurd. Can you hear me?"

"Loud and clear, Space Ranger," Willis said, a bit groggy and with his eyes still closed.

The doctor smiled and leaned in a little closer. "Can you open your eyes for me?"

Willis inhaled on cue and lifted his eyebrows, as if they would pull the lids open. He did it twice. "I guess not."

"Okay, no worries. They could be kind of glued shut with sleep, you know? You've been out for a while."

"How...how long...is a while?"

The doctor glanced at Forde and the nurse and smiled. "Long enough, my friend. It's time for you to wake up. However, we need you to do so in your own time. Your vitals are pretty high right now, so we don't want to make them get any higher."

Willis nodded his head ever so slightly and seemed content with drifting off into another round of slumber.

"Listen, Detective Willis, you have a friend here who has been looking after you...in more ways than one, I hear. If you need anything or have any questions, will you tell..." The doctor motioned at Forde. "I'm sorry. Your name is again?"

"John. We're both detectives for the same agency. He's my partner."

"So, Russell, please let John know if you need anything. Okay?"

"John is here?"

"He is. Would you like to speak with him?"

Willis nodded.

Forde stepped a little closer. "I'm here, buddy." Forde grabbed Willis's hand and held it tight for a couple of seconds. "I'm gonna stay with you until you're ready to walk out of here. Captain Harlan's orders."

Russell took a deep breath and forced it out. His vitals shot up, and in a very deliberate effort, his eyes slowly opened. It took them a few seconds to focus before they zeroed in on their hands. He followed Forde's arm up to the shoulder and then turned his head slightly so their eyes could meet.

"Man, is it good to see you, Russell," Forde said.

Russell wrinkled his brow a smidgen. "Who are you?"

Forde glanced at the doctor.

The doctor's expression switched from one of anticipated joy to skepticism.

Forde faced Russell again. "It's me, Russell. John Forde. Your partner for, like, years now?"

Russell continued to pinch his brow together until Forde finished talking. Then, he relaxed and smiled. "I was just kidding."

Forde set his jaw and peered at the two medical professionals, who had now started to laugh. "Yeah, funny. Real funny. The doc here was about to call security on me."

Willis smiled again. He opened his eyes and stared at his friend. "Sorry. Just havin' a little fun."

"Oh, you haven't changed a bit," Forde said. "Even drugged and injured, you're a piece of work."

Willis inhaled deeply. "Did I miss anything?"

Forde laughed. "You missed practically everything, Russell. But I'm glad you're still with us. I can fill you in on everything when you're ready for it."

CHAPTER 50

NATHANSEN HOLDINGS DISTRIBUTION Center
  Chicago, Illinois

The warehouse mercenaries were in custody and gone. Agent Felder had been arrested and taken to a secure facility away from where the mercenaries were being held. The plan, so far, had worked to perfection. The first two objectives, arrest the informant working for the FBI and have the mercenaries surrender without having to fire a shot and risk releasing the contagion, had been accomplished. Now, the last objective, the primary objective, remained.

Forty minutes had transpired. Blake sat in his SUV and watched as National Guard personnel, wearing biohazard suits and gear, entered the warehouse. They carried all the latest gadgetry needed to detect a contagion and a bomb. Tasked with inspecting all the packages once the building was deemed safe from any incendiary devices, Blake knew it would take some time, but he was willing to wait. If this was the antibiotic-resistant strain of the plague, then it was the mother lode. Five days of searching could finally come to an end.

As Blake allowed the others to do their jobs, he replayed the last five days in his head. The length of time he'd spent searching for the contagion...waiting for this moment...had only been five days?

Five days?

It seems like five months...

But the actual recovery process will take months...years, even...Sara and the kids...Sara and me...

Blake saw some National Guard personnel exit the warehouse and talk to some colleagues as well as some CDC officials who were waiting to enter the building.

These people will go on with their lives. Do their jobs. Punch the clock. Go home. Wake up, and do it all over again.

But what about us? Sara is not going to want me to go back to work for the Bureau after this...and we can't go home...there's no home to go back to...and there's no sense in rebuilding it...too many ugly memories reside along that stretch of coastline now...

Tears formed in his eyes.

We may never be able to go to the beach again...

Or have birthday parties in the home...

Especially for the kids...

Blake wiped his eyes. They were tired and itched, but honestly, they were wet because of how Colin Murphy had irreparably altered his life.

Forever.

And all because Murphy believed a lie.

Hundreds are dead because of his plans.

Millions more could have been, if it were not for the efforts of so many others.

And six months from now, will anyone care any longer about those, like Blake and Sara, who have to deal with the fallout?

Blake knew there would be the initial fanfare and applause from being one of the operatives who "stopped the bad guys." He also was aware of the possibility of becoming a "media favorite" to help drive up the ratings.

For his sacrifice to his country, he would be assured the government would assist with housing.

The insurance company would also step in, no doubt looking for kudos from the public, and "do everything they can" to help SSA Meyer and his family. Complete with photo ops and company logos on full display.

Blake and Sara would probably have several choices of where to live next.

There would be counseling services available.

There would be job offers, both within the Bureau and outside in the private sector.

Blake understood how it all worked, because he had seen this scenario play out before. Military heroes who get their ticker-tape parade down America's Main Street one day only to find themselves in the land of obscurity the next, only to be remembered on Memorial Day—when they are eighty-five years old and can barely walk—by the few who are not grilling hamburgers and hot dogs.

When a person took the time to contemplate it all, Blake thought, the world had everything upside down.

Men and women who could bounce a ball...or hit a ball with a stick...or who could "go to war on the gridiron" in pads and a helmet... they all got paid hundreds of thousands, even millions upon millions, for playing a game. Yet, the millions of people who work real jobs, every day...jobs which are not games...like serving their country, fighting fires, arresting bad criminals and getting them off the street...the people who literally put their lives on the line against enemies who wish ill on others...they get paid a pittance by comparison.

Children start off by wanting to be policemen and firemen...when they are little. But something happens to so many of them by the time they are teenagers. They get bit by the bug...Harrison calls it "greed" and "pride"...and they want to suddenly be in the limelight. No longer satisfied with public service, they wish to be bouncing a ball, hitting one with a stick, or throwing a pigskin. And their parents support it, because in the end, if junior becomes a gajillionaire on some field or court, then the parents will receive some of their child's "blessing."

There is no "blessing" for police officers killed in the line of duty, attempting to protect and serve...

No "blessing" for the firefighter who dies in a blaze, attempting to rescue someone from the flames...

There is no such "blessing" for those who walk off the battlefield with scars on the skin and scars on the heart and soul...

Or for the families whose son or daughter exited the battlefield in a casket...

Unless you get offered a boatload of money to tell your behind-the-scenes story...

Like I probably will...to tell my story of the last five days...

As will others...

And many will pat themselves on the back and write their memoirs, as if they ran the entire operation from some plush Washington, D.C. office...

It's all upside down...

And after these last five days, I don't see how it can be fixed...

Blake wiped his eyes again.

Harrison...I think you may be on to something, my friend—

Blake caught a motion out of the corner of his eye. He looked up and saw one of the other FBI agents waving at him and saying something.

Blake shut off the engine and exited the vehicle.

"Agent Meyer," the other agent said, walking up to him, "the commander of the guard unit says the warehouse is secure. They did not find any explosive devices, and it does not appear any of the boxes on pallets have been tampered with. Those pallets are shrink-wrapped and appear intact."

"Excellent. Tell the commander he can hand over the warehouse to the CDC officials on-site. We need them to confirm the nature of the contagion ASAP."

"Will do, sir."

* * *

Twenty minutes later, the head of the CDC team approached Blake, pulling her headgear off and removing her gloves. The look on her face had Blake puzzled.

"Please tell me it's not some bogus stunt meant to be a decoy," Blake said.

"No. Quite the contrary. It's bubonic plague. Loads of it. Perfectly packaged in air fresheners." The CDC official used her fingers to brush her hair. "It's a diabolical plan, if you ask me. Had these made it into the hands of the public...well, I don't have to tell you what a catastrophe we would have been dealing with."

"So, it's the antibiotic-resistant strain then?"

"Actually, no. It matches the specs of the contagion released in Las Vegas. We'll run some additional tests just to make sure, but our initial tests match the strain used in Nevada."

Blake, who had been rubbing his temple with his right hand, allowed his arm to drop in a perplexed manner. "That doesn't make sense. The information we received initially, five days ago, and other communiques we have received and uncovered since then have all indicated a version of the plague resistant to antibiotics. We were promised by those in control of the contagion of how it would decimate our country and others around the world, if it were released."

The CDC official pursed her lips. "Well, I'm sorry to disappoint you. I thought this would be good news."

Blake held his hands up chest high. "It is, in that it is not as harmful as we were led to believe. However, if there is a strain out there that is antibiotic-resistant—"

"Then it's still out there somewhere," the CDC official said, unzipping her biohazard suit and pulling her arms free. "And we're not out of the woods yet, like you hoped."

"Exactly." Blake snatched the cell phone out of his pocket. He held it up. "I've got some calls to make. Thank you for your quick assessment."

"You're welcome," she said with a frown. "We'll test every package to make sure they are all the same."

"Okay. Please let me know if you do find another strain."

"Will do," she said before heading back to her team.

Blake stood there for a few seconds, phone in hand.

If this isn't the strain of the plague we've been looking for, then we're dead in the water. We have no other leads on its location...

It could be anywhere.

It may not even be in the States anymore.

Blake huffed and tried to keep his blood pressure in check.

We're gonna have to go back to the beginning...comb through Sorensen's files again...

It's gonna take time...

Time we may not have...

Time I know I don't have...Sara would never go for it. She'd divorce me, for sure, if I had to tell her I need to spend another week or two—or more—looking for this contagion.

Blake accessed his contacts, scrolled through them, and dialed.

"Blakey, I'm hoping you have good news for me," Harrison said.

"No, actually, I don't. The contagion in the warehouse...it's the same contagion as Las Vegas."

"That can't be. Sorensen's files say otherwise."

"Well, I'm telling you what the CDC team leader on-site just told me. They got it right in Las Vegas, so I have to trust their expertise here. They are going to check every package, so they may find some of them laced with a different strain. However, as of right now, there is no antibiotic-resistant strain present."

"Blake, I'm telling you, I've read and reread Sorensen's files. It states, specifically, how an antibiotic-resistant strain of bubonic plague was created and produced in a lab in Novosibirsk, Russia. This same lab was responsible for finding a cure for it, so the people involved in its release could protect themselves. I even checked it out. There is a lab located in Novosibirsk. Sorensen's also got transcripts of meetings between him and this group called The Consortium. They were very meticulous, Blake. It's actually downright scary how meticulous they've been. This plan has been in the works since February of 2000. Murphy was the one leading the group in the beginning. According to Sorensen's notes, this entire plan was Murphy's idea, but when he needed money, he found people, 'investors' I guess you could call them, who bankrolled his plans.

"However, as time went on, this group took over the project, expanded it by creating what they called 'Plan B,' which involved the devices they detonated in Las Vegas and now Union Market."

"Harrison, you know I believe you, but there is no antibiotic-resistant contagion present currently in this warehouse." Blake blew out an exhausted breath through his lips. "We're missing something, Harrison."

"Whoever came up with this 'Plan B' was the driving force behind Murphy being pushed out. It started when Murphy sent the communiqué several days ago about Operation Wepwawet, which in turn, got you involved. They believed their plan would have proceeded without a hitch, if Murphy had not sent you the message.

"But make no mistake, Blakey, they believed that warehouse

contained the deadly version of the plague, same as you. Hence, the reason why top-flight mercenaries were enlisted to guard it."

Blake listened to what Harrison was saying, but his mind was running other scenarios at the same time. "Harrison, what if Sorensen and this consortium were duped? What if they were led to believe they had the deadly version but didn't?"

"Why would someone do such a thing? Wouldn't that be a deadly game to play? This consortium is a Who's Who of powerful people with tentacles spread out all over the place."

Blake walked back over to his SUV. "I'm not sure yet, but a few possible reasons come to mind. First, it could simply be a case of making the plague wrong. You think you have a deadly strain, but it turns out to be not as deadly as you thought or were led to believe. You're duped in a way, but it isn't on purpose."

"Maybe." Harrison sighed into the phone. "But again, the notes don't support it."

"The second possibility concerns how all this went down. Maybe Murphy's impatience, and my subsequent involvement, caused a change in plans somehow. Maybe those in charge of the contagion were not willing to allow it to be used, if there was such a high risk of it being found and confiscated."

"You may be onto something there, Blakey. The notes do support such a line of thinking, so maybe they did have to alter their plans, especially when we discovered air fresheners were going to be used."

Blake opened the door to the SUV and climbed into the driver's seat. "Another possibility would revolve around the person or people responsible for making it. In other words, they have it. It's lethal to the nth degree, but for some reason, they chose to supply Sorensen and his people with a different, less lethal version."

"There's nothing in the notes to indicate Sorensen or anyone else believed they had somehow been deceived."

Blake closed the door and started the engine. "But think about it, Harrison. You said it yourself. Murphy had worn out his welcome. Yet, this entire plan originated with him. Therefore, whoever was working with Murphy on the contagion, back in the days of the tests in Africa, for example, and maybe even before Africa, had to have been okay with working with Murphy. And they must have agreed to allow him to test their creation to see if it worked or not." Blake closed his eyes and lowered his head, trying to concentrate. "Now, if you're working with someone you trust, a person like Colin Murphy, to be exact, and you trust him enough to use *your* contagion...then, in a mere few years, he gets squeezed out of his own plan by others with lots of money and power, would you just switch allegiances so easily?"

Harrison grunted. "I suppose I wouldn't, no. I'd be skeptical of those people."

"Exactly. Especially if you're dealing with a contagion that could harm *you* in some way, if it found its way into the hands of people you don't trust."

"Okay," Harrison said with a little more excitement in his voice. "I'm catching your vibe now. When this bloke worked hand-in-hand with Murphy, he had assurances, but when the plan came under new management, those guarantees probably went out the window."

Blake lifted his chin and opened his eyes. He stared out the front windshield at all the commotion going on around him. "Possibly."

Harrison whistled through his teeth. "So, Blakey, you know what you're saying, right?"

"I do." Blake paused and wrinkled his brow. "Harrison, didn't you tell me a while back about a person in all those voiceprints you could not identify?"

"Yeah. Yeah, yeah, yeah, yeah. He was referred to in Sorensen's files as 'Vector," but he was never called by name. Mitchell and I did everything we could to get a match, but this guy is apparently a new player."

"I need you to drop whatever it is you're working on and figure out who this person is, if for any other reason than to rule him out."

"With nothing more than a couple of voiceprints to go on?"

"Wasn't Murphy's phone recovered when we arrested him?"

"Yes, but your techie boys in the FBI said it had been wiped. Mitchell and I already tried. And after a short confab, we believed it was James Connell who did it."

Blake muttered his dismay and let out a heavy sigh. "I caught Murphy—in the early morning, to be exact—and Connell, being the 'nice guy' that he was, suggested I head home and spend time with Sara and the kids because of Little Sara's birthday coming up. He said I could come in the next day and fill out my report, so I happily handed over everything to him."

"Yes, you did, but I wouldn't blame yourself, my friend. We didn't have any idea Connell was sleeping with the enemy back then."

Blake heard Harrison speak, but he wasn't really listening. "Connell must have taken the phone and did a factory reset before allowing it to be collected into evidence. Would have been easy enough to blame it on Murphy."

"Mitchell and I came to the same conclusion."

Blake felt his blood pressure escalate. "Listen, I need to call Julee. Let me talk to her. Maybe you and Agent Mitchell can team up on finding this 'Vector' character. In the meantime, go back through Sorensen's notes. Access his files on those servers and do a word search for 'Vector.' No stone unturned. Got it?"

Harrison faked a mellow laugh. "And I thought finding the warehouse would end this ordeal...I should have known."

CHAPTER 51

Blake Meyer hung up and slammed his fists on the steering wheel. He pounded the wheel again, and again, and threw his phone against the front windshield, growling in despair.

The thought of Connell, standing there on the tarmac in Gainesville, pretending to be caring and supportive, when all he wanted was Blake out of the way so he could allow Murphy's plan to proceed without any further interference, infuriated him.

It infuriated him, because of how Connell worked against him at every turn.

It infuriated him, because he didn't see it, when it was staring him in the face.

It infuriated him, because he'd been duped, and his family had been abducted and used against him, to distract him and keep him from getting in the way.

Now, all these days later...so many people had paid the price because of his inability to spot the enemy right in front of him.

Inside, the father, the husband, the soldier, and the FBI agent, exhausted from the wearisome trials of the last week, could no longer point their fingers at each other.

They had all failed.

Failed their country.

Failed his family.

Failed Sara.

Failed.

Blake lowered his head and covered his face with his hands.

Maybe Sara was right. Just go home and let someone else worry about it now...

We found the stockpile of contagion...let someone else figure out what to do next...

And let the chips fall...let them land where they choose to land. And if this contagion lands on our doorstep, then so be it.

Better to die together as a family, right? Than to be separated another minute, only to what? Be annihilated anyway?

"You have to finish this," came the voice of the soldier. Almost a whisper. "You may not know where the lethal strain of the contagion is, or even if there is one, but you do know who the players are."

"He's right," said the weak voice of the FBI agent. "Take them down and dismantle the entire operation. It may set them back years. They may never recover. But if you allow them to continue, and they eventually carry out their plan, you'll never be able to live with yourself."

"Besides...all that talk of 'dying together,'" the voice of the father said in a disgusted tone, "doesn't give Jacob or Little Sara much of a chance at a life of their own, now, does it?"

"Yeah," the angered voice of the husband said. "You just saved your kids. You saved Sara. And went to a lot of trouble to do it.

Doesn't make much sense to give up now. Sara would hate you more than ever, if you did."

Blake listened to the thoughts echo in his head. Every ounce of his being was sickened by his exhausted, depressed state of affairs. The despair he had allowed to engulf him, coupled with his words of defeat, incensed his soul.

The turmoil roiling inside, a cauldron of indecisiveness and hopelessness, bubbled up into a new sensation, and Blake wasn't sure how to handle it.

He always knew what to do next.

Always prided himself on being four steps ahead.

But the exhaustion was overtaking him...the synapses didn't seem to be firing on all cylinders...

Blake gripped the steering wheel as his hands gently quivered. With his eyes still closed, he breathed deeply in and out, almost to the point of passing out, but the soldier inside was determined to get him under control. So was the rest of the cast.

It took several minutes, but finally, with his breathing normalized, he could open his eyes without having them pool with tears.

He reached across the dashboard and grabbed his phone, inspecting it for damage before dialing Julee Scarfano's number. He sniffed and grabbed the back of his neck with his free hand, waiting for the line to connect.

"Well, hello, stranger," Julee said with a hint of happiness in her voice. "I hear you've been busy there in Chicago. News of the seizure of the warehouse and an errant agent's arrest has been circulating. Nothing official yet from the director, but the rumor mill has been active."

"Listen, Julee, uh, we've got a problem."

"Uh-oh...sounds serious. Are you all right?"

"We secured the warehouse, and the CDC tested the contagion. They're saying it's the same kind as the one released in Las Vegas."

Blake could hear voices in the background and what sounded like papers rustling.

"Interesting that you should say that. We just received our first two confirmed cases from the Union Market attack. An elderly woman and a small child were brought to an area hospital. They have tested positive for bubonic plague. The hospital tested the parents of the small child too. They also have it, but just haven't shown symptoms yet. And all four of them have been infected with the same strain as Vegas and are now being quarantined and treated with antibiotics."

Blake shook his head in disbelief. "Have any of the other devices been tested yet?"

"I don't think so. I haven't heard anything. But judging from what you just told me, I'm thinking all of those devices were probably supplied the same strain."

"Yeah, I would have to concur, but we need them all tested, Julee. We have to be sure. If just one of them was supplied with the more lethal strain, then it still can wreak havoc, especially if it's in a busy location, like Union Market."

"Every team working on finding those devices has been given the order to have CDC personnel test it."

"Okay then. Our next step is to follow our one last lead. And Julee, it is our only lead on finding the more lethal strain of this contagion at this point. I've got Harrison working on trying to identify the last voice in those voiceprints he and Agent Mitchell worked on. The file was labeled 'Vector,' and this person was there in the beginning, when Murphy was developing this contagion. He has to be the link to the more serious strain."

"I'll have Mitchell reach out to Harrison and see how he can help."

"Thanks, Julee."

"Are you sure you're okay? You sound tired."

Blake grunted. "I would be happy to be 'tired.' Even exhausted."

"That bad, huh? I can only imagine. I'm thoroughly wiped, and I haven't been hopping around the globe like you have."

"Yeah, well, I'll try to get some shuteye on my way back to Jacksonville, but I'm not sure I'll be able to sleep, knowing the contagion could still be out there."

"Actually, I was hoping maybe on your way back here from Chicago, you could make contact with Conrad Bowker."

"Conrad can wait."

"He's been arrested, Blake. He's in Paris and is being extradited to London as we speak.

"Arrested? What for?"

"They are accusing him of killing Major General Botinkin and some other men while he was trying to escape to the American Embassy in Paris."

"That makes zero sense. Why protect the major general for me, only to kill him and get caught doing so. Conrad's way too careful for such an uncalculated, bonehead move."

"Hey, I don't know him half as well as you do, so I have no idea what he is capable of. But according to his son, Kurt, he wasn't the golden boy you knew and loved." Julee paused. "Listen, Blake, we've uncovered a great deal of information from Kurt Bowker's computers and files. I'm going to have John send you what we have so far. Once you see it, then you'll know what I'm talking about."

Blake knew Conrad could be difficult. He also knew he and Kurt never "got on," as Conrad used to say, but he was never very specific. "Okay. I'll look it over once I'm in the air."

CHAPTER 52

Before they hung up, Blake Meyer asked Julee to authorize a video call with Conrad Bowker. Since she had talked to Conrad while he was in French custody, he believed she had the best shot at pulling it off.

An hour had transpired since he left the warehouse and drove to the airport where his Gulfstream sat refueled and awaiting his arrival.

He handed over the keys from the SUV to the agent who had accompanied him, and she left to head back to the Chicago field office.

Blake boarded the plane, asked the pilots to take him to Jacksonville, and sat down with his laptop.

For the first thirty minutes in the air, he studied the material Agent Mitchell had supplied him from Kurt Bowker's computer system. The more he read, the more bewildered he became.

Julee had warned Blake about the mountain of information Kurt Bowker amassed on his father. Much of it wasn't good.

No, most of it, Blake thought....

Just when you think you know someone...

Blake's phone rang, and he checked the screen. "Julee, were you successful?"

"I was. Took some persuading, but the contacts in London you provided proved helpful. Once I shared everything you'd been through and where we stood currently, they were much more amenable."

"Good. Now, how is this supposed to work?"

"John is going to send you a link. Open it, and follow the prompts. Make sure the sound on your computer is turned all the way up, and make sure your microphone is also turned up. Oh, and you'll need the camera on as well. I was told you have one hour. No more. It's all the time they're willing to give Bowker."

"Okay, thank you, Julee. I appreciate it. It would seem Conrad and I have some things to discuss, including how he ticked off the British government."

Julee harrumphed. "Didn't I tell you? Mr. MI-6 isn't as innocent as everyone thought he was."

"None of us are, Julee." Blake smiled at the thought. "Something Harrison's been trying to tell me for years now, and I've been too clueless to—"

"Sorry, Blake," Julee interrupted. "John is giving me the thumbs-up sign. Your link has been sent."

Blake waited a few more seconds until it arrived. "Got it."

"All right then. Give Conrad my love."

Blake nodded as if Julee could see him. "Will do." He hung up and repositioned himself in his seat as he pondered Harrison's words again.

It's all a fallacy, Blakey. You work hard at your job, because you believe there are good people in the world. And by human standards, yes, there are good people. We even say, "He's good people," or "She's a good person," but not by God's standards...

Nobody is innocent...

Not even one.

Taking a swig of water from the bottle beside him, Blake swallowed and then inhaled deeply and blew it out of his mouth. He closed his eyes.

Not even the "good people"? Blake had asked Harrison that day.

Harrison responded, *"How many 'good people' do you know who have never done something wrong, even by human standards?"*

It was a good question. No matter how "good" Blake tried to be at his job, he had a mental catalog of things he had done wrong over the years. Some of them he knew were wrong just as soon as he did it...like punching Colin Murphy...*repeatedly*...while he was cuffed to a table. All out of anger. If Murphy was still alive, Blake knew his actions would have been used against a conviction. "Police brutality!" would have been the cry of his attorney.

Even his actions against Morozov blurred the line between justice and revenge.

"Therefore," Blake responded to Harrison, *"if I cannot claim 'goodness' by trying to do the 'right thing' in defending my country, which is always viewed as a 'laudable cause' in the eyes of every patriot alive, then when can I claim to be 'good'?"*

Harrison chuckled at Blake's question. *"Never, Blakey. And that's the point. If you cannot be 'good' by human standards all the time, how can you ever be 'good enough' to meet God's standards, which are infinitely higher and more demanding?"*

Blake huffed again, opened his eyes, and clicked on the link Agent Mitchell had sent him. His duty now, to inform an old friend concerning some disturbing news, seemed apropos somehow. Based on what Harrison had taught him, Conrad served as the poster child for human failings.

He followed the instructions and waited for his laptop to make the connection until his image filled the screen.

He heard a sound like a phone dialing a number. Then, a click, followed by another, chirped from the speakers as another screen appeared, pushing his image into a small box in the upper, right-hand corner of the screen.

Staring at him with a big smile on his face was Conrad Bowker.

"Supervisory Special Agent Blake Meyer. It sure is good to see your face. I take it you have found your family, and they are safe?"

"It's good to see you, too, Conrad. And yes, they are safe now."

"Brilliant. Just brilliant." Conrad nodded his approval before holding up his hands. "So, as you can see by my 'restricted circumstances,' my situation has changed since we last spoke."

Blake noticed the computer Conrad was using sat back, several feet away from where he was sitting. He could see handcuffs on Conrad's wrists, and the room appeared to be some kind of interrogation room. "Are they detaining you at Scotland Yard?"

"MI-6 headquarters, actually."

"Are we alone, or do you have someone listening in on your end?"

"Your guess is as good as mine. They told me this conversation would be private between you and me. Julee Scarfano's request, I hear. But, since it is over the computer, who knows how many hackers, big tech companies, and government spies are listening in."

Blake shrugged. "Then, I guess we will have to trust they honored Julee's request."

"Do we have a choice, ole boy?"

"I suppose not." Blake opened his water bottle again. "Why are you in custody, Conrad?"

"According to them, I've been a naughty agent. They've accused me of killing Major General Botinkin and some hired hands I had never met prior to our one and only encounter. They said I poisoned them all."

"Poison? Well, you of all people know how that works."

"Really? I swear...you and Julee are too much."

"She say the same thing?"

"You trained her well, my friend. And you know, as well as I do, I only know about poisoning from being on the receiving end."

"That's what I meant." Blake took a swig. "How are they saying this happened?"

"They say I put it in the major general's tea and used the water bottles the hired hands brought with them."

Blake froze and stared at his bottle. It was almost empty. He swallowed slowly and put the cap back on the bottle.

Conrad chuckled. "What's wrong, Agent Meyer? Afraid I got to you too? Somehow tainted your drink from across the pond?"

"No...of course not. But you have to admit, the timing is a little, uh, interesting." Blake set the bottle down on the table beside him.

Conrad scratched his head. "Well, if you did believe such things, then you'd be no different than these imbeciles. I'm telling you, Blake, I'm being set up, and I have no clue who is behind it. There was no reason for me to kill the driver and his partner."

"What about the major general? Did you kill Botinkin?"

"No. I had every right to. I found out he was the one who approved and orchestrated the Russian's research into radioactive isotope poisoning. So, yeah...I could have killed him. Probably should have. But I also knew you were counting on him to help your cause, so I placed my personal vendetta aside." Conrad let out a relieved chuckle. "Little did I know someone felt the same way I did."

Blake stared at the screen. "I may be able to help you connect the dots and explain who was behind all this. However, before I do, I need to ask you a few questions about Operation Abydos."

"Operation *Abydos*? Never heard of it."

"Conrad, please. Don't insult my intelligence."

Conrad took a deep breath and looked away from the computer for a brief moment. "Okay, so I have heard of it."

"I know about the contagion, Conrad. The one Murphy and Clarke were trying to prevent from being released in their own country? *Yersinia pseudotuberculosis* mixed with myelin toxin."

Conrad lifted an eyebrow.

"I also know Arina Filipov facilitated its delivery to the group of IRA radicals and was going to help with its release." Blake paused and consulted his notes. "And I know it was supplied by the Russians. And I know there was a middle man. Someone who got the contagion from the Russians and delivered it to Filipov."

Conrad smirked. "You've been talking to Julee."

"Actually, yes. But I just received new information about you…" Blake whistled. "It goes way beyond what Julee told me."

Conrad cursed. "Well, since you probably know about everything there is to know, why are you asking me about Operation Abydos?"

"Because I want to know *why*, Conrad. Why did you do what you did?"

Bowker groaned at the thought of having to explain. "To put it simply, I found the spy life much easier to navigate in those years by playing both sides. It became my *modus operandi*, almost every time. Gathering intelligence was so much easier. At least, it was for me."

Blake sat stunned. He'd wondered about Conrad's allegiances over the years, especially when he went on his blogging rampage, naming every person in the book and giving away state secrets. However, the one thing he never considered was Conrad being a double agent.

"I can see I have finally left you speechless, my old friend."

Blake's head shook slowly from side to side. "I don't believe it.

You're a lot of things, Conrad, but I refuse to believe you were a double agent."

"Believe what you like, Blake. But for once, I'm finally coming clean...and you know, it feels good. If I'm going to rot in a British prison, I might as well do it with a clean conscience, eh?"

"I'll have to have proof," Blake said as he cleared his throat.

"They say confession is good for the soul, right? Well, try this one on for size, my American friend. You know about my nephew. You know how I ranted online about how the British government sacrificed him behind enemy lines, as it were?"

"I do."

"Well, what you may *not* know, Agent Meyer, is my nephew wasn't brainwashed. He didn't become disillusioned with England or 'The West,' and thus side with the communists. My blog posts were a cover. He was my protégé. He idolized me, actually...the poor kid. He told me he wanted to be *just like me*, so I showed him the ropes. Of course, he didn't know I was a double agent. He believed I had the Union Jack tattooed on my heart.

"On one particular case I was working, I learned the Russians had information we needed, so I ran my nephew in the field. His mission was easy. He was to portray himself as a disgruntled British IT employee who worked for the government, looking to score some serious cash in exchange for information. He was to hold one meeting. Share a sample of the kind of information he had to sell, arrange a buy, as well as a method for pipelining information to them in the future without having to constantly fly back and forth—"

"Because it would look too suspicious," Blake said, grabbing his water bottle again.

"Right. He did a fantastic job. Set it all up. Ferrying information to them, getting paid on the sly in the process. He was really good at the spy stuff."

Blake pinched his brow. "What was in it for you? I mean,

besides dirty money, what were you getting in return? And was the information you were selling really worth anything?"

"Patience, Agent Meyer. I was just getting to the good part." Conrad chuckled to himself. "He was to build trust, and then when the time was right, offer them his services. Leave the British government altogether and start working for the Russians. Discreetly, of course. He'd go off the grid for a bit, change his name, and then move to whichever town the Russians needed him to call home." Conrad shrugged. "This *was* the ultimate goal. Once he was firmly established, then he would start sending Russian information my way. Good intel. Priceless intel."

"So, what went wrong?" Blake took the last swig from his water bottle and placed the cap back on before tossing the empty bottle into the seat beside him. "Your blogging tirade spoke of how the British government used him, set him up to be a sacrificial lamb, et cetera, et cetera."

"Yeah, about that..." Conrad winced and wriggled in his seat. "You see, Blake, what my nephew didn't know was how he had taken the place of a contact within the Russian government I use to have. This man was actually a Russian citizen and tired of the government's propaganda, tired of all the Russian lies." Conrad pressed his eyelids together and groaned, as if recalling the details literally hurt his head. "His name was Ivan Chernov. He was the one who secured the contagion from Russia in 1999. Then, he handed it off to the middle man, who in turn, handed it off to Filipov."

Blake's eyes widened in horror. "*You? You* were the middle man? Otherwise, how would you know all of this?"

"You've always been too smart for your own good." Conrad scratched his nose and sniffed. "Aye. I was the middle man. I arranged the exchange and was to keep tabs on the contagion. The Russians desired to destabilize the region and cause the Good Friday Accords to dissolve. What I was to keep secret was my government's involvement. Nobody was to know, besides the Russian operatives involved, of how the British government also wished for the Accords to fail. Some of my superiors believed it gave too much power to the Irish.

"Ironically, those IRA radicals believed exactly the opposite, so they became unwitting participants to carry out the wishes of the Russians and the Brits."

"The entire episode is what turned Ivan's stomach...He didn't care about the Accords, per se, but he did care about all the innocent people who would die from the contagion's release. It made him rethink his dedication to the SVR and the FSB.

"It caused me to reconsider my dedication to MI6 and the Crown as well. We both came to the same conclusion independently from the other. Two rival governments. Both working together to bring about an instability to a region of the world needing peace. And all for what? To drive up the price of oil?

"So, Ivan and I made a mutual decision. Once Operation Abydos was over, our lives as agents for our respective organizations would change. Ivan became one of my informants within Russia, while I started the life of a double agent and kept him abreast of what my government was up to when it involved Russia and its allies. We saved a lot of lives over the years doing what we did.

"However, before we could change our ways, we had to carry out Operation Abydos as planned. We had no choice without exposing ourselves as traitors. So, it was Ivan who gave me the intel on the contagion's location, which I fed to my government contacts."

"And they relayed that intel to me and my team," Blake said.

"Correct. Your team receiving the intel was not part of the original plan, however. I added it to our plan in hopes your team could help stop the contagion's release. If I had not shared that information the way I did, Filipov and the radicals would have succeeded with their plan, and the region would have been plunged into at least a civil war amongst the British Isles. Not to mention how they would have become infected with the contagion itself, possibly spreading it to Europe and beyond."

Blake's tone grew sharp. "You do realize your actions are directly responsible for everything that's happened to me and my family over the last several days, right?"

"How was I to know things would transpire the way they did?" Conrad held his hands up off the table. "My friend, I hope you know I would never do anything intentionally to hurt your family. Ever."

"I can't believe you thought being a double agent would be a *logical* choice to make. Because as you can see, there was very little about the decisions you made that could be deemed logical. Lunacy? Yes. Logical? No."

Conrad smirked and stared at the screen. "Blake, I know you think of me now as a traitor, and a liar, and lump me in with the other scum of the world. However, there is one thing you do not know, or at least I don't think you do."

"Try me."

"Your government was involved as well."

Blake smiled politely, "I already know, Conrad. Filipov told me. She said the British government had a back-up plan in place, if my team failed to do its job."

"And she would be right. From whom do you think she received this information?"

"You?"

Conrad nodded. "You see, Agent Meyer. I wasn't so bad, was I? We had a Special Forces team staged nearby. Three times the size of yours. Their sole purpose was to destroy the contagion at all costs, if your team could not get it done. But, if your team was successful, then we would have the Americans involved...just not in the way they intended. Their involvement helped to keep information from being leaked. You know how all this works, Agent Meyer. When there are more hands in the cookie jar, the less likely someone will suddenly become chivalrous and feel the need to divulge anything incriminating."

Blake's face flushed red. "Your change in plans nearly got my wife and children killed." His jaw tightened. "They will be trauma-tized for the rest of their lives, because of you."

Conrad placed his hands together in a prayerful gesture. "And for that, I am truly sorry. That's why, when you called for my help, I did not hesitate. I guess it was my form of penitence."

Blake closed his eyes and grit his teeth.

Stay focused, solider...

"Let's get this over with." Blake blew out a forceful sigh, running his hand through his hair as he did. "What happened between you and Chernov after Operation Abydos concluded?"

"Ivan fed me information periodically, and I returned the favor. Like I said before, we saved a lot of lives doing what we did... until he died suddenly. Cancer, I heard. Pancreatic cancer, to be precise. Together, we had averted several major global catastro-phes, thank you very much. Then, suddenly, with his death, I was blind to half of the world."

Blake rubbed his head, angered and disheartened by what he was hearing. "So, let me guess. You didn't know if there was another 'inside man' like Ivan you could turn to...and that's when you decided to concoct your plan to send in your nephew. You created another 'Ivan' instead of having to take months, even years, to find another person disgruntled with Russian politics."

Conrad pointed at the screen. "Now you're getting the big picture, my friend. It worked for almost two years. However, what I did not anticipate was my nephew falling in love with a Russian woman." He shrugged. "Looking back, I suppose I should have. He was young and virile. He fancied himself as a bit of a 007-type, too, so that didn't help either."

Blake read through his notes. "According to the intel I received, he was contacted by a woman. Everything went sideways afterwards."

"Yes, he was contacted, but not immediately. He was firmly in place for a few months before she showed up. Allegedly, she was the daughter of an oligarch. Rich. Persuasive. Good-looking. She was working for one of the Russian bureaucrats in the Kremlin. Their paths crossed, and my nephew got swept off his feet. Despite my repeated warnings for him to do his due diligence with this woman and turn over every stone, he allowed his feelings to cloud his judgment. After a short six months of dating, they were married. Some small affair, I heard. They whisked off to some Caribbean island for their honeymoon, and when they returned, the Russian authorities greeted him at the airport. He was arrested, and the British government was notified of his espionage. They denied any involvement, which was actually true, because they didn't sanction the operation. It was completely my doing."

Blake shook his head. "And the blog which followed was your way of diverting attention from you and attempting to shift the blame toward the British government?"

"I had to save face. The British government claimed they did not know about my nephew. If that narrative went unchallenged, then they and the Russians would start looking elsewhere, and it would only be a matter of time before they determined somebody acted independently."

"So, the blog posts were solely to keep you out of prison?"

"Yes. So long as I could keep the spotlight on them, they weren't looking too deeply at other alternatives, like me. I threw accusations both ways, attempting to muddy the water as best I could. I blamed my government for denying their involvement, and I accused the Russians of brainwashing my nephew.

"Oh, they spent their time trying to save face with each other. And it worked for a long while. However, after the dust settled, and I was attacked twice for my blog rants, it became clear the Russians thought I was involved.

"I had wondered how they figured it out, until I learned my nephew's wife was actually a very skilled Russian FSB agent. She had worked with my nephew for weeks, months even, before they became an item. I always assumed she probably gained access to his computer, and I assumed they eventually were able to open his files and see where he had been sending the information. If I was right, following the digital trail to me would not have been difficult.

"However, my nephew was a computer genius. He never would have left anything to chance, and he surely would not have allowed anyone, his new wife included, to gain access to the intel he was sending. Besides, he knew it meant certain death, or at least imprisonment, if he was found out." Conrad slumped his shoulders, looking and acting the part of a tired, poison-riddled man. "I searched and searched for answers, but I never could uncover how my nephew was exposed. Hence, answers to those questions became another reason why I decided to help you, Blake. I hoped that maybe, by some slim chance, I could find some answers concerning my nephew's death."

Blake frowned. "And did you?"

"The major general didn't know anything nor did any of the contacts he supplied."

Blake cleared his throat again and winced. He clicked on a couple of things and squinted at the screen. "Well, Conrad, this is where my newly found information comes into play. I believe I can shed some light on your little story and explain who it was who actually sold you out."

CHAPTER 53

ABOARD THE GULFSTREAM
Sixty Minutes from Chicago

Blake Meyer continued to squint as he closed one file and opened another. Yes, his eyes were tired, and the small print strained his vision as he sought the correct page of information. But it was his blood pressure, soaring higher and higher, as he learned more about this friend of his. Conrad Bowker, quirky and sometimes crass, had always come across as a dedicated British agent.

Now, Blake wasn't so sure, and it angered him.

"Okay, Blake, I'm all ears," Conrad said. "Can't keep a fossil like me in suspense. The old ticker can't take it."

"Patience, Conrad. It's not like you're going anywhere."

"Ah, but were you told? We only have an hour. They are very strict on such things." Conrad mumbled some sort of expletive toward those imprisoning him, but Blake couldn't decipher it. "We spend money on all sorts of frivolities, especially when it comes to keeping the Royals on the front page of the Times, but there's a serf-like quality to life for those who have served their country and have given their lives *for* the Crown."

"Oh, but you just admitted to committing several crimes, Agent Bowker, including not always serving your 'Crown'...but I digress. Here we go. This was the page I was looking for."

"All right. On you go."

Blake repositioned himself in his seat. "Conrad, I don't know how to tell you this but to just say it. Julee Scarfano and the supervisory agent-in-charge of our FBI field office in Atlanta obtained a search warrant and stormed a condominium in Roswell, Georgia, which is a suburb of Atlanta, in conjunction with the investigation into this contagion business. The residence was owned by your son, Kurt, and his wife.

"His wife was detained for a brief while and then released, but Kurt has been arrested and is being charged with multiple counts."

"Such as?"

"Conspiracy to commit acts of terror. Espionage, attempting to detonate an incendiary device endangering members of law enforcement, and I'm not sure what else. The list is long, I hear."

"Kurt?" Conrad shook his head and pointed at Blake. "The French and the British Governments...they put you up to this, didn't they? This is their way of attempting to break me."

Blake stared at his friend. He could see the bewilderment behind the unbelieving leer. "Kurt was working with a group called The Consortium. He apparently was their go-to guy when it came to anything tech-related. I don't have time to list all the things he did, Conrad, but know this: He was working closely with the people who were responsible for releasing the contagion. The same people who were responsible for kidnapping my family and killing all the people at my own daughter's birthday party, including my sister-in-law."

"You're certain?"

"It's ironclad, Conrad. Julee informed me Kurt admitted to it all. And his hard drives are a treasure trove of damning evidence, I'm told."

"I...I, uh...I-I-I don't know what to say...I mean, I haven't spoken to Kurt in a while. We don't get on like we used to. We had a falling out. It started around the time I moved our family to London...from the only home Kurt had ever known." Conrad's gaze dropped to the table in front of him. "I saw it. I noticed the gulf developing between us, but I was too far in by then. I was a full-blown agent, and I bought the whole 'For King and Country' mantra. Our relationship unraveled, despite my protestations, and when he turned of age, he moved out. We spoke a few more times, but it was never the same. Now, we're lucky if we speak once or twice a year. Usually holidays, you know. Christmas, mostly. Then maybe sometime in the spring or summer. Often, I'd call, in between the holidays, but I'd get voicemail, and he never returned those calls."

"According to this document in front of me," Blake said, pointing at the computer, "what you just told me makes sense. He blames you for the demise of your family. The tipping point for Kurt revolves around your nephew, apparently. He was monitoring your whereabouts, Conrad. He had a huge file on you. It included a great deal of intel on your nephew."

"What? Why would he care about his cousin?"

"According to his statement, he was always curious about what his dad deemed more important than his family. He actually had a brief flirtation with joining you and British intelligence, but when he learned you were using your nephew and how, that's when he claims he 'put his foot down' and vowed to employ his skills in an effort to stop you and anyone like you." Blake paused. "He has evidence on his computer, Conrad, indicating your nephew may not have been killed by the Russians as you believed. The intel points to your nephew committing suicide."

Conrad harrumphed. "That's what the British Government said happened. It was all lies."

"Not according to Kurt. Apparently, a few days before your nephew returned from his honeymoon, Kurt sent him an encrypted file, documenting all of your dealings. He showed your nephew how you had been a double agent, and his work in Russia was solely to benefit you and how your nephew had become your new confidential informant in Russia. Kurt claimed none of the intel your nephew was amassing was ever used by British Intelligence.

"Your nephew went through with the small wedding and the honeymoon, because he truly cared for this woman. However, Conrad, your version of the Russian authorities meeting him at the airport and arresting him wasn't true. Your nephew fed you the arrest story to by himself some time. What really happened was, when your nephew found out you had been using him, he started investigating it himself with Kurt's help. When he found evidence corroborating Kurt's story, he rode out to a remote location and shot himself."

Conrad blurted out an expletive. "That's not true!"

"If you want me to supply you with the information I have, Conrad, I can send it through proper channels. But think about it, Agent Bowker. Why would I lie and make this up?" Blake leaned forward. "You've known me for years, Conrad. Have you ever had any reason to doubt me? Not believe what I've told you?"

Conrad pinched his eyes together, and the muscles in his temples bulged. "No."

"And have you ever known me to make accusations or act on intel that was piecemeal or sketchy?"

"Never."

"Then, you can trust me now." Blake paused to collect his thoughts. "Listen, I know this is really tough to hear, but I thought you should know all this. And I thought you should hear it from me. Kurt is your son. And that was your nephew in Russia. I know I'd want to know, if the tables were turned."

Conrad shook his head emphatically. "But honestly, Blake, do I look like I've benefitted financially from my work?"

"Right now, sitting where you are? No. However, your multiple accounts in the Cayman Islands tell another story."

Conrad's angry demeanor slowly melted into one of surprise.

"Kurt showed your nephew financial transactions as recent as two days prior to making initial contact. The monies originated from a deal your nephew had worked on. According to Kurt, you had used his intel to get a jump on some stock buys which proved profitable."

Conrad sniffed as the tears began to flow.

"And according to Kurt, it was the other name on one of those accounts that, quote, 'sickened him,' end quote."

Conrad's eyes widened. "No. Please, no."

"How could you, Conrad?" Blake's disbelief was written across his brow. "How could you have a relationship with your nephew's wife?"

Conrad's tears turned to groans until he could inhale and gather himself. "It wasn't like that, Blake. We met in a bar in Zurich. She was twenty at the time and worked as one of the waitresses. This was long before my nephew started his mission with me in Russia.

"It was one of those...whirlwind things, you know. You meet, and before you know it, it...it just happens." Conrad wiped his face. "We started seeing each other regularly. Wherever and whenever we could.

"Then, after a while, I believed my wife was becoming suspicious, so I ended the relationship. I knew it could never last. I was old enough to be her father." Conrad gathered himself a bit. "What I never saw coming was her crossing paths with my nephew."

"Did your nephew ever know about your relationship? In the beginning? When he first started working with you?"

"No. Not to my knowledge. And I never showed my face when my nephew and her were together. Had I done so, she would have recognized me, and my family would have unraveled."

Blake lifted one eyebrow. "Did she know about the money?"

Conrad nodded. "No. Her name is on the account as the beneficiary. She was never privy to its existence."

"So, why start it?"

"Because at the time, I loved her. And if my family did fall apart, and I had nothing left, then it was designed to be a fresh start for us." Conrad smirked at the thought now. "Looking back, I sound like a love-struck teenager, don't I?"

Blake fell back into his chair and pressed his fingertips together. "Her becoming infatuated with your nephew must have been quite the blow."

"I'll admit, it was difficult in the beginning. But the more I saw them together, the more I realized how they were meant to be together. She deserved a younger guy. Have a chance at a family, that sort of thing. And if she was to fall for someone else and never be with me, who better to leave me for than someone I know and trust will treat her well? And besides, I was being a complete idiot...being willing to throw away my family for a fling was just how far I had slid down the proverbial slope."

"What ever happened with the money?"

"Nothing. It's still there." Conrad wiped his eyes. "I left instructions for the account manager to make contact with her when I gave the word. And that was going to happen on my death bed. But she's not going to get one quid now, is she? The government is going to seize it. Claim it was produced using illegal means."

Blake pursed his lips. "And you know, Conrad, they'll want to question her about why her name is on the account. And when they learn she is Russian, and your nephew was her husband, and how he was filtering Russian intelligence back to a British agent, and how your nephew committed suicide, she's not going to be viewed in a favorable light."

"She didn't have anything to do with my decisions or my nephew's dealings with me. She was truly an innocent bystander."

"Are you so sure? She was an FSB agent. You really don't know how much she actually knew."

"No!" Conrad's outburst reverberated off the walls and echoed through the microphone.

"It seems Kurt had been working that angle, searching for evidence to either prove her guilt or her innocence when The Consortium contacted him and enlisted his services. After then, he seems to have either dropped it or just didn't commit as much time to it."

Several moments passed in silence. Blake sorted through some other documents, glancing up at the square framing Conrad in the interrogation room. He heard Conrad make some comments, groan, and cry, but all of it was unintelligible.

Blake sighed, hating to be the bearer of such devastating news. "Conrad, I have some other things to discuss with you before we run out of time."

Bowker leaned back in his chair. His shoulders slumped as if he had finally been beaten and had no desire to fight. "So, my son...my *son*...ruined everything? He's the one who ended my covert operation in Russia? And ultimately, he's the one who got me poisoned?"

"He did state how this intel about your nephew, his wife, and the offshore accounts was the final nail in the coffin, forcing him to become an enemy of the state."

"Seriously?" Conrad's eyes welled up. "I know I wasn't a good father, but isn't this just another 'blame Daddy for your troubles' excuse?"

Blake stared at Conrad. "I think you know the answer, Conrad."

"All he had to do was answer the phone and tell me all this... why didn't he just answer the phone?" The tears in Conrad's eyes dripped down his cheeks. He wiped them with his forearm. "I would have answered any questions he had...I would have...I would have. Kurt, no...I won't believe it. I won't. Kurt wouldn't turn on me like this. He had to know it would hurt his cousin..."

Blake's heart ached for his friend. The thought of hearing how Conrad's decisions in life had wrecked his family and turned his son into a terrorist must have been horrific.

"Conrad, I know you're in pain, but I have to ask you this: Did you know Kurt was working covertly and regularly with Arina Filipov?"

Conrad tilted his head and produced a new expression of disbelief. He sat up quickly and allowed his eyes to float away from Blake's. "Please don't tell me you have evidence for this too?"

"I wish I could say I don't, but he admitted to working with Filipov for years, off and on. He worked behind the scenes, in an IT sort of way. He started assisting her about five years after Operation Abydos, around the same time The Consortium made contact. Kurt supplied all of her intelligence." Blake grimaced. "Conrad, he's the main reason why she has been able to develop and maintain the moniker, The Black Mist. He's been hacking into security camera systems and erasing her from their databases. He was putting cameras on loops so she could sneak past them undetected. Before she entered a facility, he had already mapped out her escape route by supplying building schematics, locations of guards, anything she needed."

Conrad let out a defeated chuckle. "Sounds like they were quite the team."

"Yeah, and not a good one."

CHAPTER 54

ABOARD THE GULFSTREAM
Ninety Minutes from Chicago

Blake Meyer shuffled through some papers. "Conrad, I know this has been a lot, but our timer is down to fifteen minutes. And there is one more piece of information, a biggie, I need to share with you before we get disconnected."

"I'll be honest, Blake. I don't know how much more I can take."

"Well, I believe you're going to want to hear this. Better to know it now, than hear it later in court."

Conrad lifted his shoulders with a shrug. "My life is in shambles now. What could possibly make it worse?"

Blake inhaled and allowed the breath to expel loudly.

"Great. That bad, eh?"

"Were you aware Kurt was contacted by the British government early on in his IT career and invited to come work for them?"

Conrad laughed. "No. No, I wasn't, and I find it hard to believe. By the time he left home, he was already spouting some anti-government propaganda. I could tell I was losing him, but I didn't know what to do."

"Well, he was...but he turned them down cold. He claimed your demise as a father was their fault, so why would he want to follow in your footsteps. So, he took his degree in computer science and his skill set to the black market."

"So, ultimately, he really blamed me, eh?" Conrad said with a snort. "Yes, they 'ruined our family,' in his eyes, but I could have declined their offer too. But because I didn't, I chose to wreck our family. At least that's how Kurt would see it."

"Maybe. But they did offer him a chance, and he turned it down. Subsequently, they dropped it and, no doubt, monitored him from then on. But apparently, he was really good at what he did. The Harrison Kelly kind of good, you know what I mean?"

"I do."

"By the age of twenty-five, Kurt had become one of the up-and-coming IT guns for hire, as it were, like I mentioned earlier. He stated his goal was to topple nations for the highest bidder. The Consortium originally hired him, at the urging of Filipov, and one of his tasks was to dig into Harrison Kelly's files in the Pentagon. He almost succeeded at having Harrison arrested by the FBI, Conrad. Were you aware of any of this?"

"No."

"Kurt even commandeered Julee Scarfano's FBI computer— the one sitting on the desk in her office—and was spying on her, trying to gather information on what we knew about Colin Murphy, the contagion, and everything else. He was watching to find out what our next moves were. That's how the mole was able to stay one step ahead of us for so long." Blake paused again and consulted another file on his computer. "He's been responsible for data breaches in multiple countries. He's hacked into credit card companies and banks, stealing millions. He's created multiple fraudulent accounts through the Social Security Administration, the SNAP program, and Veteran's Affairs. He funneled the funds to offshore accounts so he could fund himself and others, like Filipov, radical extremists, you name it. "He's even caused accidents to cover up murders. In his computer files was information about a Línea Aérea Pájaro passenger flight going down somewhere in the vicinity of Barbados on September 12, 2009. There were ten passengers on board. The pilot called in an emergency shortly before authorities lost contact. It was later learned that the pilot's license had been suspended in 2005. According to the files, Kurt was responsible for two things. First, he forged documents which allowed the pilot to fly again. In exchange for the pilot doing exactly as he was told, of course. Comply with Kurt's orders, and his family would get the promised money. Fail to comply, and they would not live to see the news of his downed aircraft. Second, there was a passenger on board who another entity wanted dead. Hence, their hiring of Kurt and his skill set. They sabotaged the plane, causing it to malfunction. The pilot calls in the emergency, the plane goes down without a trace, and then the pilot's forged documents get exposed, making him the probable cause of the accident.

"Conrad, Kurt has seventy-six files on his computer of so-called 'accidents' just like this. They involve train derailments, car accidents, and explosions in various buildings, including the one Julee Scarfano was involved in at the InterHealth Medical Center in Jacksonville. Needless to say, Kurt is really, really good at what he does, and he's made millions in the process."

Conrad shook his head in disbelief. "What do you want me to say, Blake? I'm sorry...for being a horrible father?"

"I'm not asking you to say anything." Blake shot Conrad a serious look. "And it may be best you don't, so just listen.

"There is one more...'operation,' I guess you could call it, Kurt was involved in. This one had nothing to do with Filipov, and he was not hired by anyone. He is solely responsible for this one." Blake scrolled through a couple of pages on his computer and then stopped. "And this one, my friend, is as tough for me to tell you as I'm sure it is going to be to hear.

"Kurt was given a great deal of access to different areas during this stint with Filipov and The Consortium. He apparently took advantage of his access, and did some data dives into areas he was not supposed to see. Of course, he covered his tracks, so as far as we know, no one was the wiser until we caught him.

"His main purpose was to dig into your files, Conrad. He had an entire dossier on his computer. He knows how you were recruited by the British government. He knows what forced you to move to London. He knows about your affairs with other agents while you were still married, which almost caused your dismissal, I see. He knows everything."

Each time Blake added another piece of information to the pile already amassed, Conrad's chin dropped a little lower until his head hung helplessly. Tears dripped from his eyes, despite being pinched together, but Conrad made no attempt to wipe them away.

Blake watched his friend disintegrate before him. A shell of the man he once knew. Blake leaned over and opened the mini-fridge and grabbed another bottled water. He took several swigs before continuing, allowing Conrad time to grieve.

"You said earlier that you didn't have any contact with the men in the van before they arrived to pick you and Botinkin up from the safe house, correct?"

Conrad offered a slight nod. "Just a phone call to arrange the time and place to meet."

"And you wondered how they were poisoned, correct?"

Conrad opened his eyes and slowly lifted his head. "Yes. I said

I was being framed..." He pinched his brow and allowed his gaze to wonder off to the side. "But I didn't have any idea who was responsible..." He aimed his eyes at Blake. "No. No. No!"

Blake watched as his friend slowly pieced the information together. "I'm sorry, Conrad."

"No! Your intel is wrong."

"Conrad, *he* supplied the intel *to us*. It was in his computer, and he told us where to find it."

Conrad suddenly became animated. "But why?"

"I already told you. He viewed you and what you stood for as an enemy to be toppled. So, he learned of your whereabouts there in Paris and what you were doing with Botinkin. How he did it, we're not sure yet. But he was responsible for the blue van ramming into your transport. He hired those guys. He also had the guys you hired in the white van followed. For days, actually."

Conrad slammed his fist down on the table. "You're lying!"

"You said it yourself. You wondered how they were poisoned. You wondered how the same poison found its way into the safe house, right? He hacked into your computer, Conrad, and hired another person to scope them out. When the time was right, the hired gun stepped in and poisoned their water bottles by injecting them with a poison which takes hours to overpower its victims. He covered up the poisoning initially with the accident in order to get the men to the hospital, and by the time the doctors got around to diagnosing their injuries from the accident, the poison was given enough time to do its work.

"At the same time, Kurt had hired your two 'reliable mercenaries,' the ones from the safe house. He tripled what you paid them in exchange for adding the poison to Major General Botinkin's tea. They made him a cup right before you arrived and sent them away. They were told to make sure traces of the poison were left all around the safe house's kitchen...on the tea pot...in the tea pot...

on the cups, the saucers, the serving tray, everything, but to make sure they wore gloves and didn't leave their prints."

Conrad grabbed his head and screamed. "This can't be? There's no way they would betray me. They know I'd come looking for them and kill them on the spot."

Blake grunted. "Yeah, funny you should mention that. They told Kurt the same thing, apparently. So, Kurt shared his plan with those two men. He assured them you'd be in police custody within twenty-four hours, and Botinkin would be dead. So, all they had to do was lay low. When you were arrested and escorted by French authorities out of the hospital, some video footage from the hospital's security cameras was copied. Kurt confirmed he was responsible for the security camera footage theft. He sent it to your two guys, Sammy and whatever the other guy's name was, as confirmation. Upon receipt of the camera footage, they were in the clear, just as he had promised."

Conrad chuckled to himself in disbelief. "And to think I made the major general tea as well...thus, I put my fingerprints all over the tea pot, all over the cups we used, all over the serving tray...I literally handed my enemies evidence on a silver platter." He chuckled again. "Literally, a silver platter."

"And there is one more nugget of information, Conrad, you should know."

"Why not..."

"Kurt anonymously sent the dossier he had amassed on you to the French and British governments. They have everything now."

Bowker closed his eyes. "Now I understand why the French were so willing to allow my extradition. They know the Brits want to silence me once and for all, so let the English dogs do the dirty work for them."

Blake closed his computer and grabbed his water bottle. "Conrad, I'm so sorry to have to be the one to tell you all this."

Conrad chuckled, seemingly because he had nothing else left to do. "I've been living off of borrowed time for years, Blake. I knew deep down it was only a matter of time until my life's choices caught up to me...I just never imagined my own son being the one to tie the hangman's knot."

CHAPTER 55

Jacksonville International Airport
Jacksonville, Florida

Blake Meyer's Gulfstream touched down and taxied to a nearby aviation company's hub. It was good to be back in familiar surroundings, he thought, as the plane weaved its way toward the company's building.

"Sir," the flight attendant said, "is there anything you would like to take with you for the next leg of your journey? A bottled water, perhaps? Or one of the other beverages or snacks we have?"

Blake stood and gathered his belongings. "I'll just take this bottle of water I've already opened. But thank you. You all have been great."

"Thank you, sir. We always like to hear about a job well done. And if your plans ever involve using a plane such as this again, please remember us. We'd love to serve you again in the future."

"I'll definitely keep that in mind," Blake said as he stuffed the remainder of his belongings into his backpack, and headed for the exit.

Standing at the doorway, the two pilots awaited. "Please watch your step as you depart, sir, and thank you for using MidAir Aviation." They both held out their hands. Blake shook them, thanked them for a pleasant flight, and disembarked.

Agent Williams, standing inside the hub, enjoying the air conditioning and free complimentary coffee, watched as Blake descended the stairs, and walked across the tarmac to the main entrance. He met Blake at the door. "Man, am I glad to see you." He reached out and shook Blake's hand.

"Everything all right? Julee treating you okay?" Blake said with a wry smile.

"Oh, yeah, yeah, of course. She's been great. I meant, after everything you've been through, everything we've uncovered, I'm just glad you're alive and well. And I'm glad to hear your family is safe too."

"You and me both."

Agent Williams motioned toward the other side of the building. "Shall we?"

"Lead the way."

"Through those doors," Williams said, pointing at another large entrance straight ahead. "You know, I think Julee's chomping at the bit to have you back in the office."

"Tired of the big chair, is she?"

"More like, 'Did we miss anything? I need Agent Meyer's eyes on this.'"

"Understood. When you're the leader at the top, you always second-guess yourself, wondering if you missed something. Always a best practice to get other people's eyes on the project or the plan. Often, they think of things you never considered."

"Good advice."

"Are you looking to move up someday, Agent Williams?"

Agent Williams let a nervous laugh escape. "I've thought about it, yeah, sure. But after watching what Julee's had to deal with over these last few days, and hearing what you've been through, I'm not sure I have what it takes."

"Self-assessment is always a good process. However, it can be overdone to the point of disqualifying yourself from a position others feel you can handle. So, just like getting eyes and ears on a plan to make sure you're not missing something, it's a good idea to do the same with your life choices. If you ask people you trust to be honest with you, despite how glowing or disturbing the advice may be, at least you'll have better information when you make those life choices, because sometimes, you only get one shot at it. Turn it down prematurely, and you may never get considered for it again."

Both men exited the building, made their way over to the parking lot. "More good advice," Agent Williams said. "Now I see why Julee relies on you so much."

Blake smiled as they both climbed into the vehicle. "One more thing to consider: the AIC's chair isn't the only move up. Plenty of other positions within our field to choose from. Even shifting to other agencies." Blake shut his door and buckled up. "Say, uh, changing the topic, before we head back, I need you to take me somewhere. It won't take long."

"You name it." Agent Williams started the engine. "Where to?"

"My house."

Agent Williams shifted into gear. "You mean, the one they attacked?"

"That's the one."

"You know they have crime scene tape all over it, right? I think they may even have a patrol unit guarding the sight."

"I would expect nothing less."

"I think the whole block may be cordoned off, too, but I'm not sure."

"Just get me close. I'll take it from there."

* * *

Twenty minutes later, Agent Williams pulled up to a row of barricades and yellow crime scene tape. The entire block being cordoned off was exaggerated. Only Blake's property was off limits now. Barricades, protruding into the street about halfway across, directly in front of what remained of Blake's house, sent the necessary signal. Agent Williams shut off the engine. "Huh, no cops. I'm surprised."

"What is there to guard, honestly?" Blake could only sit and stare. He pictured in his mind's eye the home they lived in before it was destroyed. "Looters have probably already made off with any valuables by now anyway..."

"Doesn't look like there's much left, does there?"

Blake envisioned the driveway, and the sidewalk, a cobblestone path as it led from the driveway to the front door...when they were not covered with debris...

He could picture the fencing stretched out in both directions...

He could see the second story with its Spanish tile roof, buttressed against a cloudless blue sky...

The blue sky...the one he remembered that evening...as he stood out by the grill...the smell of hamburgers and hot dogs cooking to perfection...the breeze against his face...

He closed his eyes and replayed Little Sara's birthday party...

The raucous laughter of the guests...

The excitement in Little Sara's face...as she opened her gifts...

Sara urging him to go to the shed to retrieve their daughter's present...

The swell of pride, anticipating Little Sara's screams of joy when she saw what her daddy had made her...

The sting in his neck...

The dart...

The man in the green uniform, holding a gun...

The blurriness and the sudden instability in his legs—

"Blake...are you okay?" Agent Williams said.

Blake inhaled deeply, as if he'd been caught napping at work, and opened his eyes. He kept his eyes forward. "No. I'm not. Not if I'm being honest."

"What was the reason for me bringing you here, if you don't mind me asking?"

"I need to look for something. Something very important..." Blake inhaled again and exhaled loudly. "I knew I needed to do this. I've pictured this moment in my head for nearly forty-eight hours now." Blake's right leg began to shake with a nervous tension. "I thought I'd be okay, you know? Be able to handle the emotions..." His eyes pooled. "But, I guess I was wrong." Blake unbuckled his seat belt. "You stay here. I'll be right back."

"Do you want me to help you?"

"No."

"Okay. Okay. If you need me, holler."

Blake nodded and opened the door. He stepped out of the vehicle, and immediately, the smell of the ocean air overpowered the lingering hint of charred wood. Images of lying in the shed, covered in rubble, feeling like a boulder rested on his chest, flooded his memories.

Blake reached out and grabbed the side of the SUV, using it as a crutch. A wave of nausea welled up. "Get a grip, soldier," came a voice from inside. "You're not done. Not yet."

He nodded his head, as if answering without a word, and stood up straight.

"Let's find it and get out of here. This place holds nothing for you now but sorrow," came the voice of the father inside. "You're here for Little Sara. You have to be strong for her now."

He nodded again and made his way around the barricades and under the crime scene tape.

He surveyed the rubble to determine were the rooms used to stand. "It's gonna be harder than I thought," he said to himself.

The first floor is under the second...

Or at least what is left of the second.

* * *

Agent Williams watched as Blake eventually made his way to what remained of his home and began rummaging through the rubble. "What could be so important?"

He continued to keep an eye on his friend when his phone rang. He checked the screen. It was Julee Scarfano. "Williams."

"Agent Williams, where are you? I expected you back by now."

"Yeah, well, his plane was ten minutes late. Then, he requested that we stop by his old house. We're here now." Williams raised up to check on Blake. "He's digging through the debris, looking for something."

"If he's looking for something, then it must be important. Give him whatever time he needs, then head straight here. If he requests to go somewhere else, have him call me first."

"Will do. But I have to say, Julee, I'm worried about him. He's been through a lot, and before he got out of the vehicle, it was like he had gone into some kind of trance. I could tell he was fighting back tears. He seems unstable, if you ask me."

"Agent Williams, if your house had been blown up, how would you feel?"

"Ticked."

"And if your wife and children were carried off by people with ill intentions, with the plan of selling each family member into slavery?"

"I'd probably go ballistic."

"So, you chase the bad guys halfway around the world, get beat up, almost killed, finally track down your wife and children, save them—all the while finding the contagion at the same time—and you get to this very moment...where you are sitting in front of the very place where this nightmare began...what kind of condition would you be in, Agent Williams, honestly?"

He felt awful. "Point taken."

"And I didn't even mention all those poor souls who were killed at his daughter's birthday party. One of them was his sister-in-law." Julee sniffed. "His little girl will never be able to celebrate another birthday without having to relive what happened at her fifth birthday party. She may never celebrate another one ever again."

"Okay, Julee. I get it."

"Blake's been through the closest thing to hell I can imagine. So, keep an eye on him, please? If you think I need to talk to him on the ride back to the field office, call me."

"You got it."

* * *

Blake spent over thirty minutes flipping over torched two-by-fours and chunks of cinder block, shattered pieces of Spanish roof tile and damp drywall, looking for anything he felt needed to come back with him.

Miraculously, he thought, he'd found some of Sara's jewelry from their bedroom, hidden under a section of shattered bookcase. He'd also located a couple of her favorite shirts, soiled and smelling terrible, but from what he could see, were surprisingly unscathed otherwise. He even found one of Jacob's Lego creations, not put together yet, still in the box, the bag inside unopened. He remembered this was next on his son's list of things to do, right after he finished the one we was working on...

However, the main reason he came back was still buried.

It could be anywhere...

Blake continued to root around, examining broken pieces, attempting to figure out where in the house the object in his hand once resided. He was a bit amazed at how things on one side of the house before the blast were on the other side. Some of them damaged beyond repair. Others looked almost like new, like the old vase he had purchased on a whim one evening on his way home from a conference. A street vendor in New York City was slashing prices to get rid of old inventory...so the story went. There was nothing special about the vase, other than the way the colors shimmered when the sun hit it just right.

He remembered the day he brought it home, all wrapped up in old pages of *The New York Post*. Sara unwrapped it, held it out, turned it to the left and to the right, and smiled. She said she loved it. However, Blake could tell by the squint in her eyes she was just being nice.

"Here," he said to her. "Bring it over to the window and let the sunlight bounce off of it."

She did, and her smile did change a little, but not as much as he'd hoped.

The days and weeks to follow proved his suspicions, as it always managed to find itself displayed where the fewest number of people would see it. The vase never made it downstairs, and never in a window where the colors could dazzle others as they had Blake.

During the holidays, it managed to get boxed up and replaced with a cornucopia, or stuffed snowmen, or some other seasonal decoration. Now that he really thought about it, even during the summer, around the Fourth of July, it got switched for another vase filled with little American flags.

Maybe that's how it survived the blast. It was in a plastic bin or some cardboard box, shoved in a packed closet...

Blake formed a small pile of items on the only uncovered corner of the driveway available. The small items, like the jewelry, he jammed into his pockets. He knew the memories would be tough to manage when he presented these things to his family, but he'd only do it when the time was right. When Sara lamented about her jewelry being gone, or when they reminisced about the ugly vase. He'd retrieve the item then...and instead of sorrow, it would hopefully bring happiness and joy...or in the case of the vase, laughter, to their devastated lives.

As he set down the vase and turned back toward the house for another foray, something caught Blake's eye. He teetered across a portion of the shower wall from their master bathroom upstairs, stepped off of it, and zeroed in on the object peeking out from under what remained of Little Sara's closet door with the attached mirror...well, half of it anyway.

He bent down, lifted the jagged section of door, and reached under it. Grabbing the item, he could feel the fabric. Standing up with the item in his hand, he brushed it off and inspected it.

Dirty and stained, but not singed or scorched...

Give it a good wash in the washing machine, and he should be good as new.

Blake was so happy to find the reason for his impromptu archeological dig.

Mr. Panda.

Little Sara's constant companion had survived the aftermath.

Mr. Panda had been at Little Sara's side since she was a year old. Most kids had blankets. Some had other stuffed toys, but for Little Sara, Mr. Panda was special. In his little tuxedo, he was appropriately dressed for all of her tea parties. He could also attend a night out on the town with the family without having anyone make fun of his clothing, even if he was overdressed for McDonald's. He even spoke in a British accent, compliments of Little Sara's imagination after watching *Mary Poppins* for the first time last summer. When Mr. Panda spoke, it was always with the diction befitting a proper little mister.

Blake pulled the bear to his chest and allowed the sound of the ocean waves to wash away the weariness of his heart, even if it was for just a few glorious seconds.

He would miss this house...

Everything—the house, the ocean, the memories—was all tainted now...

And Blake knew this was Colin Murphy's plan all along.

Hurt Blake the same way he believed Blake had hurt him.

Problem was, Colin believed a lie...

He put me and my family through all of this because he believed a lie...

Blake hugged Mr. Panda harder, but this time, the ocean waves couldn't cleanse his aching heart.

He could feel the anger rising. The same anger he experienced in the interrogation room, questioning Murphy, listening to him boast about what he had done...the smirks...the little digs...

Blake straightened his stance. With the resoluteness of a soldier, he walked back over to his little pile of belongings, picked them up, and walked around to the back of the SUV. He opened the back door, set the items inside, and shut the door.

He climbed into the passenger seat and buckled up. "Thank you, Agent Williams. I know it took longer than I thought, but it was worth it. We can head to the field office now."

"Cool. Oh, and by the way, Julee called. She was just getting worried—"

"Because we were taking too long to show up."

"Yeah."

"Well, I have some news for her, but it's gonna have to wait until we get back to the FO. I can't risk telling her this information over the phone."

"Sounds...'ominous.'"

"More like...'explosive.'"

Williams groaned and nodded in the direction of Blake's house. "Haven't we had enough 'explosive' already?"

"We're just getting started, Agent Williams." Blake faced him. "And now, after all of this is said and done, and after our little discussion about your future with the Bureau, it may make you question your career choice."

CHAPTER 56

PROMENADE ESTATES
North Arlington, Virginia

Merina Parker turned the water off to the wonderful, long, exhilarating hot shower. She realized her "prison cell," from earlier in the day, really wasn't one. It was a holding room at the FBI field office, where people getting ready to go to jail reside. However, as she thought about the true lowlifes who had been in there before her, arrested for crimes against the government or other law-abiding citizens, all she wanted to do was scrub the filth of the room off her body.

Drying off, she thought about getting dressed and heading for the Hill, but Templeton had advised her to stay home and get some rest. He had some investigating of his own to do, and he believed having her home and "out of the way"—which were her words and not his—would allow him time to "check into some things." Besides, her status as a congresswoman had been suspended, pending a hearing with the Senate Ethics Committee anyway. Getting her reinstated and back to the Hill would only be a matter of time. But not tonight. The guards at the gate wouldn't let her inside, despite her newfound innocence, and they'd just be doing their jobs.

Merina knew Templeton was right. She hated it, but what else could she do? Make a few phone calls, send a few emails. In the end, it wouldn't speed up anything. "They aren't holding any special senate sessions tonight," she said to herself as she rummaged through her closet, wondering what to wear. "Not on a Sunday. It could be well into next week before they do…"

Staring at the rack of clothes, she dropped her arms to her side and huffed. "I might as well stay comfy."

Unwrapping the towel from around her, she grabbed her full-length robe and slipped it on. Tying it tight around her mid-section, she jabbed her toes into her slippers, slid them on fully, and marched back into the bathroom to dismantle the towel head-dress and blow dry her hair when the doorbell rang.

"Templeton? What did you forget to tell me?"

Merina plodded down the stairs and peeped out the window.

Standing at the door was a woman. Similar to her in age. Brownish-blonde hair. Average build. Holding a purse and appearing a little nervous.

Who is she? Doesn't look like any of the neighbors…

She also noticed a car parked alongside the curb in front of the house, which wasn't there when she got home.

Merina checked her robe and unlocked the door. She opened it just wide enough to be able to stand in the opening, with her left hand still on the handle and her left foot bracing it as well. "May I help you?"

"Are you the owner of this house?" the woman said.

Merina scrunched her brow even more than it already was. "Yes…"

"My name is Camila Carlton. My husband is Thomas Carlton. *Judge* Thomas Carlton?"

Merina's lifted one eyebrow, but the expression remained furrowed. "Okaaay...nice to meet you...how can I help you?"

"For the last few days, I've been in Colorado, visiting my sister. She's been battling cancer for three years now. The doctors thought they had it in remission, but she called me last week to inform me it had returned. What she didn't tell me over the phone was how bad it was. When I arrived, her husband was there. He had been by her side as much as he could, only taking time away for his job. Otherwise, he practically lived at the hospital when she was there." Camila's eyes welled up, and she reached into her sweater pocket to retrieve a wadded up tissue.

"I'm sorry to hear about your sister," Merina said. "Dealing with family members who have cancer is tough. We just went through something similar with my dad about a year ago."

Camila bit her lip and inhaled.

"So, Camila, why are you here?"

"I was at the hospital. It was around midnight there. I called Cody, I mean Thomas—we all call him Cody...a nickname from high school he's always gone by..." Camila's eyes lifted and met Merina's. "But I guess you would know that too. You apparently work with Cody a great deal. He speaks of you often, and I recognized you from the pictures on the internet."

"Camila, I'm not sure where this is going, but if you want to talk about this more, this really isn't a good time for me. I just got home from a...long...'trip,' so if you wish, I can give you a number to call to set up an appointment—"

"Not a good time for *you*? I called Cody's phone at 12:08 a.m., Colorado time...this morning. I expected him to answer, all groggy and everything, because he usually falls asleep in his lounger. He rarely comes to bed with me anymore. But he didn't answer. So, you know what I did?" Camila reached into her purse and pulled out her phone. She tapped the screen a few times and then turned it for Merina to see. "About four weeks ago, when he was asleep one night...in his lounger...drinking his booze...I installed this app. It tracks where he goes, how longs he stays there, everything."

Merina's puzzled gaze softened into one of vulnerability.

"Do you see this?" Camila said, holding her phone out for Merina to see. "It is 12:08 a.m., Colorado time. That would be 2:08 a.m. here. Ten minutes after two *this morning*. And do you see the location? It's *your* address." She pulled the phone back slightly and checked the screen. "The little blue dot shows him being here at ten minutes after two this morning. Why was my husband's phone here at this house at such an ungodly hour?"

Merina looked down. "I had called, uh, Judge Carlton about some official business that couldn't wait. I needed an official injunction to stop something from happening. Only judges can issue those, and because this particular issue was happening right here in Washington, it fell into his jurisdiction. That's why I called him...to ask for the injunction."

Camila extended her arm an inch or two and shook her phone. "At 2:10 a.m., I was calling *my husband* to inform him of the news... his sister-in-law...my sister... had passed away...from the cancer."

Merina's countenance fell completely. "I am so sorry, Camila."

Camila bit her lip again and closed her eyes briefly. She allowed the arm holding the phone to drop to her side. "I expected him to be home, in his chair, or maybe in *our* bed, since I wasn't there..." She lifted the phone and tapped the screen before holding it out again. "This is a screenshot of his total time at this address. Three hours and seventeen minutes." Her eyes pooled. "While I was standing outside my sister's room, listening to my brother-in-law mourn her death, I was calling my husband's phone—which he did not answer, ever—which was here, at this house, for three hours and seventeen minutes." Camila yanked the phone down to her side. "What would my husband possibly need to do at this house for three hours and seventeen minutes in the early hours of a Sunday morning?"

Merina withdrew slightly, pulling on the door and narrowing the opening. "Like I said, I needed an injunction. And because we were both home and not in our offices, the only way for me to get one was for me to send him the information, then he had to type it up, print it, and sign it."

"Okay, sounds harmless enough," Camila said with a deadpan stare, "and you both have fax machines, right? Email addresses? PDF? I used to work in a lawyer's office. That's how Cody and I met. I still do pro bono work even now for a charitable organization, so why not use any of those marvels of technology to get your injunction?"

"I needed it in hand when I walked into the Oval Office, which I did shortly after I received it. You can ask President Gilmore yourself, if you'd like."

"So, Cody hand-delivered it then?"

"He did."

"And does it take three hours to hand-deliver a piece of paper?"

"Listen, Camila, uh, I know how this looks, but Judge Carlton and I have known each other a long time. We've been friends for years, and yes, I don't know what else to say...I invited him in for some coffee, and we talked about—"

Camila reached into her purse again and pulled out a gun. She aimed it at Merina. "Shut up, and back away from the door!"

Merina's eyes widened in horror. She lifted her hands in surrender and backed into the house.

Camila pushed her way into the house and slammed the door shut, turning the deadbolt while she kept the gun aimed at

Merina. "Just stop! Just shut up! I'm tired of the lies. I'm tired of being married to a man who thinks I'm stupid...who said his phone's battery had died, and that's why he didn't answer it when I called from the hospital. What he doesn't know is the app I installed on his phone only works when the phone is on and active. It can't find it, if the phone is turned off. So, like I said, I'm tired of the lies."

Camila laughed and shook her head at the same time. "Oh, and by the way, you aren't the first. I've suspected there have been others. I've even been able to confirm one other woman. Six years ago. She used to work for him in his firm before he became a judge. I should have divorced him then, but he vowed 'he would change'...and I believed him. But over the years, it's gotten worse, not better. We hardly are together anymore. I even had a fling of my own, when I was out in Colorado a couple of years ago. I did it to spite Cody, and I've hated myself every minute since. That's why I don't get how you all can just go around and sleep with whoever and then walk away as if it doesn't change you, because it does, and not for the better." She eyed Merina up and down and allowed an exhausted chuckle to slip out. "I'll bet you wore that robe afterwards, didn't you?" She paused and scanned the room. "And where did it happen? Upstairs? Or was it over here on the couch?"

"Listen, Camila, I don't know what you think went on here, but—"

"Don't lie to me!" Camila gripped the gun tighter. Her hand shook with rage.

Merina lifted her hands. "Cody and I are just frie—"

Camila screamed in fury and pulled the trigger.

Merina clutched her chest as a look of shock froze on her face. Blood oozed out from under her hands and around her fingers before she collapsed to the floor.

Camila's hand quivered, and the gun suddenly weighed a hundred pounds, as the horrific reality of her fury-filled actions fell to the floor, gasping and pleading for her to call an ambulance.

Shaking, Camilla dropped the weapon and bent over at the waist with her hand over her mouth, feeling nauseated and frightened until her quivering body gave way. She fell to the floor herself, sobbing.

She'd never seen a person die before, and now, in less than twenty-four hours, she'd witnessed two.

* * *

Five minutes passed before Camila could move again. A million scenarios played and replayed in her mind, but they all ended the same way, with her in prison and her husband walking away without so much as a scratch to his sparkling career.

She mustered the strength to stand, but her emotions weren't as she expected.

I thought I'd be relieved to finally know the truth...

To finally have my vengeance...

But that was all a lie too...

She knew she could testify in court. Explain why she did what she did. However, she knew how it would play out in the tabloids...

Disgruntled Wife of Prominent Judge Loses Her Way: Falsely Accuses Member of Congress of Infidelity

She knew how it worked, after working in a law office for years as a secretary. Just because there was an app on his phone, showing him at Merina Parker's home, doesn't prove anything other than he was there.

She needed proof.

Proof.

Camila stared at Merina's lifeless body and wondered where she would most likely seduce her husband.

After a few lingering seconds, she picked up the gun, and plodded upstairs, looking for Merina's bedroom.

She peered into a couple of rooms before finding the one she wanted. And there, hanging over the armrest of a chair next to the bed was a negligee. She picked it up and sniffed it.

Her perfume, for sure.

Not something a woman does, unless she's expecting company...

But there's another scent here...

She sniffed it again. Then one last time.

A man's cologne...

Cody's favorite.

One he rarely wears around me, although he knows I like it.

She tossed it back onto the chair and faced the bed. She picked up the sheets and sniffed them.

Definitely his cologne.

Camila slumped her shoulders and stared at the bed. "So, Cody," she said, "this is where you were when my sister died in my brother-in-law's arms?"

She unlocked her phone again, turned off the password protection, and made sure the app tracking her husband's phone was open. She then crawled into the bed and positioned herself on her back, lying on the side she determined was Merina's.

With the phone in her left hand and the gun in her right, she wept.

After several minutes, wondering what Merina Parker had that she did not, she stared at the ceiling and pictured her husband standing in front of her.

"You may have fooled a lot of people in the past, Cody, but not this time. You're gonna have to live with this one for the rest of your life."

Then, with a quick, deep inhalation, she jammed the gun into her right temple and pulled the trigger.

CHAPTER 57

Blake Meyer and Agent Williams arrived at the Jacksonville field office twenty minutes later. Blake obtained a box and put all the belongings he had found at his house into it. He carried the box into Julee Scarfano's office and stood in the doorway. "Mind of I set these over there on the back table?"

Julee, startled by the sudden interruption, jumped out of her seat with a big smile on her face. "Most definitely."

Blake strolled over and set it down just in time to get a big hug from Julee.

"I am so glad you are safe, and your family."

"It's been an ordeal, for sure."

"Can I get you anything? Coffee? Can of soda?" Julee moseyed back to her desk.

"Coffee would be wonderful, but we don't have time to go get it. I have news to share with you, and you're gonna need to hear it before we take our next step."

Julee motioned to the phone. "I was gonna have someone bring it to us."

"Julee," Blake said, with his eyes pinned to hers, "after I share this information with you, you won't even trust the person bringing coffee."

Julee groaned and sat down. "Sounds serious." She motioned for Blake to have a seat as well. "Does this have anything to do with what we were talking about earlier? You said you had something you couldn't discuss over the phone."

Blake closed her office door and sat down, wincing as he did, holding his rib cage. "Yes. And now that you have Kurt Bowker in custody, my hypervigilance may be a little over exaggerated, but I'm not taking any chances."

"Trust me. I get it."

Blake leaned forward in his chair. "The mole we have been looking for...we've talked about how he seems to be everywhere, know everything, be three steps ahead?"

"Yes..."

"It's because he is. Harrison has found seventeen phone calls in Sorensen's files. They all came from the Russian phone number, 011-7-93832-555-7891. Remember it? The one Sergei Botinkin had and called several times? And it also called him?"

Julee leaned forward and rested her elbows on her desk. "I remember."

"In those files, the person on the other end of the call is referred to by Sorensen as 'Ben' in five of those seventeen calls."

"Ben?" Julee lifted her chin while a look of disbelief filtered through her expression. "As in Ben *Jenkins*? The president's chief of staff?"

Blake nodded. "Remember when I asked you to have Agent

Mitchell contact Harrison so they could get those voices matched?"

"I do."

"John and Harrison got a positive match on Ben Jenkins's voice," Blake said, pausing as a staff member walked by Julee's window. "We have enough for a warrant to search everything Jenkins has used."

"You know," Julee rubbed her face and leaned back in her chair again, "just because a person on a recorded phone conversation is referred to as 'Ben' doesn't mean it is him. His voice could have been spoofed. So, how are John and Harrison so sure? You know Ben Jenkins will claim he was framed."

"When Harrison heard the audio files and saw the Russian phone number, he placed a tracker on it. Since the moment the tracker went online, the Russian phone number's location gave us all the intel we needed to confirm Jenkins's identity and involvement."

Julee leaned forward again. Her voice became hushed. "Okay, so what are we waiting on? I want to nail this guy."

"First, I need you to call Agent Mitchell and have him come to your office. I need his help."

Julee punched the speakerphone feature on her landline and dialed.

"Mitchell."

"John, I need you to come to my office. Drop everything and make it quick."

"Yeah, sure. I need to stretch my legs anyway."

"And on your way, can you stop by the break room and pick up a couple of coffees for me and my guest?"

Mitchell gave a tired chuckle. "I'll never grow beyond a high-paid IT gopher in your eyes, will I?"

"You're not a gopher, John. You're my errand boy."

John groaned, as if he was getting out of a chair after pulling an all-nighter. "At least you didn't call me your 'cabana boy.'"

"No, no, no. You're not a cabana boy."

"Nice. Well, uh, okay then, I'll be there shortly."

"That's not what I meant—" Julee heard a click and noticed the screen on the phone went blank.

"Julee," Blake said, shaking his head, "when it comes to Men 101, you never tell a guy he's *not* a cabana boy, even if he isn't."

"I meant he's not the sleazy kind of guy who preys on bored, rich women, you know? The gigolo type?"

"I understand, but if that's what you meant, then you should have just said it."

Julee slumped her shoulders. "Noted." She picked up the land-line receiver. "So, who should I call to issue the warrants without tipping anyone off?"

Blake held up his hand. "We need to meet with Director Jameson, first, and present all of our findings...the voiceprints on all the major players from this Consortium, the voiceprints for Ben Jenkins, the mounds of documents from Kurt Bowker's computer, Sorensen's computer information, everything. Once the director sees everything, and we can tie it all together, then he will want to issue warrants for the arrest of every single person involved who is still alive. However, before he starts rounding everyone up, I suspect he will wish to present all of our findings to the president first, and not in the presence of Ben Jenkins, of course."

"When do we leave?" Julee said with a twinkle in her eye.

"That's where John comes into play."

Someone knocked on the door.

"Speaking of," Julee said, getting up and walking over to the door. She opened it, and standing there, holding two cups of coffee with a little bag of sugar, creamers, and stir sticks dangling from his finger, was John.

"Errand boy at your service, ma'am."

Julee eyed her friend with a sheepish smile. "Thank you, John," she said, stepping out of the way.

John handed Julee her a cup and stepped inside. He saw Blake and reached out his hand with the second cup in it. "Agent Meyer, it's good to see you again."

"Likewise, Agent Mitchell." Blake took the coffee and gave John a healthy handshake. "Please, sit down. We have some very, very important information to share with you. This info is to stay between the three of us and Harrison Kelly. If it gets out to anyone else, our entire operation—everything we have been working on since Monday—could be jeopardized. Do I make myself clear?"

John stared sternly at Blake before turning to Julee. "Are you sure you want to share such important intel with someone who isn't even a make-believe cabana boy?"

Julee's mouth dropped open, and a gasp of disbelief popped out at the same time.

"I'm just kidding," John said. "Maybe this wasn't the best time for a comedic interlude."

"You think?" Julee said.

Blake's eyes shifted from John to Julee and back to John as they had their little quasi spat. "Is there something going on here, between the two of you, that I need to know about?"

Julee and John gave Blake the same bewildered expression.

"Uh, no," Julee said.

"Not hardly," John said.

Blake set his coffee down on the desk. The soldier inside was about to explode. "I realize we are all tired, and fatigue often looks for ways to vent, but this is neither the place nor the time for frivolity. If these people release the contagion they claim to possess, then the human population as we know it may change beyond recognition. According to the files Harrison pulled up on Sorensen's computer, this was their overall goal—to literally change the planet's economic structure and attack what they deemed as a 'population bomb' in one fell swoop.

"Think about it. If those with money and power wipe out sixty percent or more of the world's population, then all the things deemed important and valuable—money in banks belonging to families who no longer exist, gold deposits in places like Fort Knox, prime real estate along beaches and in the mountains— everything would be up for grabs, and the only people left would be the few poor souls who happened to be immune somehow and those who have the antidote.

"This was their plan all along. And we now have the evidence to prove that portion of their plan. Now, I want to expose every player, every financial donor, every intelligentsia member who contributed to this plan, and most of all, I want those in our own government to answer for their crimes.

"Therefore, can we stop the petty bickering and get to work?"

Julee and John both said nothing. All they could do was nod.

"Good. John, I need you to go back to your office, lock the door, if you have to, and gather all the information we have amassed so far. Voiceprint analyses, all the documentation from Sorensen's files showing who the members of The Consortium are, who The Hands of Allah members are, everyone and everything Julee and I will need to present to Director Jameson, to not only show all the guilty parties, but also to prove who the mole is.

"Once we have it, Julee and I will then fly up to Washington and see the director and present to him our findings. With any luck, we should have the mole and the rest of the major players behind bars within forty-eight hours."

"I am assuming you know who the mole is?" Mitchell said.

"We do," Blake said, "but I believe keeping you in the dark on it gives you deniability."

"I'm cool with it."

"Good."

"And the contagion?" Julee said. "We still don't know where the antibiotic-resistant strain is."

"No, we don't." Blake lowered his head briefly, and pressed his index finger and middle finger into his temple to relieve some stress. "The contagion in the warehouse was just like the ones released in Las Vegas and at Union Market."

"Were they able to test all of the contagion in the warehouse?" Julee said. "Maybe it was mixed in with the less lethal kind."

"The CDC is going to test every package, but it will take days. They estimate there are over fourteen-thousand packages on those pallets."

"Fourteen *thousand*?" John said.

Blake nodded. "Just imagine if those did contain the deadly version of the plague and got distributed to stores across the U.S. By the time anybody from the medical community realized anything was happening, it would be too late. The spread of the contagion would have jumped on planes, trains, cruise ships, you name it. We would be dealing with the aftermath for years."

John stood. "I'm on it. Anything else?"

"None of this information gets transmitted over a phone, via email, via texting, faxed, made into a PDF, nothing electronic, period. I want it in a paper file, or in files. Understood?"

John nodded.

"Okay, good. I'll be down to your office in a few minutes to help sort everything."

"Sounds like a plan," John said, standing and walking out the door.

Blake looked at Julee. "As soon as Mitchell and I get all the information together, we're outta here. Got it?"

Julee nodded. "This trip is going to be one for the ages. And I get a front row seat? Oh yeah, I'm ready when you are."

JULY 14, 2014

CHAPTER 58

Situation Room
West Wing
Washington, D.C.

It took a few hours for Blake Meyer to organize all the evidence at the Jacksonville field office with the help of Agent Mitchell. Then, he and Julee Scarfano flew to the FBI headquarters and met with Director Jameson in his office a little after two o'clock in the morning.

Blake walked the director through the entire case, showcasing the evidence amassed from Sorensen's computer and the computer system of Kurt Bowker. He tied almost every thread together, and by the time he explained everything, Jameson was quiet as a mouse.

All Jameson could say every so often was how "he couldn't believe it," and "this is much bigger than anything any of us imagined."

"Do you know what this means, Agent Meyer?" Jameson

finally said when Blake concluded his presentation. "You're asking me to walk into the Oval Office and tell the president of the United States a story of how his trusted friend of...I don't know...over twenty years, thirty maybe,...maybe more...is *the mole* we've been looking for all this time? 'And, Mr. President, he's been working with some of your very own cabinet members? And some of the biggest financiers in private industry...people who are involved with green energy, space exploration, computer technologies, pharmaceutical production, world banking operations,...'" Jameson sat behind his desk bewildered. "'Then, Mr. President, there's the players on the political scene...people you have fought against, people you've struck deals with, people who are part of groups like the WHO, NATO, WEC,...'" He slammed his fist on the desk. "'Jenkins has even been working with terrorists! The very ones we have been battling up to this very moment!'"

Blake glanced over at Julee, who had a bit of a concerned face of her own, but he remained quiet. He knew it was a lot to digest all at once.

"All this time," Jameson continued, using a breathing technique to try and calm himself, "I believed—or was led to believe—foreign spies and terrorist organizations were responsible, like The Hands of Allah, for example. And I assumed there would be others caught in the fallout. But the magnitude of the planning... the size and scope of their end game...this organizational structure and the infiltration into all levels of our government and industrial societies around the world makes the efforts of Osama Bin Laden seem like a kindergartener's efforts by comparison."

"Groups like The Hands of Allah did play a part, sir, as you already know," Blake said, "but they were pawns. They were used for what they could deliver. Nothing more, nothing less. In the end, the foot soldiers for those groups were never going to be recipients of the vaccine or antidote necessary to make one immune or cure one from this plague they were going to release.

The Consortium members were saving those components for themselves and their trusted colleagues...ones needed for the next phase of the operation. If sixty percent or more of the population was to be wiped out, they would need people in strategic positions to keep chaos and anarchy from happening, while at the same time, restructure society and begin a new world order unlike anything we have ever seen in human history."

Director Jameson scratched his head as if he had to figure out some equation for quantum physics. "I assume you have a list of those who will need to be rounded up and arrested, Agent Meyer?"

Blake reached into his briefcase and pulled a thirty-eight page folder out. "I have everyone listed in alphabetical order, with their list of offenses categorized under their names. But keep in mind, sir, this is just a list of the members of The Consortium and those I have been able to link to them. It does not include all the members of The Hands of Allah, the 605 families who were being rounded up at one point early on in this investigation, nor the bit players here and there, some of which I am sure we don't have a name for yet."

Jameson thumbed through the folder. "I know a judge who will discreetly issue the arrest warrants for these people."

"Can he be trusted?"

"He's never given me any indication otherwise."

"Well, just to be sure, I'll need his name. I'll have Agent Mitchell and my other associate run it through Sorensen's files and Kurt Bowker's files, just to be sure."

"Please do. His name is Alfonzo Cardina-Bustamante. However, before we start demanding warrants and arresting every-one, we need to present all of this to President Gilmore first. Just him, you, me, and Scarfano. I think once he sees all the evidence, he will then issue a directive to have all those people arrested."

"I agree," Blake said. "And Ben Jenkins can't find out about any of this until it's too late, or most of those names on that list will suddenly disappear or die."

* * *

Less than an hour later, a private meeting had been set up with President Gilmore. He was a little perturbed the information could not have been divulged over the phone, but Director Jameson assured him he would have a different outlook, once he saw all the details.

When Director Jameson, Blake Meyer, and Julee Scarfano arrived, they were escorted to the Situation Room, per Director Jameson's request. He also requested for it be just the president in attendance, with no other cabinet members or advisors present. The president hemmed and hawed at first, but finally acquiesced.

Director Jameson, Blake, and Julee all sat down at the far end of the table, leaving the seat at the head of the table vacant for the president.

A few minutes later, President Gilmore, escorted there by secret service agents, stepped inside. Once the president gave the okay, the agent holding the door closed it and stood outside.

"This had better be good, Director Jameson. We still have a contagion out there unaccounted for, and more and more people are flooding local hospitals here in the D.C. area, complaining of symptoms related to the plague. So far, everyone who has been admitted was at the Union Market when the device was activated."

Director Jameson opened his file and pulled out the call log of the Russian phone number. "Mr. President, there was a Russian phone number discovered by Agent Meyer early on in this investigation of the plague. It came from a Russian FSB agent who was here in the States at the time. You probably remember him. His name was Sergei Botinkin."

"I do. We were working on getting his father here...and now

that I think of it, I never heard the outcome. Is his father in the States yet?"

"Sir, if you will allow me to continue, the answer to your question will be answered eventually."

Gilmore's forehead creased. "Proceed."

Jameson slid the paper over to the president for him to see. "This phone number had made contact with Sergei Botinkin on several occasions."

Gilmore took it and studied it. "What am I looking at exactly?"

"All of these calls were made by the number at the top. The Russian number. The ones highlighted in yellow were to Sergei Botinkin. The ones in pink were to Marcus Sorensen."

"Sorensen?" Gilmore said with a stern gaze. "The same Sorensen responsible for organizing the group called The Consortium?"

"Yes, sir. And as you can see, this phone number has made other calls as well. The one phone call in green was to a Russian oligarch who we know to be involved in drug distribution and human trafficking. His name is Pavel Morozov. The ones in orange are to what we believe to be the main contact for the group we know as The Hands of Allah."

Gilmore studied the paper a few seconds longer and then let his hands drop to the table. "Please tell me we know who owns or has been using this number."

"We do, actually." Jameson said. "We also have voiceprint evidence which confirms, one hundred percent—not only through voiceprint analysis, but also by Sorensen himself identifying the person by a first name in five of those calls highlighted in pink."

"So, who is it?" Gilmore glared at Jameson, then his eyes shifted to Blake, then Julee.

Director Jameson cleared his throat. "Sir, it's Ben Jenkins."

Gilmore's anxious, frustrated, and tired demeanor suddenly

froze. He slowly fell back into his chair, and his breathing became slightly erratic as if he was suffering a slight stroke. His icy stare at Jameson drifted upward and away. "What?"

"Sir," Blake said, "I can see this has caught you completely off guard. It did us as well. Trust me. But as you start to replay the events of the last several days, it all adds up. The mole we've been trying to find was here, at your side, the entire time. He knew every plan made. He heard every update on our progress." Blake pointed at the file lying in front of the director. "This is how he remained three steps ahead of us."

Gilmore swallowed hard, still gazing into his memory more than at the wall before him. "I...I, uh...don't understand...Why?" He closed his eyes and shook his head a little. "Why would he do this?"

"Sir," Jameson continued, "in addition to identifying Ben Jenkins, we also identified everyone in The Consortium, several members of The Hands of Allah, and some other players who were responsible for doing jobs for Sorensen. We now know who installed all the devices, like the ones in Las Vegas and Union Market. We still have in custody the families who were rounded up several days ago, the ones placed in the States by The Hands of Allah. And I have orders for the arrest warrants ready to go for everyone, Mr. President. All we need is your word for us to move forward."

Gilmore reached out for the file in front of Director Jameson. "May I see it?"

"Of course." Jameson slid it across the table, but when the president placed his hand on it, Jameson didn't release it. "Sir, just know...there are other names on our warrant list...who are members of your cabinet. They have been working with Ben Jenkins. The call records, the emails, the documents...they are all in there, proving it beyond a shadow of a doubt, thanks to Sorensen's computer files and the computer files of Kurt Bowker."

"Kurt Bowker?"

"Yes, sir. MI6 Agent Conrad Bowker's son. He's been working with these people too. He was the one who made the recording for Sorensen...the one sent to us, listing the demands which were said to be from The Hands of Allah? Remember those demands?"

"Oh, I remember."

"Bowker made the recording for Sorensen and was responsible for sending it to us without us being able to trace it." Jameson almost released the file, then grabbed it again. "And sir, just so you know, Kurt Bowker was also helping Arina Filipov. He has confessed to it. He helped her do everything she did, which includes killing two FBI agents in Orlando, Florida, and a Florida State Trooper near Gainesville, Florida. And, he was responsible for killing two mercenaries in Paris along with Sergei Botinkin's father, Major General Pyotr Botinkin." Jameson pursed his lips and removed his hand from the folder. "It's all in there, sir."

Gilmore sorrowfully took the file and spent almost ten minutes reading every page. With each minute, his facial expression became more hardened. The muscles in his jawline and his temples flexed and bulged. His breathing intensified in the silence, and was all Blake and the rest could hear.

When he was done, Gilmore slapped the folder shut and slid it back to Jameson. "I want them all arrested and tried in as many courts of law as needed. However, before you begin, I would like to take our meeting to the Oval Office. Once there, then I want to invite Ben to join us. I need to know, from his own lips, how he could think any of this was the right thing to do.

"Then, when we're done, Director Jameson, and I feel I've received an adequate enough answer, then you can call the secret service agents in and haul him off in handcuffs."

"Yes, sir. However, if Ben Jenkins is seen walking out of the Oval Office in cuffs, it will take the coconut telegraph about two seconds to get the information out to his co-conspirators. And once it's out, all those connected to him will bolt."

"Okay, director, what do you suggest?"

"I suggest we obtain all the arrest warrants and then enact them right after Ben Jenkins enters the Oval Office. He will not be able to alert anyone this way, and nobody gets tipped off before he arrives. We start rounding them up before he walks out in cuffs, and by the time word gets out about his arrest, we can at least have all the big dogs from your cabinet under arrest as well."

Blake lifted a finger while opening a screen on his phone. "And if I may, Director Jameson, my associates have confirmed. Your judge, Judge Cardina-Bustamante, is good to go."

Jameson faced the president. "We're ready when you are, sir."

"Do what you have to do. I don't want any of them to get away with any of this. Do I make myself clear?"

Jameson looked at Blake and Julee. They all nodded in agreement.

"Loud and clear, sir."

CHAPTER 59

A little over two hours had passed before President Gilmore sat down behind his Oval Office desk. Director Sam Jameson, Blake Meyer, and Julee Scarfano followed him in and sat down on the couches in the middle of the room.

Jameson set the folder down on the coffee table in front of him and pulled out his cell phone. He checked his messages and then gave the president a nod. "We're ready, Mr. President. All the arrest warrants have been issued, and our people are in place."

Gilmore's blood was boiling, and it took everything inside of him to keep from screaming expletives so loud, the Beltway would freeze in motion, wondering what was happening at 1600 Pennsylvania Avenue. Taking several deep breaths, he slowly calmed himself to a low roar. He picked up the receiver on his desk phone and punched a number. "Yes, get me Mr. Jenkins. I need to see him immediately. It's urgent."

"Yes, sir," the female voice on the other end said.

Gilmore hung up and waved his hand at Jameson. "Do it."

Jameson gave a quick nod and texted the words "It's a go!" to the group of numbers on his screen. He waited for a response to the directive as the three men and Julee sat in silence.

Two minutes later, as Ben Jenkins entered the room, Jameson's phone buzzed in his hand. He looked down, and the order was confirmed. He held up his phone and peered at the president. "Sir, we're good to go."

President Gilmore stood and turned his attention to his chief of staff. "Ben," he said, rounding the corner of his desk, "please come and sit down." He pointed at the couches and chairs in the middle of the room. "And you know Director Jameson, and Supervisory Special Agent Meyer."

Jenkins smiled and shook each man's hand.

"And this is Supervisory Special Agent-in-Charge Julee Scarfano of the Jacksonville Field Office in Florida. I believe you have spoken to her on the phone, but you have never met her in person."

"That is correct," Jenkins said, reaching out his hand. "It's so very nice to finally meet you, SAC Scarfano. And may I say, you have done a masterful job, in light of all the obstacles you've faced, especially stepping into the position while we were in the middle of all this mess we find ourselves in."

Julee shook his hand. "Thank you, sir."

Ben Jenkins sat down and scanned everyone's face. "So, what's up? Please tell me we have found the contagion."

"These fine folks have been busy, Ben. They have a great deal to tell us." Gilmore motioned to Director Jameson. "Let's begin."

"Sir," Jameson said, opening the file before him. "Mr. Jenkins, the reason we have called you here is to discuss your involvement in this entire ordeal involving the release of the contagion you referenced a few moments ago."

"My involvement?" Jenkins glanced at each person around the coffee table. "What are you saying exactly? It sounds menacing."

"Well, frankly, sir, to put it bluntly, it is 'menacing.' We have been tracking a phone number for several days now. It is a Russian phone number. And it has made quite a few calls to major players on the wrong side of this contagion business. Everyone from Sergei Botinkin to Marcus Sorensen to rogue operatives and Russian oligarchs."

"And what's this got to do with me?"

"Sir, we have voiceprint matches—one hundred percent matches, by the way, of the person who utilized this number. We even have Marcus Sorensen calling this individual by his first name in five of the calls made to Sorensen. And then linking the first name and the phone number to the content of those phone calls—all of which were transcribed and recorded by Sorensen himself, it became quite clear who the Russian phone number belonged to. It was you, sir."

"What? Are you high, Director Jameson?"

"Frankly, sir, I wish I was. I wish this all was a hallucination on my part, but—"

"You are hallucinating, Director...and bordering on delirium, if you ask me. You have it all wrong. I don't know how, but you do. You've misread something. Or your computers have made a mistake with their voice match." Jenkins shook his head adamantly. "You know how voiceprints can be manipulated these days. Anyone with the tech could take comments I've made to the press and use the voice data to recreate me saying anything."

"Sir, there's more."

Jenkins slammed his fist down on the coffee table. "It's not me!" He turned and faced the president. "Walter, seriously, you're not believing any of this, are you? It must be The Hands of Allah or some other group working for Sorensen. They're framing me. We are getting too close, so they are using me to get to you."

President Gilmore sat in his chair with his legs crossed and his fingers intertwined in his lap as the exchange progressed. Without moving a muscle, he watched his chief of staff squirm and yell and argue. He listened to Director Jameson explain what had already been told to him. He had read the file.

Finally, the president lifted his eyes to meet Ben's. "Ben, I'm only going to ask this once."

"Ask what?"

"Did you, in any way, help Sorensen, or any member of his 'Consortium,' or any member of The Hands of Allah, or any member of my cabinet or presidential staff commit acts of treason?"

Ben's mouth fell agape as he stared at his friend. "President Gilmore...I...I can't believe you would even think such a thing, let alone ask me such a question."

"You didn't answer my question, Ben."

"I'm not believing this. Do you all think I'm guilty?" He turned and peered at Blake. "Agent Meyer, I helped you secure funding. I allowed you to go dark and work outside the strictures of the FBI to track down Colin Murphy. I assisted you and the president at every turn. Surely, you must believe this information to be fabricated."

"May I, Mr. President?" Blake said.

The president gave a slight nod, keeping his composure.

"Mr. Jenkins, you are correct. You did assist me in those areas. However, there were other things which occurred...in a very timely manner, I might add, which could not have happened, if there wasn't someone on the inside, funneling information to Murphy and Sorensen and the rest. We knew we had a mole." Blake chuckled. "You and I have spoken about it, with the president too. We all knew we had a mole, we just didn't know who, nor did we know how the mole was accessing information and able to process it so quickly.

"Of course, we thought the person who had hacked into Agent Scarfano's computer may be the mole, but we had no evidence to put a face and name to our theory. Now, we do." Blake pointed at the folder. "The folder Director Jameson has in his possession contains evidence of events and happenings we can now tie to you, Mr. Jenkins. Such as a very specific military satellite being commandeered to camp out over *my* house so those controlling it could watch—in real time—as my family was abducted...placed in boats...and hauled out to sea," Blake said, fighting back his emotions, "while the vicious murders of innocent people, including my sister-in-law, were committed inside *my* house, as I was tranquilized in *my backyard* just long enough to stay out of the way until *my house* blew up with the explosives left behind by the abducting murderers.

"In addition to this, there are the texted orders James Connell received—from this Russian telephone number...which was the only number pre-programmed into the pay-as-you-go phone he had on him—telling him to go to Paris and hunt down Conrad Bowker and Major General Pyotr Botinkin. Once he made contact, he was supposed to murder them both and stage it so the 'details of the murder scene' could not be traced back to the president's office. Photos were supposed to be taken and sent back for confirmation purposes. Unfortunately, for you, Connell did not clear out his texts before he disappeared.

"Fortunately for us, though, Conrad Bowker hasn't been murdered. Instead, he was arrested in Paris and has since been extradited to London. He was able to tell me," Blake said, examining his watch, "a few hours ago, actually, where he left Connell's body. French authorities have since confirmed his intel and have identified the body. It is Connell. Bowker admitted to capturing Connell and interrogating him. Connell wouldn't tell him much, however, because he claimed his family had been threatened by those who sent him there."

"Connell lied. He was nothing but a liar."

Blake lifted an eyebrow. "So, what exactly did you tell Agent Connell, Mr. Jenkins?"

Ben Jenkins clinched his eyes together. He inhaled, but in an angry manner, because when he exhaled, it was accompanied by a growl. "Walter, help me out here. You knew about this Connell business. We planned it together."

Director Jameson and Blake both wrinkled their brows and turned to get a better look at the president.

President Gilmore eyed Ben Jenkins with a glare exposing his mounting rage. "Yes, Ben. We did plan it together. I even told Director Jameson about it, because he had found out I had appointed Agent Scarfano into the SAC post there in Jacksonville to replace Connell. Sam wanted to know why he had been left out of the loop. So, I told him his involvement was an oversight on my part. I was being leery, because one, we knew we had a mole in our midst, and two, I didn't know who I could trust at the time.

"However, Ben, the orders we agreed to give to Connell were to locate and bring Major General Botinkin back to the U.S., so we could pick his brain on the nature of this contagion we were battling. His son, Sergei, had told us he would know. Those were the orders, Ben. The orders we agreed to. Nowhere in those orders were the planned executions of Major General Botinkin nor Conrad Bowker. Therefore, *do not* try to pin this on me. You changed those orders to cover your tracks, because *you* are the mole we have been looking for."

Jenkins faced Director Jameson. "Connell must have been the mole. He must have changed the plans. The president is right. We planned to have the major general brought back here." Jenkins crossed his arms and rubbed his head as if a headache was expanding exponentially. "Our initial plan was to send Connell in to save the major general and bring him back to the States. But I told them not to send Connell. He was dumb as a stump. How he ever got promoted into an SAC position is just another thing wrong with this country."

"You never mentioned your reservations about Connell to me, Ben," the president said.

Blake shot a look at Director Jameson.

"So, Mr. Jenkins," Jameson said, "are you saying you were taking orders from someone else, and thus admitting to your involvement in this conspiracy to commit treason?"

Jenkins closed his eyes, clenched his jaw, but remained quiet.

"Let me inform you of this, Mr. Jenkins," Blake said. "Our FBI contacts at the scene in Paris were able to confirm every detail in Agent Bowker's story. Bowker tied him up, interrogated him, and eventually killed Connell. Then, he read the last text to come across Connell's pay-as-you-go phone. Bowker claims it came through just minutes after Connell died. Bowker was able to crack Connell's four-digit PIN and see everything for himself. He saw the orders to have Bowker and the major general killed. He retrieved the hotel information where Connell was staying. He went to his hotel room and found the file you sent Connell on the major general. And because of this file, Bowker realized Botinkin was responsible for the very technology used to poison him years ago. Of course, the major general had no idea his Russian comrades would use it on Agent Bowker years later, but the full-circle irony was not wasted on Bowker.

"In addition, our FBI contacts have since retrieved Connell's phone from the French government. All the evidence is there, just as Bowker said it would be. The received calls. The texts. The directions. Everything. Our contacts even went to the hotel room you secured for Connell and found the file Bowker referenced. This is how I knew Conrad was telling the truth. He knew about things he could only know if he had indeed been there."

Blake watched as Jenkins's expressions slowly melted from rage to remorse.

"And one more thing, Mr. Jenkins. When it was verified by your inside IT guy, Kurt Bowker—Conrad's son, by the way—that Connell had failed in his mission, you enlisted Kurt to finish the job. Which he did.

"However, Kurt Bowker failed you in one major area. He allowed his father to live as vengeance for what he perceived to be a lifetime of evil perpetrated on behalf of his father upon their family, compliments of the British government.

"Conrad now knows of his son's involvement. I informed him of all this when I spoke to him a few hours ago. In addition, Kurt has testified in a statement to SAC Scarfano and SAC Sheridan Fox at the Atlanta FO about the entire affair. He even named you by name, Mr. Jenkins. He is willing to testify in court that you are the mole we have been looking for." Blake pointed to the coffee table. "Everything is in the folder. The gig is up."

"The 'gig' isn't up until I say it's up," President Gilmore said. "Not yet, Agent Meyer. For one, we still may have a deadly contagion out there unaccounted for. And two, I need to hear from Mr. Jenkins...why he has betrayed me at what is nothing less than the deepest level." The president paused and faced his friend. "Ben, why? Why would you betray me? Why betray everything we have worked for all these years? And please, don't tell me it was for the money. I may have to kill you where you sit myself, if you say such a thing."

Ben Jenkins leaned back and slumped his shoulders. A tear dribbled down his cheek. He wiped it with his hand, trying to keep himself together. "Okay...yes, yes! I'm guilty of it all. But I had no choice."

President Gilmore faced his friend with a demeanor of skepticism. "You had no choice? Try me, Ben. If there is anything I have taught you over the years, it's how you always have a choice. It's as simple as right and wrong. And yes, sometimes, decisions are complicated and affect a great many people, but in the end, there is always a right and a wrong."

"Yeah, well, in this case, there wasn't. Right would have ended up wrong. So, wrong became the default 'right' decision. It was all about collateral damage and minimizing it."

Gilmore uncrossed his legs and leaned forward, resting his elbows on his knees while he eyed his friend. He kept his fingers intertwined, but he began to maneuver them, cracking his knuckles as he did. "We're done listening to cryptic answers, Ben. And I am all out of patience. So, you had better start being more specific."

Ben huffed. "I was doing it to protect *you*, Mr. President."

"Protect *me*? How in the world could you come to the conclusion that any of this could protect me? Can't you see? The folder in front of Sam will bring down my administration. People will look at me and declare a vote of no confidence in a heartbeat, once the content of this folder is released. They will say, 'How could he be the president and have so many people in his administration working for the bad guys and not know anything about it?' And they'd be right. So, please tell me, Ben. How does any of this *benefit* me?"

Ben Jenkins let out an expletive and stared at the president. "Not 'protect *you*,' as in 'protect your administration,' or 'protect your legacy,' or 'protect—'"

"You're talking about protecting his *life*," Blake said.

Jenkins didn't answer. He simply nodded.

President Gilmore sat up and repositioned himself in his chair. "Okay, Ben, so...tell me...how were your efforts supposed to save *my* life."

Jenkins let out a smirk and scratched the back of his head. "You've got it the wrong way around, Walter. My role and actions in all of this were not the things protecting you. They threatened to *kill* you and your family, starting with your children, then your wife, then finally you, if I *didn't do* what they told me to do."

"Why didn't you come to me?"

"If I had, I would have broken rule number one. If you found out and tried to stop me or them, they would kill me first so I could not interfere, then they would go after your family, and finally, you. They had it planned for every scenario. If you were here and your family was elsewhere. If you all were here. If you were all at home. If you were at Camp David. It didn't matter. As soon as they gave the word, your children, your wife, and then you were to be eliminated within one twenty-four-hour period.

"I was ordered to play the loyal chief of staff. They would supply me all the resources I would need to play the role of the mole. All I had to do was keep my head down, do what every normal chief of staff normally does, and keep them informed of all of our government's efforts. And when they needed me to manipulate something, then I was given a time frame for it to happen."

"So, let me ask you this, Mr. Jenkins," Blake said. "What would have happened if Colin Murphy didn't get cocky and send his communiqué, alerting me of Operation Wepwawet? I have reason to believe they may very well have been able to release the contagion before anyone knew what was happening, if Murphy had not done so. Is this a safe assumption?"

"Those in The Consortium...and I am assuming you know who they are by now?"

"We do," Director Jameson said.

"Yeah, well, those in The Consortium were furious with Murphy. They knew when you got involved, Agent Meyer, the game changed drastically. That's why they tried to kill Murphy. They already had Liam Clarke killed, because he would get drunk and blab too much. Now, Murphy had seriously jeopardized the operation for personal reasons, so they knew he could not stay in the U.S. to oversee the final steps of the operation any longer, per their original plan.

"So, they told him they would get him out of the U.S. What they didn't tell him was how the plane provided by Arina Filipov was rigged with explosives. Had you not caught him, he was going to fly out over the ocean, and when he did, there was an operative in a boat, off shore, waiting for him. This operative had some kind of device..." Jenkins shrugged. "I don't know what. But I was told all he had to do was wait for the plane to be within a certain range out over the water. Once it was, then he would shoot the plane or dial a number, or something. I'm not sure, but I was assured the plane would detonate, and Murphy would be fish food. And of course, when you caught him, they had to come up with another way to kill Murphy before he blabbed too much."

"The bridge accident."

"Yes. And if anything, the bridge accident should have demonstrated how vast and organized The Consortium's network is.

"But in answer to your question, Agent Meyer, yes. Had Murphy not done what he did, I doubt very seriously any of you would have seen the contagion's release coming."

"Do you hear yourself, Ben?" The president's voice picked up an octave. "If Agent Meyer and his people had not figured out certain things, sixty percent or more of our population, and who knows how much of the world's population, would be dead or dying right now. How does any of that benefit me? Or protect me? Protect my family? Even if they offered me the antidote or the vaccine, I'd still be an elected official on the outside, at the mercy of those in power. I don't understand how any of this benefits me in any way, shape, or form." Gilmore blurted out an expletive. "And what would make you think I would want to survive such a holocaust and live in the aftermath, my family with me or not?"

Jenkins bit his lower lip. "I guess I should have come to you at the beginning. I knew who the players were. I knew they were formidable, and I wanted to tell you. I almost did on numerous occasions. But I panicked when they said your presidency, and my placement into this position as chief of staff, was all orchestrated by them, unbeknownst to us, of course. They had me surrounded. They told me they were watching me at every turn...had greased the tracks, so to speak, helping me and you get where we were for this very moment. They painted both of us as pawns on a huge chess board, and because of the evidence they supplied to me, I was forced to believe it."

"How so?" Blake said.

"They approached me a couple of weeks after he was elected. They claimed they had manipulated the election to help him, but—"

"How?" Gilmore said.

Jenkins shrugged with a blasé expression. "They never said how. I didn't believe them at first. I want you to know that. I told them at the beginning I could not do what they were asking me to do. But then they showed me surveillance footage of my daughter, at her high school, in the afternoon, in the gymnasium, at basketball practice. The video was followed up by pictures of her driving home from practice by what appeared to be someone in a car beside her. Each picture had a caption, warning me. Then, they'd send me pictures of my wife...out and about shopping around town with her friends. They threatened to kidnap her and hand her over to the war lords in Uganda, if I refused to play ball. They even hacked into my home security system...my home!—and showed me and my wife sleeping in bed. The caption they posted with it was, 'We see you when you're sleeping...' How sick is that?" Ben faced the president. "And Walter, they showed me pictures of your children at their school too. And pictures and videos of the first lady. Private ones. Not the paparazzi-type. Ones taken by people in close proximity." He sighed. "You wanted to know why I did it. Now, you do."

President Gilmore stood and straightened his suit jacket. "Well, my friend, I wish you would have come to me. We could have turned this entire thing on its head. You could have played along, and we could have used it to our advantage. I could have employed the likes of Director Jameson, SSA Meyer and SAC Scarfano, too, and maybe, just maybe, we could have prevented so many people from being injured, killed, and made ill. All while saving my life and the life of my family...and yours.

"But now, I have no other option but to have you arrested for treason and conspiracy to commit acts of terrorism on American soil."

Ben Jenkins jumped up from his seat. "Walter! Please! Don't do this!"

Agent Meyer jumped up, as did Director Jameson. Blake stepped in between Jenkins and the president and pushed Ben back. "Don't come any closer to the president, Mr. Jenkins, or I will have to put you on the ground."

"Walter, please, listen to me," Jenkins said around Blake.

Gilmore placed his hand on Blake's shoulder and motioned for him to take a step to the side.

Blake did, and the president took the needed steps to face his long-time friend, standing almost nose to nose.

Gilmore eyed Jenkins for several awkward moments. "You want to help your cause, Ben?"

"Just tell me what I need to do to prove to you it was all about you, your family's protection, and the safety of mine as well. I see it now. I made a wrong choice. And that choice was followed by a myriad of even poorer choices. Now, let me make a right decision for a change."

"The contagion. The bad one. The one without any known cure. Not the one released in Las Vegas and Union Market. Tell me. Where is it?"

"Last word I received was it had been moved to a facility

outside of Chicago. Some warehouse. They were going to ship it to stores around the country, but after you placed the freeze on the air fresheners, they had to hold it in the warehouse and wait. That's all I know."

"That's all you've got for me?"

"Trust me. If I knew more, I would tell you. What have I got to lose at this point?"

"Mr. Jenkins," Blake said, "I just came from the warehouse you're talking about. Yes, it had the shipments of air fresheners you referenced. It had mercenaries guarding it. However, once we apprehended the mercs, the CDC tested several random batches of those air fresheners. They all contained the same contagion released in Las Vegas and Union Market."

"I-I-I don't know what to say...," Jenkins creased his brow. "That doesn't make sense. Why would they guard it so heavily if it wasn't the real deal?"

"We were wondering the same thing, Ben," Gilmore said. "Hence, my hope of you shedding some light on it for us. Guess I was wrong."

"No, wait. I can make some calls. I can get you some answers."

President Gilmore shook his head and chuckled at the same time. "It's a little late for last ditch efforts, Ben. As we speak, all of your known co-conspirators are being rounded up and arrested. Therefore, even if I was to allow you to make those calls, I doubt there would be anyone on the other end to answer."

Ben Jenkins's eyes glazed over as the weight of the information President Gilmore shared fell upon him with the impact of a thousand tons of bricks. He lost his balance and fell back into his seat.

"Oh, yes, Ben. Admiral Hoskins. Director Williamson. All the voices on all the voiceprints from all the files saved and catalogued on Sorensen's computer. All the people either helping Kurt Bowker or employed by Kurt Bowker. Arina Filipov...if we can find her. Even Guillermo Castaneda. Everyone, Ben. The headlines tonight and this week are going to be filled with stories of crime and conspiracy, espionage and treason. Government corruption at its highest levels. But trust me when I say this: When I do my press conference, once everyone is arrested, I will speak of our friendship and how disappointed and decimated I am with the choices you made over the months and years leading up to this very moment." Gilmore turned to Director Jameson. "Please, arrest this man and get him out of my sight."

"Sir." Jameson said. He plucked his phone from his coat pocket and texted someone.

"Walter, you're making a big mistake. These people are everywhere. You'll never get them all in time. They will get you and your family before you do."

"I don't take too kindly to threats, Ben. You of all people should know."

Just then, four secret service agents and two FBI agents entered the Oval Office. Jameson, Blake, and Julee stepped away, and one of the FBI agents placed Ben Jenkins in handcuffs while the other agent read him his rights.

"You're going to regret this!" Ben Jenkins said as they escorted him out of the Oval Office.

All four of them watched the agents escort Jenkins through the doorway, and then the door closed.

"What do you think he means exactly?" Julee said, shooting a look at each of them. "'You're going to regret this?'"

Gilmore, who had worked his way back around behind his desk, huffed a huge sigh and sat down. "He's either a good friend, and he's truly worried about how the people he was working for will carry out their initial threats against me and my family, or... he's more aligned with their treasonous ideology than I care to admit, and he's *hoping* for my demise." The president's weary appearance suddenly changed. "Either way, Director Jameson, please coordinate with the Secret Service to have my family's comings and goings limited to only necessary trips until further notice. And I think ordering extra agents to protect my family is warranted, wouldn't you agree?"

"Yes, sir."

"And I'll explain everything to my family later. But for now, let me know when we have every one of our own on the list arrested and in custody. I need to set up a press conference, but I want to make sure everyone on our end is behind bars first."

"What about Filipov, Castaneda, and the others outside the country?" Julee said. "They could be the ones posing the danger to your family Mr. Jenkins was referring to."

"True, SAC Scarfano, but if I cowered behind this desk every time there was an international threat leveled at this office, I'd spend my entire presidency here. So, we will take care of our own, and then mention in the presser we have others who are being actively sought as well. Maybe such news will deter their efforts to try and get close to me, especially when we release their photos to every news outlet and every law enforcement agency on the planet."

CHAPTER 60

THE WHITE HOUSE ROSE GARDEN
Washington, D.C.

It was Monday, the Fourteenth of July. Exactly a week since it all began. Or at least, a week since proper authorities caught wind something was brewing.

Whispers in the data...

A cryptic message...

Seemed so long ago now.

Mid-morning in the Rose Garden proved to be another beautiful setting. The temperature was heading to ninety degrees on this day, so those who plan such events believed getting it done while the sun was not at its zenith would be best. However, despite their pleas to move the event into the Capitol Rotunda, both for temperature and safety concerns, President Gilmore wasn't having it. If anything, he was a traditionalist at heart. Such events always took place in the Rose Garden. This was why hundreds had gathered there already.

It was to be a somber and festive time all at once, and unfortunately for President Gilmore, his presidency would go down in history as not only one having to deal with a major attack on American soil, but it also would be remembered for the corruption which rose to the highest ranks and brought all of those attacks to bear.

This moment was not wasted on Walter Gilmore as he stood behind the desk in the Oval Office, making sure his neck tie was straight. He buttoned his coat and lifted his arms out from his side. "How do I look?"

"As dapper as ever, sir," Jonas McCormick said.

The president lifted his chin a little and turned his head to the left, held it there, and then to the right. "No hair is out of place, right?"

"Sir, despite the lack of sleep over the last week, and the amount of stress you have been under, you look great, if I do say so myself," Blake Meyer said. "I wish I felt half as good as you look right now."

"Well," Gilmore said, pointing at Blake, "*you* get a pass, my friend. I may have put a lot of thought equity and planning equity into this entire ordeal, but I did the majority of it from behind this desk. I wasn't putting in the sweat equity and physical exertion you were out there in the field. Your efforts, Agent Meyer, they will be commended on this day."

"Sir, if I may, please commend everyone who helped me, but exclude me and the one person who chooses to remain anonymous from your speech."

"You and your infamous IT guy." The president picked up his briefing folder and notes. "I will make sure his name is lumped together with 'all the other people too numerous to list at this gathering' part of the speech. I really don't want to name anyone just yet, not while the investigation is still ongoing."

"Thank you, sir," Blake said.

Jonas McCormick received a phone call. "Yes...okay...thanks." He ended the call and faced the president. "Sir, they are ready when you are."

* * *

President Gilmore exited the Oval Office and wound his way out to the lectern centered on the stage. No chairs were set up behind him, a precautionary decision on the part of the Secret Service. Instead, all the dignitaries and people to be honored stood "off stage," if you will, only to be seen when their time had come.

Without teleprompters this time, the president chose to go "old school" and use his prepared notes. He opened his comments with the typical pleasantries and traditional remarks. Then, he jumped right into the events leading up to this very moment. He replayed each day, giving some detailed information which had already been released to the press while also speaking in more vague terms and painting images for the mind's eye to fill in obvious gaps.

"There have also been some developments of late I wish to remark upon, for no other reason but to speak to the enormity of this terrorist activity and the depths by which these people were willing to go to bring about the end they desired.

"First, as many of you know, Congresswoman Merina Parker was recently arrested for what was believed to be her involvement in the attack on the Bahama Bay Hotel and Casino in Las Vegas. After further investigation, those accusations were found to be false, and she was released from custody. However, I have just learned over the last few hours that Congresswoman Parker was shot and killed in her home. According to the Capitol Hill Police and the FBI, the perpetrator was Camila Carlton, the wife of Judge Thomas Carlton. And for now, those are all the details I can offer, as this is an ongoing investigation. But please know, as of this very moment, law enforcement authorities do not, I repeat, do not believe Congresswoman Parker's death was related to her earlier arrest nor do they believe, at this time, it has any connection with all of this terrorist activity our country has experienced. They believe it to be another matter entirely.

"Second, we have another late development in our fight against those wishing to bring harm upon our dear country. We now believe we have gained a major upper hand in the battle. Although we have yet to locate the contagion originally threatened against us, which was not supposed to have any known cure, the contagions used against us thus far have been determined by the CDC to be completely curable, if we can treat the victims soon enough. This belief has been proven with the cases in Las Vegas. Therefore, we continue to urge anyone, particularly those who were at the Bahama Bay Hotel and Casino in Las Vegas in and around the time of one a.m., Las Vegas time, yesterday, Sunday, July 13th, or anyone who was at the Union Market here in Washington, D.C. also yesterday, Sunday, July 13th, around noon, Washington, D.C. time, to report to your nearest local hospital or clinic and get checked out. Both of these outbreaks have been determined to be regular strains of bubonic plague, which can be cured with the proper antibiotics with no lingering side effects, if one gets detected early enough. Hence, our urging of those near those infected areas to report to a local hospital or clinic as soon as possible. I cannot reiterate this enough.

"My heart is beyond broken for all the victims in Las Vegas who did not survive these attacks, and for those who may not, although they are battling for their lives as we speak. Our heartfelt condolences go out to their families. In addition, we have lost some city, state, and national government personnel in this fight. Our condolences go out to the families of all those who served their country bravely during this time."

President Gilmore flipped a page in his notes. "In addition to all of this, however, I do wish to update you on what we know so far concerning those behind these attacks. Some news outlets reported some things late last night, however, they did not receive any of their information from the Office of the Presidency. Therefore, I wish to share the *correct* information with you now.

"Over the last twenty-four hours, I learned of a serious and thorough international cabal operating both in our country and abroad. This cabal had penetrated and infiltrated some of the highest places in our government. Through these 'chess pieces' I am calling them, this cabal was able to manipulate and intercept information flowing into and out of all branches and agencies of our American government. This cabal also spread its tentacles into other countries and their governments as well. Their plan, as diabolical as it sounds, was to release a contagion so deadly—one with no known cure—for the purpose of literally reorganizing and restructuring human society around the world.

"Imagine, for a moment, a world where six out of every ten people around you die within the span of the next three months. The death rate could even reach seven or eight out of ten by the end of six months. For the remaining twenty to forty percent who survive, human civilization—with its structures of banking, food production and distribution, energy production and distribution, water purification and distribution, health care systems, transportation systems, media outlets, electrical power grids, as well as other sources of power, like nuclear reactors...namely, everything we rely on in our day-to-day lives—would grind to a halt. There simply would not be enough people left, with the knowledge and skills needed, to keep all of these structures operational. Anarchy would most assuredly ensue, and it would turn into a gross and inconceivable test of survival of the fittest among those left behind.

"Those conditions I just described for you would be the new norm, if nobody made any contingency plans.

"However, this cabal did. Behind the scenes, they had formulated an antidote and are working on a vaccine, we believe. They were going to inoculate their own, the best and the brightest of those who were willing to go along with their plan. They would seize the banking system after the dust settled and operate it the way they chose to, benefitting their own supporters, of course, along the way. Everything would be redesigned. Even military personnel with access to all the weapons would become the new unifying force. If you chose to stand up and fight against the new world order, you would die. There would be no courts of law. No legal recourse. The new norm would be, 'do their bidding or be eradicated.'

"This cabal had meticulously planned all of this for more than fifteen years. Every step strategically orchestrated. Every person carefully placed into crucial positions of power with a distinct purpose. Rogue organizations—like The Hands of Allah, for example...a group used for their skills at getting people into our country undetected—were, no doubt, promised a seat at the table of this new world order as well.

"The cabal's plan was quite simple, actually. Plant over six hundred families into our most populated areas of the lower forty-eight. Then, in one synchronized moment, they were to release the contagion into the homes of those families. The families would never know. They were simply the delivery system.

"These families would become infected and go about their day as usual...the husband going to work...the children going to school or day care or the playground...the mother going to work, or the grocery store, or the post office...each one spreading the disease as he or she went. Even some of the husbands of these families were being trained as airline pilots, so they could take the disease overseas undetected.

"Within two to four days, these family members would show symptoms, be told to go to local area clinics or hospitals. Because medical officials would have no idea what they were dealing with, these infected family members would spread the disease to health care workers and sick patients already in those locations.

"To add to this chaos, this cabal had disguised its contagion in air fresheners, of all things, and had plans to have thousands of these air fresheners either delivered to stores across the country or sent through the mail system as freebies to try out in the comfort of your own home.

"When we learned of this portion of the cabal's plan, I enacted a ban on all air fresheners in an attempt to slow our enemy down, and we did." The president paused as the audience applauded. "I can say it now. We have found the air fresheners they were going to use, stored in a warehouse in south Chicago. They are now in the possession of the federal government and will be destroyed, once their investigative purposes as evidence is no longer required.

"So, as you can imagine, if this cabal had released these air fresheners into the stores and homes of unsuspecting consumers, these poor souls would have activated them, and in the process, would have unwittingly infected their own families.

"As you can see, this cabal was well-organized, well-funded, and we know they had even more horrendous plans, but I will not bore you, nor do I wish to frighten you, with all the details, as I may have said too much already. Suffice it to say, I wanted you to know how deadly this cabal is, and how we have been fighting against their plans to save countless tens of thousands of lives, both here and overseas."

President Gilmore flipped to another page of his notes. "Now, you may be asking how we know all of this. How did we find out about this cabal and their plans? Well, I can tell you...not without a high cost. As I said before, we have lost some great men and women at every level of law enforcement who were just doing their jobs and died as a result, because they were getting too close.

Others even had their families abducted and sold into human trafficking rings as a means of inflicting pain and preventing these law enforcement officials from doing their jobs. This kind of savagery speaks to the level of evil this cabal was willing to incorporate into their organization.

"But, I am happy to report how these brave men and women did not die in vain, and many, many others like them, have persevered and continue to do so. They never stopped. They never faltered. They persisted at great risk to themselves and their families, and with their help, we were able to uncover a series of two computer networks containing all of the cabal's plans. Once we had access, all the chess pieces were identified, except one—and we are still working on this individual. Once we gained this information, it gave us the upper hand, and we were able to start tracking down every other member of this cabal.

"We have learned through our current investigation that some of these members of the cabal have been killed. Others have been arrested or will be very soon. We will track every last one of them down and bring them to justice. You have my word."

President Gilmore looked away from his notes, and waited for the crowd's applause to subside. "Now, before I get to all the questions you must have, I would like to take time to honor the law enforcement officers who lost their lives in the course of this investigation. I am going to ask my press secretary, Jonas McCormick, to come forward and read the names and bios of each of these brave men and women.

"At a later time, after this cabal business is settled once and for all, we will invite the family members of these individuals to come to Washington, and hold a proper gathering, complete with Medals of Honor." The president gathered his notes, slipped them into the folder, and stepped back as Jonas McCormick took the podium.

CHAPTER 61

The Rose Garden ceremony concluded with a thirty-minute barrage of questions from the press corps. Finally, exhausted and hot from standing in the blazing sun, the president thanked everyone for coming, exited the stage, and made a beeline for the Oval Office.

President Gilmore tossed his folder of notes on the desk and plopped down into his office chair. He loosened his tie, picked up the phone, and called for his secretary to have a supply of cold drinks brought in for those who had accompanied him.

He leaned back and watched as Jonas McCormick, Sam Jameson, Blake Meyer, Julee Scarfano, several high-ranking members of Congress, and some other cabinet members entered the room and sat down in the extra chairs provided. The entourage formed a semi-circle around the president's desk, with the couches and chairs normally in the room filled as well.

"Ladies and Gentlemen," the president said, "we're not quite out of the woods yet, and as you know, it's truly a dark day, figuratively speaking, for our country. The men and women missing from this gathering speaks volumes to the corruption we are rooting out at this very moment.

"However, in light of all the deception and devilish deeds done by so many, the good news is, we have stopped this cabal. We have saved millions of American lives, and who knows how many lives abroad."

The little group nodded their approval and voiced it as well. A couple even quietly applauded the president's words.

"So, I am sure some of you must have questions I did not already answer for the media mob out there." The president, still leaning back in his chair, lifted his hands. "Now's the time, if you have any."

Several members of Congress asked questions about the arrests and where his administration would go from here. Others in the room seemed more interested in how these members of the cabal had been able to accomplish so much while going undetected. A couple of others wanted to know if he had any plans to resign, in light of Ben Jenkins's arrest.

"I have no plans to resign. I simply want to rebuild the trust of this office with the American people." Gilmore paused as the drinks he ordered were delivered. "Whether I run again, for this office, or any office, for that matter, well...today's probably not the best day to ponder such things."

The collective group allowed nervous chuckles and guffaws to escape as they nodded their understanding.

Drinks were passed around to those who desired one.

"Sir," Blake Meyer said, sitting on one of the couches, "there is still one lingering thread gnawing at me. It's been doing so since early in this investigation."

"Only one?" The president looked around the room and laughed. Others joined in. "Must be nice."

"Well, actually, sir, there are two. The first is not knowing who the last unidentified member of the cabal is. We only have a code name, and the man seems to be a ghost. Of course, we will continue to investigate him, but until we can locate him and arrest him, the release of a more lethal strain of the plague is going to always be a threat."

"And you will catch him, Agent Meyer. I have the utmost confidence in you and your team. If it wasn't for you, it is a real possibility sixty or seventy percent of us in this room would not survive the end of the year." Gilmore scanned the room. "Quite a sobering thought, isn't it?"

Everyone in the room nodded or voiced their agreement.

"Thank you, sir. It was definitely a concerted effort. Which brings me to the second lingering thread. A phone number has been popping up here and there in our investigation. It was found on several phones we confiscated along the way."

"Ah, yes, the infamous Russian phone number Mr. Jenkins was using."

While the president spoke, Blake pulled an evidence bag from his right coat pocket, containing a cell phone. "No, sir, I wasn't referring to the number Mr. Jenkins used. We already know everything there is to know about it and have ample evidence to make the case against Mr. Jenkins." Blake removed the phone from the bag and powered it up. "This phone number is a different one. It has a Chicago area code, not a Russian one. The number is 773-555-4532."

"Oh, I see. Chicago area code? Probably tied to those mercenaries guarding the warehouse full of air fresheners, I am assuming?"

"No, sir. This number was in operation for a considerable amount of time before the mercenaries were hired to guard the warehouse. We have reason to believe this phone number is tied to The Consortium, or the cabal, as you called them. We now know this organization has been operational since the early to mid-year 2000s." Blake accessed the phone's contacts and chose the 773 number. He pressed the green icon and waited for it to connect.

"So, do you have any leads?" Gilmore said as a soft, almost incoherent ringing sound emanated from his pocket. He reached inside and pressed a button, silencing the call.

"Well, sir, I believe we do," Blake said, pulling out another evidence bag. He pulled a second phone from it and booted it up as well, while pressing the green icon on the first phone again. "You see, this first phone here, on the coffee table, belonged to Colin Murphy."

"Murphy?" the president said as his pocket made the same sound again. He pulled the phone out, examined the screen, then silenced it. He held it up and chuckled. "It's the wife. She always calls at the most inopportune times."

"Probably wants you to bring home some milk," one of the senators said.

Everyone chuckled and laughed.

Blake retrieved the contact list from the second phone, selected the 773 number, and pressed its green icon.

The phone on the president's desk vibrated and rang again. He picked it up and ended the call. "And my wife wants bread, too, it would seem."

The room of dignitaries laughed again, but a tentacle of tension slithered into the room.

"As I said before, the first phone here belonged to Colin Murphy," Blake continued, pointing to it. "As we know, he was the major architect in the development of the contagion which was to be used against us. We originally found his phone when I captured him in Gainesville, Florida, but we later learned there was nothing on it whatsoever, as if a factory reset had been performed. Even his prints had been wiped clean.

"We now have reason to believe Supervisory Special Agent-in-Charge James Connell of the Jacksonville field office of the FBI was responsible for doing this, in an attempt to keep Murphy from being tied to The Consortium. However, what Connell did not know was Murphy had a second phone stashed away in a safe house we have since located, courtesy of Kurt Bowker and all the valuable information he amassed. This first phone sitting here is the one I am referencing."

Blake paused and pointed at the second phone. "This second phone, Mr. President, belonged to Marcus Sorensen." He chose the 773 number and pressed its green icon.

The president's phone rang again. He stared at it, picked it up, silenced it, and dropped it on the desk. He then lifted his eyes to meet Blake's with an icy stare.

"For the good of the group in this room," Blake continued, "Marcus Sorensen was one of the members of The Consortium. He was the one who organized the group. Mr. President, you referred to them as a 'cabal' in this morning's speech, and you were right to do so. They have several members. High-ranking political and military members, as well as well-to-do businessmen and women across the globe. Some thirty-two members in all. We found out from Sorensen's files who every member was—minus the one person I referenced earlier—and as you know, every last one of them has been or is being rounded up and arrested as we speak."

Blake pulled out a third and last evidence bag. All eyes were on him now as he conducted the same initiation process to this phone before selecting a caller and pressing the green icon. "This third phone, Mr. President, belonged to a man by the name of Pavel Morozov."

The president's phone rang one last time. He snatched it off the desk, powered it down, and tossed it on the desk. He glanced around the room as the mounting tension had completely engulfed its occupants.

"For those of you who do not know," Blake continued, "Pavel Morozov is a newly minted Russian oligarch who made his money via drug trafficking. However, he has diversified his empire in recent years. In an effort to launder his illegal money, he 'acquired,' with the help of Russian President Bischkov, the Miklos Oil Company.

"This purchase allowed Morozov to expand his empire as well. He is using his drug trafficking network to traffic human beings now. I know this first hand, Mr. President, because he was the one who worked in concert with Colin Murphy to have my family abducted and sold to human traffickers. My team and I were the ones who caught Morozov. It was on his mega yacht where I found my wife and rescued her. Unfortunately, my children, who had been on the yacht as well, had already been sold by Morozov to the next set of traffickers in the pipeline."

"Please tell me you were able to retrieve your children alive," said a female congresswoman.

"Yes, ma'am. I was. We finally caught up to them in Albania."

"Oh, my," the female congresswoman said. "We all know what a hotbed Albania is for traffickers."

"Yes, ma'am."

"And your point would be, Agent Meyer?" the president said.

Blake glanced at Director Jameson and picked up the first phone. He held it up for everyone to see. "My point, Mr. President, in front of this group of witnesses, is to explain how the phone number, 773-555-4532, has been tied to a person who was at the heart of this entire ordeal. This mysterious phone number was in contact with Colin Murphy for many years. There are multiple calls in Murphy's phone records to and from this number. Murphy was also in touch with multiple other members of the group you called a cabal, known as The Consortium.

"This same phone number, 773-555-4532," Blake said, setting down the first phone and picking up the second one, "has made multiple calls to Marcus Sorensen and received multiple calls from Sorensen on this device as well." Blake pointed at the third phone while he set the second one down. "And as you might expect at this point, the same goes for Pavel Morozov's phone number."

"However," Blake said, finally picking up the third phone, "the last call from Morozov's phone to the 773-555-4532 number wasn't made by Morozov. It was made by me, after we had apprehended Morozov. I called the number, and the person on the other end sounded 'robotic.' They were using some kind of voice-altering application, but we could tell it was a male voice.

"The person on the other end knew all about my family's abduction, and even knew about the attempted murder of me and a Russian spy by the name of Arina Filipov. He stated we were both supposed to be killed in Tbilisi, so he was shocked to learn I was still alive."

"And do you have this phone conversation recorded?" one of the dignitaries said.

"I do, actually." Blake paused, watching the president's slight expression of care melt away into one of mounting depression. "I can supply it upon request.

"Needless to say, this 773 number has been tied to several other phones, owned by unsavory types, like Joe Ricatelli, for example. Ricatelli is a man who gets hired to organize and set up all sorts of things, from peaceful protests to finding bomb makers, capable of blowing up half of the InterHealth Medical Center in Jacksonville.

"However, the big piece of information," Blake said, holding the third phone a little higher, "which was gathered from the phone call I made with this device, posing as Morozov, was the *location* of the phone. It was tracked, and the tracking app placed the phone using the 773 number inside this very building, which was yesterday morning, at 3:38 a.m. Specifically, it determined its location inside this very *room*. And yes, the tracking app used is precise. Very precise, actually. This particular program uses the building's Wi-Fi as well as the phone's wireless network to triangulate the signal. It can pinpoint its location within ten feet of its exact location." Blake reached out and took a folder from Director Jameson. "Mr. President, according to the White House logs, you were inside the Oval Office from the time I made the call from Pavel Morozov's phone at 3:38 a.m. until 5:05 a.m., when you called for a meeting in the Situation Room, to discuss the attack on the Bahama Bay Hotel and Casino, is that correct?

"I believe I left a couple of times to stretch my legs. And yes, there was a meeting in the Situation Room a little after five yesterday morning."

"And where did you go when you stretched your legs?"

The president looked around the room, expecting everyone to grow weary of the questions like he was. Instead, everyone was listening intently. "I vaguely remember going to see Jonas McCormick about something. I think the other time was to simply get up and walk...stretch my legs, you know? And probably help me stay awake. But frankly, I can't remember exactly."

"Do you recall what time those trips were made?"

"No." The president felt the pulse of the room react to his curt response. "I mean,...no, not the exact time. In my defense, it's been a little busy around here. The days have kind of run together."

Blake stood. "Mr. President, I have noticed, as the others in this room probably have as well, that you have two cell phones. The one on your desk," Blake pointed at it. "And the one you use for your family."

"No, you're mistaken, Agent Meyer." Gilmore picked up the phone from his desk. "This is the one my wife uses."

Blake pulled out his personal cell phone and swiped the screen until he accessed the number he needed. "For the benefit of everyone in this room, I am dialing the number provided to me by President Gilmore's wife. This number is supposed to be his personal cell phone number. It is the one she uses exclusively to reach the president. Blake hit the green icon.

"Wait!" the president said as his left coat pocket began to ring. He stood and held his hands up. "Listen, I can explain."

"Aren't you going to answer it, Mr. President?" Blake said.

The president's somewhat playful demeanor took offense. "Agent Meyer, I hope you understand the fire you're playing with."

"The only fire I see, Mr. President, is the firestorm you are about to face when you have to answer in a court of law as to why you were calling Colin Murphy, Marcus Sorensen, Pavel Morozov, Sergei Botinkin, Joseph Ricatelli, and another dozen members of The Consortium on a regular basis. One of which was a Chinese businessman named Ju-Long Zou—who attempted to take over The Consortium. And most recently, an FBI agent named Edgerrin Felder from the Chicago FO—who was just arrested for conspiring with the mercenaries guarding the warehouse in Chicago.

"It has also been proven how Agent Felder was conspiring with members of The Hands of Allah, and most importantly, Ben Jenkins.

"All of these evil people made contact with the phone on your desk, Mr. President, which we all see now is the phone number 773-555-4532."

"Uh, Mr. President," Congressman Bill Waldegon said, "why would you call Ben Jenkins from the phone on your desk when you have your own personal cell phone as well as the landline?"

The president hesitated.

"I can answer your inquiry, Congressman," Blake said. "As many of you know, Ben Jenkins was arrested for admitting to being the mole we all had been looking for. He had his own special cell phone with a Russian phone number. We were able to track Mr. Jenkins's phone to the same perpetrators—Murphy, Sorensen, and the rest. What we also learned was how Jenkins's Russian number had called this 773-555-4532 number, and vice versa. We just did not know who this other number belonged to until now."

"Which means, Congressman Waldegon," Director Jameson said, standing up and stepping forward to address the group, "we have a direct link between the man who confessed to being the mole, Ben Jenkins, and this 773-555-4532 number, which apparently belongs to President Gilmore. We have since traced the server of this number to a server farm on the Iraqi-Iran border. When we contacted them to gain access to the phone call records, they happily obliged." Director Jameson smiled. "You know, you just can't trust those Iraqis and Iranians when it comes to espionage. They may say they are working with you, but they ultimately hate westerners more. They view us as infidels who need to be extermi-nated. So any time they can eliminate one of us, they take advan-tage of the opportunity, especially when the westerner in question is a big fish, such as the President of the United States."

A senator taking notes stood up and stepped forward as well and faced Jameson. "Are you officially stating, for the record, Presi-dent Gilmore was involved in the attack on our country, Director Jameson?"

"Yes, Senator. We have documentation now, courtesy of another informant, showing President Gilmore was actually a *member* of The Consortium...the very cabal he referenced and condemned this morning."

"And in addition," Blake said, "after Ben Jenkins was arrested, Supervisory Special Agent-in-Charge Julee Scarfano and I confronted Ben Jenkins with this information I have shared with you here.

472   C. KEVIN THOMPSON

"At first Mr. Jenkins denied any knowledge of the president's involvement. However, when I told him the president would not be able to help him once he was arrested, Jenkins confessed and signed an affidavit, in the presence of his lawyer, in exchange for a plea deal, which is life in prison, with a chance at parole in twenty-five years, instead of possibly facing the death penalty.

"In his affidavit," Blake said, pulling a series of papers from the folder, "which I have right here, Mr. Jenkins explained the entire plan he and the president had concocted. If things went awry, and our investigation got close to uncovering everything, Jenkins would take the fall and portray himself as the mole.

"Then, if the contagion was released, the president would ensure Jenkins got the vaccine or the antidote while in prison, so when the dust settled and the new world order took over, Jenkins had a seat at the table for all of his hard work.

"If the plans for the release of the contagion were foiled in some way, then Jenkins would receive a full pardon from the president at the end of his presidency. Either way, Jenkins was promised a golden parachute, of sorts."

The president slammed his fist on the top of the desk. "Agent Meyer, what do you intend to do with all this information? For I would tread very lightly."

Blake motioned to the Attorney General. "I believe the attorney general can answer your question, Mr. President."

The attorney general, standing in the background, motioned at another man standing by the door as he walked up to the desk. Within seconds, four secret service agents and two FBI agents entered the room. "President Gilmore, you are under arrest for violating the Espionage Act, for planning, conspiring, and committing acts of terrorism on U.S. soil. In addition, you are being arrested for treason, conspiracy to murder and the attempted murder of federal agents, namely Special Agent Blake Meyer, conspiracy to kidnapping, i.e., Agent Meyer's children and wife, conspiracy to commit human trafficking...and that's just for starters. I'm sure there will be more charges before it's all said and done." The AG then motioned for Director Jameson to read the president his rights.

Blake stepped back and watched as Gilmore was placed in handcuffs.

"All of you are going to regret this," Gilmore said. "You don't know who you are dealing with."

"Actually, Mr. President," Blake said, walking up to him, "we know exactly who we are dealing with. As of an hour ago, all but two Consortium members had been arrested. Well, three, if we include you."

"These are powerful people, Agent Meyer. Way out of your league."

Blake leaned in close. "Maybe. But I doubt they are out of the reach of The Black Mist. I hear she has all of their addresses, dossiers, everything, compliments of Marcus Sorensen and his laptop. So, you know as well as I do that it's only a matter of time before she pays each and every one of them a visit. And since you are on Sorensen's list,...well, you can figure it out."

President Gilmore grinned. "But you know how this works, Agent Meyer. I'll never go to prison. I'll get permanent house arrest at the very worst." He allowed a cocky smirk to escape. "At my villa on Martha's Vineyard, more than likely. Surrounded by secret service agents, no less."

Blake nodded his understanding and leaned a little closer. "One thing I do know about The Black Mist...she *loves* a challenge. The harder, the better. So, if I was you, I'd ask for prison time— there's better protection in there, but hey, I hear Martha's Vineyard is pretty this time of year, too, so enjoy it while you can. And pay my regards to Agent Filipov when you meet. I'm sure you two have *a lot* of catching up to do." Blake smiled and stepped away as President Gilmore was escorted out of the Oval Office.

CHAPTER 62

GENFORMA LABORATORIES

Outskirts of Novosibirsk, Russian Federation

Two men in full biosuits entered Lazar Nicolescu's lab and searched it for personnel before enduring the second decontamination chamber between the lab and Lazar's office.

When the door finally chimed and opened, the men rushed in and found Vladimir Klebnikov sitting on Lazar's cot. He was holding a torn portion of Lazar's bedsheet against his face, and the fabric was nearly all red.

"Sir, are you okay?"

Klebnikov blotted his nose and checked the rag. "Do not take off your biosuits. This room is infected."

The first man glanced at his comrade. "How do you know, sir?"

Klebnikov gave them a tired chuckled and held the rag out for them to see. As he did, blood trickled from his nose and ran over his top lip. "Is this not enough evidence?"

"I am sorry, sir. I thought you had been struck in the nose somehow."

Klebnikov wiped his nose again. "I wish, but I have my friend over there to thank." He motioned toward the box on the floor, containing the almost dead rodent. "It would seem Dr. Nicolescu did not approve any longer of our mission. Have you found him?"

"Yes, sir. He was locked inside the security camera room. It is believed he committed suicide. There was an empty bottle of pills on the desk next to him."

"Are we still under quarantine?"

"We were able to disable the protocols from inside the facility. One of our scientists was in a hallway when it started," the first man said. "He was able to eventually gain access to the main control room and shut down as much as he could. However, we have bigger issues. We received word the government has set up a quarantine zone around the facility and has enacted an evacuation process for all civilians. Some are saying the radius is currently at twenty miles, but we have not been able to confirm it."

"Twenty *miles*?" Klebnikov closed his eyes and let out a heavy sigh as he covered his face with his rag. He knew the process would take hours, maybe even days before everyone inside was cleared to leave. And he didn't have days. He barely had hours.

He also knew Lazar must have somehow leaked to the Ministry of Health what he had been developing to cause them to activate such a cautious and preventative action.

"Have you found my cell phone?"

"Yes, sir. Dr. Nicolescu had it as well." The second man reached into the bag he was holding and pulled out the phone.

Klebnikov took it from him and checked it. There were twenty-five missed calls, seventeen of which were from Ma'mun Khawaji. He entered the password and dialed.

"Vladimir, where have you been?" Khawaji said. "I have been calling you for hours."

"I have been...incapacitated."

"What does that mean?"

"It would appear Dr. Nicolescu did not agree with our acceleration of the timeline." Klebnikov wiped his nose again. "Lazar drugged me when I met with him. I have been out for hours, apparently. And now, I was just informed Lazar committed suicide."

"Lazar is dead? Who else knew about this?"

"I do not think this involves anyone else. This was all Nicolescu's doing. It was his plan. He has been lamenting his involvement and the conditions of our arrangement for months. The sudden change in the timeline must have pushed him over the edge."

"Where is the human test subject?"

"I have no idea. As I said, I have been out for a while, but our people are searching the lab as we speak, I think."

"You *'think'*? Finding him needs to be your first priority, Vladimir. The test subject holds the key to our success. Surely you have logs of everyone in and out of your facility."

"We do, but honestly, I have no clue where the young man is at this moment." Klebnikov paused and coughed. He winced as the new symptom confirmed another step in the plague's progression. "When I arrived, I demanded to collect all of his notes and take possession of the young man, so Lazar led me to his office. While I was checking to see if all the notes where in the notebook, he stabbed me in the neck with something. When I awoke, I was locked inside his office. The landline had been disabled, my biosuit helmet was missing, as was my cell phone. Lazar also had hidden in his office an infected marmot, which was, obviously, part of his research, and—"

"So, you are now infected?"

Klebnikov coughed again. "Yes. And after he locked me in here, Lazar locked down the facility and placed it under quarantine, preventing anyone from leaving or entering the facility. He also must have made contact with the Ministry of Health. They are setting up an evacuation zone around Novosibirsk as we speak, I understand."

Khawaji blurted an expletive. "We need the human test subject, Vladimir. Without him, we are back to almost square one. Someone needs to review the security cameras and find out where he went."

Klebnikov pulled the phone away from his ear. "The young man who was in this lab with Dr. Nicolescu, has anyone seen him?"

"No, sir," the first man said.

"Has anyone checked the cameras?"

"Yes. They have been disabled. There are some people working on them now. However, they believe the footage was erased from the company server, dating back to last year. Maybe even further back. And because of the nature of the testing here, all of the recorded security camera footage was stored only on the local server in this facility. Mr. Sorensen was very adamant about limiting this lab's connectivity to the outside world."

Klebnikov spouted a curse word in Russian and put the phone to his ear again. "Did you hear what he said?"

"Yes, and it is unacceptable, Vladimir. Not only does the test subject pose a significant risk of outbreak, if he is *not* completely cured from the testing he was undergoing, but without him, all we have are Lazar's notes."

Klebnikov, knowing where his colleague was going with his reasoning, walked over to the notebook on the desk and thumbed through the pages. "I am looking at his notes right now. It appears he omitted key sections from it. Sections I was not able to ask about before he attacked me."

"So, you are telling me Lazar's notes are incomplete?"

"Yes. It would appear all of his notes relating to the human test subject have been removed, and key parts to the earlier stages as well."

Khawaji allowed more expletives to escape. "Lazar did not leave the facility, so those notes must be somewhere."

"We will look," Klebnikov said with a tired sigh, "but if Lazar was this thorough in his planning, I have to believe he has made sure those notes are destroyed to prevent us from retrieving them."

"Sir, if I may interrupt?" the first man said.

"What?" Klebnikov said in a huff.

"When we found Dr. Nicolescu, a small closet off to the side was filled with smoke when we opened the door. A trash can was found inside, and some papers had been recently burned." The man wrinkled his face. "Could those have been the notes you are referring to?"

"Possibly. I will need you all to see if any of the pages burned can be retrieved to determine what they were. But knowing Lazar like I do, he knew he was going to die, so he was not afraid of a little smoke inhalation."

Khawaji groaned. "Did I hear him correctly? Lazar burned the missing notes?"

"We do not have confirmation, but it would seem logical to assume so."

Khawaji let out a huge sigh. "How much time do you have left, Vladimir?"

Klebnikov walked into the bathroom and peered into the mirror. He pulled the rag away from his face and examined it. He watched, and the trickle of blood from his nose was more persistent now. "Hours, not days."

"I am so sorry, Vladimir. Can you use the antidote Lazar used on the human subject? Perhaps it is not too late."

"We can check to see if there is anything left in the lab, but I am pretty sure he took it to the grave with him as well."

"Have you heard from Zou?" Khawaji said.

"Not since before I arrived here. Why?"

"He's not answering his phone, either, which means he's gone dark, committed suicide, or has been killed."

"He could have been arrested."

"Zou? In China? Not a chance." Khawaji cleared his throat. "This is why I must go dark now, Vladimir. You're severely compromised. Zou is missing. And I am hearing through the chatter something about President Gilmore's chief of staff having been arrested, and most of The Consortium members are on the run, dead, or have been arrested too."

Klebnikov sat back down on the cot. "What is happening, Ma'mun? Are we finished?"

"It would appear so." Khawaji allowed an exhausted chuckle to escape. "I warned you...and Murphy...and Sorensen...about involving Blake Meyer. I warned you all about allowing Zou into The Consortium, and how it was a bad idea. I pleaded with you all to give Lazar the necessary facilities and the necessary help to speed up his part of the plan, especially when it was running behind schedule. Had we released this contagion on time, on July 4th when it was originally planned, we'd be in the middle of the greatest reorganization of humanity the world has ever seen. Our new empire would have made the Roman Empire look puny by comparison." He snorted into the phone. "I feared all of this was going to happen. Too many bosses and not enough employees, as they say. You all started overthinking the plan. Adding this, wanting that. It became too top heavy. Therefore, it would seem my gut feeling was accurate. I'm glad I did what I did now."

"Did what...?"

"I supplied your group with the regular strain of the bubonic plague only. Sorensen ordered the Plan B devices, and he wanted them filled with regular, run-of-the-mill plague. So, that's what I did...well, it was still militarized, but could be cured, if caught soon enough. But then I found out Sorensen had given control of the Plan B devices to Zou. I disagreed with his decision vehemently, but Sorensen did not care. He said he had too many things on his plate, and Zou offered to help.

"What Sorensen did not know was I had worked with Zou before. He cannot be trusted, and he proved it again by releasing one of the Plan B devices in the United States. He has too much communism running through his veins. He'd never betray the Chinese government. He wanted to bring his politics along for the ride into the sunrise of the new world order. So, when it came time to fill the air fresheners in Novosibirsk with the deadly strain, I refused to play along."

Klebnikov closed his eyes and fought back the growing sensation to vomit. "What did you do, Ma'mun?"

"I filled the air fresheners with the same Plan B bacterium. It is all the same stuff." Khawaji laughed. "You see, Vladimir, I told Colin, more than once, starting in Africa, about how I had a purpose for helping him. I even reiterated it with more details when we met in Florida a few days ago, before he was arrested. Had he stayed with the original plan, I would have been all in. However, the changes to the original plan, the addition of people like Zou, and now your revelations about Lazar and his lab work, coupled with everyone else's incompetence, have proven the point I was trying to make to Colin all those months and years ago.

"I do not believe in Jihad. Killing people who do not believe as you do is a recipe for destruction. I believe we can all coexist, but you have to eradicate the likes of Zou and Sorensen. You cannot allow hordes who wish to dominate, pillage, kill, and conquer to run governments. We need a fresh start. We need a remnant of people, left from a major holocaust like a plague, to band together and create a new world order, based on cooperation and mutually agreed upon beliefs. Under such conditions, survivors will be forced to help each other."

Klebnikov walked back into the office and ripped a new

portion of Lazar's bed sheet away from the rest of it. "Sounds like a dream to me. A bad dream, yes?"

"Only for those who do not survive. But with any attempt to save the masses, there is always fallout."

"And why are you telling me this, Ma'mun?" Klebnikov folded the newly made rag and pressed it against his nose.

"I am not sure. By the time I implement my plan, you'll be dead, and those associated with you will be as well, or incarcerated. Either way, they won't be able to get in the way next time. They served their purpose."

"Meaning?"

"When I made the decision to not play along any more, I continued to be a part just to see how the government agencies, the politicians, law enforcement, and the rest reacted to the release of a contagion. Now I know. Now I understand how the air fresheners will work. This was the plan all along. It was the original plan. Then, Colin wanted things added and other things changed. He became vengeful, unhinged. Then, Sorensen convinced Murphy Plan B devices would be a good addition." Khawaji chuckled. "It went off the rails shortly thereafter, and I am glad I got off that train when I did, or I'd be rounded up with all of you.

"So, I will wait, Vladimir. Bide my time. Allow the governments and people to handle the ramifications of The Consortium's foiled plans. And if I can't get my hands on Lazar's notes soon, I will begin working on the antidote myself.

"And thanks to you, I have the blueprint, now, for how the contagion can be packaged. In other countries where air fresheners are not used, there are other means I can utilize, like replacing surface cleaners with an aromatic version of my creation. Cleaning crews will spray to their hearts content, wiping down surfaces in hospitals, offices, homes, schools, you name it, with products designed to be green and good for the environment.

And all the while, the particles will fly through the air and be inhaled by unsuspecting people.

"And I will order more air fresheners for America, too, but this time, I will fill them with the deadly plague bacterium. By the time the governments realize a synchronized attack has materialized around the globe, it will be far too late.

"Once you all changed the plans, I decided to change mine. You all have done my homework for me. All I had to do was play along and gather intel. So, thank you."

Klebnikov coughed into the new rag and noticed fresh blood. He closed his eyes and lamented the progression of the contagion. "You'll never get away with it, Ma'mun."

"I beg to differ, but you won't be around when I release the contagion anyway, so I'm sure you won't care. But to honor you and your efforts, I have sent you the final installment of our arranged monetary agreement. Of course, I sent it before I knew you had been infected. Sorry, comrade. Maybe you have a relative or mistress you can give it to, perhaps?"

Klebnikov placed Ma'mun on speakerphone and checked his bank statement.

"I assume your silence means you are wondering if I am telling the truth. Trust me, Vladimir. It's there. I sent it out over twelve hours ago. That was one of the reasons why I was calling you."

Klebnikov tapped the screen and waited for the account information to upload.

"You're welcome, Vladimir. Thank you for your help." Khawaji ended the call.

Finally, a PDF of the statement dinged its arrival. Klebnikov opened it, and there, at the top of the document was the latest deposit. Time stamped twelve hours earlier. Nine million rubles and change from Khawaji's company account: Vector Research and Development.

CHAPTER 63

THE HOME of Pavel Morozov
  Mykolaiv, Ukraine

Pavel Morozov spent hours—too many of them—at a naval base in Jacksonville, Florida, being dragged back and forth between his tiny cell and an interrogation room. He kept telling them he wasn't going to give up any information, and because he was a Russian citizen with newly minted diplomatic status, he gloated about how untouchable he was.

After several attempts to get him to divulge anything he knew, naval officials were ordered to release Morozov into the custody of two CIA agents, who in turn, would escort him to Jacksonville International Airport and book him an all-expenses-paid trip back to the country of Ukraine.

Morozov laughed almost the entire ride from the naval base to the airport, making fun of "The Americans" and how soft they had become. He also shouted at how they would repay him for his confiscated mega yacht. "They are not cheap," he said. "And to keep it as 'evidence' is preposterous. You will be hearing from my lawyers and the Russian government. I will have a new one by the time all of this is over!"

He did praise Agent Meyer for his cleverness, though. "Boarding my boat in the middle of the Atlantic without anyone noticing was quite the feat, I must admit," he said to one of the CIA agents. "And of course, I will be filing charges in an international court of law about my injuries suffered during Agent Meyer's act of piracy as well as the illegal interrogation techniques he used. I know your American government would not approve. Shooting someone's ears, shooting a knee, shooting an elbow...this is definitely cruel and unusual punishment, yes? And then there's the assault at the hands of Agent Meyer himself, *and* his wife. Oh, yes. She will be part of the lawsuit as well. I think my sternum is fractured, and you can see all the marks on my face." Morozov stared into the face of one of the agents. "But in Agent Meyer's defense, he did not bite my nose. The wrath of the female species did this. They tend to get angry when you confirm their status as a commodity and not as anything 'special.' And when they are not, uh...how do you say it? 'Housebroken?' Then, they do this," he said, pointing at his face. "I am sure you can see the teeth marks, yes?"

"Sir," one of the agents said, "all I know is, Agent Meyer should have shoved you from the deck of your boat and let you swim with the fishes. So, it's a good thing we are taking a commercial flight and not a military escort. For if we were, I'd throw you out the door over the Atlantic myself."

"Big words from such a small agent." Morozov flared his eyebrows, loving how he could taunt them without retribution. "If you were not so small, you would not be babysitting me, yes? This is the kind of job for a peasant laborer."

The CIA agent started to say something but paused himself as he pulled into the parking lot. He hit the brakes more forcefully than usual, and threw the car into Park with a huff. He composed himself and turned his head toward their "prisoner." "Yes, sir. We've been tasked with taking out the trash."

"I guess I am to be offended by your words?" Morozov said with a smile. "Better to be Russian trash than American peasant scum, yes?"

For fear of physical retaliation against their "prisoner" which would cost them more than their jobs, he and his partner escorted Morozov to the gate in a wheelchair onto his flight without another word.

Exaggerating, so as to garner the attention of the other passengers, Morozov hobbled down the aisle, using a cane to balance himself, putting most of his weight on the left leg while his right arm was in a sling. Two bandages, one on each ear, along with the wrapped knee and sling, made the other passengers wrinkle their brows and slink away as he passed by.

Morozov spoke brashly to the other passengers about how he had a golden ticket and how "these two very good CIA agents are in tow, just to make sure he was a good little boy on his flight from Jacksonville to his home country of Ukraine."

The CIA agents motioned to the passengers about how crazy Morozov was and simply told them all to ignore him.

Morozov laughed even more, causing some to understand what the agents were saying, while others were leery of the arrangement.

* * *

Several hours later, after arriving in Kiev, Morozov exited the plane blew kisses to the CIA agents as he shifted from a cane back to a wheelchair, held and made ready by a political grunt of one of the local politicians close to Morozov.

The agents pointed their fingers at Morozov, pretending to

shoot him, before waving and smiling with the biggest, fake grins they could muster.

Morozov wasn't sure why, but their actions made him feel immediately unsafe and paranoid as they exited through the nearest doorway and disappeared.

But they have no jurisdiction here...

He checked his watch.

10:01 p.m., local time.

I am probably just tired.

* * *

In the next two hours, Morozov flew from Kiev to the Mykolaiv International Airport near Balovne. He then paid handsomely for a luxury taxi to take him the thirteen miles to his home on the Southern Bug River.

When he arrived, he paid the cabbie extra for not only being compliant with his wishes for a safe and quiet ride, with only Tchaikovsky playing through the sedan's speakers, but for also helping him walk to the front door of his home.

Offering to help Morozov inside, the cabbie was told his services were no longer needed, so he hopped back inside his vehicle, circled around the spacious driveway, and exited through the front gate.

Morozov reached into his pocket and remembered he no longer possessed his keys. He cursed under his breath and rang the doorbell, awaiting his young servant to open the door.

However, nobody answered.

Wonderful. She must be asleep.

Morozov set his bag of clothes down and hobbled around to the back of the house, cursing his condition every other step.

He located the spare key and limped back to the front door. He opened it, and the alarm sounded, giving him twenty seconds to silence it before the police were dispatched. He closed the front door and shut it down.

Scanning the foyer, everything appeared to be in its place. "Lidiya!"

No answer.

"Lidiya! Are you home?"

No answer.

He shuffled into the kitchen and saw a note on the counter.

Pavel,

Went to my sister's house for a short vacation. Will be back on Friday.

Lidiya

"Ah, this explains your absence. But my girl, which Friday?" Morozov chuckled at the thought. "She's not much good for thinking, but she serves me well." He tossed the note back on the counter and opened the refrigerator. He grabbed a beer and shut the door.

Using a bottle opener to remove the cap with one hand proved frustrating, but he managed before flipping the cap into the sink. He tossed the opener on the counter, and took a swig, allowing the fluid to swish around inside his mouth. He swallowed finally and set the beer down on the counter. He grabbed his bag of clothes, slinging the shoulder strap around his neck and feeding his one good arm through. "I need a shower...and a nurse."

He picked up his beer and angled toward the stairs, allowing expletives to escape with every other step. Reaching the edge, he stopped and looked up the flight of stairs, realizing he'd never make it all the way up in his condition. More expletives flowed as he hobbled to the built-in elevator, waited for the door to open, and entered.

Spewing more expletives as rode it to the third floor, he stepped out, limped down the hallway and entered his master suite. He flipped on the light, and sitting in the chair in the far corner, with a full view of the bedroom door was Arina Filipov.

She held a pistol in each hand, and both were aimed at Morozov's torso. "Hello, Pavel. I hear you desired to take your chances with The Black Mist instead of plunging to the bottom of the ocean?"

Morozov froze.

"All I can say is," Filipov continued, "be careful what you desire. Desires often are the things which destroy us, yes?" Filipov lowered the aim of the weapon in her right hand. "It appears someone already shot your right knee, so I'll take the left one." She pulled the trigger.

Morozov collapsed to the ground, dropping his beer and spilling it on the hardwood floor. He grimaced in pain, spouting expletives in Russian and grasping his knee. He rolled to his side and glared at his attacker. "What have you done to Lidiya?!"

"Lidiya? Oh, you mean your *seventeen-year-old slave*? I sent her away. She left you a note, yes? Telling you where she was going?" Filipov slowly stood with her aim now zeroed in on Morozov's head. "I also gave her the money in your bank account. Payment for a job well done, I assumed. Well, to be honest, not all of the money went to her, but almost all of it. I took the rest. It paid for my little one day layover here in your pretty little town. The company I am using to fly all over the place does not come cheap. And I thought, since you wanted to meet me, you should pay for my flight." Filipov smiled with a shrug of her shoulders. "Hope you do not mind."

"You will pay for this!"

"In the afterlife, maybe, but not at your hands, Pavel."

Morozov snarled at his predicament. "So...Lidiya...you think she is safe at her sister's house, yes? I know where her sister lives."

"Yes. You probably do." Filipov aimed the weapon in her left hand at Morozov's right ankle and fired.

Morozov bellowed at the pain and howled in fury at the same time.

"However, Lidiya is safe. Forever, actually. From you, I mean." Filipov tucked one weapon into her waistband while she set the other down on the bed. She then pulled out a knife and held it out for Morozov to see. She gazed at it, as if admiring its design. "I sent her away, because I did not want her to witness what I was going to do to you." She knelt down and pressed the knife into Morozov's throat. "Have you ever heard of the expression, 'Death by a thousand cuts'? For the girls you traffic and use, like Lidiya, your actions feel like death by a thousand cuts. So, now, Pavel, here in your last hours on earth, I wish to help you experience *physically* what they feel *emotionally* every day...for the rest of their lives."

JULY 15, 2014

CHAPTER 64

LAZAR NICOLESCU'S Vacation Home
Bystrovka, Russia

Two days had passed, and Karina Kuznetsova noticed how much Peter Zakayev had improved and was seemingly asymptomatic. She couldn't take blood samples to monitor the antidote's effectiveness like Lazar Nicolescu had done in the lab, but she did monitor his breathing, his body temperature, his heart rate, and his blood pressure meticulously. By the afternoon on Tuesday, July 15th, she felt the time had come. She had to trust her instincts.

She concluded two viable choices remained. One was to allow Peter to remove his mask and see how his vitals responded. This would put everyone in the house, namely her, at risk, if he was not one-hundred-percent cured. The second option involved keeping Peter in the mask for at least one more day, simply to play it safe, since so much was at stake.

As she mulled over her options, a news alert came across her smartphone, forced through the telecommunication company's system as a government-directed state of emergency. Russian authorities from the Ministry of Health had been ordered to investigate a private lab in Novosibirsk for a possible containment breach. At this time, they were ordering everyone within a twenty-mile radius to evacuate the area immediately. Those outside the twenty-mile radius up to a one-hundred-mile radius were to be vigilant and stay tuned to the news for updates on the evacuation protocols.

Karina used her smartphone to calculate how far away they were.

Less than forty miles...

As the bird flies—

"Am I interrupting something?" Peter said, standing in the doorway, his voice muffled by the mask.

Holding her smartphone in her hand, Karina dropped her hands into her lap and looked up at Peter. "It appears we have a problem. A 'private lab' in Novosibirsk has been placed on lockdown by the Ministry of Health. They are ordering evacuations for everyone living within twenty miles of the lab."

Peter stepped through the doorway. "Doctor Nicolescu?"

"Who else could it be?"

Peter sat down on the couch and stared at the floor with his elbows on his knees. "He told me he did not have much longer to live shortly after I arrived. Something about his former life and how 'his sins had chased him down.' I did not know what he was talking about, but he seemed at peace with dying there, at the lab."

Karina rubbed the screen of her phone with her thumb as her thoughts were definitely elsewhere. "He was very sick. It was truly a wonder he was still alive. Maybe he was kept alive for this very moment. To save you, Peter. To have mercy on you and get you to Germany so his friend can use your blood to save the world."

"Maybe. But if I stay here, surely the Ministry of Health will come knocking, yes? To check on people to see if they are infected."

Karina scooted up to the edge of her seat. "And if they do, they will ask questions."

"And if they find out my real name, or recognize me, then I am a dead man, yes?"

"There is no doubt." She pointed to her face. "Which begs the question: How are you feeling? Do you think you are asymptomatic enough to remove the mask? I mean, you have been through this before. You know how you felt the first time you were infected, as well as when you recovered, and Lazar declared you cured. So, compare the experiences. Where are you in the process by comparison? For we cannot travel through checkpoints and make border crossings while you sit in the passenger seat with a hospital-grade, infectious mask on. And yet, if we stay here much longer, you are right. They will come to check on us all. The guard at the entrance to the lab in Novosibirsk will surely tell them of our departure."

Peter inhaled deeply and allowed it to escape like a slow leak in a balloon. "I have to admit. This mask has definitely strengthened my lungs. And as for the dizziness, the headaches, the lethargy...they all seem to be gone. I feel like I could walk out the front door and run. Honestly. I am not just saying this in order to escape. I, too, understand the gravity of our circumstances." He pointed at her phone. "Now, more than ever."

"Your vitals look good. They all seem to have normalized," Karina said, checking her notepad.

Peter lifted his hands, as if negotiating for something. "Then, I say, let us take the mask off and see how things go. In the vehicle, we can keep the windows rolled down, or just roll them down on my side."

Karina studied her friend and quickly searched her mind for other options. "I wish we could stay one more day, but with Lazar's lab undergoing quarantine protocols, it would be best for us to leave as soon as possible."

Peter nodded emphatically. "When?"

Karina checked her smartphone. "I think it would be best if we travel as much as we can in the early evening and at night. Not during the day."

"Agreed. So, we leave soon, yes? It is almost dusk now." Peter tapped his mask with his finger. "I have a better idea. I will keep this on as long as possible, just to be on the safe side. If we do not cross any checkpoints or borders, it could be well into tomorrow before I am forced to remove it."

Karina stood and slipped her phone into her back pocket. "I think that would be a good idea. We cannot be too safe."

Peter sprang up from the couch and patted Karina on the shoulder. "I am excited to get as far away from Lazar's lab as possible. And I would start packing now, but I do not have any other clothes."

"I am in the same predicament. I guess we should have had Igor get us some other clothes when he was out purchasing supplies, yes?"

"Hindsight is always twenty-twenty, my grandmother used to tell me."

"Go ahead and get ready," Karina said. "Get your mask supplies packed up. I'll make some sandwiches for the trip and see if there is a cooler we can use for some cold drinks."

* * *

An hour later, Karina and Peter strapped themselves into Karina's SUV, and did one final mental checklist, knowing they could not come back, even if they had forgotten something.

Satisfied there was nothing else they needed nor wanted, Karina backed the vehicle up, shifted into Drive, and pulled into the lane, heading for the main road. Olga and Igor stood on their front porch, waving goodbye, having already wished Karina well.

As they turned onto the road and headed west, Karina checked the time. "Well, Pforzheim, Germany, here we come."

"And how far away is this place you are taking me?" Peter said, still wearing his mask.

"My driving app says it is 5,900 kilometers away and will take us almost three days. Of course, that is without any stops."

Peter used his fingers to count off the days. "And how do you expect to get me across borders without papers?"

Karina motioned toward the back seat with her head. "In the briefcase. Igor said he had a friend of a friend who could help us out. Inside, you have a passport as well as a driver's license. I got a passport too. I did not have time to go back to my house and retrieve mine. And besides, as Igor said, if the authorities search my house and find my passport, they will be less likely to search for me at airports, bus terminals, ports, even borders, thinking I cannot get away from the region without it."

"I feel like an international spy now."

"Yeah, well, if we get caught," Karina said, checking her mirrors, "you will wish you had the resources of a spy, because they will probably view you as an enemy of the state instead."

"Even with my new passport?

"It depends on how good Igor's friend is at making false passports."

Peter lifted a lever and reclined back in his seat. "Let us hope he is good at what he does."

Karina smiled at the thought. "If he is not, this will be a very short trip."

Peter rolled down his window, leaving an inch-wide crack at the top. "Short trip or not, let me know when you need me to drive. In the meantime, I'm going to grab some sleep."

"Do not sleep too much when we are driving," Karina said, "or you will never be able to sleep during the day when we are stopped."

"With all due respect," Peter said with his eyes closed. "I think me being awake during the day while you sleep may be better. I can be a lookout in the daytime. You act as one at night while we are on the road."

Karina tapped her finger on the steering wheel while she contemplated his proposal. "We can surely try."

"And does this doctor in Germany know we are coming?"

"Yes. Lazar gave me his email address, so I sent him a message. I told him we would be leaving within the next twenty-four hours, so to please have everything ready to go when we arrive."

Peter pursed his lips and grunted. "His lab cannot be any worse than Lazar's. At least I will not be strapped to a table, wearing leg irons, nor threatened to be shot and tossed outside with the rest of the refuse, if I do not comply."

"Lazar told you this?"

Peter laughed. "No. No. Lazar was kind. The dogs who dragged me into the lab threatened me."

Karina shook her head in disgust. "I am sorry you had to endure such things. Just know, this is not what I signed up for either." She gripped the steering wheel tighter. "But we are going to set things right. Once and for all. We are going to save the world, Peter. Mark my words."

CHAPTER 65

FBI H<small>EADQUARTERS</small>
Washington, D.C.

Julee Scarfano remembered a tour of HQ when she was attending Quantico years ago. As a new, wanna-be FBI agent, she walked through the halls with eyes as big as Buick hubcaps. She soaked it all in and imagined sitting in the director's chair one day, calling the shots.

Now, sitting in the director's office at a few minutes after eight o'clock, the morning after the president was arrested and tossed into an interrogation room on these very premises...and after going through the week she hoped would never happen again, Julee wanted anything *but* the director's chair.

They couldn't pay me enough. Jameson can have it, Julee thought, as he literally walked through the door.

She stood.

"No, please, Scarfano. Sit. You've earned it," Sam Jameson said as he closed the door and walked around his desk. He sat down with an exhausted huff. "We've all earned a quick rest, wouldn't you say?"

"Yes, sir. It's been a week."

"A week from hell, you mean?" He motioned at all the files piled on his desk. "Every one of these has something to do with this week. Half of them got added yesterday after Gilmore got arrested. So, it appears I'll be sleeping in my office for the foreseeable future."

"Anything I can do to help?"

"I wish, but most of it is reading and signing stuff...and preparing for the barrage of congressional investigations to come in the next few months."

"Above my pay grade then."

Jameson smiled and leaned forward, placing his elbows on his desk. "Yes. But enough about my career choice. Instead, let's talk about yours, shall we? The reason I asked you here concerns how you handled yourself during this crisis, Julee. I must say, I had some question marks at the beginning, but in the end, you came through and proved you can sit in the SAC's chair."

"Thank you, sir. I appreciate the vote of confidence. And yes, it was definitely a learning curve, for sure."

"Well, if there is one thing I pride myself on, it is recognizing good employees and good work. And when it is the appropriate time, rewarding said employees and work. And since you were already here in D.C., I thought I'd better take advantage of the opportunity. Therefore, tell me...are you happy in Jacksonville?"

"It's a good FO. Lots of good agents there. Ones you can trust."

"Which is a pleasant and wonderful situation, in light of all the bad eggs we've had to root out this past week."

"Most definitely."

"So, if I left you there as the official SAC, you'd be okay with it? You'd be willing to take on the challenge?"

"I would, but I believe Agent Meyer would be the better choice, sir. Besides, he would be the next in line."

Jameson bounced his head slightly from side to side. "Technically, you are correct. However, Agent Meyer informed me a few hours after we arrested Gilmore about his plans to retire from the FBI."

"He's retiring? What's he going to do?"

"He didn't say, but knowing Blake, he already has something lined up. The only thing he did mention was he was retiring to be able to spend more time with his wife and children."

Julee nodded with a big smile. "Of course."

"Which brings me back to you. The obvious choice would be to have you remain in Jacksonville and continue to keep some continuity there. However, because of your performance, and the vote of confidence Agent Meyer gave you, I am prepared to entertain other considerations, should you be interested."

Julee turned her head and peered at the director with a bit of a sideways stare. "Other considerations? Such as?"

"Other field offices, for example. I've been planning on shuffling some people around, so if it was in the cards for you, what's one more move? Also, there are positions within the HQ here as well. I could even see you sitting here one day," Jameson said, patting the armrests of his chair.

Julee laughed and pointed in Jameson's direction. "No, sir. I was thinking about that very question when you walked in a few minutes ago. I thought about everything you've had to deal with over the last few days..." Julee shook her head emphatically. "I don't know how you do it, sir. There's too much politics involved for my taste." She waved her hand dismissively. "It's all yours."

"I didn't mean you could have it right now, Scarfano. I'm still okay with the job...for now."

Julee looked away and peered out the window. "It's funny you should bring all of this up, though. I have been giving a move some thought. You see, my dad...he's been ill lately. He's been dealing with cancer, and he lives in the Boston area. My mom passed away a couple of years ago, so it's just Dad. My sister lives close. She's about a hundred miles away, but I'm in Jacksonville. I often use long weekends to fly up and see him when I can."

Jameson placed his hands on top of the desk and stood. "Say no more. I'll see what I can do. The Boston FO is a big gig, but so is Jacksonville these days, especially after this past week. You handled it okay. So, I'm confident you can handle Boston. And you're from that area, right?"

"Yes, sir." Julee stood as well. "Irish-Italian. Irish on my mom's side of the family. Italian on my dad's side. Both families, interestingly enough, immigrated to the States in the 1890s."

"I'll tell you what," Jameson said as he made his way out from behind his desk. "Head back to Jacksonville and wrap up this contagion business on your end. Give me a couple of weeks to do the same here, then we'll be in touch. Fair enough?" He reached out his hand for a shake. "If everything goes smoothly, we could have you in Boston in time to see the leaves change."

Julee shook it with a beaming smile. "Sounds like a plan, sir. Thank you."

CHAPTER 66

Home of Joseph & Ann Jensen
  7147 Vance Hill Road
  Newport, Vermont

Blake Meyer stepped off the Gulfstream at 12:28 p.m. The skies were cloudy, messaging to the inhabitants below a storm was brewing to the south and east. Blake allowed the breeze to waft across his face while he stood on the tarmac. It felt good to be on solid ground. The kind of *terra firma* which promised a different future. No more clandestine treks into enemy territory. No more off-the-books, international missions to far away destinations.

He had officially decided to retire from such a life. His paperwork would go into the system next week.

The soldier inside officially stood down, too, and could finally stand at ease.

The husband's anxiety melted away with each gust of wind and was hopeful.

The father, exhausted emotionally, experienced a newfound energy growing inside.

The FBI agent—the final piece of Blake's personality—felt complete, as he watched President Gilmore get escorted out of the Oval Office by a growing assemblage of FBI and secret service agents. Blake had followed the director out as they stayed close behind the individual who turned out to be not only the actual mole, but the mastermind inside The Consortium. He was the one who promised Colin Murphy safe haven until the dust settled... after two-hundred-million people in the U.S....possibly many more...men and women...children...babies...all fell victim to the biologically and militarily engineered plague bacterium with no known cure.

Director Jameson and Blake had both agreed. The president could not be trusted to a mere one or two agents. He surely had contingency plans for such an event. So, Jameson vowed to be part of the police transport until he had Walter Gilmore in protective custody within the walls of FBI headquarters.

Once there, Jameson had several trusted agents who would be assigned a twenty-four rotation to ensure none of the remaining Consortium members could silence the president once and for all.

Outside the building, Jameson arranged for a military unit to set up a three-block perimeter around HQ, including the nearby rooftops with orders to arrest and detain anyone who looked or acted suspicious.

When Gilmore's head was shoved down into the back seat of a black Ford Expedition, Blake turned to the director, and with a pre-determined handshake, handed him his gun and his credentials.

"SSA Meyer," Jameson said, "I'm not sure if our country can repay you for your service, especially for these last few days."

Blake chuckled. "Ironically, the president promised me any position I wanted, if I brought this situation to a satisfactory conclusion." He peered at the black SUV holding Gilmore. "Not that I want one now, but some retirement compensation would come in handy, since I don't have enough years in the Bureau for any pensions, and I'm not old enough for social security yet."

"Blake, I have a feeling once you put your name out there, the speaking gigs and consultant offers will pour in. You'll have to pick and choose. I have no doubt you'll do just fine."

"Maybe you're right."

"There's no maybe about it. With your expertise, you'll be able to demand just about any price. And who knows," Jameson said, pointing at the black SUV, "once all this business finally washes itself through the court system, I have a feeling someone will be knocking on your door about a book deal."

"You're probably right," Blake said with his hand extended for one final goodbye. "I guess I now have some food for thought on the plane ride home."

Jameson shook his hand again. "If you ever change your mind about retirement, please make me your first phone call. I could use a guy like you to train these young'uns."

"Yeah, well, Connell and I were working on that very deal the day all of this broke. I'm not interested now," Blake said with a smirk.

"Amazing how a week's worth of days can shape your future."

Blake nodded. "Best of luck, sir."

"To you as well."

* * *

On the flight from Washington, D.C., Blake asked himself over and over again if retirement suited him. Was it a good idea? And is what Jameson suggested, about speaking and being a consultant, true? How much does one of those people make?

Ultimately, it boiled down to one question. What would he do now, with all the free time he'll have on his hands? With each iteration of the same question, asked in different ways, each with a different option to consider, he found himself returning to the same, final answer...

It doesn't matter, so long as I can be home every night with Sara and the kids.

This sentiment continued to flood his emotions as he stood on the tarmac, next to the plane, awaiting his ride. He had promised Sara one last five-year stint with the Bureau in 2009. Before the plague business surfaced, he was sitting in James Connell's office, talking about his future, with three months remaining on his five-year promise...

Blake smiled. *Looks like Christmas came a little early, Sara...*

He opened his eyes and stared across the runway at the vehicle heading his direction. He slipped his left arm through the strap of his backpack and held it in place.

But man, how things have changed in a week...

Before, it was a mere question of finances and supporting his family.

Now, there was no amount of money, no accolade to chase, no "attaboy" worth another day on the job. Even the peace of his country took a backseat. There were others on the job, fighting crime. Peace could be their concern. The peace of his family was his number one priority now.

He took a fifteen-minute taxi ride from the Northeast Kingdom International Airport to the home of his in-laws, unannounced on purpose. He wanted to surprise Sara and the kids, first with his presence, and secondly, with his news of retirement.

The taxi approached the house, and Blake asked the driver to stop a quarter mile down the road. "Here. Let me out here. I want to walk the rest of the way."

He handed the driver his fare times two, and exited the vehicle.

Blake waited alongside the road until the taxi did a U-turn and headed east, back toward town.

Ten minutes later, he meandered up the driveway and walked up to the side of the house facing the small trout pond on the five-acre parcel.

He quietly made his way up the back porch steps and knocked on the door. He waited off to one side with his backpack over his left shoulder.

Blake could hear his mother-in-law, Ann Jensen, ask who it could be. He then heard his father-in-law answer back, "Probably one of those UPS drivers. They could drive to our house blindfolded."

Ann growled playfully. "Oh, you be quiet, Joe. Half the stuff they deliver is from your online fishing stores. And besides, where is Captain Davis? And the other men? Are they outside?"

"They're not in here," Joe said. "Maybe you locked them out of the house again."

She peeked out the window, and a loud gasp escaped.

"Is everything okay?" Joe said.

"Oh, bless you, Lord!" Ann said, frantically opening the door, pushing the screen door open, and lurching at Blake to give him a big hug.

"Hi, Ann," Blake said as he hugged her back. "Can I come in?"

"Sara! Kids! Look who's here!"

From around the corner of the living room, Jacob slid to a stop on the hardwood floors in his sock-covered feet and peered at his dad. "Daddy!"

Blake knelt down, and Jacob ran and plowed into him with considerable force.

Close behind was Little Sara, and when she saw her father, she squealed his name and ran into his arms.

Joe Jensen stepped into the hallway between the foyer and the kitchen and watched the celebration with a smile.

Blake squeezed his children and kissed them both on the cheek just as Sara came down the stairs in a hurry. As soon as she recognized the visitor, she flew to him.

Blake gave the kids one last hug and stood just in time to envelope his wife with his arms. They kissed. And hugged. And kissed and hugged again.

"You didn't tell us you were coming," Sara finally said, her chin still over Blake's shoulder.

"I wanted it to be a surprise."

Sara leaned back to look Blake squarely in the eyes. "Where's Captain Davis and the other men?"

Blake smiled, turned, and pressed his fingers to his lips. "I asked them to hide." He blew out a loud whistle, and from the outbuilding next to the garage, the five men exited with smiles across the board.

Sara watched the men head in their direction, then faced her husband again. "Is it over?"

"Haven't you been watching the news, Sara?" Joe said. "President Gilmore has been arrested. So has his chief of staff and about half his cabinet." He smiled and jammed his hands into his pants pockets. "And now, out of the blue, Blake turns up unexpected? It don't take a Phi Beta Kappa to figure out the answer, does it?"

"Is it true?"

Blake nodded as his five friends climbed the steps to the porch. "Yes. It's over."

"Over?" Sara's eyes glistened. "How over is 'over'?"

"I have retired. Paperwork officially goes into the Bureau next week."

Sara's eyes widened, and a smile like nothing he had seen in years spread across her face. She hugged him around the neck. Hard.

"Uh, honey," Blake said in a raspy voice. "I'd like to enjoy retirement and not be asphyxiated on the first day."

Sara loosened her grip and started to jump up and down a little. "I can't believe it." She ran her hand through his hair before cupping the side of his face with it. "Are you sure it's official? Are you really sure? I have to know it's for real."

Blake held his arms out away from his body. "Look. No weapon. No FBI credentials. No suit and tie. I'm all yours. All day. Everyday."

"That's wonderful!" Ann said, clasping her hands together.

"It won't last," Joe said.

Ann scowled at her husband. "Give it a rest, Joe. Will ya?"

"I'm just sayin'...guy like Blake...all the stuff he knows...somebody will come calling, asking him for his expertise."

Blake kissed Sara and turned to face his father-in-law. "Yes, Joe, they probably will, but the good thing is, I can pick and choose where I go and what I do now. And when I do decide to go speak somewhere, I can take Sara and the kids with me. But those decisions are not for now. They're for later. Right now, I just want to be with Sara and my children."

"Hear, hear!" Captain Davis said.

"Hear, hear!" the other four soldiers said in unison.

Blake spent the next hour listening to updates on how everyone was. Sara and the kids regaled him with stories from the last two days, and thankfully, Captain Davis and the five-member team never ran into any opposition. All had remained quiet, and their services were never needed.

"Sara," Blake finally said, "can you give me a few minutes, I need to send my team home. They've been through enough, and they have families to get back to as well."

"Oh, yeah, sure. Of course."

Blake led the five men outside, and they circled up in the

driveway. "Gentlemen, you will never know how much I appreciate your help. Without you, I'd have no idea where my children would be right now, not to mention my marriage."

"Blake," Alwin Nefarje said, "you would have done the same for us, if we came calling."

"You're right. I would have. And I still will...but let's hope you never have to call me."

"Amen, brother!"

"I have the Gulfstream fueled and waiting for you. Take the rental back and check it in. All arrangements for it have been made. Then, simply tell the plane crew where you need to be dropped off. They'll need a little bit of time to work out a flight plan, based on the locations you give them. Once they have it figured out, you'll be on your way home."

Each man reached out and shook Blake's hand.

"Oh, and by the way," Blake said, placing his hands in his pockets, "I made sure each of you were compensated for your time and trouble. When you get home and see your bank accounts substantially larger, don't be alarmed. I had an associate help me with the transactions."

"This 'associate' of yours....he wouldn't happen to have an Aussie accent, would he?" Davis said.

"Possibly." Blake smiled.

"And where did the money come from, if you don't mind me asking?" Nefarje said.

"Harrison did help me deposit the funds into your accounts." Blake lifted his eyebrows as he allowed a confident grin to spread across his face. "As for the funding source...it's better if you don't know where it came from. Just know it is *not* stolen 'evidence,' nor is it money from ill-gotten gains. Let's just say I had a few leftover bucks from my operational expenses I cannot give back now. The person who gave the funds to me has been arrested." Blake held up his hands. "Not because of this money, mind you. But now that he is arrested and going to jail for a very long time, and because the monies were deemed 'black ops funds,' for me to hand them back would create more red tape and paperwork than anybody wants to deal with. So, I took the balance and split it amongst all the people who helped me this past week. And I did not take a dime, just so you are aware."

"Thank you," Davis and the other men said.

"You're welcome. Now, get to the airport and get home, gentlemen. I'll take over here."

CHAPTER 67

Home of Joseph & Ann Jensen
7147 Vance Hill Road
Newport, Vermont

Blake Meyer had spent the last three hours with his family, simply enjoying their presence. If Colin Murphy's personal vendetta had been successful, he never would have seen Sara and the kids again. If Murphy's overall plan had been implemented, there was a six-in-ten chance Sara's parents would not have survived the aftermath. Pondering those statistics helped cement Blake's perspective on everything.

Finally, Blake grew weary of sitting. "Jacob, Sara, want to go outside? Throw a ball around or something?"

"Can we play soccer?" Jacob said.

"Bring it on, little man." Blake stood and winced as he did.

"Honey, are you okay?" Sara reached out, pulled up Blake's shirt, and gasped.

"Daddy, yur hurt," Little Sara said.

Sara stood and pulled his shirt back down. "Blake, you need to see a doctor. Those are serious bruises. And are there any broken bones?"

"As for the doctor, I've already seen one. These bruises are old. Happened several days ago. And as for the broken bones...I have some cracked ribs. And a gunshot wound to my shoulder."

Sara's expression became concerned. "Which one?"

Blake lifted his sleeve and exposed the now sealed and healing damage.

Sara whimpered as tears pooled. She wrapped her arms around Blake's neck and held him for a long moment until finally inhaling deeply to regain some composure. She pushed him back a little and gazed into his eyes. "I'm worried about blood clots. Aren't you?"

"I was, but I think I'm out of the woods now." Blake took Sara by the hands. "Listen, let me play with the children for a bit. Then, I'll rest for as long as you say." He leaned forward and kissed her. "You're the boss now."

"Well, if that's the case, then I think you should go rest *now*."

"Mom, please?" Jacob said with his palms together. "Just for a little while? We'll go easy on him."

Blake laughed as much as the ribs would allow. "Yes, please do, little man."

Ann leaned into the conversation from her sitting chair. "Honey, I don't think thirty minutes is going to cause any issues, do you?"

Little Sara starting jumping up and down. "Thur-dee-minits! Thur-dee-minits!"

Jacob joined his sister in the chant.

Then Grampa Joe added his voice.

Sara motioned toward the door. "Fine, but I'm setting a timer."

Jacob shot out of the door with Little Sara close behind.

DEVIL OF A CRIME 513

Blake patted Sara on the shoulder and gave her a peck on the cheek. "Thur-dee-minits! Thur-dee-minits!"

Sara smiled and smacked Blake on the buttocks. "You better get a move on. You're down to twenty-nine 'minits,' mister."

* * *

Blake enjoyed kicking the ball back and forth between his children, being careful not to knock it into the trout pond in the corner of the property.

When the timer had sounded, Sara came out on the porch. "Okay, soccer fans, time's up. Time to come inside and take a shower before supper."

Blake kicked the ball to Jacob, and before he picked it up, he pointed toward the road. "Dad, somebody's here."

"Jacob, take the ball and your sister into the house while I see what this is about."

"Yes, sir."

Blake kept a wary eye on the vehicle creeping toward him while he waited for Jacob and Little Sara to get inside.

The car stopped, and the dust, kicked up from the tires, drifted away. The glare of the late afternoon sun glimmered off the windshield, blocking the driver's face.

Blake took a couple of steps forward as the driver's side door opened.

"You know, Blakey, you really should be resting," Harrison Kelly said, climbing out of the car and slamming the door shut. "Playing soccer is a great way to dislodge some clots."

"Have you been talking to Sara?" Blake said, walking over to the vehicle.

"No. But I did hack into your phone's speakerphone feature recently. Would be a shame to go through everything we've been through, only to die from playing a pickup game of soccer."

Blake reached out his hand, but Harrison pushed it aside and gave his friend a hug.

"Am I glad to see you, my friend. Clots and all."

"You too. Been a pretty amazing few days, hasn't it?"

Harrison brushed his hair with both hands, trying to get any dust dislodged. "'Amazing' isn't the word I would've used, but it works—"

"And who might this be, Blake?" Sara said, closing the door to the house and working her way to the edge of the back porch.

"Sara, this is Harrison Kelly. Harrison, my wife, Sara."

"Mrs. Meyer, I have heard a great deal about you, all of it good, by the way. You are what keeps this man sane, in case you were wondering. Nice to formally meet you."

Sara smiled. "So, you're the infamous Harrison Kelly? I've heard your voice on the phone a few times. Blake has told me about you a little bit as well. Hopefully, nothing that will jeopardize national security."

"No worries, love. I haven't worked for Uncle Sam in years. And if what I have heard is true, neither does your husband any longer."

Sara crossed her arms. "That's what I've heard as well. I do believe, though, it will be up to the both of us to help my husband keep it that way. If you know him like I do, he's not one for idle hands and sedentary lifestyles."

Harrison slapped Blake on the back of the shoulder. "I've known you longer than she has, but I do believe she knows you better, mate."

"Oh, she does. She does. But we won't go there." Blake winked at Sara. "So, what brings you by, Harrison?"

Harrison pointed at the car. "I was heading back to my house in Maryland. I received word from a trusted source, namely Agent Mitchell, about how my name has been cleared, so they won't be looking to arrest me anytime soon."

"Good to know."

"Yes, I thought you would appreciate the update, seeing how you are the bloke who initiated the process of exoneration." Harrison cleared his throat. "I also hear the director of the FBI is interested in my services, as are some other alphabet entities within the government. You wouldn't happen to know anything about those offers, would you, Blakey?"

"Nope."

"He's lying, Harrison," Sara said, her arms still crossed. "He was never good at it."

"An admirable trait, for sure, Mrs. Blakey, but I already knew the answer. Director Jameson contacted me himself. He sold you out, Blakey, me boy."

Blake glanced at Sara and then at Harrison. "Okay, so he asked about you, but I told the director you'd never go for it. I know how you feel about working for the government. But he said he had to ask."

"I rest my case, Your Honor," Harrison said, while bowing toward Sara. "But enough of this friendly banter. I also stopped by for two other things. First, I think I mentioned this before, but we were a little busy at the time, so it may not have sunk in. And of course, Sara wasn't there." He paused and took a deep breath to slow himself down. "My mum owns a bed and breakfast in Avalon, Australia. Avalon is north of Sydney, and the bed and breakfast is near Stokes Point and sits right on the bay. I spoke to her on the way down here from Maine. She said whenever you're ready, you can stay at her place. I told her to book you for a month when the time comes. You don't have to stay a whole month, but it would give you plenty of time to take in Sydney and the entire coast up to Brisbane, if you're interested. You could even book a cruise to New Zealand. Anyway, my gift to your family. Just let me know when you want to do it, and I'll make all the arrangements."

"Harrison, that is most generous," Sara said, uncrossing her arms and placing her hands in her back pockets. "I'm not sure now is the best time, but I think sometime in the near future might be. I'd love to just get away from it all, you know?"

"Of course, however, I can understand how *now* is probably not the best time. Besides, it's winter there right now. Best time to go is when fall and winter hits here."

"Thank you, my friend." Blake extended his hand. "It's almost dinnertime. Why don't you join us? We'll order some pizzas. At least let us feed you before you leave."

Harrison checked his smartphone for the time. "Actually, that works. I booked a hotel in town. I knew I wouldn't get much farther than this today anyway."

"Perfect," Sara said. "Come on in. I hope you like pepperoni. That's all this family eats."

"My favorite."

Blake wrapped his right arm around his friend and gave him a firm side hug. "And what was the second thing you wanted to talk to us about?"

Harrison shot a look up at Sara as she entered the house. "For that one, let's order the pizza first, then we can talk. Alone."

CHAPTER 68

HOME OF JOSEPH & Ann Jensen
  7147 Vance Hill Road
  Newport, Vermont

Blake could tell Harrison's demeanor had changed, and the information he wished to share wasn't for the little ears in his family. After the pizzas were ordered, he asked Sara to allow the kiddos to take a shower and stay inside. He made sure the front door was closed tight as he and Harrison made their way outside and sat on the front porch, waiting for the pizza to be delivered. Both men held coffee mugs in their hands.

"There's something on your mind, my old friend. What is it?"

Harrison repositioned himself in his Adirondack chair. "I heard you spoke to Conrad Bowker recently. Via video call."

"I did. He'd been arrested by the French authorities, and then was extradited to London. On my way back to Jacksonville from Chicago, I was tasked with filling him in on all the new information we had received from his son."

"Were you aware they allowed Conrad to speak to Kurt? After Conrad spoke to you?" Harrison took a swig of his coffee.

"Uh, no. Didn't get the memo."

"Yesterday morning, they rigged up another video call at the request of Conrad, I was told. He somehow convinced them to allow him the privilege. Something about it being the last time he'd ever get to see his son again."

"I'm surprised Kurt took the call." Blake pulled the mug to his lips. "From everything Julee told me, Kurt Bowker blamed Conrad for all of his boyhood traumas." He finally took a drink.

"True. He did blame Conrad. And judging by the mountains of data I saw, Kurt did have some legitimate grievances. Nevertheless, he did speak to Conrad."

Blake set his mug down on the table between them. "How did it go?"

"Blake, according to what I was told, Conrad wanted to hear from Kurt's own mouth if any of what you told him was true. Kurt not only confirmed everything, but he also added some information even you didn't disclose to Conrad. It wasn't in any of Kurt's files either." Harrison huffed and peered out through the pine trees, separating the road from the front of the house. "I don't know how to tell you this, but Conrad committed suicide less than an hour after the call ended. Apparently, Kurt's confirmation of your information, and his additional information, was more than Conrad could bear."

"What intel could Kurt provide that could be worse than what I shared?"

Harrison took one last gulp before setting his mug next to Blake's. He leaned a little closer to his friend. "Conrad's wife, Kurt's mother, had an affair, shortly after Conrad became a constable. As it turns out, Kurt wasn't Conrad's son after all. Kurt was the product of an illicit affair between Conrad's wife and an old boyfriend. While Conrad worked his shift as a new constable, she was meeting up with the old flame. When she got pregnant, she ended the relationship. She claimed the baby was Conrad's, and he was none the wiser.

"However, at some point during Kurt's early-twenty-something, 'rage against the machine' years, he had a DNA test done. I'm not sure what prompted him to do it, but he figured out from the results Conrad was not his dad. I suspect he questioned his mother about it, and maybe that's how he found out who his father really was."

Blake stared ahead, toward the pine trees, but his mind was elsewhere. "So, Conrad finds out his son Kurt has been working against him...and is responsible for framing him for several murders, all because he blames his 'father' for ruining their family. Then, on top of all this, he informs Conrad he isn't even his father after all." He blew out a heavy sigh, "And he did all these things, knowing Conrad wasn't his real dad?"

"Yes, but it gets worse," Harrison said. "One of the last things he told Conrad on that video call was how horrible of a cop he was. He berated Conrad on how he'd allowed his wife to have an affair right under his nose and never knew anything about it. And if he was such a bad cop, he must have been an even more pathetic spy."

"That must have crushed Conrad."

"I think the news of Kurt betraying him did. Conrad's subsequent suicide is obviously evidence of his overwhelming grief. However, before the call ended, Conrad shared a little newsflash of his own."

Blake's ears perked up. He picked up his coffee. "I'm listening."

"Conrad informed Kurt he *did know* about the affair. He *knew* Kurt wasn't his blood relative. But, he decided to forgive his wife as best he could—which explained their strained relationship—and raise Kurt as his own son. He did it, because Kurt's real father had been arrested about the same time he was born. Kurt's biological father, as it turns out, was a lackey for a crime syndicate in London. He got pinched, and the syndicate was planning on getting him out of jail. But when they heard he had been having a relationship with a copper's wife, and she was having his baby, they disowned him. And six months later, another inmate stabbed him to death inside the prison, compliments of the syndicate bosses. Turns out, they didn't want a possible snitch giving away family secrets in exchange for cigarettes and bags of crisps."

Blake lifted his coffee cup as a toast of sorts to his friend. "As you have said before, Harrison, 'If you choose to sleep with the devil, expect to get burned,' right?"

"So true. So true."

"I'm sorry to hear about Conrad. He had a rough life, but unfortunately, his choices contributed to it in many ways."

"To his credit, however," Harrison said, lifting his hands in Bowker's defense, "Conrad did admit to Kurt he wasn't the best father, and he knew it. He apologized for his failures before he hung up. And within an hour, Conrad committed suicide. When the news got back to Kurt, he attempted to do the same, but was saved before he bled out."

"That's not good. Kurt Bowker is a major piece of evidence for the justice department."

"You're tellin' me. I hear they have him on a twenty-four-hour, suicide surveillance watch until his trials are over, for there will be many, I suspect."

Blake leaned back in his chair and sighed heavily, setting the mug down on the arm of his chair. "I am so glad I am not part of that world anymore, Harrison. I've been out of it for what? Twenty-four hours? And already, I feel a huge weight off my shoulders."

"I bet you do. But Blakey, you feel that way because you no longer have to be the one handling all the intel. You worked your entire life trying to save America. Trying to save other countries.

Trying to keep terrorists and other bad *hombres* from stealing our freedoms. Now, others will carry on the work, doing the exact same things."

"It was time. The world has changed, Harrison. You know it as well as I do. The boundaries of where the bad guys reside isn't so clear anymore. They don't stay behind fences and borders like they used to. What used to be nationalistic ideologies have jumped those barriers and have morphed into political and religious ideologies. Those can reside anywhere. A line on a map doesn't mean what it used to mean anymore."

"You're right, my friend. And I keep asking the question, 'For what purpose? Why did we do what we did for so long?'" Harrison brushed some fuzz off his pant leg. "We knew if anything ever happened to us, they'd fill our spot by week's end. So, why did we risk our lives and our freedom for the sake of other people's freedom?"

"For the greater good, I suppose. Ultimately, what everyone wants is peace. With peace, all the other things fall into place. Freedom. Autonomy. Free markets. The lot. Without peace, all of those are in jeopardy."

"True. And yet, even in peacetime, those things can be limited. You say you're free, Blakey, but speak out against the wrong people, and see how free you really are. Or, you think you own something, like your house, for example."

"Well, I used to."

"Oh, yeah, bad example." Harrison winced and clicked his tongue at the same time. "Sorry. So, take your in-laws house here. Have them stop paying taxes on it and see how long they own it. You get where I'm coming from? This world promises freedom and peace, but it cannot deliver on its promise."

Blake closed his eyes and continued to lean back. "And you're point would be, Harrison?"

"I'm talking about *true peace*, Blake. Not the kind of peace that only occurs because everyone has prepared for war in some kind of nuclear standoff. That isn't peace, Blake. That's just 'quiet' while everyone reloads." Harrison slid to the edge of his chair. "You know me, Blake. We've been together a long time. And I have been praying for you and Sara and the kids during this entire ordeal. But the one thing I have prayed about more than anything else is your relationship to God.

"The peace we've worked so diligently to achieve our entire careers is a false peace. People, like the members of The Consortium, for example, are 'Exhibit A.' They desire money, power, and prestige. So do most people, if the truth be known. We all like our raises. We all like it when our employer adds to our benefits. We all are affected—or maybe 'infected' is the better word—by what the Bible calls 'the sinful nature.'"

Blake opened his eyes and eyed his friend. "We've had this conversation before, you know. I remember you saying how we'd never have to teach Jacob and Little Sara how to do wrong. They come by it naturally. Instead, we spend much of our time teaching them to do the right thing."

Harrison smiled. "So, you *were* listening. Brilliant! And because of the sinful nature, there can never be true peace in this life apart from God. Case in point: Riddle me this, my friend. How many peace treaties over the centuries have been made?"

"Thousands. Tens of thousands, probably."

"And how many of those have been broken?"

"A bunch, I'm sure."

"More than 'a bunch.' The answer is, all of them. Every last one of them. And if any are made today, they will be broken soon enough. You know why? Because the peace mankind *offers* is a false peace. Any peace we *experience* in this world is a false peace. It will never last, and that is because we are ultimately at enmity with God. Another way to say it is, we are 'at war' with God. Therefore, because we are, we do things which are in direct opposition to His commands. The Bible calls it 'sin.' Sinful beliefs bring about sinful acts. Sinful acts bring about 'Consortiums,' Blakey. Sinful acts breed terrorists. They breed corrupt politicians. They breed murder, strife, lying, stealing, coveting, hatred, and division. They breed everything evil we see around us that attempts to tear society apart and demolish *true* peace.

"However, when a person recognizes this dilemma...when a person realizes that no matter how 'good' he or she is, he or she can never be good enough to satisfy the penalty for sin, and thus, God's wrath, then that individual determines in his or her heart there must be another answer. There must be another way. And he or she would be correct. There is something else needed to pay the penalty for this sinful nature—"

"And that is where the blood of Jesus Christ comes in," Sara said as she opened the screen door.

Harrison looked up and smiled at her. "Exactly. He paid the penalty for sin. His sacrifice becomes the bridge to true peace. His blood satisfies God's wrath against us. So, if you want peace, Blake, and I mean *true peace*...the kind which transcends human understanding...the kind which brings true joy...the kind which can allow you to sleep soundly at night when others are fearful of what tomorrow may bring, then Jesus has the answer. He knows the way, because He is The Way."

Sara walked over and stood next to Blake. "I used to believe, Harrison. Years ago. When I was young. I was older than Little Sara and Jacob but not yet a teenager. But somewhere, along the way, I went astray. I stopped reading the Bible. Stopped going to church. Stopped everything."

Blake slipped his arm around Sara's waist. "And then you met this old goat, and he pulled you even farther away, is that it?"

"Hardly. I was already far away, and I've been far away our entire marriage. And you know, I've never had a moment's peace, Blake. I always worried about your safety. Always worried about what would happen to me and the kids, especially if something happened to you. Always wondered when the next monster would surface and force you to trek around the world again, trying to combat it."

Harrison, sitting and listening, was nodding more and more emphatically. "Worry is the absence of true peace. When we worry about the kinds of things you just mentioned, we cease to trust in God. Instead, we're trusting our own efforts. It's no wonder we never have peace when we live such lives. Peace does not exist apart from God. Not *true* peace. Never has. Never will."

A vehicle with a Mario's Pizza sign illuminated on top pulled into the driveway and parked with the motor still running.

"Well, fellas, looks like our dinner has arrived," Sara said. "But I would like to talk about this more, Harrison. I don't know about Blake, but I want true peace. The kind the Bible talks about. The kind that...how does it go? It surpasses understanding?"

"Yes." Harrison stood up. "Philippians, chapter four. 'Be anxious for nothing, but in everything by prayer and petition with thanksgiving, let your requests be known to God. And the peace of God, which surpasses all understanding, will guard your hearts and your minds in Christ Jesus."

Sara pointed at Harrison while Blake went down the stairs to meet the pizza delivery boy. "That's the one. I want that peace. Especially after this past week. Now more than ever."

"Oh, I hear you. Loud and clear."

CHAPTER 69

Home of Joseph & Ann Jensen
   7147 Vance Hill Road
   Newport, Vermont

Blake Meyer and his family ate pizza with his friend, Harrison Kelly, until everyone felt like a Thanksgiving turkey. Stuffed, cooked, and done. There was a great deal of laughter as Blake and Harrison entertained the family with stories from their past, keeping it light and staying away from the tales which would certainly chill their blood and take away their appetites.

Finally, Harrison glanced at his watch. "Crikey. I had better get a wiggle on, or you lot will have to feed me brekky."

Sara peered at Blake, and then at her parents before breaking out into a laugh. "You have to do what?"

"Oh, that's just Harrison getting all Australian on us," Blake said. "He defaults into his Aussie slang, sometimes. He forgets we Yanks have no clue what he's saying."

Harrison offered a shamefaced grin. "Sorry." He scanned his

watch again. "Oh my," he said in a fake American voice, "look at the time. I must be going, or all of you are going to have to feed me breakfast."

"See how much better that sounds?" Blake said. "And everyone understood you."

"Seriously, Yank, I should be going. I have a long drive ahead of me tomorrow."

Blake slid his chair out and stood. "I'll take you on a walkabout."

Harrison shook his head. "Please stop. You can't use the slang, if you're not going to use it correctly."

"Harrison, thank you for praying with me," Sara said. "I already feel wonderful. Turning my life over to Jesus...I can't explain it. I feel like I did when I was younger, but it's different too. It seems more real somehow."

"Probably because you are more sincere now. When we realize we are desperate beggars, deserving nothing but death, as Romans 6:23 says, it is at that moment our eyes start to open. We see ourselves for who we are—sinners—in light of who God is—holy, holy, holy."

"Harrison, thank you for sharing the gospel truth with my family," Ann said. "I've been praying for them all for so long."

"Continue to do so, Mrs. Jensen. Satan is not a fan of new believers. He wants them to shipwreck their faith and be useless. He'll attack from every which way."

"Don't worry. Already on it."

Harrison faced Sara. "And Sara, I know it feels liberating right now. Just remember how feelings can be deceptive. It's the truth of God's Word that keeps you grounded. It is in Him where you find true peace, and it is what liberates you from sin. In Him, we live, move and have our being."

Sara stood and gave Harrison a hug. "Don't be a stranger. Once we get settled somewhere, Blake will give you the address."

Harrison nodded. "Thank you for dinner. Goodbye, everyone."

Blake escorted his friend out the back door and walked to the car with him. "Harrison, about all that back there...uh, I would like to talk to you more about it. I never grew up around church folk. Growing up, our family never went to church, so all of this is new to me. But seeing I have more time on my hands now, I would like to discuss it further with you."

"I'd love to, Blakey, but please, don't wait too long. I appreciate you and how you are 'counting the cost,' as the Bible puts it, but you of all people know we are never guaranteed tomorrow. Wait too long, and it may be too late. God doesn't allow 'do overs.' There's no 'overtime' in this game of life. When the final horn sounds, it's game over for all the people who said 'no' to God and 'yes' to sin."

"Call me when you get back home, and we can talk more. Trust me. I've had a great deal of time to think about this 'sin' thing over the last few days." Blake reached out his hand. "Be safe. And let me know what needs to be replaced along with the replacement costs. I already told Jameson about how things went down at your house there in Maryland. He said send him the bill, and he'll take care of it."

Harrison shook Blake's hand and winked. "Right. I'll believe that, retired SSA Meyer, when I see the check with my own two eyes."

CHAPTER 70

Home of Joseph & Ann Jensen
  7147 Vance Hill Road
  Newport, Vermont

Blake Meyer waved as Harrison Kelly backed out of the driveway and took off down Vance Hill Road. He smiled at the thought of having such a good friend. When he stopped and gave it some serious consideration, he had a lot of good friends. Many of which had been instrumental in bringing him and his family home. Bringing them together. And for that, he would be forever grateful.

He turned to walk back to the house, and standing at the top of the stairs was Sara, leaning against the post, arms folded. He suspected she'd been watching him and his friend interact and now was watching him from afar.

He stopped and just admired her beauty. *What did I do to deserve such a person?*

He smiled.

She smiled back.

"Well, Mrs. Blakey," he said, walking up the stairs and grabbing her around the waist. "How do you feel about getting away from it all for a few days? Nothing special. Not Stokes Point in Australia. Not yet. Instead...maybe a week-long getaway to a beach somewhere, perhaps? Or a mountain cabin? It matters to me not where we go, so long as it is with you and the kids."

Sara's eyes sparkled as they slowly twirled around in a silent dance. "Did you get some kind of special bonus I don't know about, Blakey?"

"*Au contraire.* I have about two gazillion frequent flyer miles that need to be used up. The plane tickets shouldn't cost us anything."

"But what about the cost of the room? If you're retired, you should have some kind of pension coming, correct?"

"From the Bureau? I doubt it because of the way I was enlisted. I should get a military pension, however. And I did ask for a special compensation, of sorts...kind of a repayment for all that we've been through, you know? At first, I was led to believe such a request would be a longshot and not to get my hopes up. However, earlier today, on my way here, I got a text. The director stated a 'travel voucher' was waiting to be deposited into our bank account. It's designed to give us living expenses for up to three months until we can find a place of our own. It is enough to pay our bills, then when we sell our other property in Jacksonville, Uncle Sam is going to pay the balance of whatever the new home costs, up to a certain amount, of course, if needed."

"Up to what amount, exactly?"

"I was told up to $250,000. So, sell our property, put that towards a new place, and if there is still a balance, we can use those funds to cover the balance up to that amount. They know we would have sold our property for a lot more if the house was still intact."

Sara frowned but nodded. "I'm gonna miss that house."

"I know. We all will."

"And what happens if we purchase a house and there is no balance to pay off?"

"In essence, the quarter of a million is my compensation from the Bureau, so 'spend it wisely' was the message I received when I read between the lines."

Sara brushed her fingers against the hair on Blake's temple. "I'd love to get way tomorrow, but we can't. Sally's funeral is next week. The casket is supposed to arrive by plane the day after tomorrow, and the funeral director has to be there to pick it up. We have been requested to be present to observe the transition."

"Why next week?"

"Mom and Dad wanted to give all the relatives some time to make plans to attend."

Blake nodded.

"And also, I don't know if anyone told you, but Mom and Dad just got back from Florida last night. They flew down first thing yesterday morning, identified her body, and flew back all in one day. Mom said she didn't want to leave me and the kids alone, but I think they didn't want to stay in Florida any longer than they had to. Like our house, Florida is now the state where their daughter died."

Blake closed his eyes and shook his head slightly. He fought back some tears. "I am so sorry. All this is my fault."

Sara brushed Blake's hair again. "You know, I got to talk to Captain Davis and the other men after you left us at the airport. They filled me in on some of the details of what you all went through to get me and the kids back. Those men love you, Blake, you know that, right? They spoke so highly of you. They told me stories of when you all met, and how you had helped them become the men they are today. It was good for me to hear it, because I wasn't in a good place. You and me...we weren't in a good place after all that had happened." She kissed Blake on the cheek. "I just want you to know...hearing them explain what was going on behind the scenes, and all the things you endured," she said, pulling up his shirt again to examine his midsection, "like all these bruises...they told me you were beat up by a group of men and then tied up and almost killed? Is that true?"

Blake bit his lip and could only nod.

"I understand now. I know you didn't ask for any of this. What Colin Murphy did to us wasn't your fault, and I just want you to know how sorry I am...for my behavior...for the words I said when we were on that ship...for everything. I never thought I could love you more than the day we got married, but boy, was I wrong." She clutched his face and kissed him.

Blake pulled her body close and allowed her love to wash away the pain.

Sara finally relinquished her husband and smiled. Her eyes glimmered even more. "So, about this vacation...where did you have in mind?"

Blake chuckled and then pretended to be thinking hard. "Hawaii, perhaps? Or some beach on the west coast? I suspect the kids would prefer an ocean over a mountain. And probably nothing extravagant, either, like Monaco or Marseille or Barcelona." Blake gave Sara a quick kiss. "And I think we should save the mountain cabin for us. I know of a great place in Switzerland. A friend of mine owes me a favor. We could go there when the Alps are all covered in snow. But that's for later."

Sara shivered at the prospect. "I agree. The beach would be better for the kids."

"And if you want to invite your parents along, I'm good with that too. Oh, and, uh, I did promise Jacob I would take him to a hotel with a pool, so we'll need to make sure the hotel we choose has one."

Suddenly, the screen door flew open. "Did I hear someone say something about a pool?" Jacob said.

Blake and Sara turned enough to see their son without relinquishing each other.

"Yes, son," Blake said. "I promised you a hotel with a pool. Remember?"

"Yes, sir, I do." Jacob started to bounce a little as the excitement was building inside him. "Can we go now?"

"Well, we first have to decide where we want to go, and once we do, then we can look for hotels with pools."

"I don't care where we go. Just as long as it has a pool, Daddy, I'm good."

Blake and Sara laughed.

"Well, son, I do care where we go," his mother said. "So, I will have a little say in the decision. But I'm sure we can figure it out."

Just then, Little Sara walked out onto the porch. "Is Harwison gone?"

"Yes, honey," Sara said. "He had to go. He wanted to go home too."

Little Sara's face changed from sorrowful to distraught. "But we don't haf a home to go to anymore."

Sara stared at Blake, and he allowed her to slip out of his arms.

She knelt down and picked up her daughter. "Houses can be rebuilt, honey. Homes are where your heart is. And right now, my home is here, with you, your brother, your daddy, and your Grandma and Grandpa J. All of you are the ones who make Mommy happy. And someday soon, we will go find another house we can turn into a home."

Little Sara hugged her mom, but Sara and Blake could tell the words didn't mend all the hurt.

"Oh, wait. I have something for the two of you," Blake said. "Wait here. Wait here. I almost forgot. I'll be right back."

He raced inside the house and up the stairs to retrieve his backpack from the bedroom. He unzipped it, checked its contents, and then went downstairs.

He carried it out onto the porch. "Okay, Jacob, come stand over here," he said, pointing to a spot on the porch. "And Sara, you come stand next to your brother."

Jacob zoomed to his spot and shook with a nervous energy.

Little Sara climbed down out of her mother's arms and sidled over next to her brother. She watched him shake with emotion, and it caused her to act excited as well.

"Jacob, close your eyes and hold out your hands."

Jacob did so, and Blake pulled out a Lego set yet to be put together. He set it in Jacob's hands. "You can open your eyes now."

Jacob did so, and he grabbed it with both hands, hopping up and down in place. "My Lego set! I thought it was destroyed." He flew to his daddy and gave him a big hug. "Where did you find it?"

Blake lifted his finger to his lips. "Hold that thought. I'll tell you in a sec." Blake turned to Little Sara. "Your turn, sweetheart. Close your eyes and hold out your hands."

Little Sara did so with her eyes clenched as tight as possible.

Blake reached into his backpack and pulled out her item.

Sara allowed a quick gasp to escape before she covered her mouth with her hand.

Blake placed the item in Little Sara's hands. "You can open your eyes now."

Little Sara did so. "Mistuh Panda! Mistuh Panda!" She jumped up and down with her best friend held out at arm's length for all to see. "Wook, Mommy! Daddy found Mistuh Panda!" She hugged the stuffed bear as hard as she could and let out a squeal.

Sara peered at Blake with tears in her eyes. She mouthed the words "Thank you" as she allowed her eyes to drift back to her children's happiness.

Little Sara ran to her father and gave him a huge hug. "Fank you, Daddy! Fur finding Mistuh Panda. And he wooks so kwean." At once, she stopped and became more serious. "Did you haf to buy me a new one?"

Blake chuckled. "Nope. He's the real deal. I gave him a bath yesterday, so he'd be presentable for you, my dear."

"Fank you, Daddy."

"I went back to our old house and found him. That's where I found your Lego set, too, buddy," he said, reaching out for his son.

Jacob hugged his dad again. "Thank you. I'm gonna put this together tonight."

"Well, it's late, buddy. That will be up to your mom. She knows how late you can stay up these days."

Ann and Joe had stepped out onto the porch soon enough to see all the joy transpire.

"Honey," Ann said, "it's okay with us if he stays up past his bedtime tonight. His daddy just got home tonight. And besides, what happens at Grandma's stays at Grandma's." She gave an obvious wink.

Jacob listened intently and then turned toward his mother. He just grinned and sheepishly held the box up for his mother to see.

Sara smiled, and the smiles turned into laughter. "Go on, you goon. Go put your Legos together. And maybe Grandpa Joe can give you a hand."

Off like a shot, Jacob flew past everyone and barreled up the stairs.

Grandpa Joe lumbered behind him. "Wait up, buckaroo. Takes the old man longer these days to climb these stairs than it used to."

"I'll go finish cleaning up the kitchen," Ann said.

Blake tossed his backpack into the closest chair and slipped his arms around Sara again.

"You have anything in that backpack for me, Blakey?" she said.

Blake frowned. "I was going to put it in the backpack, but I was afraid it would get broken. So, I left it in a box along with some other trinkets I found. Julee Scarfano said she would ship it to me, once we get our own address."

"What was it?"

"Remember the vase I brought home from New York City? The one that shimmers when the light hits it just right?"

"Are you serious? It survived?"

Blake nodded with a silly grin.

"Of course, it did." Sara chuckled in defeat. "I don't mean to be mean, but if you hadn't noticed, I was not a fan of that vase."

"I noticed. It probably survived because you probably had it stuffed in a bin or a box."

"You're right. It's all my fault it survived."

"Well, you will have it again soon."

Sara rolled her eyes. "I can't wait. In the meantime, please tell me you brought me something else in your backpack?"

"I have something, but it's not in my backpack any longer." Blake reached into his pants pocket and pulled out a necklace. "I think you lost this, miss."

Sara's eyes pooled again, and she took it from Blake. She held it in her hand and admired it before draping it around her neck, clasping the ends together. "My grandmother gave me this when I was a little girl."

"Glad I found it," Blake said, just as he felt the arm of Little Sara hug his leg.

They both looked down, and she had her other arm around Sara's leg, holding Mr. Panda.

Little Sara's eyes were closed, and she was smiling. "I wuv gwoup hugs."

Blake gazed into Sara's eyes and kissed her.

Sara smiled as a tear trickled down her cheek. "So do we, kiddo," she said, caressing the back of her daughter's head. "So do we."

ACKNOWLEDGMENTS

It is *finally* finished.

Thirteen years in the making.

So many stops and starts.

So many steps forward, and so many setbacks.

Writing a series like this is not something I would recommend for just one person, for it is clear why TV shows and mini-series use teams of writers, each one writing an episode or two while collaborating with the others to keep the storylines straight.

I was the team. A writing team of one.

The Blake Meyer Thriller Series became one huge story. Some twenty-three storylines, woven together into six, action-packed novels, in a TV-show-esque fashion (Think Jack Bauer and 24). A whopping 373 chapters. Nearly 2,900 pages total. It could be "binge read" just like a series of shows can be binge-watched.

During this process, I produced an Excel spreadsheet which helped me keep all the chapters in order chronologically. It became a great resource. When printed—with each chapter summarized in a little two-inch square, storyboard-style—it covers half of a wall in my study, and the "days" with multiple chapters run down to the floor and roll out across my room like a red carpet.

Yet, despite everything that has transpired during the development of this series, one thing has become abundantly clear...

The "fiction" of this series is anything but fiction alone.

The events which have occurred over the last five years prove there are "evil people" out there, and their plans do not include the majority of us. We are in the way, so we need to be exterminated, eliminated, or at least incarcerated. And it takes people who are willing to risk everything and stand up for what is right to keep our world from plunging into the abyss of no return.

We need the Blake Meyers of the world to take their stands, and we must support them. They don't care about political affiliations, per se. They simply want justice, based on a logical set of moral principles designed to keep society sane and criminals in check. Laws and rules which apply to all instead of just the serfs and lower classes.

Oh, how I wish we had more Blake Meyers alive today. And maybe we do. Maybe they are fighting behind the scenes, never gaining the accolades or the press coverage due their service because of a biased press who thinks communistic ideals are somehow good. We could use more Blake Meyers, nevertheless.

So, for all the fans out there who have been with us from the beginning and have been more than patient, while I strived toward this final goal, thank you, from the bottom of my heart. Your desire to "find out what happens next" became a driving force for me.

For all the newer fans, who heard more recently about Blake Meyer and the cast of characters who comprise this thriller series, thank you, too, for joining the party.

For all my family members and friends, who have been so supportive through the entire project, thank you for your encouragement. This last book is for you.

For my fellow writers within my critique group, thank you for your encouragement as well as your eyes and ears, helping me all along the way. I know I said I was a team of one, and in regards to writing the story, I was. However, I could not have worked through a great many conundrums without picking your brains and having you read and reread certain sections. Some of you have expertise I do not possess. It became invaluable.

For my editor, Katelyn Wiggins, thank you for challenging so much, forcing me to go back and "figure it out," especially when it came to tying up all the storylines with as many nice, tidy, little bows as possible.

For my wife, Cindy, it's done. It. Is. Done. Thank you for sticking with me through it all. In a lot of ways, I see a lot of Blake and Sara in us, or maybe it's vice-versa. In some ways, we became their template.

And for my Heavenly Father, it is now completely in Your hands. Bless it as You see fit.

* * *

I'm not a prophet, nor am I the son of one. But I did ask a question one summer day in 2012: "If I was a terrorist, and I was going to take out a country as powerful as America, how would I go about doing it?"

This series answers such a question.

The scary part is, apparently, others have been asking the same question and came to similar conclusions.

In 2020, I believe they performed a Beta test, of sorts, with COVID-19. They have been doing "Gain of Function" testing for years. This is not news. However, it must be remembered that there are only two reasons anyone would seek to conduct such testing, as many of these viruses never jump species on their own. Either, you wish to create it, or you want to learn how to combat it, if it ever was released.

In 2009, we had the H1N1 Swine Flu, and everyone got scared. It was touted as the next pandemic, and those of us within secondary education were wondering how it would affect schools. Between seven-hundred thousand and 1.4 million people worldwide supposedly contracted the disease. Yet, less than nineteen thousand died. By comparison to COVID-19, the

Spanish Flu, and other similar pandemics, those numbers were small.

However, one thing occurred the makers of swine flu never anticipated. A vaccine quickly emerged (which tells us a lot, as it takes months, sometimes years to create one) and everyone was urged to get vaccinated. Many did, and children started dying from the injections.

Within weeks, the vaccines were pulled, and magically, the threat of the swine flu dissipated. By Christmas, you heard very little about it. By August of 2010, The World Health Organization declared it was cured. The CDC conducted a study in 2012, and their numbers from the 2009 outbreak were much higher. Shocker.

Personally, I believe children were not the H1N1 target, and because of the horrible track record of the vaccine, officials had to scuttle the plan.

Then, the Avian Bird Flu was a thing. Scientists admitted it was created in a lab. COVID experienced several iterations, like SARS, before COVID-19 became a thing.

My point is, this kind of warfare is strategic and intentional. Many elderly people died during COVID-19. Many are still affected and dying even to this day. I personally know many who contracted the virus, and their health has deteriorated significantly, even though they are "well" and "COVID-free." Many who received the vaccine are also experiencing horrible side effects.

I'm sure this "just happened to help" the Social Security Administration and the Veteran's Affairs administration, saving each entity a great deal of money. The hidden goals of "Obama Care" and it's so called "death panels" were carried out without anyone even bringing it up. Doctor's offices were thinned out. Many elderly voters were cleared off the voter registration rolls (although some would say they changed parties after their death).

And these are just some of the effects America experienced. Who knows what other countries have experienced.

I know it sounds like a conspiracy theory, but one must admit they literally controlled the world for almost a year while making billions of dollars from the proliferation of a vaccine with dubious results and horrific side effects. This was also part of the "Beta Test," I believe.

You see, all of these "pandemics" are building up to something bigger.

This is why true peace is so important. This world is spinning out of control in so many ways. Its moral degeneration is picking up speed. Its physical rotation on its axis is slowing down. There are "wars and rumors of wars. Earthquakes in various places." I am simply watching the birth pangs in real time, waiting on the One who will come back and recreate everything anew. In the meantime, I am letting others know about the God who created the heavens and the earth the first time. He is the only One we can trust, besides his Son, of course.

For the one who "rules" this world we live in, the *diabolos*, is like a rebellious prince given dominion over a parcel of land by the king, and he has only one goal: To see all of his subjects follow him to perdition's flames. It's not about you. It's not about me. It's about his hatred of Almighty God, and his followers exhibit the same, virulent, vehement detestation toward the God of the Bible. So long as he can keep his followers in the dark, he is happy. He only wishes to destroy that which God created, from the soil and sky to the body and souls of mankind.

Always has. Always will.

And this is why I don't think the virus makers are done trying either.

They work for *Abaddon, Apollyon,* that is, the Destroyer (Revelation 9:11).

ABOUT THE AUTHOR

C. Kevin Thompson is an award-winning author of several books, including *The Serpent's Grasp* (winner of an award), *30 Days Hath Revenge* (winner of a second-place award), and *The Letters* (winner of two awards). His novella, titled, *The Near Distant: Eye of the Beholder*, was a finalist for the 2023 BRMCWC Selah Awards as well.

Kevin has served as a pastor and has been an educator for over twenty years. He lives with his wife in the central Florida area, where he's busy researching and writing a new middle grades fiction series! And he's also written a blog series of Bible studies which will eventually become a book of their own, titled *The King and His Kingdom: Viewing This Life Through the Eyes of the Almighty*. You can find everything on his website!

You can find out more about Kevin at these locations on the web (and he truly appreciates the "follows"):

Website: www.ckevinthompson.com
Facebook: CKevinThompson.AuthorPage/
X: @CKevinThompson
Instagram: instagram.com/ckevinthompson/
Bookbub: bookbub.com/authors/c-kevin-thompson

SELECTED BIBLIOGRAPHY

The Blake Meyer Thriller series is complete. Although there were countless articles used in the writing of this series, in addition to segments of many other books, it was decided a selected group of books and articles might help the reader understand how the author shaped and molded the stories of all the characters. In doing so, the bibliography would not be any more daunting than it already is. However, as Kevin worked on the series, new articles came to light, giving more credence to the notion that maybe this "fiction" isn't really fiction after all.

One such article is the one listed below by Meghan Roos. Written nine years after *30 Days Hath Revenge* was completed...

Another such article, a press release by the Department of Justice - Eastern District of Michigan, happened recently, in June of 2025, showing how "bad actors" may have read this series after all...

BOOKS & ARTICLES USED

Alibek, Ken. *Biohazard: The Chilling True Story of the Largest Covert Biological Weapons Program in the World—Told from Inside by the Man Who Ran It.* (New York, NY; Random House, 1999). NOTE: This by far was the most informative, yet scary, book I read in preparation of this series. You see the contents of this book being played out in the current affairs of the world as we speak.

Aslan, Reza. *How to Win a Cosmic War: God, Globalization, and the End of the War on Terror.* (New York, NY; Random House, 2009).

Bales, Kevin, and Ron Soodalter. *The Slave Next Door: Human Trafficking and Slavery in America Today.* (Berkeley, CA; University of California Press, 2009).

Carroll, Michael Christopher. *Lab 257: The Disturbing Story of the Government's Secret Germ Laboratory.* (New York, NY; Harper, 2004). NOTE: This book is the (somewhat) American version of Ken Alibek's book referenced above. The key difference being Alibek lived it (and almost died from it). This author just researched it and wrote about it.

Cartwright, Frederick F. *Disease and History.* (New York, NY; Dorset Press, 1972).

"Chinese Nationals Charged with Conspiracy and Smuggling a Dangerous Biological Pathogen into the U.S. for their Work at a University of Michigan Laboratory." *United States Attorney's Office: Eastern District of Michigan: Press Release.* 03 June 2025. <https://www.justice.gov/usao-edmi/pr/chinese-nationals-charged-conspiracy-and-smuggling-dangerous-biological-pathogen-us>

Cross Giblin, James. *When Plague Strikes: The Black Death, Smallpox, AIDS.* (New York, NY; Harper Collins, 1997), pp.11-53.

Ellison, Bryan J. and Peter H. Duesberg. *Why We Will Never Win the War on AIDS.* (El Cerrito, CA; Inside Story Communications, 1994).

Flores, Theresa L. *The Slave Across the Street: The True Story of How an American Teen Survived the World of Human Trafficking.* (Boise, ID; Ampelon Publishing, 2010).

Gibson, Jim. "Dealing in Flesh." *Lake & Sumter Style*, March 2012, pp. 47-53.

Harris, Shane. *The Watchers: The Rise of America's Surveillance State.* (New York, NY; Penguin Press, 2010).

Jacques, Martin. *When China Rules the World: The End of the Western World and the Birth of a New Global Order.* (New York, NY; Penguin Press, 2009).

Kara, Siddharth. *Sex Trafficking: Inside the Business of Modern Slavery.* (New York, NY; Columbia University Press, 2009).

Kelly, John. *The Great Mortality: An Intimate History of the Black Death, the Most Devastating Plague of All Time.* (New York, NY; Harper Collins, 2005). NOTE: Of all the historical accounts of the plague, this book was the best read.

Kessler, Ronald. *The Secrets of the FBI.* (New York, NY; Crown Publishers, 2011).

Kirby, Reid. "Using the flea as a weapon." *U.S. Army Chemical Review.* July-December 2005. <https://www.scribd.com/document/43529768/Using-the-Flea-as-a-Weapon>

Levine, Steve. *Putin's Labyrinth: Spies, Murder, and the Dark Heart of the New Russia.* (New York, NY; Random House, 2008).

Lewis, C.S. *Mere Christianity.* (New York, NY; Collier Books, 1943).

Miller, Judith, Stephen Engelberg, and William Broad. *Germs: Biological Weapons and America's Secret War.* (New York, NY; Simon & Schuster, 2001).

Orent, Wendy. Plague: *The Mysterious Past and Terrifying Future of the World's Most Dangerous Disease.* (New York, NY; Free Press, 2004).

Riedel, Stefan. "Plague: from natural disease to bioterrorism." Baylor University Medical Center. *Proceedings.* April 2005. Vol. 18; pp. 116-124.

Ritter, Malcolm. "Panel backs sharing studies of lab-made bird flu." *Phys.org.* 30 March 2012. <https://phys.org/news/2012-03-panel-lab-made-bird-flu.html>

Roos, Meghan. "18 States' Walmart Stores Hit by Recall of Aromatherapy Spray Linked to Deadly Bacteria." *Newsweek.* 27 Oct. 2021 <https://www.newsweek.com/18-states-walmart-stores-hit-recall-aromatherapy-spray-linked-deadly-bacteria-1643176>

Singh, Jyotsna. "Plague confirmed in northern india." *News.BBC.co.* 19 Feb. 2002, <http://news.bbc.co.uk/2/hi/health/1830034.stm>

Skinner, E. Benjamin. *A Crime So Monstrous: Face-to-Face with Modern-Day Slavery.* (New York, NY; Free Press, 2008).

"Vaccine To Protect Against Black Plague Bioterror Attack Being Developed." *Science Daily.* 31 July 2008. <http://www.sciencedaily.com/releases/2008/07/080730140829.htm>